HAUNTING BEAUTY

K. LORAINE

USA TODAY BESTSELLING AUTHORS

MEG ANNE

Edited by Mo Sytsma of Comma Sutra Editorial

Cover Design by CReya-tive Book Design

To everyone who wished the Beast never turned back into Prince Adam.
(You know Belle wished the same thing)

"But I don't want to go among mad people," Alice remarked.

"Oh, you can't help that," said the Cat, "we're all mad here. I'm mad. You're mad."

"How do you know I'm mad?" said Alice.

"You must be," said the Cat, "or you wouldn't have come here."

— LEWIS CARROLL, ALICE IN WONDERLAND

HAUNTING
BEAUTY

Authors' Note

Haunting Beauty contains mature and graphic content that is not suitable for all audiences. Such content includes scenes of attempted sexual assault, child abuse, ritual sacrifice, cults, drugging, mentions of mental illness and more. **Reader discretion is advised.**

As always, a detailed list of content and trigger warnings is available on our website.

SESSION TRANSCRIPT: OCTOBER 31ST

Dr. Masterson: And rolling. This is Dr. Elizabeth Masterson. It is October thirty-first, and the time is 10:00 a.m. Today marks the first session of our latest peer accountability group. Please go around the room one by one, introducing yourselves and telling us what led you to Blackwood. We'll start with you, Cain.

<<dead air>>

Dr. Masterson: Cain?

Cain: *Clears throat* Oh, right. That's me.

Caspian: Poor sod doesn't even know his own name.

Dr. Masterson: Caspian, wait your turn. Please continue, Cain.

Cain: So they tell me my name's Cain, uh, Alexander. I don't know what the fuck I'm doing here. I can't remember a damn thing before I woke up tied to a bed here in this hellhole.

Tor: Sounds blissful.

Dr. Masterson: Tor, thank you for volunteering. You can go next.

Tor: Hello. I'm Tor Nordson. Prince of Novasgard. Thor-blessed demigod. Berserker. And I'm here because it was this or prison.

Kai: Novasgard, huh? *snickers* Where's that located? The star beside Neverland?

Caspian: That's Ravenndel, and Novasgard is fictional.

<<chair clatters to floor>>

Tor: *growls and heavy breathing* Watch your tone when you speak of my homeland.

Cain: Holy shit, is he getting bigger?

Dr. Masterson: Tor, remember the breathing exercises you learned in anger management?

Tor: *indecipherable muttering followed by measured breaths*

Dr. Masterson: Perfect. Let's carry on shall we? Malakai, would you like to go next?

Kai: I've told you to call me Kai.

Dr. Masterson: So you have. Please continue.

Kai: *heavy sigh* I'm Kai Nash. I'm here because I found myself trapped in my dragon form after a drunken rage, the remnants of a little village smoldering in the distance. Apparently it's frowned upon to murder townsfolk while they're asleep in their beds.

<<clothes rustling>>

Cain: Jesus, and I thought I was going to be the most fucked-up member of this little boy band. What's our name again?

Caspian: The Blackwood Villains . . . obviously.

Tor: Original.

Caspian: I think you mean iconic.

Dr. Masterson: We seem to have gotten off topic.

Caspian: Welcome to the party, darling. We have the good drugs.

Dr. Masterson: Caspian, what have I told you about calling me darling?

Caspian: *whispers* That it makes you wet?

Dr. Masterson: Don't make me send you to isolation again.

Caspian: Oh, all right. I'll behave. Is it my turn, then? Although, honestly, I don't see why I should have to introduce myself. Everyone already knows who I am.

Cain: I don't.

Caspian: I am Caspian Hook. As in . . . *Captain* Hook.

Cain: For fuck's sake, you're all delusional.

Tor: And you're not? You don't even know your name.

Cain: At least I'm not going around telling people I'm a god.

Tor: Demigod.

Dr. Masterson: Gentlemen, the point of this exercise isn't to shame anyone. As you may have gathered, we're all in the same boat here.

Caspian: It's called a ship, darling. Especially one of this size.

<<groans>>

Dahlia: You certainly think highly of yourself.

Caspian: Give me five minutes, and you'll think highly of me too, love.

Dr. Masterson: Dahlia, your turn.

<<clothes rustling>>

Dahlia: Hi. Um . . . I'm Dahlia Moore. And honestly, I don't know what I'm doing here. I seem to be the only one who doesn't think I'm some sort of fairytale hero.

Caspian: Villain, love.

Dahlia: Yeah, whatever. Anyway, I don't belong here.

Dr. Masterson: Oh, Dahlia, we both know that's a lie. The only way forward is to take accountability. Now tell us what got you in this situation.

Caspian: I want to know all your secrets, darling.

<<chair scrapes against floor>>

Dr. Masterson: Tor, no!

<<static>>

End of transcript.

CHAPTER
ONE
DAHLIA

One week earlier

Ball gowns are bullshit.

If I never had to squeeze myself into a formal gown and this much underwear again, it would be too soon. I was more of a yoga pants and oversized sweat-shirts kind of gal. Messy buns and glasses. Mismatched fuzzy socks and two-day-old Cheeto stains. Not red silk numbers trimmed in black lace, with matching opera-length gloves and murder skis (a.k.a. stilettos).

Shifting in my seat as the limo pulled up to the line of cars dropping people off at the theater, I forced my mind off the way my ass was currently eating the shapewear keeping the jiggle at bay. Honestly, I liked the jiggle. I liked being soft and cozy.

"I look ridiculous," I grumbled.

"You look hot. I'd fuck you," my editor and best friend

Kiki said, handing me the beaded clutch she'd let me borrow. It was only large enough for my phone and a tube of lipstick, but she insisted it completed the look.

She was so much better at all . . . this. Kiki walked through life as though the spotlight was meant to shine on her. But then, she was the extrovert in our pairing while I was the happy hermit. A bridge troll, if you will.

And I liked it that way. I was a recluse for a reason.

"I thought the whole point of a pseudonym was that I wouldn't have to show up at these things."

"That was before you went and got Twilight famous, Ms. Spector."

"Don't start," I groaned, just like I always did when she referred to me by my other persona.

Kiki laughed, pulling out a compact and checking her perfectly powdered face. "I can't help it if you're a hotshot author, dollface. Rebel changed your life in basically every way. That means public appearances but also a fuck ton of money."

She was right. I'd written Rebel and the Haunts with zero expectations and was met with a worldwide phenomenon. Traditional publishers had a bidding war over my sexy ghost smut after it had taken the indie publishing world by storm, then came the offers from producers for film rights. I'd gone from unknown to a household name in the blink of an eye. Well, Ruby Spector had. Most people didn't realize I was actually boring old Dahlia Moore, daughter of Jacob Moore. Yes, *that* Jacob Moore. The infamous cult leader who murdered his flock.

If the world got wind of that little morsel, things would be drastically different—in a bad way. We wouldn't be talking about my books anymore. I'd be splashed all over the news as the broken little girl who'd survived a terrifying ordeal instead.

Hard pass.

I'd take this kind of media circus over that one any day of the week.

So yes, the money was nice, but the rest of it threw me so far out of my comfort zone I'd need GPS to get home.

"Stop."

"I'm not doing anything."

"Yes you are. You're doing that broody, woe-is-me thing you do whenever I have to dress you up and parade you around."

"Maybe one of us should learn our lesson and break the cycle."

Kiki laughed. "I don't learn lessons as a rule."

I snickered, amused despite myself. "How's that working out for you?"

"No regrets," she said, running her hand down the strawberry blonde hair high on top of her head. It was styled in what she'd called a bubble braid. I stood by the assertion it looked like anal beads.

Her eyes landed on the necklace I always wore, and on instinct, I clutched the penny, the worn surface instantly calming me.

"Babes, you can't wear that."

"I always wear it."

"Trust me, I know, but this is a red carpet. You can't wear a dingy old coin around your neck. Here, give it to me. I'll keep it safe until we leave."

I scoffed, gesturing to her highlighter-pink gown as I unclasped the chain. "Where are you going to put it?"

She winked before taking the necklace from me and

slipping one hand into a hidden pocket in the skirt. "Pockets. Always go for the pockets."

My heart galloped beneath my ribs. I felt oddly exposed without my little coin. My good luck charm. I could barely remember the woman who gave it to me, but I could still hear her kind voice murmuring as she dropped the chain over my head. "This will keep you safe. It's your good luck charm, okay? Nothing bad can happen to you while you wear it."

I'd clung to that damn bit of copper like it was a lifeline. I knew now, of course, that it had just been a bit of foolishness a nice woman told a traumatized child, but it didn't change how vulnerable I felt letting go of it. Some people had a security blanket; I had my necklace.

Realizing I'd gone awkwardly silent, I cleared my throat and tried to pick up the threads of our conversation.

"I didn't exactly get a choice. You picked out my gown."

"Well then, next time maybe you should go with me when I invite you shopping."

"You know I don't go shopping."

Not in stores, that is. I was all about Instacart and free two-day shipping. They were the best thing that ever happened to me, truth be told. I didn't even have to leave my house for groceries anymore.

I'm what we refer to as a people person.

Yeah, I couldn't say that with a straight face either. More like anti-people person.

The car stopped, and my heart lurched as the driver opened our door, a hand held out to assist us each. Stepping onto the red carpet was like falling through the looking glass. Instant overwhelm hit me, making my chest tight.

Cacophony is the word I'd use to describe what greeted

me as Kiki nearly dragged me toward the crowd. Ahead of us I saw some of the production team, decked out in tuxedos and gowns. A few of the actors who made up the supporting cast were having photos taken, smoldering for the cameras like they were born for it. God, did I have to smolder? I didn't smolder. I barely knew what to do with my hands on a good day.

Dammit, why didn't Kiki get me a dress with pockets?

Maybe I could slink away and stand in the back. Hide behind the sexy actors who made up Rebel's ghost harem.

Sure, Dahlia. That would totally work if you weren't five-eleven and wearing heels. But go ahead, give it a try.

My head buzzed as the raging nervousness I was trying and failing to beat into submission continued pressing forward.

"Almost there, babes. Just a few pictures, and then we can go inside," Kiki whispered, giving my hand a squeeze.

I bit down on the inside of my cheek and gave her what I hoped was a reassuring nod. I winced as people shouted my name, begging me to look at their cameras and answer their questions.

"Ruby, when will we get a sequel?"

"What's next for Rebel and her guys?"

"What are you working on?"

I squinted beneath the bright lights, worried I was sweating so badly it would show through my dress.

"Um . . ." I said, mouth unbelievably dry.

Kiki came to my rescue. She always did. "We're not here to talk about that. We're here to go watch some ghost dick."

As expected, the crowd burst into peals of laughter at her irreverent description.

"Stand right here—relaxed fingers, no claw hands. Stare just over their heads and think of the latest cover shoot you went to. Remember how hot he was? That's the face you need to make."

"I don't look like him."

"Not the face he made. The face *you* made when you let yourself be a little thirsty." Kiki's eyes never left mine as she instructed me, and once I nodded in understanding, she left.

I did my best, but there was no way in Hades I was successful. I was pretty sure I looked constipated rather than thirsty, but I didn't care. I just wanted to get away from these people.

My first mistake was looking directly at one of the photographers. He grinned at me, his eyes glittering. Out of sheer reflex, I looked away, and a jolt went through me as my gaze flitted to someone else. This man made my blood run cold. He didn't have a camera raised and ready; he held a dagger, and his skin was pale, eyes filled with rage and familiarity.

"Dad?" I whispered as terror gripped every cell.

He shouldn't be here. I hadn't seen him since that day when I was little. Not because he'd abandoned me or been taken to jail. But because he died.

"No, no, no," I murmured, attempting to back away, but the cast had gathered around me for another photo op.

The beauty playing Rebel put her hand on my shoulder, and I turned to her, expecting to see a smile. Instead her eyes bugged wide, and she gasped before she fell to the crimson carpet. One by one, everyone around me dropped, eyes vacant, chests still. And all I could do as they died was scream.

I dropped into a crouch, my arms raised protectively around my head while my keening cries filled the night.

Images assaulted me. Memories I'd locked away.

Memories of the night my father had tried to—No.
I wouldn't let myself go back there.
Not again.
Never.
Again.

I heard the voices before I opened my eyes. One British and unfamiliar, the other a frustrated Kiki.

"Why would you want to send her to rehab?" Kiki asked. "She's not on drugs."

"Blackwood is a discreet, prestigious, and world-renowned wellness center."

"It's rehab."

"She needs rest and rejuvenation. A chance to recover from a clear psychotic break."

"Right, so . . . rehab."

At this, I finally cracked open my eyes, not needing more than a second to discern I was in some sort of hospital. Stark white walls, horrible fluorescent lighting, a small TV mounted in the corner, and lots of machines with wires running to the various places they were attached to me.

Kiki was seated beside me. She must have stopped by her house to get some clothes because she was no longer in the hot pink velvet dress she'd been rocking. Her glamazon makeup and Barbie-pink lipstick were still on, but that didn't mean much. That was pretty typical for her.

"That may be the word you choose to use, but here we call it a wellness center."

"More like an asylum," I croaked. "That's where they send the crazy people, right?"

My doctor—my *hot* British doctor—winced. "We don't use that word anymore, Ms. Moore."

"Crazy, or asylum?"

"Both. Mental illness is not something to stigmatize. But it is something we can treat."

"I'm not mentally ill."

"You're showing signs of severe burnout and exhaustion, and your delusional episode last night only confirms my diagnosis. The best course of treatment will be provided at Blackwood."

As if his words opened up the floodgates, everything came rushing back. The screaming. The dead bodies. My father's ghost.

"Oh my God, I killed them all," I shrieked, trying to jerk upright. Trying, because my arms were shackled to the hospital bed. Oh yeah, they definitely thought I was a nutcase.

Even though I didn't say it out loud, this time *I* winced. Maybe the hot doc was right about being more selective about my terminology. It seemed I was less 'sane' than I once believed, and they'd cuffed me to keep me safe from myself. Shit.

"Shh, it's okay, Dee. I'm right here, see. You didn't kill anybody. You just had a panic attack." The last part was hissed at the doctor, Kiki's eyes narrowed with censure. She hadn't liked the 'delusional' part any more than I had.

"Kiki, what happened? How did I get here?"

She reached over and brushed some damp hair off my forehead. "You freaked out. Then blacked out. Paramedics showed up and ambulanced you off. Brought you here to run some tests and make sure everything was all right."

"Ambulanced? Not a word, Keeks."

She waved a hand. "You skipped right over the hot paramedics rushing to your rescue part. Typical."

"Oh God," I groaned, already imagining the reactions to the videos of my very public meltdown that were surely already posted. "How bad is it?"

Kiki bit down on her bottom lip, weighing her words. She wasn't one to hold back, so if she was treading carefully, things had to be worse than she wanted to admit. "Bad enough that the publisher is breathing down my neck, demanding we comment on it." Kiki's phone chimed, drawing her attention to the slim device and away from me. I watched her expression go from impassive to concerned.

"Maybe we should take a look at Blackwood, babes."

"What? You were just saying I didn't need rehab."

"That was before your agent emailed me. Last night wasn't a good look. They want you to make a public statement addressing it. Leaning on your mental health and the toll this took on you will make them sympathetic rather than judgemental. If you own up to burnout getting the better of you, we can spin this as a good thing." She scrolled on her phone and then looked at the doctor. "Blackwood Estate is in Scotland?"

He nodded. "Yes. It's in the Highlands, on a beautiful parcel of land with a lake, rolling hills, and stunning scenery. The Scots don't say there's magic in the hills for nothing."

Kiki looked at me and waggled her brows, her voice low like she was whispering during a lecture. "Hear that, dollface? Magic. We could do with a bit of that right about now."

I shook my head while the doctor continued his sales pitch. "It's a place for restoration and rejuvenation, along with the best doctors on staff who will assist with any mental health needs you have."

Kiki smacked me on the arm, calling my focus away from Hot Doc. "Oh, listen to this, Blackwood Estate, formerly known as Blackwood Asylum, has a dark and sordid past going all the way back to the 1500s—"

"Told you it was an asylum."

"—now, newly renovated and under the ownership of The Donoghue Trust, Blackwood Estate is committed to serving its guests the best care possible and sending them back to their lives equipped with all the tools they need to flourish once they return home."

I sighed. "Sounds too good to be true."

Doctor Hiddleston—because he was hot and British and I didn't know his name yet—smiled at me, the glimmer in his eyes unmistakable. "Would it help if I told you I did a rotation at Blackwood myself? I wouldn't recommend a single one of my patients stay there if I didn't trust Dr. Masterson. She is singularly responsible for helping me reach my own potential. You'll thrive once you settle in."

"What kind of doctor is she?" I asked, though I had a strong suspicion based on where she worked.

"Psychiatrist."

The woman was going to have a field day with me. Daughter of a cult leader. Orphaned at twelve in the middle of what the media dubbed a mass suicide ritual gone wrong. Aversion to people and leaving her house with crippling anxiety and a swiss cheese memory.

Christ, they were going to lock me up and throw away the key.

I reached for my necklace, needing its familiar weight between my fingers, only to come up empty.

"It's in my purse," Kiki whispered, correctly interpreting the little whimper that left me.

Without warning, the atmosphere in the room changed, the air growing heavy, like everything was underwater. I couldn't breathe, the pressure on my chest so great tears came to my eyes. Out of the corner of my eye, I caught sight of a deathly pale woman standing in the glass doorway. A patient? Why did she look so sad, and what did she want with me? She was staring right at me with her mouth open in a silent scream.

My heart began racing, the beeping on the monitor betraying the oncoming panic attack. Squeezing my eyes shut tight, I breathed slow and deep, desperate for the woman in the door to leave me alone.

"It's okay. Look, here it is. You're fine." Kiki pressed my necklace into my hand, and I swear, it felt like she'd lifted an elephant off my lungs.

"Thank you," I whispered weakly.

She winked at me.

"Code blue, room 210. Code blue, room 210," blared on the intercom along with an alarm.

"I'm sorry, I have to go. That's my patient." Doctor Hiddleston left the two of us in a rush, calling over his shoulder, "I'll check on you a little later."

"Thank you, Dr. Temperance," Kiki offered as she fluffed my pillow.

"Temperance. That's so much better than what I've been calling him in my head."

"Hot Doc?" Kiki guessed, knowing me too well.

"That and Dr. Hiddleston."

She snorted. "He did have a nice ass."

"Kiki!"

"What? He dropped his pen and bent over right in front of me. What was I supposed to do? Pretend he wasn't waving it in my face? It's not like I reached out and pinched it."

"Don't you dare take my doctor for a ride."

Her giggle was near maniacal. "Maybe that should be your next series. Hot hospital drama. Her Doctor Daddies."

"Stop."

"Dicked by the Docs?"

"I'm begging you."

"Dr. Good Dick?"

"I hate you."

"But you're feeling better, so it's worth it," she said as she took the necklace from my hand and gently fastened it around my neck.

I was. I was still scared and reeling from the absolute shit show of the night before, but for the first time since setting foot out of that limo, I felt a bit more like my usual self.

"So, Blackwood, huh?" I asked.

"Think of it as a long overdue vacation."

"I hate vacation. I get bored. I like to work."

"So work," she said with a shrug. "You've been struggling to come up with your next project. Maybe you'll get inspired by the Highlands and all those castles."

"You mean all the ones I won't get to see because I'll be in the looney bin."

"Wellness center."

"Prison."

"Retreat."

"You say potato . . ."

She took my hand and squeezed. "It'll be good for you.

Maybe you can work through some of your struggles with anxiety while you're there? Wouldn't it be nice to be able to go to lunch with me without being wound so tight?"

As close as we were sitting, there was no way Kiki missed my flinch.

"You know I didn't mean it like that . . ." she started.

And I did. I did know that. But deep down, I feared that one day she'd grow tired of me and my 'struggles.' That being my friend was more work than it was worth.

"Fine. When do I leave?"

Her gentle smile said she'd already booked my stay at Blackwood. I couldn't be angry with her for it. I'd always been one who needed a push to get started. This was the same thing.

"A few days. That gives us time to get you packed and book your flight."

"Can't wait."

THREE

DAHLIA

"I guess they weren't kidding when they said Gothic castle," I muttered, staring at the black lacquered monstrosity masquerading as a door.

Was this a doorbell situation, or was I supposed to use the ancient gargoyle knocker staring me down? The faces were obscene, all bulgy eyes and forked tongues. Yes, multiple faces. There were three of these little fuckers stacked on top of each other totem style. I immediately named the ugly creatures Tom, Dick, and Harry. Appropriate names for gargoyles, if I do say so myself.

Reaching out, I moved to grab the knocker, but the massive door creaked open, revealing . . . a pirate? What the hell?

"Are you my mail-order bride, then?"

I blinked at the, dare I say, dashing scoundrel. "Excuse me?"

He grinned, and I was momentarily blinded by the perfection of his teeth. They were Hollywood actor white. *Definitely not a real pirate, then, but maybe he plays one on TV.*

To be fair, everything about the man was perfection. He was sex on a stick hot. If I were describing one of my fictional heroes, I'd say he was an invitation to sin. All chiseled features, tousled hair, intense eyes a shade so blue it couldn't possibly be real, and the guyliner . . . have I mentioned the guyliner? Oh shit, was that a dimple? And an earring. Fuck me. He wasn't stacked like a Viking, but I bet he could pick me up and throw me around, which was saying something, given my height and more than ample curves.

"Honestly, I was only having a laugh when I placed my order, but if you're here to tie me down, I'm your willing captive, love." He held his hands out, wrists together as if waiting for me to bind them.

My mouth hung open as I tried to figure out how to respond.

"All right there, darling?" He leaned one arm against the doorframe, brow raised, his crooked grin making that dimple deepen. "Have I already scandalized you?"

"N-no, I'm fine. I . . ." Jesus, I had to clear my throat just to talk to this man. "My name is Dahlia Moore. You should be expecting me."

His eyes dropped to the bags by my feet and then slowly made their way back up my body. I tried not to fidget in my black leggings and off-the-shoulder *Never Meet a Man* sweater, which didn't do anything for my figure.

"Moving in, then? Excellent. I can show you to my room."

"Thank you, that would be"—I paused as his words sank in—"Wait. Your room?"

He held out a hand for my bag and continued smirking. "Well, it'll be so much lonelier if you stay in yours. I'm a cuddler."

My mind immediately populated with images of his body twined around mine. I couldn't help but shiver as a wave of heat rolled through me.

"Uh, I'm not. Sorry."

Lies.

Filthy, filthy lies.

I'd cuddle the fuck out of this guy. Cuddle fucks all day. Mmm, yup.

Offering me his arm, he gave a soft chuckle when I hesitated before taking it. Sure, he was eccentric, but wasn't I as well? He smelled of clean ocean and a hint of patchouli, and I had to fight the urge to lean a little closer so I could breathe him in deeper.

"Do you work here?" I asked.

"Darling, I'm a captain. I don't work."

"A captain? Like in the navy?"

He laughed, a loud, sensual rumble that rolled down my spine and had me clenching my thighs. Holy balls, what was with this guy? He was throwing off pheromones like it was his purpose in life.

"Caspian, I've told you not to answer the door," a diminutive woman with a delightful Scottish brogue called out from the end of the hallway. She wore a pair of black-rimmed spectacles with a bejeweled chain attached to them that glittered in the light. And the way she was dressed, in a pair of black slacks, a crisp pink button down, and a white doctor's coat, made it clear she was in charge.

"What would you have me do? Allow this exquisite little lamb to molder on our stoop?"

The doctor wasn't nearly as charmed by my escort as I was. Her lips tilted down in a frown, her brown eyes narrowing in annoyance. "If you truly wanted to be helpful, you could flag down an orderly. Or summon me. Lord knows you're always looking for a reason to sneak into my office."

"I am a pirate, love. Sneaking is part of the job description."

She rolled her eyes and approached me. "Dahlia?"

"Yes."

"You're earlier than expected. Come with me, and we'll get you settled in."

Caspian slipped his arm around my waist, giving me a squeeze before bringing his lips to my ear and whispering, "I'll find you later, darling. We'll have some fun."

"Caspian, don't think I won't revoke your outside privileges."

He let out a low laugh. "Yes, mummy dearest."

He sauntered off with entirely too much swagger. Something about the movement, the way he sort of rolled from side to side, made me think he really was used to moving about a ship at sea.

"So I take it he's a patient, then?" I asked once he'd disappeared around a corner.

The doctor sighed and removed her glasses, using the edge of her coat to clean the lenses. "What gave it away? The pirate garb? I'm Dr. Elizabeth Masterson, by the way. We'll be working closely together in the days to come."

"Do I need to be worried about him, Doctor?"

"Only in the sense of protecting your virtue," she said with a surprisingly bubbly laugh. "He's mostly harmless. Just mischievous. And charming. He'll talk you out of your trousers if you're not careful."

Oh dear. But also, why did that thought send a thrill through my body?

Because you're a virgin romance novelist, and you're dying to live your fantasies but too afraid to actually let someone touch you.

I do enough touching myself, thankyouverymuch. I might be a virgin, but I was far from innocent. My toy collection was extensive, and I had a very colorful search history. You don't write polyamory without learning a thing or two. One woman and four men required a vivid imagination, especially since a girl only had so many holes.

"Miss Moore, are you quite all right?" The doctor's voice snapped me out of my defensive spiral.

"Yes. Of course. So, um . . . the patients here are just allowed to wander?"

Her warm laugh eased something inside me. "They're not patients. We call them residents. And yes, for the most part. Anyone you see roaming the grounds has been deemed in control enough of themselves to be allowed the privilege."

In control enough? That was an odd way of phrasing it.

"So I don't need to worry about a psychopath chasing me down one of these endless corridors with a shank made from their toothbrush?"

Dr. Masterson stopped with a hand pressed to her chest. "My, what do you think this place is? A prison?"

Isn't it?

"You'll find all the common areas are shank-free. Now, let me show you around, shall I?" Before I could ask her about my bags, she glanced down at them. "Leave those next to the door, and someone will be along to take them to your quarters."

Quarters. A bitch is not in Kansas anymore.

Though the Gothic castle I was currently standing in sort of gave that away.

21

"Follow me, and please remember we have strict rules for a reason. Chief among them is locked doors are there for your safety. Do not, by any means, open one."

I swallowed hard, but simply nodded and followed behind her. The castle was sprawling. I was going to need a map if I had any hope of finding my way around. Blackwood wasn't the dreary place I'd expected. Nor was it anything like the posh LA rehabs you see in magazines or on TMZ. It was . . . quaint. Warm. A bit dated in terms of furnishing, but everything had been chosen with care and was clearly expensive. If I was being honest, I felt a bit like Belle stumbling into the Beast's house. All I was missing was a chipper housekeeper to show me the ropes. And a library . . . obviously.

She showed me to various rooms, one a sun porch with soft pillows positioned around the space, a few other residents sitting on them with their eyes closed as they were led in a guided meditation.

"You're free to join in any of the group activities you wish, but I will also make my recommendations after we have our first session."

"And when will that be?"

"Tomorrow morning, once you get settled and get some rest."

"Can't wait," I said, my tone betraying my words.

My focus raked over the meditators, taking them all in. They looked like normal people: a willowy woman with dark ebony skin and long lavender hair dressed in yoga pants and a sports bra, a pale as bone man with cheekbones that could cut glass, a tiny woman with elfin features wearing a gown that looked like it was made from leaves, and then . . . him. The least normal of the bunch.

Even seated, he towered over the others. His body was insane. Muscle stacked upon muscle. I think his bicep was the size of my head, and his thigh was basically a whole-ass watermelon. And then there was his hair. Thick golden strands streaked with black and a stubbled jawline in the same shade, the angle so sharp it could make a sculptor weep. There was one section of his hair in particular—what they referred to as the money piece at the salon where I sometimes braved getting mine done—that was pure inky darkness. I'd thought Caspian was perfection, but this guy was . . . godly. There was no other word for it.

I sucked in a sharp breath as his eyes snapped open and locked on me. Piercing blue orbs framed by dark lashes set in a face I could only liken to a Norse god. He was rugged, striking, and beautiful.

His nostrils flared as we stared at each other, and he whispered, "Kærasta."

What the fuck did that mean?

"That's enough mediation for you, Miss Moore."

A soft tug on my elbow pulled me from the trance I seemed to have gotten locked in. It was hard to look away from the guy. There was no way he didn't feel it too, not with the way his gaze tracked my every step through the room. I knew the second I was out of his sight because I immediately felt the lack of it. Like it was a physical thing.

I'd written about it so many times, but didn't know it was real.

That a look *could* be physical. A claiming. No, a branding. That's what it had felt like. As if the second his eyes landed on me, something inside woke up and shouted, "Mine." I just wasn't sure if it was his voice or my own.

"Who was that?" I breathed.

"I assume you're asking about Tor Nordson. He's quite the pretty picture, isn't he? Comes from a long line of Vikings. Berserkers, if you believe the lore."

I could believe it. That man probably made firewood with his bare hands and hurled entire tree trunks for funsies.

"What's he in for?"

A sly smile spread across her lips. "That's not my story to tell, lass. Doctor/patient confidentiality, you know."

"But you told me Caspian's story."

"Did I? He's a different case. He tells everyone who meets him exactly who he is."

Thinking back on our brief but memorable interaction, I gathered he'd done just that.

"Fair enough," I grumbled.

A short, stocky man met us when we finally arrived at the base of the stairs. He clearly worked here, dressed in white trousers and a white button-down. I always thought white an interesting choice for any medical facility, to be honest. Bodily fluids, you know?

"Ah, Joffrey, right on time."

"No relation to the Game of Thrones tyrant, I hope," I said, eyeing the short man's red beard and shock of red hair. He reminded me a bit of a life-size Troll doll. I wondered if he had a little gem in his belly button. Maybe he'd let me rub it for luck, and I'd wake up back at home in the safety of my own bed.

This was the problem with writers. We sort of ran away with our imaginations in the middle of important conversations. Or at least this one did.

"Follow me, Miss Moore," he grumbled, not answering my question, I noticed. Suspish.

"I'll see you tomorrow at noon for your private session.

Don't be late. My schedule is quite full." Dr. Masterson turned and walked away without giving me the chance to respond.

"Lead the way, I guess," I said to Joffrey, who was already heading up the stairs.

He wasn't what I'd call chatty, so our silent trek gave me the opportunity to take in the worn carpet running down the center of what had to be genuine hardwood floors. The walls were stark, but not entirely bare. Every few feet, there was a random pastoral painting or portrait of some long-dead person. The banisters were hand-carved and had a natural shine after centuries of hands running along them. I had a feeling if I listened hard enough—or could converse with inanimate objects—the walls would tell me some wild stories. There had to be a mad king who stayed here once upon a time, right?

"Farmer George," I whispered to myself.

"What's that?" Joffrey asked.

"Nothing." Then I glanced behind me at the arches with panes of stained glass in the entryway. "You don't have an observatory, do you?"

"Yes. Why?"

I smirked, thinking of my favorite comfort series on Netflix. "No reason."

He shook his head and continued leading me down the long as fuck hallway. Each door had a number mounted at eye level and three locks on each one. I was waiting for Joff to pull out a huge iron key ring at any moment. Instead we stopped in front of room number seven, and he shot me a look.

"What?"

His eyes went from my hand to the door, but he said nothing.

"You're gonna have to help me out here, Joff. I cannot, in fact, read minds."

"Touch the handle, miss."

"A secret compartment isn't going to slide open so a needle can pop out and steal some of my blood, is it?"

He looked at me as if I was high. Considering where he worked, I was a bit surprised he found the question out of line. That couldn't have been the weirdest thing a patient ever asked him. Unless he was new here. Maybe this was his orientation, poor dude.

"Blood is precious, so no."

I shuddered. Creep.

Pressing my thumb to the center of the doorknob, I waited as the whirring of each lock disengaging filled the air. Then the door opened, and I let out a soft "Whoa."

"Look at that. It worked. Thanks, Jof—"

"One last thing, miss," the orderly said, apparently not wanting my gratitude.

I raised a brow, waiting for him to fill me in. If he could be a rude shit, so could I.

"You need to surrender all prohibited items."

"Prohibited items?" I repeated with a snort. "Do you think I'm hiding a gun in these leggings? Or is this like TSA, and I'm not allowed to cross the threshold with any of my own fluids?" A little shiver rolled down my spine as I remembered his comment about blood.

He just stared at me, still entirely unamused. "No weapons are permitted in these halls."

"Good thing I'm fresh out."

"Your necklace, miss. It's a talisman of ancient protection. A weapon. Hand it over."

"I'm sorry, how is a penny a weapon?" I asked, skipping

right over the BS about it being a talisman of protection, whatever the fuck that was supposed to mean.

"It's made of iron."

"It's made of copper."

"No. It looks like a penny to you, but it's not. That is iron, and I must confiscate it."

I clutched the penny like it was my lifeline. "You can't have it."

"I will take it from you by force if necessary."

I was at least two heads taller than him. I could take him. Removing the necklace, I held it as high as my arm would stretch. "If you can get it, you can have it. Otherwise, kick rocks."

He blinked at me and then shocked the hell out of me by bounding into the air. I swear the guy had a spring-loaded ass. He snatched the necklace from my hand and kept on walking as if he hadn't just leapt four feet.

It seemed silly; it was just a necklace, but I felt wrong without the little bauble. Before I could close my door, a figure appeared right where Joff had been standing, startling the hell out of me. My chest hollowed out, that same persistent buzzing I'd felt at the hospital and the premiere filling my ears. The man looked . . . wrong. His eyes were a burning acid green, and an animalistic growl rumbled from his throat.

"I-I think you have the wrong room," I spluttered.

He reached for me, forearm sprouting fucking fur as claws—actual claws—in the place of fingernails came *this-close* to slashing across my throat.

"Holy shit!" I jumped back, narrowly avoiding him.

Then he turned around and—oh God, I *was* crazy—walked through the wall like it wasn't even there.

I must have closed the door behind me—but I don't

remember doing it—because my knees gave out, and I slid down the panel of wood as my entire body shook.

Jesus fucking Christ.

I was losing my mind.

I had to be, because . . . it was one thing to write about ghosts, but another thing entirely to see them.

T rolled out of my bed the next morning intent on finding my one true love. Coffee, obviously. I never slept well when I wasn't in my own space, but last night had been epically terrible. Every noise in my room woke me: the creak of the bed frame, the sounds of the old pipes groaning, the scream of the wind in the rafters. Each one brought back the memory of that freaky as fuck wolfy man who'd walked through the wall.

Half of me expected him to make an encore appearance, this time showing me what he could do with those claws of his. Suddenly I was living my own Red Riding Hood fantasy, except I was the one in the bed with the sheets pulled up to my nose, and my visitor didn't bother hiding the fact that he was the Big Bad Wolf. Metaphorically, of course. In reality, I was alone—so far as I could tell—and standing in the middle of my room in my PJs. But you get the idea.

"Get it together, Dahlia. You're going to put on some clothes, go downstairs, and caffeinate. Then, you'll do everything you can to get yourself phone and computer privileges."

Which probably meant I shouldn't mention the wolf-man. I was no expert, but hallucinations didn't tend to win people any brownie points.

Pulling on a soft oversized sweatshirt with *Buy me books and tell me to STFUATTDLAGG* on the front, followed by a pair of black yoga pants, I slipped my feet into a pair of Chucks and gave myself a cursory once over in the mirror. There was no saving my hair, so I didn't even bother brushing the heavy white-blonde mass and pulled it up in my signature sloppy bun. As far as the dark circles under my eyes, it wasn't like I had any makeup to fix that, and honestly, I really didn't give a shit. I wasn't here to make friends or find my future husband.

A memory of Caspian and the godly Viking flitted through my brain and sent little tingles to my bathing suit parts. The thought of running into them looking like this sent a pang of apprehension through me, but then I shrugged. There was no hiding the truth. This was my status quo.

"Bridge troll mode activated. That's right, what you see is what you get, Blackwood. Don't like it, send me back."

My hand trembled when I reached for the doorknob, the fear that wolfman was going to be on the other side of the wood getting the better of me. But in the end, coffee won out, and I yanked it open, tense and ready to somehow defend myself. Laughable, I know. What would I be able to do against a ragey hallucination?

Usually when I was dealing with figments of my imagi-nation, I was the one in control. I was the one killing them off or making them fall in love. This time I was at their mercy, and I didn't like it. Not a single bit.

I survived by being in control of myself and my environ-ment. But in the last week, that had all been tossed on its head. Now I had zero control, which resulted in nervous breakdowns that led to me being sent away.

You should have stayed home. None of this would have happened if you'd just skipped the premiere like you'd wanted to.

But there was no putting the genie back in the bottle, as they say, so instead I had to find a way to deal with my new circumstances.

As luck would have it, the hallway was empty. Nothing but a long stretch of pastoral paintings and wall sconces greeted me, and I sighed in pure relief. God, I was a chicken. I couldn't even look at a corridor without being scared.

What is wrong with you? You write about way scarier stuff than this. Strap on your lady balls and handle your shit, Dahlia.

The pep talk rolled through my mind in Kiki's voice. She always called me on my BS. It was one of the things I loved most about her. She knew when to coddle me and when to throw my ass to the wolves. *Oh, wolves . . . shudder. Way to go, brain. I was just getting my poop in a group.*

Hustling as fast as my feet would take me without actually running—that was reserved for escaping death—I darted for the stairs, eyes focused straight ahead as I pushed away the irrational fears in my mind.

I was starting to feel good about myself and even a little silly for how stressed out I was over the simple act of leaving my room when I ran into him. I'd just made it to the first floor and was turning a corner, trying to remember which way led to the dining hall, when I collided with what felt like a brick wall.

"Watch where yer going," the wall grumbled. Though, when his hand gripped my bicep to steady me, I realized it wasn't a wall. I'd run smack into a very tall, very fucking hot, man. A hot *Scotsman* by the accent.

Fuck me, what was in the water here? Was it a prerequisite for all the men here to be insanely gorgeous? His eyes were purple. Like real purple. The color of the violets Kiki kept bringing me for my desk and I kept killing. And the color was only emphasized by a thick fringe of stupidly long dark eyelashes. I'd have said they were extensions if he'd been a woman. Men always got the good lashes. What a waste.

"Sorry, I didn't see you," I said, proud of myself for keeping my cool enough to speak to him.

"I don't know how that's possible. I'm hard to miss."

I looked him up and down, taking in his tall frame and heavily muscled torso. His shoulders were easily double the width of mine. And then there was the inky black hair that fell into his eyes. My fingers itched to push it back so I could see more of him.

I knew I was staring, but I couldn't help myself. He was just so damn beautiful. Perfect in a way humans usually weren't. Even the tattoo swirling on the side of his neck seemed to shimmer. As I watched the scaled head of a . . . dragon? rippled, and then the eye—the same shade as his —popped open.

I stumbled back, or tried to. The hot Scot was still holding me in place.

"Are you afraid of me, lass?"

I shook my head, but the slight twitch of his lips made me think he was calling me a liar. As did his next words.

"I haven't done anything to you . . . yet."

"Is that a threat?"

He released me at the question, and I took a step away from him.

"Watch where you're going next time. There are far worse creatures you could run into than me."

I couldn't help but notice he didn't say no.

I also couldn't help but stare after him as he walked away, the muscles of his back and ass flexing deliciously beneath his fitted shirt and joggers.

"So you met Kai," a soft, hesitant male voice pulled my focus from the retreating book boyfriend come to life.

"Kai?" I repeated stupidly, finding another walking stereotype waiting for me. If Kai was the book boyfriend, then the newcomer was a cute nerd. With black-rimmed glasses emphasizing hazel eyes, windswept red-brown hair in desperate need of a trim, and a crooked smile he looked like he belonged on a college campus, not in an asylum. Sorry, wellness center.

"Malakai, but don't tell him I told you that." The cute nerd leaned in and winked. "He hates it."

"I don't blame him. Makes him sound like some sort of super villain. It must be a family name."

"It's something. I'm Oz. And you're Dahlia." Holding out his hand, Oz waited for me to shake. I was still caught up on the part where he already knew my name.

"I wouldn't touch him if I were you. Oz knows better than to look into minds here, but a new creature in our midst might prove too tempting." A statuesque woman with sleek black hair and startling amber eyes placed her palm on my outstretched arm, stopping me before I returned the gesture Oz was offering.

"I wasn't going to read her mind, Sorcha. I just wanted a little peek. She's a mystery." Oz pouted and shoved his hand into his pocket.

"And what good would it do for you to peek?"

"Maybe she knows something about the Ripper. She was out there in the world, and no one tells us anything useful."

"The Ripper? As in Jack the?" I asked, feeling more confused by the second.

Sorcha laughed, her smile flashing frighteningly sharp canines. Oh God, did she think she was a vampire or something? Her Morticia Addams attire certainly pointed to it. Black on black, with enough cleavage I was in danger of falling in and never escaping.

"Precisely. Although I doubt he's the original. Bloody copycats can't even come up with their own creative ways to murder anymore."

"And he's here?"

"Don't worry. You're not his type," Oz said.

"Well, that's a relief." The sarcasm dripped from every word out of my mouth.

"The Blackthornes are tracking him."

"And who are they?"

Sorcha stared at me like she couldn't believe I had to ask and then laughed, the sound bordering on maniacal. "Only the most famous vampires in existence. Don't worry, my family won't let him get away with this for long. My brothers love a good hunt."

Yep. Delusions of being a vampire. And a famous one at that. Cool. Cool.

This place was officially the worst.

I took a step away from Sorcha, which put me closer to Oz, but at this point, I'd take a guy who fancied himself a mind reader over a woman who'd had her teeth sharpened into fangs. Kiki was in so much trouble for sending me here.

"So a serial killer's on the loose? Anything else I need to know?"

Oz blinked his owlish eyes at me, pushing his glasses up his nose. "You're supposed to be the one bringing us news, but I suppose we can provide you with a little orientation."

He cleared his throat as if preparing to launch into a full speech. "Welcome to Blackwood Asylum. Home of the criminally insane."

"What, really?" I balked.

He winked at me. "No. Not insane anyway. Criminal might be debatable. Not many of us are in here by choice. We get stuck in here when we misbehave."

"You mean when our power misbehaves," Sorcha corrected.

A vampire with power? I was so lost. Not to mention terrified.

"Case in point, Sorcha Blackthorne has a reputation for abusing her compulsion powers. Oh, and she killed her husband."

"Arranged his murder," Sorcha corrected before blithely adding, "But I did the world a favor. He was a lecherous creature."

I mentally broke out into a rendition of *Cell Block Tango*.

"And you?" I asked Oz, pretending I didn't currently have six versions of Sorcha performing Fosse in my mind.

"I melted a few brains and left them vegetables. It was an accident."

I mouthed, 'It was an accident,' and then blinked. "Of course," I eventually managed, beginning to plot my escape. I could not stay here with these people. There was no way it was safe.

Oz stared me down, not a hint of amusement on his face. "You're pretty judgy for someone in your position, doll. I'm sure *you* didn't mean to kill all those people."

"I didn't kill anyone."

"Sure."

"I swear."

"You know, I'm surprised they didn't lock you up in No Man's Land."

"What's that?" I couldn't help it. I needed to know.

"It's where they put the truly dangerous ones," Sorcha threaded her arm through mine and began walking, dragging me through the maze of halls and rooms. "No Man's Land is the only place the most deadly of us can be housed safely. If they were to escape, the world would bleed."

"Sounds great," I deadpanned.

"It's not. I should know," Oz said, his voice small and hard. "It's like solitary confinement on crack. No windows. No company. No entertainment of any kind. Just you, a cell, and a warded room. And we can't forget the *treatments*."

"Jesus," I breathed.

"Oh, he doesn't care about you," Oz said. "No one does. We're the forgotten ones, don't you know? Blips in history. The family embarrassments, hidden away from the public eye."

God, that was dark.

This conversation was doing nothing for my chill. All my anxiety from the night before came roaring back to the foreground of my mind. I was so keyed up I felt like I had ants crawling beneath my skin.

"Thanks for that cherry on my shit sundae."

Sorcha chuckled. "Oh, I like her. She's feisty. Reminds me of, well, me."

An alarm blared through the castle, lights flashing as the shrill alert bounced off the walls.

"Fuck! What's that?"

"New resident," Oz muttered. "Coming this way. Get back against the wall and give them space."

Coming this way. Meaning No Man's Land.

The new resident was a dangerous one.

Part of my brain screamed at me that this was a running moment. That I should sprint up the stairs and not stop until I reach the safety of my room, coffee be damned.

The other part of me was curious what someone that dangerous looked like. Some of the most notorious serial killers were undeniably attractive. And clearly, everyone here seemed to have been slapped with the beauty stick a few extra times. Or would this new person be the exception? Would they be horribly disfigured? Chained up? Foaming at the mouth?

I blamed the writer in me for my curiosity, but I stayed put. I *needed* to know.

My answer came in a rush of white coats and snarls as two orderlies escorted our newest addition. He fought them every step of the way, eyes flashing a vivid, burning azure. Oh, also, he was totally hot. His dark blond hair was windswept, his bone structure classically perfect, and even in a straightjacket, there was no hiding his muscular build. So . . . hot. Definitely. But in an 'I belong in a slasher movie' kind of way.

Figures.

I've always had a thing for villains.

Morally gray is my favorite flavor, and red my favorite color. Flag, that is.

We'll just call them daddy issues and leave it at that.

CHAPTER
FIVE
CAIN

Warm skin slid over mine, her legs tangling in the sheets as she buried her beloved face in my chest. I could smell her all around me, sweet and succulent. Like a night-blooming garden in the summer mixed with fresh pomegranate and the earthy notes of teakwood. Fuck, the woman could take me under in one soft sigh.

She's always been my weakness. Ever since I first laid eyes on her. She represented everything good and wholesome. Everything I was not. My opposite. My perfect counterpart. My one true obsession. And I finally had her in my bed.

Her hair splayed across me, a silken blanket I wanted to wrap around my fist so I could hold her to me forever. She was my goddess and always would be.

She moaned and layered tender kisses across my shoulder as her hand snaked beneath the sheet covering my waist.

"Insatiable little thing, aren't you?" I rumbled, not opening my eyes for fear of breaking the spell.

"When it comes to you, always," she whispered, taking me in her firm hold.

I groaned and rutted into her grasp, seeking more of that sweet friction.

"You will be my undoing."

"You were already mine," she said with a soft laugh. "Defiler of innocence. Thief of virtue."

I nipped her on the side of her neck. "Love of your life."

"That too."

"Stop playing with me, mate. Take me into you."

"Open your eyes and look at me first," she demanded.

No.

My soul protested even as my eyelids sought to obey.

The dream always happened this way. As soon as my eyes opened, she'd disappear, and I would be alone again. Eternally lost. Endlessly searching.

"Open, my heart. Please?"

I couldn't deny her. My eyelids lifted, and shocked gray irises found mine, but before I could memorize her face, she was gone, and I was met with four white walls and an empty room.

The first thing that registered was the throbbing ache behind my eyes. The second was the fluffy ball of fur at the end of my bed. And the third was that I had no fucking clue where—or who—I was.

"Well, isn't this a pickle?" I muttered as I sat up and frowned at the dog. "What the fuck are you supposed to be? A bichon?"

The dog gave a tiny yip before resuming its seated, quivering position. The little pink tongue never quite found its way back inside the dog's mouth, instead lolling to the right, a pearl of drool threatening to fall on my leg.

"Asshole," I muttered on pure principle.

What kind of place was this that they locked you up but left you a puppy on your pillow instead of a mint?

Asshole yipped again, then got to his?—yes, definitely his—paws, sniffed a few times, circled, and . . . "Oh, come on, fella. You just met me. Don't you dare take a piss on my bed."

Bored of me already, Asshole scooted away from the puddle he'd left me and yawned before promptly falling asleep, his little chin tucked between two tiny paws.

"Well, aren't you fucking useless," I grumbled, climbing out of the narrow cot they were trying to pass off as a bed.

"Hey!" I yelled, spying the solid metal door with its bolted peephole. "Let me out of here. I'm innocent."

I couldn't possibly know whether that was true, and something told me I was far from innocent, but it seemed like the sort of thing a man in my position would say. Reaching for the handle, I wrapped my palm around the cool metal, but a painful shock passed through me, jolting hard enough I was thrown backward.

Asshole began barking fiercely, his little tail sticking straight out and his ears back in a failed attempt to look vicious.

"If that's your way of sounding the alarm, you're about thirty seconds too late, you good-for-nothing mongrel."

Asshole cocked his head, not understanding a damn word I said. It was probably for the best.

I plopped down on the cot again, sighing and dropping my head in my hands. How the hell did I end up here? My shoulders and wrists were both sore, like I'd been bound and struggled. Honestly, I probably had. You didn't wake up in a padded cell without having been restrained.

"What are you in for?" I asked the dog.

He sidled up next to me, laying down with his head on my thigh, then huffing.

"Disorderly conduct and public urination. I see. Let's throw in a noise complaint too."

Had it been a different breed—say a Doberman or a shepherd of some variety—I might say I was in good company. Those were the sorts of misdeeds one might have after a memorable night on the town and a few too many bourbons.

"I wonder what I'm in here for," I said after a beat, absently rubbing my wrists. "Must be a hell of a humdinger if I can't even remember." Standing, I paced the small room, desperate for a way out. I might not remember much, but I definitely didn't like confined spaces. "Maybe you're here as a kind of insurance. They have to feed you sometime. Right? They can't leave us in here alone together forever."

As if proving me right, there was a hard rap on the door a second before it opened.

A small woman in a white lab coat with a pile of red curls peered at me through her spectacles. "Ah, good to see you're awake, Cain."

Cain. I guess that was me.

"I'd love to say it's good to see you again, Doctor . . ."

She adjusted her glasses, then stepped over the threshold, one palm out, waiting for me to shake her hand. "Dr. Elizabeth Masterson. Welcome to Blackwood. Apologies for the somewhat . . . abrupt nature of your admission."

"I don't remember a lick of it. How did I end up here?"

The tiny woman let out a rather indelicate snort. "Ye damn near blew up a hospital."

"Come again?"

"You're lucky a colleague of mine was in the middle of contacting me about another patient. He recognized the symptoms immediately and was able to transfer you here rather than handing you to the authorities."

My gut twisted. "Authorities? Symptoms?"

"Your episode left an entire wing of the hospital decimated, Cain. But we got you out before the police found you. We're going to help you figure out how to control yourself. You won't be a danger to anyone once you're finished with treatment here."

"Treatment?" The headache that had already been a steady presence since I woke up turned into a full-blown migraine. Not a single word coming out of this woman's mouth made any sense. "I don't . . . I don't remember any of that."

"Ah yes," she said with a sympathetic nod, "that tracks. A power burst like yours often results in short-term dissociative amnesia. One of the things you and I will work on together is getting those memories back."

Fuck, my head hurt. Asshole hopped off the bed and sat next to me, leaning his tiny body against my ankle. I wasn't too proud to admit I appreciated his warmth.

"Why am I in this cell? When can I leave?"

"That's what I'm here to determine. As long as you don't pose a risk to yourself or others, I'll let you out of here on a temporary pass. If you prove yourself safe, I'll assign you a room in our main residence hall."

"But when can I go home?"

Her brow lifted in challenge. "You don't even know where home is, so for now, you'd do best to consider Blackwood your home."

Fuck.

Her eyes dropped down to the furball at my feet. "How did you get in here?"

Asshole growled.

"We don't allow pets, Cain."

"He was here on my bed when I opened my eyes. He's not my pet. "

"Have you told him that? I'll take him and do . . . something with him." She leaned down and reached for Asshole, but the fluff ball snapped at her and gave a warning snarl. Tiny but fierce. Ish. I could work with that.

I also couldn't let her take him. Every protective instinct in my body told me he belonged with me. Scooping him into one arm, I held the pup like a football and said, "Looks like you're making an exception for this one."

"Familiar," she murmured.

"What is?"

She blinked as if she hadn't realized she'd spoken out loud. "Hmm? Oh, nothing. I suppose you're correct. And what are we to call him?"

"I've been calling him Asshole."

Her lips twitched with laughter. "I see. Very well, you may keep him. But, I draw the line at bringing your . . . dog with you to therapy. Find something to do with him for your appointment."

"What appointment?"

"The one starting in"—she checked her wristwatch—"half an hour."

"I don't need fucking therapy."

One corner of her mouth lifted as she stepped away from me and my new best friend. "Why don't you let me be the judge of that? I'll see you in thirty minutes."

"Where am I supposed to go? And can I get something to eat? Or a shower?"

She stepped over the threshold again and pulled the door nearly closed with her. "Joffrey will be along shortly to fetch you."

"Wait! Can I at least—" I didn't finish my question as the door closed and the nearly inaudible hum of that electric barrier snapped back into place.

Asshole yawned in my arms, pulling my attention to him. "Well, buddy, I guess it's just you and me."

The puppy leaned forward, that wet tongue darting out, but not to lick me. No. The little fucker earned his name as he bit down on my thumb, sealing our bond in blood and a string of curses.

CHAPTER
SIX
TOR

S weat dripped into my eyes as I pushed my body to its limits. I wasn't allowed weights, so I had to improvise and use my body weight instead. Thankfully I had that in spades, and pushing myself up and down while in a handstand position worked almost as well as a barbell.

"Five more minutes, Nordson," my babysitter called from his corner of the room. Bruno had been my assigned mage since the day I arrived in this godsdamned place. I couldn't take a piss without checking in with the man. Which was a smart move on Dr. Masterson's part, because he was the only one strong enough to bind me when my beast took over.

I'd been so jealous of my twin when he'd found his Berserker . . . until mine was awakened. Now I understood what he'd tried to explain. This was no blessing from the gods. It was a curse.

Quite literally, in my case.

I was never supposed to be a monster. I was Thor-blessed. A hero.

49

But now I was a hero no longer. I was nothing more than a beast.

The black rose inked into my chest proved it.

I dropped my feet to the floor and then straightened from my crouched position to study myself in the mirror. My formerly golden hair was streaked with black; my ice-blue eyes, once mirrors of my brother's, were now a midnight blue so dark as to be obsidian. And right in the center of my chest was a tattooed rose choked by thorns. Each time my beast took over, a petal withered and fell. That was thanks to Lilith, the demon proprietress of *Iniquity*, who'd taken an interest in me long before the Shadow Court administered their version of justice for a crime I didn't commit. She'd learned of my . . . affliction and connected me with Kai, the famed magical tattoo artist. Now I had a physical reminder of my folly.

I ran a hand over my chest but couldn't bring myself to count the fallen petals. One was too many. It didn't bear contemplating what would happen when the final petal fell. There wasn't an option that resulted in anything good.

My whole life, all I'd ever wanted was to bring honor to my family's name. To follow in my father's footsteps. Now, I'd bring only shame.

It was best I remained locked up here, far from their reach.

I never wanted them to learn about the monster I'd become.

"Time's up, Beast," Bruno grunted, approaching me with magic swirling between his palms. "Don't make me bind you."

With one final glance at my tattoo, I pulled the tie out of my hair and released the long locks, only to catch them all in my hand and secure them into a fresh bun.

"Keep your shirt on, Bruno. I've finished. I wouldn't dare be late for another of Dr. Masterson's rousing chats."

He smirked. "This one's going to be a little different."

"Different how?" Unease skittered up my spine. Not because I was afraid, but my beast was unpredictable. Changes to my well-maintained schedule meant possible triggers. Triggers resulted in dangerous consequences.

"I'll leave the explaining to her," he said, flinging the T-shirt I'd discarded at me. "You might want to put this on, though."

"Why? Can't stand the sight of all these glistening muscles?" I goaded. Bruno was the closest thing I had to a friend in this place, which meant I had to take the piss out of him. It was my love language, according to that little witch Moira I'd spent a few months with.

Bruno blushed but quickly recovered. "You're not going to be alone for this one."

"Not another group session. Do you recall what happened with the last group? Kai and I scared them off."

"Try not to do that this time, then."

"You say that like I'm the one to blame."

"Aren't you?"

I pulled my shirt on. "I am the picture of well-behaved."

"Since when?"

Since birth, actually. But I'd changed a bit since then. Instead of saying any of that, I sighed. "It's not my fault people try their hardest to provoke me."

"The last one that set you off was a loud chewer."

"You can't honestly say eating while in a group session is polite, let alone chewing loud enough to be heard."

"The one before that was a 'popper' if I recall."

"He was popping his gum in my face. He had it coming."

51

"And the pen clicker?"

"No explanation needed."

"And yet, they're the problem."

"Obviously."

Bruno shook his head. "You are ridiculous. And deluded."

"And you're a pain in my arse."

"Here I was thinking you were a pain in mine."

If my brother were here, he'd snap back with something snarky like, 'Not yet, but I could be if you play your cards right.' My heart gave a little pang. I missed my twin. But this was for the best, for all their sakes.

Clapping Bruno on the shoulder hard enough he grimaced, I shored up my self-control and nodded. "Do I have time for a shower, or do they get the Beast of Novasgard in all his sweaty glory?"

"You wasted any time you had complaining about your fellow residents."

I glared at him. "You started it."

Bruno's hands began to glow. "You might want to think twice about picking a fight with me, beastie. I'll set you on your arse."

I towered over him, but he was gifted in ways my physical strength couldn't compete with.

"Put your magic back in your pockets."

"That's not where I keep it," he said with a wink.

"What the hell is that supposed to mean?"

Bruno shrugged as he led the way toward the sunroom. "Dunno. Just sounded good."

"Did anyone ever tell you that you have a very punchable face?"

"Only my mum."

I laughed. "I think I'd quite like to meet her."

"You can't. We lost her to the Death Rattle before you arrived."

"Never say never. You know as well as I that ghosts come and go as they please."

Bruno shuddered. "Don't even joke about it. The last thing I need is my mom showing up while I'm rubbing one out in the shower."

"I'm going to have so much to contribute to group today. Thanks, Bru."

"You leave me and my mum out of it."

"You're the one that brought her up."

"How'd you like it if I started telling stories about your mum?"

Any hint of laughter faded as I gripped Bruno by the neck of his shirt and shoved him up against the wall. My voice was pure growl as I got into his face. "You keep my mother's name out of your mouth. She's a godsdamned saint among women."

Bruno's eyes got wide, but all he did was press those glowing hands against my wrists, zapping me and freeing himself in the process. "Firstly, I don't even know your mother's name. Secondly, now you see how it feels."

The rage that had spiked so suddenly returned to a low simmer. Which was basically its default state these days. Ever since my Berserker appeared, it never diminished entirely, though these flare-ups were occurring more and more frequently.

"Sorry," I grunted.

He shrugged. "It's what I'm here for."

The sunroom door opened, and Dr. Masterson greeted me with a warm smile. "Tor, thank you for joining us. Take a seat. The rest of the group should be here momentarily."

Bruno's gaze met mine, and he offered a slight nod. "I'll be right outside."

I returned his nod with one of my own and followed the doctor inside. Kai was already here, along with Caspian and a new guy I hadn't met yet.

My temper tugged against its restraints at the smug-as-shit smirk curling Caspian's lips. He was manspread in a chair, his eyes tracking my entrance into the room.

"Got a seat for you right here, Herc."

A little growl slipped free. "How many times must I tell you I am a *Norse* demigod?"

"At least one more," the pirate taunted. "Besides, aren't all demigods the same? They all have daddy issues."

I glared at him as I took the empty seat across the circle from him, between Kai and the newcomer. "My father could murder you in his sleep."

Caspian pretended to shake. "I'm so scared."

"You should be."

Kai sat up a little straighter, his gaze on mine. "Caspian, you know better than to rile him up before we've even started. Give the doctor a chance today, would you?"

"Where's the fun in that? This is the highlight of my day."

We all fell silent as the stunning blonde I'd noticed yesterday appeared in the doorway.

"Uh, is this the right room?" she asked.

"I stand corrected," Caspian murmured, his smile stretching at the sight of her.

Mine.

That same primal need I'd felt during meditation when she'd peered into the room hit hard and fast. Gods, what was this? My soul cried out for her, and I didn't even know the woman's name.

"Come sit by me, darling. I've been saving a chair for you," Caspian drawled as he stood, playing at being a gentleman.

Her cheeks turned a fetching shade of pink, and she tucked a lock of hair behind her ear as she cast her eyes down. "O-okay."

She made to sit, but he stopped her and slowly twirled her around. "Hang on, let me take a good look at you today. I missed you at breakfast." Was the dastardly pirate flirting with her? Of bloody course he was. "Do enlighten us, love. What does that jumper say?"

Her cheeks blazed crimson now. "Uh . . . I'd rather not say."

"Oh, but now I'm even more curious. You must tell us. We don't keep secrets from one another, do we, lads?"

I couldn't help but notice that Kai and the newcomer were staring at her with as much interest as me and the pirate.

Fuck. This didn't bode well. Already my Berserker was rattling his chains.

"Shut the fuck up and take that dick like a good girl," the stranger said, his southern accent surprising me. I wasn't sure why; Blackwood's prisoners came from all over the globe.

The woman stared at him with wide eyes while Caspian cackled with glee. "Oh, I'll call you a good girl any time you want, sweetheart."

"How did you know that?" she asked.

The stranger shrugged. "I have no fucking clue."

"I'm mortified." She sat next to Caspian, arms crossed over her chest as though trying to hide.

"Don't be. Everyone should wear their kinks on their chest. It would make things so much easier." Caspian went around the circle, pointing at each of us in turn, starting with me and ending with himself. "Primal, bondage, Daddy Dom, role playing. Oh, and group activities," he added with a wink. "But I think that might go for all of us."

I didn't bother acknowledging his statement. He was clearly making shit up. Or so I thought, until Kai coughed and crossed his arms.

"Nothing wrong with consensual rope play."

"I'm not judging you." Caspian slid his palm over my girl's knee, and I saw red.

"How can you possibly know I'm a, what did you call me, Daddy Dom, when *I* don't even know that?" the new guy asked.

The pirate shrugged. "You've got that whole protective and tortured vibe going on. And you look like you need a cuddle."

Before we could continue, the doctor strode in again, taking her seat next to my mystery woman.

"All right, now that we're all sorted, let's begin." She placed a recording device on the small table beside her and turned it on. "This is Dr. Elizabeth Masterson. It is October thirty-first, and the time is 10:00 a.m."

The session was a blur. I went through the motions, responding when necessary. I'd been through this before. I knew what to say to appease the doctor.

But then she turned to the new woman in our midst, and I was suddenly riveted.

"Dahlia, your turn."

Dahlia shifted in her chair, smiling shyly as she flicked her gaze to mine. Gods, it felt like she was speaking directly to me. "Hi. Um . . . I'm Dahlia Moore. And honestly, I don't know what I'm doing here. I seem to be the only one who doesn't think I'm some sort of fairytale hero."

Caspian leaned close and murmured, "Villain, love."

I hated that he was close to her, that he could bring out that lovely flush on her cheeks, but my focus was on her, my Dahlia. And she was mine. There was no doubt about it. *Kærasta*. The word whispered through my mind again.

I knew what it meant, what it signified. Of course I did. This woman was my fated mate, as impossible as that was.

Caspian trailed one lazy finger over her wrist, and I nearly lost control when she shuddered in response.

"Yeah . . . whatever. Anyway, I don't belong here."

Dr. Masterson tutted. "Oh, Dahlia, we both know that's a lie. The only way forward is to take accountability. Now tell us what got you in this situation."

Caspian tilted his head, still far too close to her, and feathered his lips on her neck as he whispered, "I want to know all your secrets, darling."

The thin hold I had on my rage snapped. Before he'd finished speaking, I was out of my chair and across the room, my body transforming into that of my beast. I would have his blood for this.

"Tor, no!" Dr. Masterson cried.

But before she could so much as attempt to stop me, Bruno had me bound in chains made of the strongest magic he possessed and was hauling me out of the room. Away from my mate, away from the pirate attempting to win her, and back toward the solitary cell that had become a sort of home to me while we waited out my rage.

Disbelief clutched at me, stopping any sound from leaving my lips as I watched Tor's skin change from the sun-kissed gold it had been to a disconcerting and unnatural deep gray. That wasn't all that changed, but my brain refused to accept what my eyes were seeing. Because instead of skin, it seemed as if he'd sprouted scales. But that was impossible. Maybe it was just some sort of rash. Yeah, a rash that ran up his arms and disappeared beneath his shirt.

Okay, but how do you explain the horns?

Yeah . . . there was no way to explain the thick black horns curving up and back from his temples. He was like some mythical goat shifter. But like . . . a sexy, scary version? Because despite the scales and horns, he had an almost fae-like quality about him. His face grew more sculpted, and his body became larger and bulkier with heavy muscle that made veins pop all along his arms. And I would have sworn lightning flashed in the obsidian pools of his eyes. But even with those changes, he was undeniably handsome. Regal. Wild—no, feral. That was the word.

Something in me was desperate to go to him and soothe the beast, even if he could kill me with one swipe of his hand. But before I could make that idiotic hormone-addled choice, he was captured in an electric blue haze that bound him. Dr. Masterson followed behind the orderly who'd taken charge of Tor, and the only two stable people in the room left me with . . . them.

Well, this was awkward. Were we supposed to talk about the crazed beast that just left the room or pretend it never happened?

Another thought occurred to me, and my stomach churned. They did *see* that, right? His transformation wasn't just another hallucination?

"So touchy. It's always the Vikings who fly off the handle at the most minor of perceived slights," Caspian said, sitting back in his chair and spreading his knees wide, as though he were a king on his throne.

"And what do you know of Vikings, pirate?" Kai asked.

"They're basically my distant cousins, are they not? They have their ships and their raids. It's practically the same thing as piracy."

Kai lifted a dubious brow. "Sure it is. I can't wait to let Tor know his *cousin* is here."

"Does he do this often?" Was my voice squeaky? I didn't want them to think I was some weakling, but Jesus, the guy was an actual monster.

"Beast out? Aye, lass. He's been doing well, but I've seen it a time or two. It hasn't gotten to the horns stage in a while, though."

Oh, thank God. They saw the horns too. I wasn't hallucinating.

Oh shiiit. That meant this place was even more fucked than I thought. Because if I wasn't hallucinating, then this was real. Which meant monsters actually roamed around. Holy crap, did that mean Sorcha really was a vampire?

"What's wrong with her?" Cain asked.

"She's hyperventilating," Kai answered.

"Easy, love. Take a deep breath." Caspian rubbed circles between my shoulder blades. "The only one who should be making you pant is me, but in pleasure."

"Do you ever get tired of hearing yourself talk?" Cain's muttered question might have been rhetorical, but Caspian answered him anyway.

"No."

"Pity," Cain drawled, filling the word with so much disdain I would have laughed if I hadn't been freaked the fuck out.

"I need to know something," I finally rasped.

"Is it how to get to my bedroom? I can show you the way." Caspian should have made me uncomfortable with the way he was trying to push my buttons. Instead, a twinge of arousal awakened in my belly. I clung to it, welcoming anything that would pull me out of my panic spiral.

"Did they put meds in our morning coffee or something? I'm seeing shit. This can't be real. First the wolfman, now Tor."

"The wolfman?" Kai's Scottish brogue didn't do a damn thing to diminish my desire. "You might need to be a bit more specific. Blackwood has a number of wolf shifters on its premises."

What.

The.

Fuck.

"This one walked through walls."

"Oh, a ghost then," Caspian said, with entirely too

much glee for my liking. "We have plenty of those. Poor sods. Trapped between worlds. I, unfortunately, am far too familiar with the concept." Then he winked at me. "Thank the stars I'm far more than a misty apparition. Go on, touch me. Feel for yourself. One hundred percent real and fully functioning."

"Give it a rest, man." Cain got to his feet, unfolding his long legs and providing me with a full view of his tall frame.

"You look good without the straightjacket," I blurted.

"I'd look even better with a glass of bourbon. Who do I have to kill to get a drink around here?"

Kai's low, rumbled laugh pulled my attention to him. "You'll have to take that up with Dr. Masterson. It's a privilege. Just like going outside, technology, and . . . physical connections with other residents."

"I'm sorry, physical wha—oh my fucking God, your tattoo is moving." I nearly swallowed my tongue as the dragon tattoo on Kai's neck worked its way from one side to the other. I hadn't made that up.

"Of course it is. It's magic." Kai looked at me like I wasn't firing on all cylinders.

"Magic?" I said the word slowly, trying to let it sink in.

"Aye. That's my specialty. Magic tattoos."

Caspian chuckled. "Well, don't be coy. Tell her what else you can do. Oh, right . . . nothing. You've been neutered."

Kai growled—honest to God growled—the rounded pupils of his violet eyes turning to reptilian slits. "Keep poking me, pirate. See where it gets you."

Was it my imagination, or had his voice gotten even deeper?

"I'm not scared of you, dragon."

"You should be."

"Maybe if you had access to your beast, I might take those threats of yours a little more seriously."

Dragon? Access to his beast?

These guys were nuts. The only one who seemed in his right mind was the man who didn't remember his own name. I had to get out of here.

"I thought Captain Hook was supposed to be afraid of crocodiles," Cain muttered from where he leaned against the wall, looking far too sinful to be good for me. "Isn't a dragon basically the same thing? But bigger and with wings?"

Caspian shot him a withering look. "An expert now, are you?"

"Couldn't rightly say. Don't know where that came from. But am I wrong?"

Caspian bared his teeth but surprised me by admitting, "No. Dreadful beasts."

"Are you seriously telling us your nemesis is a crocodile?" I asked, surprised that Caspian would admit to being afraid of anything. He seemed to have way too much pride to show any vulnerability.

"My nemesis is Peter Pan. The crocodile is just a constant barnacle on my arse."

"If you're Captain Hook, why do you have both hands?" Cain asked.

"I don't know. Why do you smell like dog piss?"

"Asshole," Cain grunted. It didn't sound like he was calling Caspian an asshole, more like he was answering the question. I think. This conversation was officially out of my wheelhouse. I'd peopled too much. Time for me to go.

"Well, as interesting as watching you all devolve into your own delusions is, I'd better be going. Nice to . . . um . . . meet you?"

"Oh, she doesn't know," Caspian mused, but I didn't want any further clarity.

Standing, I made for the door, but Kai's hot grip on my elbow stopped me. His eyes blazed as he pinned me with that eerie stare. "They're no delusions, lass. The sooner you accept that, the safer you'll be. You cannae go wandering around these grounds thinking we're all harmless humans."

A twist of fear took hold in my gut. "What do you mean?"

"You've lived your life thinking the world is one way, but it's time you understand the truth of it. Supernatural creatures are very real, and you are one of us. You wouldnae be here otherwise."

I shook my head, but my protests died on my lips. As much as I wanted to deny his claims, too much had happened recently for me to ignore. The premiere. The ghosts popping up all around me. Tor and his horns.

"Think about it," he insisted, bending down until we were at eye level. "This is a place where those who cannae control their power are locked away to protect the world. So what have you done to scare them? Why do they think you're a threat?"

"This is crazy. I feel like I've fallen through the looking glass," I murmured under my breath, hand reaching for the door.

Caspian chuckled. "Welcome to Wonderland, little rabbit. We're all mad here."

INSTEAD OF RETURNING to my room so I could sit on my bed and stare at the walls as I slowly went insane, I headed for the fresh, clean air of the Highlands in hopes of finding some peace. Unfortunately for me, not even the stunning garden could distract me from the conversation I'd had with Kai, Cain, and Caspian.

The words they said made sense and didn't all at the same time. How could the supernatural world be real? It was fiction. It always had been. I should know, I wrote it. I'd grown up reading fantastical tales of the fae, mermaids, vampires, things that went bump in the night. But that's all they were: tales. I'd always known none of it was true.

Maybe I was in my own fictional world right now. Drugged and sleeping after my episode at the premiere? Trapped in my own head, conjuring up sexy beasts and swashbuckling pirates as a way to cope with what I'd done. Of course the figments of my imagination would tell me I *wasn't* crazy. They were on my side. The mental equivalent of a stuffed animal, offering comfort and solace.

I tried to imagine snuggling up to Tor in his beast form and shuddered. Warm and cuddly he was not. More like hard and stabby.

He'll give you something hard and stabby.

Shut up, brain.

"You shouldn't be out here, Dahlia." Dr. Masterson's smooth Scottish brogue took me by surprise as she came up behind me.

"Christ on a bike!" I shouted, flinching.

To her credit, the good doctor didn't laugh at me. She stayed a discreet distance from me and the giant yew tree I'd taken refuge beside.

"Did I break a rule or something? No one tried to stop me when I left," I said, willing my racing heart to return to a normal rate.

"No, not technically. However it's not safe to roam outside unaccompanied. Especially not for young ladies."

My spine stiffened at the unexpectedly misogynistic excuse. "But the men are—"

"Not the target of the Ripper."

I gulped. Right. That guy. "He's here?"

"Who knows where he lurks? But I'll not have my residents putting themselves at risk of being snared by him if I can help it."

Now seemed like a good time to test the waters. Speaking of, the earthy scent of lake water filled my nose as it drifted on the breeze, pulling my gaze from the woman before me to the . . . entire fucking lake—or I guess it was considered a loch—beyond Blackwood's walls. That had definitely not been there when I'd arrived.

"But I thought your residents were here because they had uncontrollable powers. Surely they can protect themselves against a mortal man."

Could she tell I was totally bluffing my way through this? I tried to unobtrusively look at her to see if she was buying it. It felt like I was speaking in some sort of code but didn't have the decoder ring.

The sparrow is red! Repeat, the sparrow is red!

"Who told you that?"

"One of the hot guys in the group session."

She arched a brow. "Then they should have also told you the Ripper only targets powerful creatures."

I snorted. "Then I'm off his list."

"Oh, Dahlia, you're very much wrong about that."

"Okay, you can drop the Morticia Addams act now. It's a very funny joke bringing me to the Haunted Mansion and dropping me in this weird game of Clue, but I'm about done with all the games. I don't have powers. I can barely get myself into a bra most days."

Her brows furrowed. "Do you regularly make a habit of mixing your metaphors, Dahlia? As an author, I expected a bit more from you."

Well, fuck you with a rusty spoon, lady. Consider the friendship bracelet I was going to make you officially off the list.

"I'll show you a mixed metaphor . . ."

"You have power. That's why you're here. It's why all of them are."

There went my snort again. "So everyone in this place is off their rocker? Including you?"

"We aren't going to get very far unless you see the truth for yourself. Here," she said, reaching beneath the collar of her shirt and pulling out a heavy chain. She lifted it over her head and presented me with an ancient-looking key.

"What am I supposed to do with this?" I asked, accepting it from her warily.

"It's my skeleton key. With it, I can open anything."

"Anything?"

She nodded.

"What about this tree?"

Before the question fully left my lips, a blue glow emanated from the trunk of the yew tree. As it faded, a keyhole was left in its wake.

"What the holy fuck?"

Dr. Masterson nodded and said, "Go on, then."

"Uh, I think I'm good."

"For pity's sake, lass. You wanted proof. Now you're refusing it?"

Huffing, I inserted the key and turned it clockwise.

There was a loud crack, like rocks breaking off a mountain, and then the bark hinged, opening up like a . . . door.

That glow was back, only this time it was golden and accompanied by several high-pitched shrieks.

"Gah!" a shrill feminine voice cried.

"Jax!" a second shouted.

"Cover yer dangly bits, my love. No one's getting a free show here."

"What's dangly about them? I was mid-thrust."

"You know, in most polite societies, it's customary to knock when interrupting an orgy."

I could only watch in rapidly growing mortification as the tree fully opened to reveal some sort of Polly Pocket fantasy. Or Pixie Pocket, I guess. It was a whole-ass tree house, complete with six tiny creatures with gossamer fairy wings. Naked creatures. Naked *aroused* creatures.

I had to avert my eyes. It seemed rude to stare, even though one of the males continued to jerk off as if nothing untoward had happened. One of the females glared at me, her purple strap-on bobbing ridiculously as she did.

"Erm, sorry. My bad."

"You say you want us to repopulate Scotland with pixies, but you literally tear us apart during breeding season? I'm going tae have tae take this up with the Fae Council."

"Not yet, Owen. I'm just about to finish. Come on, Polly, get over here and present for me, love."

Polly. One of them was actually named Polly. And she was in the middle of an orgy. I couldn't help but wonder if her last name was Amory. Get it? Polly Amory. God, that would make a great drag name.

I lost it then, a totally inappropriate laugh bubbling up as a sputtering guffaw.

"Right, that's enough fairy porn for the day."

"Ye'd be so lucky to watch magic in the making. Begone giant, you werenae invited."

Doctor Masterson removed the key from the split-open piece of wood, and the door slowly swung shut. The tiny voices shouted orders at each other to get back into position.

"Right then, Polly, spread those thighs, I'm coming in hot."

"Where'd ye put the uni-porn? I'm drying up over here!"

The door sealed shut then, cutting off whatever the response was, but I would have sworn in a court of law that I could still hear their phantom moans.

"I think I need a shower."

"Mmm, we do have excellent water pressure in the castle. Just be careful. The ghosts like to watch."

I frowned, waiting for her to crack a smile and tell me she was kidding. She didn't, and I shuddered.

"Do you believe now?" she asked.

It was tempting to say she must have spiked my afternoon tea with psychedelic mushrooms, but . . .

"I sort of have to after that."

"Lovely, and all it took was an orgy."

"To be fair, it had more to do with the tree and the, oh, never mind."

Looking across the grounds toward the window I'd clocked as mine, I abandoned the idea of a shower. My fingers itched to open my laptop and jot down the scene these randy pixies had just inspired before I forgot any of the details.

"Can I have my computer back?"

"I'm afraid not. Not until you have your first session with me."

"When's that? We were supposed to do it today, but Tor monstered out on everyone."

"I've rescheduled us for tomorrow. Until then, you will have to make do with a pen and paper, my dear."

"Old school. I guess I can deal with that."

At least it would give me a way to pass the time.

"Good. And from now on, when you want to use your outside privileges, please ensure you're not alone. I know at least three residents who've already taken a shine to you who I'm certain would be happy to escort you."

The reminder of Kai, Caspian, and Tor—or did she mean Cain—had me squirming. Just that fast, the hazy characters in my mind took shape, and I found myself even more inspired.

I was all but panting as I jogged away from her. "You got it. Whatever you say."

Maybe when I was finished with my scene, I'd test out that water pressure after all.

EIGHT

DAHLIA

"Come on, Ruby. Put that dirty mind to good use like you know you can," I muttered, hyping my alter ego up as I stared at the blank page, the tap tap tap of my pen on the paper taunting me an hour later.

It'd be easy to blame the unfamiliar materials for my writer's block. My ritual had been changed—location, equipment, even the music I liked to listen to. All I had was my usual uniform of a comfy oversized shirt and soft socks. But the truth was, even if everything had been in place as usual, I was too amped up to get my mind to form the prose such a scene required. It certainly wasn't for lack of inspiration. If anything, I had an abundance of it. I was caught up in the images unfolding in my mind, like a kaleidoscope of carnal delights. But for whatever reason, the words wouldn't come.

Come...

Maybe that's what I needed. A little release. Something to get the creativity flowing. All this pent-up tension couldn't be good for my brain, right?

I bit down on my lip. I was sadly lacking my toy drawer, so I was going to have to get creative. A hand between the legs would get the job done, but I wanted something a bit more . . . stimulating. Living on my own meant that my sex life was a full-time party of one. That got boring fast, so I had an extensive collection of fantasy-inspired dildos, vibrators, and other party favors to keep things interesting. Tentacle porn was a thing for a reason. Don't knock it till you try it.

But for now, since I was unfortunately sans tentacle, I'd make do with what I had at my disposal. Recalling the fancy detachable shower head and claw-foot tub in my bathroom, I shot to my feet.

"Eureka."

Dr. Masterson's warning about ghosts enjoying a bit of voyeurism flashed in my brain, but I pushed it back. Let them watch. They probably needed something fun in their afterlives if the best they could do was spy on me getting myself off.

As the tub filled, I let my mind wander, visualizing my characters in the scene I wanted to write. A dimly lit room, a nest of pillows and blankets, the soft slide of clothes hitting the floor. Just like it had back in the garden, the shadowy figures were quickly replaced by the four men I'd spent the afternoon with.

A hulking blond demigod. A broody tattooed bad boy. A filthy-mouthed pirate. And the silent sentinel. Mysterious. Captivating. Dangerous.

My hands became Tor's as he lifted the hem of my shirt and bared my form to everyone in the room, making me very aware that the only thing hiding my nudity from them was my bra and boyshorts.

Even though it was a fantasy and I could put myself in

any number of sexy outfits, there was something to be said for picturing it happening in my standard comfy apparel. It made it more real somehow. Like the rough scrape of hands up my ribs wasn't my own, but was actually Kai's as he reached behind me to unhook my bra and slide it down my arms. Or that the fingertips plucking my already hard nipples were actually Caspian's while Cain tugged down the stretchy fabric around my hips.

Here, in the safety of my imagination, I didn't feel self-conscious about the softness of my full figure. I was in control, and just like my heroine, I would let these men worship my body.

Cain's fingers played between my thighs, trailing over sensitive flesh until my breath came in rapid pants. I closed my eyes and threw my head back, loving the feel of Tor's bearded jaw scraping along my shoulder before his lips found my neck.

I'd written scenes like this more times than I could count, but this was the first time I'd ever put myself in the center of the sexy sandwich.

It was hotter than I'd expected. The thought of four different men solely focused on me and my pleasure. I felt like a goddess.

Pausing my fantasy just long enough to slide into the steaming water, I turned off the faucet, settled back, and allowed my mind to wander. This time adding the sensual growl of their voices to the mix.

"Lie back. Part your pretty thighs. Let me see you," Cain said as he stood at the end of the tub, intense stare trained on me.

My breath hitched as I did as he said, my eyes rolling back as my fingers slid between my thighs.

"Not so fast. Eyes on me," he chided.

"Relax and let us take care of you, Kærasta," Tor murmured, moving to stand behind me, his strong hands massaging my neck as he began to wash my hair.

"What he means, darling, is we're going to torture you with pleasure," Caspian breathed in my ear, his hands replacing mine as he soaped up my body.

"What did I say about your eyes, Dahlia? Look at me. Only me. I'm not touching you, but I'm going to feel you all the same." Cain's palm rested over his crotch, fingers curling around the sizeable bulge there.

"You might have to look at him, lass, but you can still put your hands on me." Kai's deep rumble sent electricity zinging straight to my clit, and it was all I could do not to look away from Cain.

He caught my wrist and pulled my arm over until my palm rested on his belly, leaving me to choose whether I traced the ridge of warm muscles up . . . or down.

I chose down.

Obviously.

Don't tell me you wouldn't have done the same.

"Your skin is so hot," I whispered, finding him bare and straining toward me. I wondered if I could take him into my mouth without tearing my gaze from Cain.

Before I could test that theory, Kai sank to his knees, his hand bringing mine across his torso until it rested over his heart.

"It's because of you."

Caspian snorted. "Go on. Say it."

"Say what?"

"I burn for you," he said in a put-on growl.

"I'm a dragon. I run hot," he deadpanned, but then his lips met my ear. "It's true, though. You set my soul on fire."

God, I'm good. That was so going in the book.

I groaned when Caspian's fingers parted me and he sank one inside, the pressure wonderful but not near enough. Tor's hands trailed away from my hair and down to the full mounds of my breasts, caressing them as he sucked on my earlobe.

The combination of Tor's gentle suction and Caspian's wicked fingers set off tiny explosions in my veins. My orgasm was close, and it felt like we were only just getting started.

"Tip her over the edge, Kai. Make our pretty little writer come so I can see what her face looks like when she does. I want to learn the exact shade of pink her pussy turns when she comes."

Cain's words were just filthy enough to heat my cheeks. God, what would it be like to have that broody man really talk to me like that? Or any of them, for that matter.

Kai grabbed the detachable shower head and switched the flow of water to a powerful stream before he positioned it over my aching clit. I writhed, but Tor and Caspian held me in place.

"Eyes. On. Me," Cain reminded me.

I had to swallow a moan as Caspian curled his fingers, finding the perfect spot inside me.

"That's right, chase your pleasure, darling. We want to see you fall. We want you to shatter."

"Give it to us, Kærasta. I need it." Tor's teeth sank into the place my neck and shoulder met, and that sharp sting of pain sent me spiraling into a toe-curling orgasm.

I couldn't follow Cain's orders, even though I wanted to be his good girl and give him everything he asked for. My eyes closed as the pleasure bled through every inch of me, and I moaned for all four of them.

By the time my climax had finished washing through

me, I felt decidedly more relaxed. I blinked open my eyes, body languid and heavy from my release.

Well . . . that was fun. We were *so* going to do that again. Maybe I could get Kiki to send me Dr. Tentacles. (That's tent-a-clees, like Hercules, in case you were wondering. Yes, I name my toys. Deal with it. At least it's more inspired than BOB. *insert superior side eye here*)

Or . . . maybe I could order one of those dragon-phallus-inspired dildos I'd been eyeing. Fleetingly, I wondered if they were based on the real thing. If supernaturals were real, maybe someone out there was capitalizing on unknowing smut readers everywhere. Brilliant.

I was still breathing hard as I stepped out of the draining tub and wrapped myself in a towel. Lord almighty, if these men knew what I got up to in my head, they'd probably run screaming. Though Caspian might just strip and offer himself as tribute.

It was harder to imagine the others jumping at the chance to share me. Not because they didn't or couldn't want me. I didn't make up the desire burning in Tor's midnight gaze. They just seemed a bit too snarly caveman to agree to enter into a group situation.

A girl could dream, though. And write it down.

I mean, Cain looked at me like something he simply wanted out of his way and barely said two words to me. My insta-connection with Tor was a little scary, if I was honest. It felt a lot like he was about to pin me down and mark me as his mate, like this was some paranormal romance. Although, now that I knew the truth, maybe that wasn't such a stretch.

And then there was Kai . . .

A knock at my door interrupted me before I could follow that thought to its conclusion.

"Uh, just a second," I called, scrambling to find my robe and knotting it around my waist as I moved to answer.

"Please, lass, take your time. I have all day."

Oh Jesus, am I a witch? Did I summon him?

I opened the door and found Kai standing there, one arm braced on the top of the frame because he was so freaking tall. His gaze was trained on the floor, but after inhaling deeply, his lips twisted into a lascivious grin.

"Am I interrupting something?"

Why did I get the feeling he knew exactly what I'd been doing before he showed up? Was it the nostril flare? The darkening of his irises? Did his voice get a bit deeper?

Or maybe I was just reading into things, and he was responding to my wet hair and robe.

Like a normal person.

Not a dragon-shifting sex machine.

My eyes dropped to his crotch. Annnd now I was wondering if that bulge had ridges.

"Can I help you?" I asked after two attempts to get my words out.

"I think I should be asking you that."

He could not be flirting with me right now. Not after the things he did to me in my bathtub fantasy.

"You're the one knocking on my door. You came to me."

And I just came for you.

Dammit, Dahlia. Stop. It. Right. Now.

No dragon dick for you.

At least not until you write your chapter.

Look at me, being responsible. Kiki would be so proud.

Actually, Kiki would totally be pro-ride the dragon. For research purposes, obviously.

"Dahlia?"

His voice snapped me out of my spiral. "Huh?"

"I said I heard a noise as I was passing by and wanted to check on you. I know today's session was . . . eye-opening. Needed to make sure you were okay."

The possibility that he'd just heard me coming while fantasizing about him had me praying the ground was about to open up and swallow me whole.

"Uh yeah. You know. As well as can be. If Dorothy could handle Oz, I can deal with this."

"Did you know that story originated in the fae courts?"

I gaped at him. "No. I did not know that."

"Aye, it did. Except in truth, Dorothy was the wicked one, and the witch was an innocent bystander. She tried to overthrow the Summer Queen. Stole her shoes for their power. Nasty creature she was."

My jaw dropped open, and I listened to his story like it was an episode of Jerry Springer. "Get out of here."

He shrugged as if to say, 'it's the truth.'

"And the flying monkeys?"

"Members of the court. She was mocking them for their blind obedience to their monarch when she relayed her story to the author."

I was fascinated. Instead of making him leave me alone, I invited him into my room and took a seat on the bed. "Tell me more. What about the wizard?"

"A sorceress called The White Lady. She didn't give Dorothy what she wanted, so the brat made her into a weak fraud."

"The Tin Man?"

"A lover who scorned her."

"How do you know all of this, Kai? Are you teasing me?"

He leaned his perfect ass on my dresser and crossed his arms over his chest. "I'm fae. My father was the guardian of the lost Shadow Queen's crown. Trapped as a dragon until she reclaimed it."

I stared at him, more than a little aware I probably had stars in my eyes. Or little red hearts. He was a fairytale come true. A writer's dream.

This writer's fantasy.

I cleared my throat, forcing myself to look away. "Cool."

A soft huff of laughter was his only response, and my cheeks burned at the notion he was totally on to me.

"So . . . there's nothing you need me to help you with tonight, then?" he asked, gaze raking over my silk robe.

Jesus, my nipples were so hard I worried they'd shred the fabric.

"Not unless you want to write my next chapter."

Or help me act it out.

Stop it, brain. You're supposed to be the rational one.

"Did you really stop by just to make sure I was okay?" I asked, getting to my feet and tying my robe a little tighter.

"No. Actually . . ." he hesitated, looking a little embarrassed as he pulled my 'Hand necklaces are my favorite accessory' notebook from his back pocket. "You left this in your rush to get out of the session. You were pretty rattled."

I'd completely forgotten about it.

"Oh, um, thank you," I spluttered, snatching it out of his hand and promptly sitting on it. Like that might do something to erase the memory of it from his mind.

"What's a hand necklace?" he asked, tipping his head to the side quizzically.

Before my brain could catch up with my body, I'd already taken him by the wrist and lifted his hand until it was resting against my throat.

"Getting the idea yet?" I asked, panic and excitement causing my pulse to race. God, I was sure he could feel it.

His fingers flexed, closing around the delicate column and digging in just enough that I had to press my thighs together.

I was staring at him so hard I didn't miss the way his throat bobbed or his pupils dilated.

"I think it's my favorite accessory too," he said, stepping back and dropping his arm.

Je-sus.

"Between your jumper and notebook, I've sure learned a lot about you today."

"My jumper?" I parroted stupidly.

Then it hit me, and my cheeks blazed crimson. The guy probably thought I was a filthy whore. He'd die laughing if he found out I was just a super horny virgin with one hell of an imagination.

"Shut the fuck up and take my dick like a good girl."

If I'd had water in my mouth, I'd have choked. As it was, I think I started hyperventilating.

"That."

"Excuse me?"

I had to clear my throat. "It's um, take *that* dick like a good girl."

He winked at me. "I think I like my version better."

Me too.

He grinned, and I might have whimpered. It was hard to know for certain. I'm pretty sure I was going to wake up and find out this was all one sexy-as-hell fever dream. What happened to the silent, broody guy I'd met in the hall yesterday?

Reaching out, he tucked some hair behind my ear. "Goodnight, lass."

"Night," I said, staring after him and forcing myself not to tackle him and ride him to glorious orgasmic victory.

I looked over my shoulder at the desk and chair, note-book open and staring at me with guilt-inducing empty pages. Then my gaze went to the bed. I had such fresh inspiration in Kai. I should write, but . . .

Heaving a sigh, I told my pussy to stand down. Delayed gratification made everything better, anyway.

The slip of silk over my nipples had to go, though. It was way too distracting. I'd be back in the tub screaming my way through a second orgasm before you could say Gandalf.

I turned toward my hamper and the pair of leggings and aforementioned sweatshirt resting on top of it. The leggings were there, but the sweatshirt was gone.

What in the actual fuck?

"Casper, you better not be a fucking klepto!" I growled into the silence.

That was the last thing I needed. A bunch of sticky-fingered ghosts running around.

Snatching the leggings, I started tugging them on when a young, sassy voice hit my ears.

"Don't blame me. I didn't touch your ugly jumper."

I spun around, almost tipping over in the tangle of my leggings as my eyes landed on the ghost in the doorway to my bathroom.

Sticking her tongue out at me, she vanished, and I collapsed to the ground.

"Ugh, I hate it here," I groaned, kicking my legs out and rolling over onto my back dramatically.

Except the truth was, after my fantasy and with the scent of Kai still lingering in my room, I had to admit there was a whole hell of a lot I didn't hate.

Dare I say, a few more run-ins like this, and I might even start to enjoy it.

Go figure.

CHAPTER
NINE
HOOK

Pixie dust was good for many reasons—chief among them its addictive qualities. Plus, it barely weighed anything, which was another boon for me as I fished a small vial filled with glittering sand-like grains.

"You, my beauty, are as good as gold."

Better, really, since it was far more rare. And I was the only man around who knew how to harvest it. Grueling work, that, but one must suffer for one's art. Pixie orgies and all. Regardless of how I got the stuff, it was the only way I could achieve my goal of a quick and easy escape from Blackwood.

I couldn't have predicted Tor's freak-out during our session this afternoon, but it worked out in my favor. Everyone was so distracted by him that no one noticed me sneaking away. Now, under the cover of dark, I could take care of business. Perhaps I should thank him. Send him a fruit basket?

As I neared the end of the dank tunnel that ran beneath

the main courtyard, I could see slivers of moonlight filtering in from the bars. A shadow passed in front of them.

Someone's eager.

True, this passage was always guarded, but usually they'd remain hidden. Guess he was worried I wasn't going to show up.

Ah, addicts. So predictably depraved.

He was itching for his next taste, and it had only been a week since last we met. There was enough in these vials to last for at least twice that. Either he'd been sharing, or he was far more eager to escape his life than I'd thought. Not that I could blame him. This place was hardly fit for habitation. I could only imagine what crimes he must've committed to get himself assigned to a post like this one.

Deciding to toy with him for just a moment, I threw my voice and mimicked the screech of an owl. The git flinched and covered his head with his hands in anticipation of an attack. I didn't blame him; owls were vicious.

My dark chuckle preceded me as I gave myself away.

"Hook, you bastard."

I dipped into my deepest bow. "That's *Captain* Hook to you. At your service."

"You ain't captain of a damn thing these days, pretty boy."

I snarled at the reminder. "Best you watch the way you speak to me, *boy*. I'm the one with your treat."

"And I'm the one with the key."

This cocksure prat thought he had something over me, but I knew better. I had everything he wanted in the literal palm of my hand. Raising my fist, I opened it and displayed the faintly glowing vial.

"So, I suppose you don't care if I just . . . let the wind

take this precious magic away then?" I popped the top, and a few grains floated into the air.

"No!" he screeched as I began to tip my vial.

Not through proving my point, I performed a bit of sleight of hand, dumping the contents into my pocket and making the vial appear empty.

"What have you done?" he cried.

I rolled my eyes. "Pull yourself together, man. Such bad form, crying like a child who lost his favorite toy."

I pinched a bit of the pixie dust between my fingers and held them out so he could see I was still in possession of it. The magic tingled on my skin, but I'd grown tolerant to it after a lifetime of exposure. He, however, was near feral in his hunger for the stuff.

Pouring it back into the vial, I chuckled at his whimper of frustration when more of the glittering granules flew away on the breeze.

"Now, if you want what's left, you'll be a good lad and stop this alpha posturing."

He grumbled some, but unlocked the gate.

"Good man."

Snatching the vial from me, he spat, "I hope you trip and land face-first in a pile of satyr shit."

I shuddered, equally repulsed by the visual and impressed with the man's creativity.

If you thought pirates were randy bastards, you've clearly never met a satyr. The half-men, half-goat creatures with their permanent erections and insatiable sexual appetites didn't do anything in moderation. Not even shit. And then there was the constant masturbation. Satyr semen was worse than tree sap. No, I'm not sharing how I found out. Just trust me.

I heard the guard's groan of pleasure as I dashed away

from the cage of Blackwood and into the forest beyond, out of sight of prying eyes. He couldn't even wait to be off duty. Typical.

But, honestly, it suited my purposes just fine.

A quick stop by my hidden stash, and I'd be onto the evening's true festivities. A rendezvous with a deadman. Adonis D. Edman, to be exact.

It didn't take me long to find the hollowed-out stump where my transportation was secreted away. I was a pirate, after all. Deception ran through my veins in equal measure to my very blood. Brushing aside the covering, I smiled down at the multitude of colorful orbs nestled within the rotted wood. Pixie dust, you serve your master so well. The witch who'd spelled these for me had been only too happy to take three vials as payment.

Why was I hiding them out here, you might ask? Well, it's not like Dr. Masterson would be pleased to know I can come and go at my leisure, would she? Oh. You thought I was like those other unfortunate souls. The ones who weren't here by choice.

Allow me to disabuse you of that notion.

No one takes Captain Hook without his permission. I am here because I choose to be. Because I have a mission to accomplish. A crew to return to and a ship to captain.

When Pestilence's hellmouth closed, the portal between realms closed with it, leaving us stranded in a godforsaken little town in Alaska with no way back to Ravenndel.

Neverland to you.

My home.

And that simply would not do for reasons I'd prefer not to get into. A pirate does love his secrets. Suffice it to say, the only thing stopping us from returning was my lack of key. A key that was hidden away on Blackwood's grounds.

Somewhere.

I simply had to find it. If there was one thing pirates were good at, it was locating buried treasure.

Snagging an azure orb, I held it high before thinking of my chosen destination and releasing it. As soon as the ball connected with the forest floor, the magic was released and a portal opened, allowing me to step into The Hag's Tooth as though I'd used the door.

It was busier than normal, and it took a second for me to register why.

All Hallows' Eve.

The witches would be out celebrating Samhain with their covens in the forest, but the rest of the supernatural world would gather in pubs until the clock struck midnight and they could freely walk amongst mortals. Some of us passed easily with nothing more than a glamour. Others used the thinning of the veil as an opportunity to remove their masks and play the sorts of games that would strengthen them for another year.

All tricks, plenty of treats.

"And there she was, standing at the top of the stairs in her bloodied shift. Her eyes were sightless, mouth open in a silent scream as the thunder boomed and shook the walls of the house. Pointing one pale finger at the bloodstain on the floor below, she finally let out a howl that broke the windows."

I leaned against the wall nearest the door of the pub, eyebrows raised, not doing a single thing to mask the annoyance on my face as I watched the old showboat draw out his fabricated tale of a banshee.

The thing that made Adonis such an asset was the same

thing that made him a pain in my arse. He loved to talk. Loudly. At great length. To anyone he could con into listening.

And bugger it all, he was a masterful storyteller.

Pity for his crowd, most didn't realize he was feeding on them while he did it. Stealing sips of their essence to bolster his own. It was the only reason a spirit such as him could appear mostly corporeal.

As he finished his tale, he caught my gaze, his eyes reflecting the lamplight and flashing with an eerie inhuman glow. The audience applauded, and he hopped down from the table where he'd held them all captive before floating toward me. Well, to the casual observer, he walked, but I noted how his feet never truly made purchase with the floor.

"Adonis." I acknowledged him with a dip of my head.

"If it isn't the famed captain of the fae sea."

I rolled my eyes, though I inwardly preened. It was nice to be addressed as befitting my rather infamous station instead of mocked.

"No need to butter me up. I'm here for a bit of gossip, nothing more."

"Spirits trade in gossip like no other creatures."

Sighing, I fought to rein in the irritation coursing through me. Ghosts always played games rather than getting to the bloody point. Similar to the fae. Or . . . pirates, for that matter.

"They do. I've been known to have a few secrets to sell myself. What would it take for someone as powerful as you to be persuaded to connect me with Charlie Higgins?"

He tilted his face a bit away, casting himself in shadow. When his eyes swung back toward me, they glowed silver. I couldn't be sure if it was due to the soft flicker of candlelight or if it was simply a side effect of his long-dead status. Either way, he painted a macabre picture, with his raven wing top hat and faded Victorian coat, an ornate walking stick resting beneath his palms. Adonis belonged in another time.

Or an Edgar Allan Poe poem.

"What do you want with that good-for-nothing poltergeist?"

"That's really none of your business, is it?"

"Agree to disagree. I make it a habit to know who I'm getting into bed with and why."

"If we were getting into bed, this would be an entirely different bargain. Now, if you're not interested in a bit of tit-for-tat, I'll leave you to your adoring crowd. I have other means to get what I'm after."

The cold shackle of his fingers around my wrist stopped me from leaving even as I turned away. I had to school my expression so he didn't see my knowing smirk before I turned back to him, skin tingling with an uncomfortable pressure from his touch. Most spirits weren't strong enough for physical contact, and certainly not prolonged touch. Adonis could be dangerous if he wanted. This simple gesture proved my point.

"You promised me payment, pirate. I intend to collect. Now tell me what you want with Charlie-boy, and I'll do my best to help you."

"He knows Blackwood better than any living soul. Therefore, it stands to reason he will have the information I need."

Adonis hummed. "And what is that?"

"None of your concern."

Anger darkened his gaze, turning the silver orbs nearly

black. "Keep your secrets. For now. I'll get them out of you eventually. I always do."

Adonis D. Edman was proof the old adage that dead men tell no tales was wrong.

He told plenty of tales. Usually ones that didn't belong to him.

I had no trouble believing he'd ferret out my secrets one way or another. Which meant I needed to watch what I said when I met Charlie. It wouldn't surprise me to learn he worked out some sort of deal where anything I told him would find its way back to the ghost before me.

"You'll find him skulking about his tomb two nights hence. Careful, though, lad. He's stronger now the veil is thin. Samhain is only the start. These next three moonrises bring my kind closer to the living than the dead, and he's not as friendly as I am."

I didn't bother acknowledging his warning. It wasn't anything I didn't already know.

"You'll make sure he's amenable to a meeting with me?"

Adonis slowly dipped his chin, the move causing that weird trick of the light to play in his eyes again.

"Then I guess we're done here. Happy All Hallows, spirit."

"Don't you mean happy haunting?"

"Sure."

Adonis lifted his raven-winged hat and offered me an affected bow before turning on his heels and joining the crowd once more.

"All right, my wee deadlings. Who wants another terrifying tale?"

I claimed a seat, settling in for the show now that I had what I'd come for. I was in no hurry to get back to my prison cell. Might as well enjoy myself while I could. I'd certainly worked hard enough to escape. As long as I was back before dawn, no one would ever be the wiser.

Signaling a delightful barmaid, I called out, "A bottle of your finest rum, wench."

"She's not a wench, she's my wife," a burly Scot snarled. The two were not mutually exclusive, but an uncommon burst of self-preservation kept me from pointing it out. The man was a shifter by the look of him. I'd seen his type before, in Aurora Springs, where the rest of my life was waiting for me.

Thankfully Adonis was in full swing, his cackle interrupting the tense moment. "Now listen well and hold on to someone, because the tale I'm about to tell is so bone-chilling, so bloodcurdling, so terrifying, it may well turn your hair white before I finish."

TEN

KAI

T he scrape of charcoal across paper typically soothed me the instant my pencil made contact with my sketch pad. Not today. I couldn't focus on the tattoo commission to save my life. Water lapped at the loch's shore as ducks swam in a neat line toward the cluster of lily pads to my right. It should have been inspirational for the siren I was supposed to be creating. But so far the only inspiration on my mind was her.

Dahlia.

My newest obsession.

My dragon craved her like she was the rarest treasure. He wanted me to throw her over my shoulder and take her to the tower, locking her up with the rest of my hoard.

I couldn't do that to her.

Not yet.

Closing my eyes, I ceded all creative control to my subconscious, allowing the pencil to go where it would. My hand moved quickly, seeming to know exactly what it wanted to draw, while my ears were filled with the soft scrape of the lead over the paper.

I let my eyes flutter open, and my focus trained on what my brain had conjured. Not a mischievous mermaid, but a captivating beauty all the same.

She was naked in the bathtub, her head thrown back, eyes closed, brow furrowed in pleasured concentration as one hand delved between her parted thighs and bubbles tastefully hid her nipples from view.

Dahlia.

"Good christ, man," I groaned as I made to tear the page from my book and crumple it before someone saw my fixation for what it was.

Madness.

Taking a deep breath, I tried again. This time when I reopened my eyes, my muse wasn't pleasuring herself in a bathtub. She was on her knees, eyes squeezed shut, teeth biting into her delectable lower lip while I railed her from behind, one of my hands wrapped around her throat, the other tangled in her hair.

I let out a low string of curses as my brain helpfully supplied the term she'd taught me last night.

Hand necklace.

The second she'd placed my palm to her throat, I'd gone rock hard. I'd been able to think of little else since. Clearly.

Disgusted with myself, I flipped the page, unable to destroy that particular image, as a soft, husky voice hit my ears.

"Whatcha drawing?"

Goddess help me, I flinched even as my dick swelled once her scent caught up to her voice. "Hasn't anyone ever told you it's rude to sneak up on a man while he's working?"

She sat beside me, her soft rose-colored jumper brushing my arm and making me wish it was her bare skin instead. My gaze was instantly drawn to the writing across the front of the fabric stating, *It's Always 'WYD' Never DYWMTCOAEYPTYCOMF*. What the bloody hell did that one mean?

The first bit was easy enough: WYD, what you doing. The rest . . . not as much.

"Sorry, I didn't realize it was work. I recognized the expression on your face and wanted to see what put it there."

"What expression?" I asked, snapping the sketchbook closed and placing it on my other side, far away from her prying eyes. The last thing I needed was for her to take a good look at my depravity, especially while I was distracted trying to unscramble the meaning behind the letters across her chest.

"Creative genius at work? A man who's found his muse?"

A slight snort of surprise escaped me. I wondered what she'd think if she realized she was talking about herself. "My muse . . . interesting."

Don't you want me to come on . . . No, that wasn't right.

"So, can I see?"

"Do *you* let strangers look at *your* work in progress?"

Her eyes widened just enough to let me know I'd hit a nerve, but she quickly schooled her expression. "Point taken."

"Perhaps one day I'll let you see inside my mind, lass. But not today." I waved a dismissive hand at my sketch-book. "It's all crap anyway. Not worth seeing."

Do you want me to come over and empty my penis . . . Nae. First, no one would ever say that. And second, it's a Y, not an M.

She tipped her head, eyes narrowing in thought. "I doubt that. We're always our harshest critic."

Her fingertip trailed across my exposed forearm, tracing the swirling lines of my intricate ink depicting my father's dragon form. Fuck, I liked her touch. I craved it. My chest burned with a fire I'd never felt.

I needed to change the subject. Pulling my arm away, I focused on her chest—shirt. I focused on her shirt—again as I tried to parse out the secret romance reader code.

This time it was like something unlocked, and I found myself blurting it out like an absolute fucking arse.

"Do you want me to come over and eat your pussy until you come all over my face?"

Her soft gasp was followed by laughter, then, "I mean, with an offer like that . . ."

For the first time maybe ever, I blushed. "No, I mean your jumper." I pointed at her tits like a git. "The secret phrase."

She glanced down, laughing. "Well, it's not that much of a secret. You seem to have guessed it easily enough. Or maybe you just like to go around offering your services to poor, unsuspecting women."

"More like women in need," I countered, my embarrassment easing in light of the teasing twinkle in her eye.

"And do you think I'm in need, Kai?"

I swallowed thickly, not letting the truth rush to my lips. That it wasn't her in need, it was me. Our eyes held for a few seconds before she took my arm and pointed to the tattoo again.

"So, if you're not making good on that offer, why don't you tell me a little about this? You don't seem like the kind of man who inks something into his skin unless it has a meaning."

I dragged a hand down my forearm and the series of tattoos that represented my family. "Everything on this arm is tied to my history." I traced over the dragon, saying as I did, "This is for my father, Valor." Then the dark clouds interspersed with stars. "The Shadow Court." The Scottish thistle. "My home." After a beat, I added, "And my mum, Joss. She loves thistle. She's always saying that prickly things can still be beautiful. And then she usually looks at my dad and winks."

For the love of God, man, shut yer gob.

I was rambling on like I was getting paid by the word. It wasn't like me. At all. I didn't bare my soul to relative strangers. Or become so singularly fixated on a woman that I couldn't focus on anything else. Usually I was secretive. Reclusive. Suspicious. Never trusting and rarely flirtatious. But this blonde beauty had somehow turned all of that on its head in a matter of days. Was this a wicked trick of sorcery or something else?

Before I could follow the train of thought, her voice pulled me back to our conversation.

"So that's where they are? In the Shadow Court?"

I shook my head. "Nae. They're here, in the Highlands. Mum could never return, human as she is. It's too much strain on human bodies to live in Faerie. Dad got called back to serve our queen a few years ago when the Apocalypse was looming and our people were endangered. I went in his place."

"Why?"

"I wouldn't see them separated. They're mates. It wouldn't have been right."

A gentleness filled her eyes as she threaded our fingers. "You're a good son."

Bitterness filled me, my thoughts taking a dark turn. "Not good enough."

"Why would you say that?"

"Because of my lack of control, my dad has no choice but to return to Faerie. The Shadow Court's dragon has to stand guard until this threat is handled."

Her brows furrowed in confusion, but I could tell the second she pieced it together. "The incident that brought you here, that's what you're referring to, isn't it?"

My dragon shifted restlessly on my back, responding to my discomfort.

"If you can call razing an entire village filled with innocent people an incident, then aye."

"Did you do it on purpose?"

I stared at her, pure confusion swirling within me. Why was she being so compassionate?

"No. My dragon was out of control. I have no memory of it save the fire burning in my chest."

"Then you aren't solely responsible. And you are making amends."

If you call locking away my dragon making amends.

It was hell, living with a part of my soul locked away. Denying a primal part of myself. But it had to be done. I couldnae be trusted. Never again would I be the reason for the slaughter of so many innocents. To this day, their souls weighed heavily on me. Thousands snuffed out in a matter of seconds. Never. Again.

"I appreciate you saying that, lass, but it doesn't change what I've done. I'm not to be trusted with fragile things. All I do is turn them to ash."

Which was why I could not entertain my obsession with her. She deserved better. More.

Or at the very least, a man not haunted by the ghosts of his victims.

I stood, pulling away from her because I couldn't take the strange hum of connection between us anymore. It was nearly painful, the need to have her in my arms and at my side. My dragon writhed, protesting the separation and snarling for me to make her mine. I was on the edge of losing control. Until I figured out exactly why I felt this way, it would be best if I kept my distance.

Before I could come up with an excuse for my sudden departure, Dahlia gasped. My gaze dropped to her, noting her skin had leached of color.

"What's wrong?" I asked, going on high alert.

"D-do you see him? The old man trailing behind Tor and that other guy?"

Following her focus, I caught sight of the big Viking as he walked the courtyard's perimeter. The only person near him was his guard, Bru.

I shook my head slowly. "No."

"That's what I was afraid of." Her shoulders slumped in defeat. "Great, more ghosts."

Or at least that's what I think she said, the words laced with frustration and spoken mostly under her breath.

"Ghosts?"

"Yes." She loosed a heavy sigh. "I see dead people."

"Wicked."

"You might think so, except they're the reason I'm here . . . I think."

"So you're a medium. Nothing wrong with that."

"According to Dr. Masterson, I'm a psychic." She scrunched up her nose, looking adorably confused. "Which doesn't make any sense, honestly, because don't psychics see the future and shit? I don't have visions. Hell, up until a few weeks ago, I thought I was totally normal. Well, maybe not exactly normal, but a run of the mill neurotic human."

"There's nothing run of the mill about you, lass. Nothing at all."

She swallowed, twin bright spots blooming on her cheeks and bringing some color back to her face. "Um. Thanks?"

Fuck, I had to get out of here or I was going to kiss her, and it was too damn soon for that. Or it would be too soon if I could even entertain the thought of pursuing her. Which I couldn't. So I really needed to go and remove myself from temptation.

Tor's attention shifted from his path out of No Man's Land to zero in on Dahlia, standing next to me, palm outstretched like she was going to touch me again. His expression was pure jealousy, and my dragon tensed, ready to fight the Beast. Before I could do a damn thing, Bru placed a palm on Tor's shoulder and said something that made the Viking pause, take a breath and avert his stare. A second later, he stalked off, hands balled into fists but still fully in his human form.

Dahlia tracked him with her gaze. "I should go talk to him. Warn him that he's being haunted or whatever. Maybe that's what's causing him to turn into a beast. Ohmygod! Do you think he might be possessed?"

"I have no bloody clue, but if anyone can help him figure it out, it's the girl who can see ghosts."

"You're right." She nodded her head decisively, already heading after Tor's retreating form. "I'll see you around, Kai."

As much as sending her into Tor's arms got my back up, I knew it was the right choice. I wasn't ready for her. Not yet.

And honestly, I may never be.

CHAPTER
ELEVEN

TOR

The meditation room was blessedly silent and empty as I slipped off my shoes and stepped inside, leaving Bru at the door so I could reclaim my self-control. He trusted me; gods knew why. Instead of handling my shit, as Dr. Masterson promised I would be able to do, I was worse off than when I'd first arrived at Blackwood.

Every time I gave into the bloodlust and ceded control to the beast inside me, it was as if my tenuous hold on my humanity slipped a little further out of reach.

I was getting worse, not better. More monster than man.

Even now, my hands shook with the need to go back to the courtyard and tear Malakai limb from limb. All because he smiled at her.

My mate.

Mine.

He dared to look at her, knowing I was right there, knowing I'd see. And she'd touched him.

Rage boiled in my blood at the thought of anyone taking her from me. Rationally, I knew I was out of line. I'd made no moves to claim her. I hadn't even spoken with her. But the beast was far from rational. He was all violence and primal instinct. Domination and greed.

As far as he was concerned, Dahlia was his. May the gods have mercy on anyone who tried to stand between them.

Us.

Fuck.

I paced the room, my breaths more snarls than anything else. If I gave in and touched her, I'd never be the same. I'd seen a Berserker separated from his mate before, taunted him even from behind the safety of a magic cell. I'd been such a fucking fool. The fates were punishing me for my hubris now. Dangling my mate before me now that she was the one thing I could never have.

Why can't you? She's yours. The fates chose you for her.

I stilled and followed the tempting thought.

Could I take the chance of being with her and losing myself to my beast? Clearly, she unsettled him. What if I hurt her? Broke her spirit or, worse, destroyed her fragile human body?

No. It could never be. I could not risk her safety.

My fingers dragged through the length of my hair as I resumed pacing like a caged animal searching the room for a weak spot. I could fucking feel her even though she wasn't anywhere near me.

My heart cried out her name.

How pathetic was I? Yearning for a woman I'd never even spoken to. Mourning a soul bond that could never be complete.

But you could complete it. Take her and make her yours.

I shook my head, fighting the temptation to do exactly what my instincts begged for. The horrors that have come to pass at my hand would be nothing compared to the ones I'd unleash if I lost her.

I'd simply have to stay away from her. You can't lose something you never had. Right? I could work her out of my system and keep myself away. Perhaps I'd plead my case with Dr. Masterson and ask for a transfer to a different accountability group, a different wing of the castle. She might do it if I could convince her it was for everyone's safety.

Instead of relief at the thought, despair gnawed at me.

I didn't *want* to distance myself from her.

"But you must," I growled.

"Must what?"

I stopped dead, my muscles knotting with tension as her voice crashed into me. My heart raced, slamming against my ribs like a creature caught in a hunter's snare. I breathed deep, drawing the scent of her into my lungs.

Hers was a complex scent. Bright and warm, with a hint of tartness. Honeysuckle, night blooming jasmine, and . . . pomegranate. Unique. Sensual. Delicious, just like the woman herself. My cock stood at attention, ready for the claiming my nature demanded. At the sound of the door shutting, I adjusted myself in a futile attempt to hide my reaction to my mate's proximity. I had to face her. There was no avoiding it.

Turning around slowly, with more restraint than I thought I possessed in this moment, our gazes collided. Everything in me was screaming to wrap my hand around her pretty throat and shove her against the wall so I could take my fill of her.

She must have sensed it because her eyes widened slightly in challenge.

"Am I bothering you?" she asked, one hand on her hip and not a hint of apology in her question. "This isn't a private meditation session. Your boyfriend let me in."

"He's not my boyfriend."

"Glad we cleared that up."

"Get out of here, beauty."

Her brows rose in challenge. "Beauty? Is that my name now? Does that mean I get to call you beast?"

"If you so choose. It wouldn't be the first time."

My godsdamned heart was racing with every word, every cell in my body aching to close the distance between us. I needed to touch her, to feel the flutter of her pulse under my fingers, taste the salt of her skin and drink down her moans. Thank the gods my joggers were a deep gray. My length was weeping for her.

"Maybe you should reflect on why that is, big guy."

A growl built in the base of my throat.

"I'm not scared of you."

"You should be."

She rolled her eyes. "And here I was trying to do you a favor."

"A favor?"

Her eyes narrowed for a second as she considered me. "I'm not sure if I should bother now. You seem like the type to eat the messenger."

If she allowed me, I'd eat her all night and into the next morning. As much as I loved this spirited back and forth between us, all she was doing was feeding my need for her.

"You are aware this room is for meditation?" I asked, forcing myself to sit on one of the large cushions on the floor and closing my eyes.

"Yes."

"*Silent* meditation."

"You were the one pacing and talking to yourself. I just followed your lead."

I found myself fighting the urge to laugh. It was rare anyone called me out, especially after I was cursed. The last time had been when I'd met that little witch, Moira.

Cracking open one eye, I watched her move to the pillow next to me, her frown doing nothing to minimize my attraction.

"Fine, I'm sitting. We'll meditate together, okay? You, me, and the ghost attached to you."

My brow raised at that. I gave the room a curious once over, but the only being I sensed besides myself was the beauty next to me.

"What ghost?"

"The old guy with the cane. Real distinguished looking. He's got a whole Patrick Stewart thing going on."

There was only one man I knew of who matched that description. Uncle Alistair. Well, technically, he was my great-uncle who died before I was born, but he'd been like a father to my mother. My brother had been named after him, while I'd been named for my grandfather.

"Alistair?"

"That would be the one. He just nodded."

Glancing around the room again, I searched for some indication of where he was. A glimmer or ripple in reality, perhaps. All I saw was the serene, minimalist space. Nothing out of the ordinary.

"He's on your right. Just watching you. I can see him, but he isn't speaking to me."

I pondered the implication of that. My mother had been a ghost once upon a time, and she'd told my twin and me what she remembered of the experience. Ghosts were usually stuck to a single geographic location. So Alistair's presence here likely had to do with the thinning of the veil and my being the relative in closest proximity to his resting place.

He'd died brutally in Edinburgh. It had been a tragic end for a wonderful man. And while he may not have been a Viking, I'd hoped he'd ended up in Valhalla for the bravery he'd shown while protecting my mother. It was because of him that she lived, that my brother and I were able to be born. Without his loyalty, we'd all be nothing more than severed threads in fate's mighty weave.

"I never met him, but it would stand to reason he'd reach out now."

"Why?"

"Last night was Samhain. Tomorrow is All Souls. That makes today All Saints' Day. These are the three dates each year the veil between worlds is the thinnest." I frowned at her. "Don't you know this? You're clearly a medium."

Her smile was self-deprecating, and it made me wish I could do something to make it real. "I'm probably the latest bloomer this community has ever had. Until today, I really thought I was nuts. Now I realize the truth. I see ghosts. I have for a long time."

I wasn't sure what I was supposed to say to that, so I grunted in what I hoped came across as understanding instead of the loss for words it was.

She studied me for a second, and I fought not to squirm under the scrutiny. What did she see when she looked at me? Did she realize what I was to her?

"For a guy who's being haunted, you don't seem all that torn up about it. I feel like most people would be at least a little creeped out."

I huffed out a laugh. "My twin has enough fear of ghosts for the both of us."

"Twin? There are two of you?"

I couldn't quite contain my snarl of jealousy. "He's a mated man."

"Mated? Is that like married?"

I had to approach this delicately, and surprisingly, I had the control to do it. The frenzied buzz beneath my skin vanished with her so near. It was like all the noise was cut off the instant she was with me, talking to me, mine.

"Yes. But so much more. It's rare for a Novasgardian to find their true mate, but when they do, nothing can break the bond between them. It's a lightning strike when their souls recognize each other."

Her lips twitched. "So . . . instalove?"

"I suppose you could call it that. Seems like a gross simplification for a divine act of the goddess, but sure."

"How do you know when you've found yours? Do you have one?"

Fuck.

Reaching out, I dared to press my palm to her chest, right over her heart. She gave a little gasp of surprise, but her eyes flicked to mine again. Voice rough with the weight of this moment, I said, "You feel it. Right there. Undeniable."

And it was.

The second I touched her, an electric current raced between us, confirming what my soul had already known. It was a full heartbeat before I could pull my hand away.

She was mine.

My Kærasta.

I hadn't realized I'd said it out loud until she blinked at

me, absently rubbing at her chest like she could still feel the imprint of my touch against her skin.

"I've heard you say that before. What does it mean?"

The words crowded my mouth, desperate to be spoken, but instinct warned me it was not the time. This bond could not be allowed to strengthen more than it already had. It wasn't safe.

"It's personal."

Dahlia's face fell, a mask of self-preservation sliding into place at my rebuff. "Cool. Great. Well, your ghost seems to have left the building, so I guess since it's *personal* and all, I'll leave you to it."

It was on the tip of my tongue to beg her not to go, but it was better this way.

Safer.

Inside, my beast rattled his chains, growling his displeasure as she stood and started for the exit. She paused when she reached the door, her hand resting on the handle.

"You're really not going to tell me?" she asked, glancing back at me over her shoulder.

I hated the wounded expression in her eyes. I hated even more that I was the one who put it there. As her mate, it was my privilege to care for and protect her. Never harm.

My heart yearned for me to confess everything, to give her the truth and replace that look in her eyes with something else, but my head wouldn't allow it. Gritting my teeth, I took a long breath before I said, "Not yet."

I hadn't intended to give her even that small bit of hope, but it would seem my beast had a bit more control over me than I'd thought. Or were the two of us in agreement on Dahlia? We both wanted her. Perhaps there was no separation between us on this.

"Not yet," she repeated, her eyes narrowing as she mulled my words over. "Well, Beast, I guess I'll have to live with that."

Me too, beauty.

Me too.

SESSION TRANSCRIPT: NOVEMBER 1ST

Dr. Masterson: This is Dr. Elizabeth Masterson. It is November first, and the time is 1:00 p.m. This is a recorded session with Cain Alexander, newest arrival here at Blackwood. Cain, why don't you tell me how you're settling in?

<<dog yips>>

Cain: Quiet, Asshole.

<<clothes rustle. Dog growls.>>

Cain: Asshole, no. Down. Do you want your treats?

<<dog yips>>

Cain: That's what I thought. Sit there and be quiet, or next time I'll leave you in the room. Sorry, Doc. What did you ask me?

Dr. Masterson: How you were settling in.

Cain: It's fine, I guess.

Dr. Masterson: You seem to have acclimated well enough. No one has ended up bloodied so far.

Cain: *chuckles* There's always tomorrow. That Caspian character is cruisin' for a bruisin'.

Dr. Masterson: Tell me more about that. What's he done?

Cain: If it's all the same, I'd rather not.

Dr. Masterson: That's not how this works, Cain.

Cain: *sighs* Fine. I don't like the way he looks at Dahlia. Or talks to her, for that matter.

Dr. Masterson: How does he talk to her?

Cain: Like she's his. He hasn't earned the right to treat her that way.

Dr. Masterson: Let's delve deeper into this. Why do you care so much?

Cain: I don't.

Dr. Masterson: Clearly you do, or you wouldn't have an emotional response to his behavior.

Cain: You're the expert.

Dr. Masterson: Well, why do you think it bothers you? What makes you think he hasn't earned the right, as you say?

Cain: How is any of this relevant to my being thrown in here?

<<clothes rustle, footsteps back and forth>>

Cain: I think the most important thing for us to talk about is how the hell I got here in the first place.

Dr. Masterson: Didn't you just say I was the expert, Mr. Alexander? Why don't you trust the process and allow me to decide how these sessions need to go?

Cain: *grumbles* I get the feeling I'm not used to being questioned.

Dr. Masterson: Why's that?

Cain: I don't fucking like it.

Dr. Masterson: Okay, let's try something different. Think back to the last thing you remember before you arrived here. What can you recall?

Cain: *low hum* I remember a hospital waiting room. Lights flickering. And dreams.

Dr. Masterson: Dreams?

Cain: Yes. I can't escape them. Every time I close my eyes, I see death, darkness, and . . . her.

Dr. Masterson: Who?

Cain: I don't know. I can't see her face. But I . . .

Dr. Masterson: Yes?

Cain: *heavy exhale* But I think I loved her.

Dr. Masterson: Loved, past tense? Do you think she's gone, Cain?

Cain: It's hard to say. I just have this sense that I'm searching for her. That I've always been searching for her. Maybe even across lifetimes. Does that sound crazy? *chuckle* Hell, maybe I am in the right place.

Dr. Masterson: There's nothing crazy about it. We're all searching for something, and it's common enough for supernaturals to have soulmates, which is what you're describing. What do you think you'd do if you found her, Cain? Your dream girl?

Cain: *growl* Tie her to me. Make sure she never leaves me again.

Dr. Masterson: Cain, what are you doing?

<<dog barking defensively>>

Dr. Masterson: Cain, calm down. I need you to calm down. Cain!

<<static>>

End of transcript.

TWELVE

DAHLIA

The echo of Tor's heated palm on my chest was so strong I could practically still feel him touching me. I'd played it cool at the end, but all that stuff he said about lightning and soul mates had hit me . . . well, like lightning.

I hoped my meeting with Dr. Masterson went well today. I could really use my cell phone. I needed to talk to Kiki stat. She was going to die when she heard about my run-in with the God of Thunder.

Almost unbidden, Tor's voice floated through my mind, correcting me. *Demigod.*

Fuck me, he was hot. Demigod or regular human, Tor was . . . intense.

All big and muscley with eyes that peered straight into my soul. I was willing to bet the guy could pick me up and throw me around without breaking a sweat. Fuck, my panties were damp just thinking about it. A girl my size rarely got to experience that. I'd never felt delicate a day in my life, but damn if the way he looked at me didn't do just that.

The clang of bells from the tower announced the time, making my heart skip a beat in response because I was all the way over here, standing outside the meditation room with Tor's guard watching me pull myself together. The problem was, I should be across the grounds at my one-on-one session with Dr. Masterson.

"Shit. Hope you enjoyed the show, Bruno. Gotta run!" I dashed away, my skin still tingling where Tor had touched me, and bolted toward No Man's Land and the doctor's private office.

"Don't worry about me, watch where the bloody hell you're going! You think he's ridiculous now, just wait and see what happens if you get so much as a splinter."

I was about to holler back that I was fine, just as I noticed I was racing headlong toward a fountain. So maybe he was on to something.

Offering him a harried wave, I adjusted course and ran as fast as I could manage toward my appointment. It wasn't that fast, mind you. Boobs were not made for running. And my girls were doing their damnedest to punch me in the chin.

"Honestly, Dahlia, show a little restraint," Sorcha Blackthorne said as I passed her where she sat on the edge of the fountain reading.

I stopped, breaths—let's be honest, they were gasps—coming hard and fast. "How . . . do I . . . get . . . to—"

She rolled her eyes. "Oh goddess, just spit it out."

"Dr. Masterson's office."

"Sorcha, don't be a twat." Oz rested his palm on my shoulder. "It's just around the bend there. She has a special access door apart from the entrance to No Man's Land. Safety first, and all that."

I gave him a beleaguered smile. "Thanks. I might . . . die here, though. Send Kiki . . . my love."

I wasn't a runner as a rule. I liked a long walk, or even a swim. Running was sweaty business. These clothes were too cute for sweat.

Without another word, I started to move in the direction Oz had pointed, this time at a more manageable power walk. I literally might keel over if I tried to run again.

Before I could turn the corner, a tiny white puppy came zooming in my direction.

"Asshole, get back here!"

The dog paused in front of me, a quivering ball of excited energy.

"Aw, hi sweetie, what are you doing all by yourself? Making a break for it?" I asked, scooping the bundle of fur up and giggling as he immediately began to lick my face. He was warm and soft and just the sweetest little thing. "You're not an asshole at all, are you? No, you're not. You're the sweetest, most bestest baby."

"Put my dog down before he bites your pretty face off." Cain's smoky velvet voice made my blood heat. It wasn't fair for him to sound like that and have the looks to match.

What was with this place? I was one meet cute away from a bingo or Yahtzee. Oh, or a punch card like my favorite sandwich shop at home had. One more to go until I get a free quadruple-decker surprise.

I tried to meet his gaze but found myself instantly returning my attention to the puppy cradled in my arms. Something about Cain made me all kinds of nervous.

The dude was intimidating as fuck. Tall, broad shoulders, just a hint of sexy stubble lining his angular jaw. Where Tor belonged in some sort of bodybuilding competition, Cain looked like he'd be right at home in a boardroom. You know how they say someone had Big Dick Energy? Cain had Biggest Dick In The Room Energy. If I was casting him in one of my books, he'd be the billionaire CEO. As soon as I pictured him behind a big desk, I saw myself spread out on top of it, skirt rucked up to my waist as he drove into me. Or, better yet, below it, kneeling between his legs while he sipped a glass of bourbon or smoked a cigar, free hand tangled in my hair.

Jesus fucking Christ.

Worried he might be able to read my thoughts, I had to train my focus between his brows to keep my gaze off those fiery blue eyes as I forced out, "He would never. He's a lover, not a fighter."

"He's a piss all over your bed-er," Cain said, his brow furrowing a bit at the end, as if he couldn't believe he'd just said that.

"That might be your kink. I don't judge. Personally, I don't think I'm into watersports. Hand necklaces, sure. Maybe a little daddy kink here and there. And I haven't dabbled in the breeding thing yet, but the idea gives me the flutters. But what really gets me going is exhibitionism . . ." Shit, I just word-vomited my kinks all over this dark and dangerous man who stared at me like he had no clue what to do with me.

Well, to be fair, the spark of interest in his gaze made me think he had an idea. Or maybe that was just wishful thinking, what with the desk fantasy still playing rent-free in the back of my mind.

He coughed before holding out his hands. "May I?"

May he? May he what? Breed me in front of everyone here while he choked me and I called him Daddy? "I'm sorry? I don't even know you."

As if that would really stop you, girlfriend. One crook of that sexy finger, and you'd be face-first in his crotch.

"My dog, doll. May I have my dog?"

Doll? That was a new one. It was sort of close to Dahlia; maybe he just forgot my name.

"It's Dahlia," I helpfully corrected.

He blinked at me. "I know."

I still hadn't handed over the puppy. He was so cozy in my arms, his face tucked into the side of my neck as he chewed my hair.

"You keep letting him do that, you'll have no hair left. I call him Asshole for a reason."

"You need to name him something different. He doesn't deserve this one."

"You've known him for five seconds. Trust me on this one. The name is entirely deserved."

"I've known you for five seconds. Should I call you asshole too?"

His brow quirked up, his expression so stern and unamused that I squirmed, waiting for him to start pulling off his belt so he could punish me for my smart mouth. Good lord. What was wrong with me? Had I been dosed with pheromones or something? Was I ovulating? This was getting ridiculous. I was liable to start humping a wall at this rate. At the very least, I'd need to change my panties after my session with … shit.

"I need to go. Here," I said, shoving the dog at Cain. "Think of a better name for him."

"No."

"Okay, I will. I'll send you my notes."

"I won't read them."

"Something tells me you will. I've heard my writing is captivating."

"Shouldn't you be on your way to wherever you were going?"

God, the handsome jerk got under my skin. "Shouldn't you be . . . doing . . . something broody?"

He stared at me.

"Statue practice it is. Hold that pose. You're doing great. Now don't speak or move."

A sexy-as-hell chuckle escaped him before he shook his head and turned away from me.

"You lost! That's not how the game of statue works!"

I hated to see him go, but I loved watching him walk away.

"Miss Moore? Did you get lost?"

Dr. Masterson's voice had me jumping like I'd just been caught with my hand in the cookie jar. "Sorry, yeah. This place is a maze."

From the amused twitch of her lips, she wasn't buying my excuse, but she was kind enough not to call me out. "This way, please. We've already lost valuable time."

I don't know what I expected when I walked into her office, but something I would see in an LA psychiatrist's practice was definitely not it. The walls were a quiet taupe, and the decor a modern minimalist style so juxtaposed with the Gothic castle that housed the residents of Blackwood I had to look out the door and make sure I hadn't stepped through a portal or something.

There was a sleek leather couch, a couple of bookcases filled with books and various odds and ends, the doctor's desk, a couple of plush armchairs, and oddly enough, a wall of carnivorous plants. Their pots were attached to wood slats, sort of like a succulent or living garden.

"Get a lot of flies in here?" I asked, taking a few tentative steps toward what I recognized as a Venus flytrap.

"Not anymore," she said with a smile.

I couldn't decide if I was impressed or concerned. Maybe a bit of both.

"Have a seat, Dahlia." The doctor gestured to the room and the multiple seating options available.

I chose the couch, instantly snagging a throw pillow and holding it to my front so I could squeeze it for comfort. I was a sucker for anything soft and cuddly. My house was filled with stuffed animals and fuzzy blankets for that exact reason. I don't think I ever met a blanket I could say no to.

"You seem to be finding your footing," she said, taking a seat in the chair nearest to me.

Shrugging, I toyed with one of the tassels on the end of the pillow. "It was a lot of change in a short period of time."

"How do you feel about that?"

"Like I don't know who I am. Like my whole life has been one big lie."

"What makes you think it was a lie?"

I scoffed, glancing at her calm and controlled face. "Oh, I don't know, the whole I see ghosts thing? The supernatural world is real? The . . . oh fuck, I see ghosts. That means I really saw him at the premiere, doesn't it?"

"Him?"

"My father."

Her expression didn't change. She was far too professional for that, but the second the admission left me, I knew she'd latch onto it. What therapist didn't love to dig into mommy and daddy issues?

"Had he come to you before?"

"No."

"Why do you think he appeared to you in that moment?"

"Your guess is as good as mine, doc. I'm hardly a ghost

whisperer."

"When was the last time you'd seen a ghost prior to that night?"

"I don't think I had."

"Are you certain? This type of power is usually something you're born with. Children are even more sensitive and typically have more frequent encounters until they learn how to manage the energy."

I took my shoes off and splayed out on the couch, thinking back through the years. Recalling what my dad had looked like, as well as the other ghosts I had come into contact with since being here, I searched through my hazy recollections. As expected, there were large patches of my past that were a complete mystery to me. It was a trauma response from my days in the cult, or so I'm told. But there were a few decades-old memories I'd retained. And it was there that I came across a figure that resembled the spirits I'd seen more recently.

Holy shit, my playmate hadn't been a child from a neighboring farm. He'd been a ghost! But it had all stopped the day I'd been found.

"I was a kid. I don't remember much. It's all very fuzzy. My memories are spotty."

"They're likely locked away to protect your psyche. There is a method I'd like to try if you're willing. It's called hypnotherapy. It can unlock repressed memories and help with healing. In order for you to come into your power, you'll have to heal those parts of you."

"I don't know, doc. I suppressed them for a reason. What if it backfires and I end up crazier than I started?"

Even as I admitted my fear out loud, another part of me couldn't deny being curious. Hadn't I always wondered about those patches in my past? About what had happened that night? She was offering me a chance to finally get answers. Could I really puss out?

"Why would you think it will backfire? You're not crazy. That's not a word we use here. This is about your power. It is desperate to be released. If you don't get a handle on it now, the pressure will grow until it bursts from you in a way that could be harmful."

I sighed. She was right, and I could not let fear rule me any longer. I'd already spent too many years of my life that way. This was my chance to do better.

"Okay."

"I'll be right here the entire time. Consider me your co-pilot, okay?"

I laughed a little at that. "Okay."

"All right, now I want you to close your eyes and take a series of deep breaths. With every exhale, I want you to remind yourself that you are safe." Her voice was softer now, her words slow and measured. Soothing.

As my eyes slid shut, the deep click of a metronome filled the room, rhythmic and slow. Exactly what I needed to focus on.

"Let your body sink down into the comfort of your surroundings. Feel each of your muscles relax, starting with your toes, now your feet, ankles, calves."

She continued on, not stopping until I'd relaxed the muscles of my forehead and was nearly asleep.

"How do you feel, Dahlia?"

"Calm."

"Perfect. That's exactly what we want. Hold on to that feeling as we move into this next part, okay? If at any time your calm feels threatened, I want you to take a deep breath and remind yourself that you are safe. That I'm right here and I will not let anything happen to you."

"Okay."

"Right. Now, I want you to imagine you are standing at the top of a staircase. Can you picture it?"

I didn't require more than her suggestion to visualize a nondescript white staircase. It was dimly lit, leading into darkness, but I wasn't scared. It wasn't frightening, just plain.

"Yes."

"Perfect. You're going to take a step down, and as you do, I want you to remember the night of your premiere."

My body tried to tense, but I breathed through it as she'd instructed me and then did as she'd asked.

"Okay."

I saw it all: the flashes of the cameras, the cast and crew, Kiki, my father's face in the crowd. I knew what was coming; that horrible moment everyone dropped dead.

"Take another step down, Dahlia. Remember back farther, to the first day you were able to live on your own."

Again, I did as I was told, remembering how excited I was to hold the keys in my hand. That I finally had a place that was mine where I could be alone and away from everyone else. A safe space where I didn't have to play by anyone's rules but my own. Where my idiosyncrasies couldn't be judged or used against me.

"Very good. Now, we're going back farther. Take one more step down into your childhood. The night you were rescued. We're going to be here a while. Remember, I'm with you. You're safe. Nothing you see can hurt you. It's already happened, we're just observers passing through on our way to the first emergence of your power."

I gave a slow nod as the memory took hold.

I was twelve years old, dressed in nothing but a pure white shift, my long hair cascading down my back as my "mother" escorted me out of the room where she and the other women had been preparing me. We all knew she wasn't really my mom. She was the chosen woman Papa had assigned to my care because he was too busy tending his flock.

My belly was filled with nervous flutters. It was my first time being allowed to participate in the ritual. A great honor, they said. One they were granting me because I'd just bled for the first time two weeks earlier and was ripe.

I didn't know what that meant exactly, but they were all very excited about it. And I wanted nothing more than to make Papa proud. Maybe he'd spend more time with me now. That's all I'd ever wanted. To not be left alone, locked in my room while everyone else gathered together. To belong.

They said I would herald the coming of the goddess.

I was destined to see her return and would carry her with me.

All I knew was pleasing Papa meant everything to me.

So I wore the scratchy, shapeless dress. I let them comb my long hair and anoint me with stinky oils. And I followed behind Mother Carol as she led me to my destiny, trying hard to hide the trembling in my fingers. I was a woman now; I couldn't act like a scared little girl.

Mother Carol squeezed my hand as we approached the sacred chamber. "It's going to hurt. Lie still. Don't make a sound. It will be over soon."

My belly quivered in the same way it did when I got sick.

The door opened, and we entered the circular space. The sleek black walls were illuminated by strategically placed torches. In the center was an altar made of bones, their pallor matching my dress. Together, we were the only white in the room. Behind the altar, taking up nearly the entirety of the north curve of the room, was a stained glass window. It was a full moon tonight, and the image in the glass seemed to glow because of it.

It was our goddess.

Death.

She stood atop a pile of bones, a crown on her head, a scepter made from yet more bones in her hand.

Her eyes twinkled like endless night, and her smile was not warm exactly, but knowing. Inevitable. Eternal.

Just like her.

I shivered.

Something powerful was going to happen here. Powerful and terrible.

Papa entered from a side door which must've led to an antechamber. He was dressed in black robes, and behind him was a boy I'd seen only a handful of times. He had to be fifteen, maybe sixteen now. His eyes were wide with fear as he looked from me to the altar.

"Come here to me, Dahlia," Papa called, taking position on one side of the altar.

I hesitated, my nerves getting the best of me.

Mother Carol gave my shoulder a little shove. "Don't make him ask again."

Swallowing hard, I walked on trembling legs, distantly aware of the people filling the room behind me.

Papa held out his hand as I joined him on the dais. "Tonight, we witness the relinquishing of innocence. The manifestation of pure power. The sacrifice of blood and breath to the Eternal One. Tonight, we open the door and welcome our goddess into our realm. This is what we have been waiting for. This is what Dahlia gives us. My firstborn. My greatest gift."

He gripped my hand and guided me until I was laid out on the altar. In moments, I was bound to the table, feet unshackled but placed in shallow grooves so my knees were bent.

"Take your position, Brother Sam. She's ready for you."

Brother Sam joined me on the altar, parting my clenched knees as he fumbled with his robe.

"Papa," I whispered. He silenced me with a glare. I was so scared. I didn't want to be a sacrifice.

With wild eyes, I glanced around at the members of my father's flock, who were watching this unfold. They were chanting in a language I didn't understand, none of them looking directly at me.

Except one.

A blonde woman I didn't recognize. She'd removed her hood, her long hair gleaming in the moonlight. Her eyes caught and held mine, and right as Brother Sam began to slide my dress up my legs, she mouthed a single word.

Scream.

I did.

I unleashed a scream so loud the window shattered, glass raining down onto the stone floor. Brother Sam released my legs, and I kicked out with all my might, knocking him from the table. Soon my scream was joined by others until we were a single ghastly chorus.

One by one, the screams faded, blood dripping from the eyes and ears of everyone in attendance as they dropped to the floor. Including my father.

I screamed until there was no one left standing. Until my body gave out and I let myself be consumed by the comforting blanket of oblivion. Anything was better than remaining conscious in the nightmare of my reality.

THIRTEEN

DAHLIA

I powered on my laptop with a happy sigh. The return of my electronics was worth the cost of admission. Namely, my absolute freak out during my session yesterday.

That's what I was telling myself, anyway. Even if the return of one of my suppressed memories had been absolute nightmare fuel. Dr. Masterson had brought me out of the trance as quickly as possible, but I'd been a snotty, sobbing mess. It had taken hours—and a heavy dose of valium—to calm back down.

Almost twenty-four hours later, I could still recall the pressure of the bindings, the unwanted touch, the crippling dread and sense of betrayal. It was as fresh in my mind as if it had just happened. I guess that was the danger of unveiling lost memories. They weren't dulled by time. Nope, they were as sharp as knives and just as harmful. I thought hypnotherapy was supposed to help, not make me sick to my stomach.

Once I came out of hypnosis, there was no continuing on with our session. Dr. Masterson hadn't even tried. She'd sent me to my room, and I hadn't left since. Joffrey appeared every once in a while to deliver food and check for proof of life. This last time, he'd also delivered my phone and computer. Of course, the first thing I did was text Kiki. Her reply was nearly instantaneous.

KIKI:

She lives!

KIKI:

Emergency bestie venting sesh, coming right up. Let me grab some wine. I'll be right there.

My computer rang with a video call two minutes later. Kiki'd been working. I knew it by her thick black-rimmed glasses and high, no-nonsense bun.

"You didn't have to drop everything," I said.

"Pfft, I'm just reading a manuscript. It'll keep." She propped her elbows on her desk and leaned forward, peering at me. "So tell me about therapy. What happened?"

"It's like I said in my text. I don't want to unpack anything else. I want to send it all back. Full refund."

"Dee, you're deflecting. I can see how upset you are from here. Talk to me."

It was now or never.

"I had a one-on-one session yesterday."

"And?"

"She hypnotized me . . ."

"I take it you didn't suddenly start barking like a dog?"

I laughed, but it was hollow. "Not quite. I went back into my repressed memories. To right before I was found."

"Oh Jesus. Dee, are you okay? That had to have been awful."

I took a deep breath, wishing I had my own glass of

wine to help me get through this. Then I exhaled and word-vomited the whole thing.

"Fuck," she whispered when I was done. If I wasn't mistaken, some of the color left her cheeks. "I knew it was bad, but I didn't think it was *that* bad."

"Cults . . . am I right?" I muttered bleakly.

"God," she said, still shaking her head. "I just . . . there are no words. Whoever that woman was, she has my undying gratitude for helping you when you needed it most."

My thoughts drifted back to the stranger, wondering for the hundredth time who she was and how she'd gotten there. I didn't recognize her as one of the Scythe Society. But she had to have been, right? Why else would she have been there?

"Well, she's dead. They all are. Every. Last. One."

She shivered. "Good?"

I nodded grimly. That about summed up my thoughts on the matter as well.

"Do you want me to come get you? I can. I'll book a fucking ticket right now. I already have the tab open. We'll figure something else out."

I appreciated the offer more than she'd ever know, but I couldn't give in to the temptation. There was so much more going on here than just my fucked-up past. Blackwood may be my only chance to figure out how the hell to use this power of mine. I couldn't run from that, and something told me I would only be a liability to myself until I learned how to control my 'gift.'

"No. I need to see this through. Get some answers." Tired of the heaviness in my chest, I dangled a carrot I knew she wouldn't be able to resist. "I guess it isn't all bad, though. The men here are like a beefcake buffet."

"A what now?"

"It's ridiculous. They're like . . . paranormal romance level hot."

I needed to tell her about the ghost thing, and the supernatural thing, and . . . fuck, the mate thing. No time like the present, right?

"In other news, I might be married."

Kiki spit out a mouthful of wine. I couldn't help but laugh, even as I winced apologetically.

"I'm sorry, what *the* actual fuck?"

"You should sit down."

"I am."

"You should lie down."

"You're freaking me out. Start talking, Dee."

"Um. Well. So vampires are real, and like . . . all the other supernaturals too. I saw this pixie orgy, and Captain Hook is here, another guy is a dragon, I might be the God of Thunder's mate, he calls me Kærasta, and when he touched me, there were like full-on tingles and lightning in my veins, and like . . . there's this other guy with an asshole, I mean a dog he calls Asshole. Also, I can see dead people."

"That's it. I'm getting on a plane."

"Keeks, I'm serious. I know it sounds insane, but it's true. This isn't rehab. Well, it is. It's a supernatural rehab. Everyone here is some kind of paranormal."

"I . . . okay, setting aside the fact that paranormal creatures are fiction, why would you be there? You're human."

"About that. Turns out I'm some kind of psychic. It's why I can see ghosts and like, interact with them and stuff. Or that's what my doctor tells me. I'm a little fuzzy on the details, to be honest."

She frowned, shoving her glasses up the bridge of her

nose. "So you're a ghost whisperer, like Jennifer Love Hewitt. And you're married."

"I know that face. That's the face you made when I wanted to kill off Ren permanently and never let him dick her down."

"We don't kill off the love interests, Dee. You know the rules. Romances must end with an HEA or a happily for now. Killing off the sexy British rockstar would have been the worst choice you could have made."

"He was already dead!"

"Not perma-dead. He still had that ghost dick."

I huffed and shook my head. "This isn't even the point. I can see you don't believe me."

"Can you blame me? You're at rehab because you had a mental breakdown. A public one. Now you're telling me about ghosts and vampires and dragons."

"And demigods."

"Yes, those too. I just . . . it's a lot to take in."

"Fine. I'll prove it to you." I shoved off my bed and made a beeline for the door. Yanking it open, I grabbed the first person who was passing by. Lucky me, it was our resident dragon, Kai.

"I'm happy to see you too, lass, but there's no need to get handsy."

I ignored him and gently shoved him in front of my computer's webcam. Kiki's mouth dropped open the second Kai came into frame.

"Jesus, is this the one you're married to?"

"Married? You're married?" Kai asked, shock clear in his voice.

"No. Maybe. I'm not sure how all this works."

"All what? You either married someone or you didn't, lass. There's not a maybe in the mix here."

"Oh my God, he's SCOTTISH? You need to lead with the good stuff. How tall are you? Six-two? Six-three?" Kiki asked.

"Six-four."

She fanned her face. "I might be pregnant."

"Keeks!"

"What? Have you seen this guy? Good lord. He's like a walking fertility clinic. I bet he could knock up an octogenarian."

"There's only one person I'll be knocking up, and it's not you." Kai stared at Kiki from the screen.

"Is it Dahlia? Oh, this is delicious."

It took everything in me not to slam the computer shut. "Kai, I brought you in here for a reason."

"And that is?"

"I need you to show her your tattoo."

"You need to be more specific, lass. I'm covered in them."

"Is it my birthday?" Kiki whispered. "This feels like a present."

"The moving one. It's usually here," I said, reaching up and tracing the edge of his collar.

The man gave a soft grunt that I felt in my lady business. Fuck.

Without a word, he reached behind his head and pulled his shirt off.

Kiki gasped. "Oh fuck, I was such a good girl, wasn't I?"

"Kiki . . ."

"Where do I sign up for the powers?"

I didn't bother responding to that one because my attention was consumed by the wall of sexy muscle in front of me. And the tail of his magic tattoo, which was currently peeking out of the waistband of his jeans.

"Um . . . where is it?" I asked through a tight throat.

"Wrapped around my thigh."

"Sweet baby Jesus in a manger with the donkey," Kiki muttered.

Kai chuckled. "I haven't heard that one before. Usually it's Moses in the basket."

"Do you . . . uh . . . need to take off your pants too?" Oh my God, what was wrong with me?

"Is that what you're after, lass?"

My cheeks were on literal fire.

His hands went to unfasten the button, but he stopped and grinned wickedly. "I'm just having a laugh. Here you go."

The dragon's head slithered upward, moving its winged form across the ridges of his abdomen, the flat planes of his chest, across the thick muscles of his built shoulders, and then finally settled by resting on his bicep. Lips hitching up in a soft smirk, Kai turned around, revealing his back . . . and the rest of the dragon's impressive body.

"Did someone drug me? Am I drugged?" Kiki whispered.

"No, Keeks. It's magic."

"Wow."

"I get that reaction a lot," Kai joked, already tugging his shirt back on.

"Well, hello. What are we doing? Playing strip poker?" Caspian said from my still open door. God, he was devastating, dressed head to toe in black, guyliner firmly smudged, and a dusting of rakish stubble across his jaw. "Looks like I'm late to the party. I'll catch up."

He pulled his shirt off and tossed it at me. I caught it and did *not* simper like a twitterpated idiot.

"Okay, tell me *this* is the one you're married to."

"What's all this about marriage?" Caspian asked, pausing in the act of removing his belt.

"Yeah, let's get back to that. Why do you think you're married?" Kai asked, crossing his arms.

"No, Keeks. This one's the pirate."

"Captain."

"Captain," I amended, mentally rolling my eyes.

"I thought you were supposed to have a hook," Kiki said, eyeing him up and down.

"Who says I don't?" he replied with a wink. "It curves to the left."

"I'm waiting, gem."

"Oooh, who's Gem? Is she a fairy?" Kiki asked.

But Kai's eyes were on me. Blazing. Serious. Intense. Oh, *I* was gem. I liked that. A whole fucking lot.

"Um, it's nothing, I guess. Or maybe it's not. It's just something Tor said. And . . . the lightning effect."

"Lightning effect?" Caspian repeated, finally seeming to take the conversation seriously.

"Yeah, when he, uh, touched me . . ."

"He fucking touched you?" Kai's voice was more growl than anything. Shit.

"Not like that. Not inappropriately. It was more of a connection thing. He was explaining mates to me and said it was like lightning striking. We both felt it. I could see it in his eyes."

"You sure that wasn't his Berserker? Sometimes lightning flickers in his eyes," Kai asked while Caspian sulked.

"Bad form. I saw her first. You were supposed to be mine, Dahlia darling. I thought we had a connection."

"Jesus, Dee. You need to stay there. Definitely. I'd be a bad friend if I let you leave all this. You're starring in your own freaking romance novel."

"She's not going anywhere," Kai grumbled.

"He's one growled *mine* away from claiming you. This is so good. I should have made popcorn."

I squirmed under the scrutiny of my best friend and the two insanely gorgeous men standing beside me. Things had really devolved quickly. It was like they were both ganging up on me and staking their claims at the same time.

I hardly knew what to do with one of them. What was I supposed to do with four?

Wait, four? No, Dahlia, you don't get to count the hottie with the dog. He doesn't even like you.

"Maybe you two should wrestle for her. Have you ever seen the videos of Turkish oil wrestling? Really get in there an—"

Caspian slammed my laptop closed, cutting off the conversation before she could finish.

Knowing my best friend, I wasn't surprised when my phone vibrated with an incoming call. I'd just have to call her back later. Caspian saw it too and shook his head.

"Not yet, darling. We need to have a little chat about exactly how exclusive you are with the Viking."

"I-I'm not. With him, that is. He sort of shut me down after."

"Even better," Caspian crooned, taking me by the hand.

Without the Kiki buffer in the conversation, I was painfully aware of how attractive these men were. And that one of them was currently shirtless and touching me.

Kai must have picked up on my sudden discomfort because he grabbed Caspian by the back of the neck. "Come on, Hook. We're late for our workout."

"Workout? What workout? I don't exercise. I was born this way."

Undeterred, Kai shoved him out my door, and they left

me standing alone, a little aroused and, honestly, a lot flustered. I had way too much energy running through my system, but the last thing I wanted to do was leave my sanctuary and possibly encounter them or the others when I was so wound up.

My phone vibrated again, this time a text alert.

KIKI:

> If you're not being bent into a pretzel by those two hot men, you should at least be writing this down.

The lady had a point. If I wasn't getting any, my heroine absolutely should. Someone deserved a couple of good orgasms.

ME:

> On it. 📖 ✏️ 🖋️

KIKI:

> Damn. I was hoping for the former.

I was smiling as I sat my phone down, absently reaching for my scrunchie, when I realized that the heavy cloud I'd been lost in since my session yesterday had vanished. There was a sudden pang of fear that it would return now that I'd recognized it. Sort of like a monster who'd been summoned, but . . . it didn't.

I wondered if that was because of Kiki or the guys.

Shrugging, I decided it didn't matter. I was just thankful it was true.

I squared my shoulders and shook out my hair to prepare for my pre-writing ritual. Playlist, socks, bun. I already had the socks on, so all that was left was to turn on my music and get this mess of hair wrangled. Unfortunately, my cute baby pink silk scrunchie was missing.

"Damn," I muttered, disappointed because it was one of my favorites and it kept my hair from tangling.

Shit, that was the second time recently I'd gone hunting for something only to come up missing.

I scowled into the empty corner of my room, silently cursing this place and sticky-fingered ghosts. One of these days, I'd catch them in the act. But until then, I'd just have to deal. I had a scene to write, and I knew exactly which two men would be starring in it.

CHAPTER
FOURTEEN
HOOK

"Call," I said, staring over my fan of cards at Cain from across the table.

He eyed the pile of chips in front of me and then the one in front of him. A warning yip came from the dog at his feet, and he tossed his cards face down with a scowl. "I'm out."

"You're not using that ball of fur of yours to cheat, are you?" Kit asked, eyes narrowed in suspicion. The demon frowned down at the dog as if he wanted to kick the fluffball.

"Asshole can't even see the table. What use could he possibly be?"

"Then what's the matter, Cain? You aren't even interested in seeing what he has first?" Drax taunted. I didn't know much about the burly denizen of the underworld except that he liked to pick fights.

The broody southerner snorted. "I may not know much these days, but I do know demons are crafty and have the best poker faces around."

"I beg your pardon. I. Am. A. Bloody. Pirate. My poker face is immaculate." How very dare he insinuate otherwise.

"Was I talking about you?" Cain asked with a lift of his brow. "I didn't realize you dabbled in souls, Caspian."

"What use is a soul? Virtue. Panties. Those are far more interesting."

Kit let out a wistful sigh. "Oh, I do miss stealing virtue and panties. In my day, I was more of a demon in the sack than actual hellspawn. Why do you think I kept up the Christopher Marlowe act as long as I did? The ladies love a playwright. Willie and I, we were the original rock stars."

"As I said, those are of far greater interest to me than souls."

Cain rolled his eyes but remained silent, choosing instead to pick up his dog and idly pet him while Drax snorted.

He leaned forward, obsidian eyes intent on me as he snarled, "You only say that because you've never experienced the rush of claiming a contracted one."

"I've experienced plenty of rushes. You haven't lived until your fingers have been covered in a woman's . . ." My words faded as Dahlia walked into the room, her hair piled on top of her head, hips swaying as she moved through the space with a quiet focus.

"Eyes on your own paper, pirate," Cain grumbled, his voice a low warning.

"Who says that's not mine?"

"The fact that you're here and she's there."

"Oh, who is *she*? Can I play?" Kit asked, leaning in conspiratorially. "Perhaps we turn this from a game of cards with nothing but gummy bears as the prize to a wager for her heart? Much more fun with higher stakes."

"No," Cain snapped before I could tell the demon to fuck off.

"Aw, don't be like that, Cain-y boy, secrets don't make friends."

This came from Drax, who was smirking like the cat who caught the canary.

Cain and I shared a rare look of mutual annoyance. Neither one of us appreciated the interest these two numb-skulls were showing Dahlia. She was ours.

No, mine. Ours only in the sense that she was part of our little therapy crew. But she was mine in every other way that mattered. I could still picture the subtle flare of her pupils while I'd undressed before her. That sweet flutter of her pulse against her neck when I'd caught her looking. Oh yes . . . the pretty little psychic was a bud ripe for the plucking.

"What's he doing?" Drax asked, dubious stare on me.

"Don't ask. I doubt any of us want inside a dirty pirate's mind." Cain leaned back in his chair, absently stroking the animal in his lap. I wondered if he realized how ridiculous he looked, big and stormy and cradling a tiny ball of fluff in his arms.

As though he could sense my disdain, Asshole growled at me.

What are you, little beastie? A familiar or just a plain old pooch?

There was far too much intelligence shining in those beady little eyes for me to discount him entirely. The runt was out to get me.

My focus, however, was pulled away from the game, the dog, and the men around the table. Dahlia drew me to her. She had from the moment I opened the door and let her inside. The woman was exactly my type of challenge. A complex puzzle I alone could solve.

"Excuse me, gentlemen. It's time I officially throw my hat into the ring."

"We're in the middle of a game," Drax complained.

"Fine, I'm all in, mates." I shoved every one of my chips into the pot. Then I tossed my hand on top of it, face down. "And I fold."

Kit cackled gleefully, since he was the last player standing. If you asked me, the demon had a bit of a sweet tooth. He was entirely too excited about the prospect of his two-pound bag of contraband.

Asshole growled at me as I stood, and Cain shot me a warning glare. "What are you doing?"

"Didn't you hear me the first time? I'm making my intentions known. You should try it sometime. You look like you're in desperate need of a shag."

"I'm not the only one," Cain muttered, jerking his chin toward Kai, who was seated at a window seat, intently staring at his open sketch pad. As we all turned our attention to him, Dahlia sidled up to him, a smile tilting up her lips.

"Oh, what a cunt. He's smarter than we all give him credit for with those charcoal-stained fingers and that brooding artist facade."

I didn't want to look too closely at the annoyance that bubbled up within me as I watched Dahlia and Kai converse. Lucky for me, I was a champion cockblocker. I just needed to remind my sweet little rabbit exactly how much she liked me before Kai got a chance to show her his dragon.

Without another word, I strode from the table and

beelined for the pair, only to be immediately intercepted by a gossip of merfolk. Five of them, to be exact.

"Hook! Do you need something? Your brow is furrowed in that special way again."

"I got you a water. You seem dehydrated."

"Hook hates sparkling water. I'll get him some rum."

"I got you a cookie."

"Me too. It's in my room. If you follow me, I'll lie back and let you eat it."

Usually I loved my adoring fan club. Today I wanted to stab each and every one of them in the eye.

"Leave him alone. You know he's not a fish eater. Get out of here and go swim into a net or something," Oz said, approaching me with big, soulful eyes. "I'll get him whatever he needs."

The mermaids hissed, the first one stepping up like she might be a match for him. "And what makes you think you even know what that is?"

Oz raised a brow, entirely unfazed. "Did you forget what I can do, you overgrown sea cucumber?"

The mermaid blanched, her silvery-blue skin mottling with anger. But before she could throw herself at him, one of the others grabbed her around the waist and hauled her back.

A flash of blonde in my periphery had me glancing past the group to where Dahlia was currently making her way out of the room.

"Shit."

"What is it, my love? What can I help you with?" One of the other mermaids asked, reaching for me as I peeled away from them.

"Back, you creatures!" Oz shouted, jumping in front of

me with his arms out on either side of him. "Go, Hook, now's your chance. I'll hold them off."

I had to bite back a laugh as he started waving his hands in front of him, threatening each mermaid who tried to get past with his touch—and the mind reading ability that came with it. Smart play. He looked utterly ridiculous, but there was no denying the effectiveness of his rather inventive ploy.

A curt nod of thanks was all I offered him before I followed after her, a strange sense of anxiety unfurling in my chest. I'd never lost before, but with the way she and Kai looked at each other, I wondered if I might this time.

I guess I'd just have to give her the Caspian Hook treatment. Then she'd have no reason to look at anyone other than me ever again.

~

CAIN

IF IT HADN'T BEEN for Asshole sitting on my lap like a lead weight, I might've snagged Hook by his collar and forced him to sit his ass down and leave Dahlia be. The fact that I even had the impulse was alarming. The girl was nothing to me. Less than nothing. We'd spoken for all of fifteen minutes in total.

And yet . . .

I couldn't even get myself to supply the words that came after. That would require me to admit to truths I was not yet ready to acknowledge.

Asshole pranced on my thighs, his attention on her and

the dragon shifter as they talked and he made her smile. The pirate was hot on the trail to her as well, and I felt . . . threatened? Competitive? Jealous? None of that made sense. If she'd been anyone important to me prior to my memory loss, surely she would have said something. But the uncomfortable twisting in my gut said I needed to defend my territory, whether or not I understood why.

Since arriving at Blackwood, I've been plagued with these unexplainable feelings, things that seemed instinctual, muscle memory perhaps. I've just gone with it, let them take the reins, and trusted my gut because that was all I had.

I don't know what I was expecting in under a week, but sadly, one session with the good doctor had brought me no closer to learning the truth of my identity or tenure here. Apparently, I'd lost control.

Control of what, exactly? My temper? I wasn't a hulking brute like Kai or Tor, so a loss of control in that regard seemed unlikely to cause significant damage. As soon as the thought registered, a darkness slithered through my mind, seeming to negate it. All at once, I knew my truth—I wasn't physically stronger than a human man, but I wasn't without power.

Dark power.

Shadow power.

I didn't know where the correction came from, only that my bones acknowledged the rightness of it.

"Bloody hell, this is like playing cards with a dead man. Oi! Cain! Your turn, mate," Kit said, waving a hand in front of my face.

Drax chuckled under his breath. "He doesn't even know what the bid is."

I didn't give a damn. The last thing I wanted was a

fucking bag of gummy bears. Especially not when Dahlia got up and all but ran out of the room, intently focused on something I couldn't see.

Of course that motherfucking pirate followed her, like a snake in the grass.

Asshole growled and hopped off my lap, his body tense and gaze darting from me to the woman I shouldn't fixate on.

Taking a page from the pirate's book, I shoved all my chips in and stood before saying, "I'm all in."

Then I left the table, my sole focus on uncovering the mystery of Dahlia Moore. It was true; I hardly knew a single thing about myself, but that same innate sense of knowing told me she was the key to unlocking everything.

FIFTEEN

DAHLIA

H ave you ever been plunged into a pool of ice water? And not like a refreshing pool, where it's a super hot day and you're desperate to cool off, but an arctic fishing hole. Like dead of winter, hypothermia imminent levels of bone-deep cold.

That's where I was at the moment.

One second, I'm doing my best to flirt with a Scottish hottie. The next, all the air left my lungs, the sounds around me were muffled and unintelligible, and I felt like I was moving through molasses on a winter day. The atmosphere was thick with malevolent energy, heavy and oppressive. Just like when I was at the hospital.

Gaze slowly shifting from the handsome dragon in front of me, I followed the pull from the other end of the room. Despite being early afternoon, the hallway at the far end seemed to be cloaked in shadows from the dead of night. No one else reacted to the sinister darkness.

No one but me.

Heart racing, breaths coming in shallow pants, I watched as the shadow seemed to writhe and curl in on itself, little tendrils of inky black peeling away piece by piece. Terror raced along my veins, but I couldn't keep from stepping forward. I had to find out what this was. The draw was too strong to deny, and now that I understood what I could do, I'd be a fool to ignore it.

Are you sure you aren't a fool for running headlong after it?

I vaguely heard Caspian call my name as I passed in a trance-like state, my only thought to follow wherever the shadow led. Because it was clearly leading me. Every time I paused, it did too. Writhing. Waiting. A maelstrom on the verge of breaking.

My pulse thrummed in my ears, a surge of white noise getting louder and more frantic with every step I took, reminding me I was still human. I needed this fragile organ to keep me alive, and as much as I wanted to know the answer to this menacing riddle, I wouldn't solve anything if my heart gave out from fright.

The shadow spoke in hisses I couldn't understand, harsh and sibilant, painful to my ears.

"What are you saying?" I asked, needing it to stop but desperate to know.

In answer, it moved deeper into the castle, winding its way through a labyrinth of hallways I'd never find my way out of.

"Where are we going? What do you want?"

The figure within stopped, then solidified just enough I could make out a human shape but not much more. It turned where it stood at the end of the hallway and fixed its focus on me. The weight of its fury and desperation nearly brought me to my knees.

My lungs seized, and my heart stuttered and ached as the ghost flickered in and out of the solid form. Gasping for air, I reached out to support myself on the wall. If I fell, I wouldn't get up again.

"Stop," I croaked. "Please."

With a scream of absolute savagery, the ghost rushed me, claw-like hands outstretched and reaching.

I threw my arms up in a sorry attempt to protect myself. I couldn't run if I tried; I was locked in place, my muscles knotted with terror.

If she touched me, I would die.

"No!" I wailed, the word bursting out of me in a voice I barely recognized as the ghost closed in.

I closed my eyes, as though somehow not seeing the spirit would keep me safe. When a hand clamped down on my shoulder, I let out a bloodcurdling scream and collapsed to my knees like a marionette whose strings had just been severed. Whatever unearthly power had just held me captive was gone. The anger, the evil, the soul-crushing energy. All of it was gone, and in its place, the scent of the sea and wind.

"Hush now, love. You're all right. I've got you."

My eyes fluttered open, clammy palms pressed to the hardwood floor, gaze trained on the polished wood between my hands. I couldn't look up. If I did, I'd see her again, and she'd take me.

"Come now, you're all right. I'm here. You're safe."

Caspian's soothing voice washed over me, but it still wasn't enough to pull me from my terror. As if he could sense it, he forced the issue by pulling me up by my shoulders and into his arms. I didn't fight him. To be honest, there wasn't a single cell in my body that wanted to push him away. I nestled my face against his strong, warm chest and clung to him for dear life.

161

"You're trembling, darling. What's wrong? What scared you so?"

"G-g-ghost," I stuttered. Though that felt like far too tame a word for what I'd just experienced. Thus far, they'd been creepy and a bit annoying, but nothing like this. Nothing that radiated danger. None had struck me with this much terror.

"Pesky nuisances. Is it still here?" He stroked my hair and pressed his lips to the crown of my head, waiting for my answer.

"N-no. God, Caspian, she was . . . evil."

I couldn't see his face, but I could feel the change in him. The subtle tensing of his arms around me, the sudden alertness as if his attentions had shifted from me to our surroundings, a harsh inhale. All of these things told me he was preparing to face a threat. That he was taking me seriously, even if he hadn't witnessed what I had.

I didn't know how badly I needed someone to believe me until that moment. So many times before, I'd been treated like I was losing my mind. Even with Kiki, she never immediately took me at face value; I always had to prove myself. Case in point: our earlier conversation.

"I won't let anything happen to you, Dahlia. I swear to you."

He knelt before me and crooked his finger under my chin just before he tipped my face up so I had to look at him. Lord, he was handsome with his sharp jaw with a hint of stubble, cut cheekbones, and perfectly shaped brows. He was model pretty, but the glint of the metal hoop that pierced one nostril and the earring in his ear gave him a rakish edge. Not to mention all the rings, tattoos, and black clothing. His usual flirtatious air was missing, though.

He was surprisingly serious and, dare I say, protective.

Two words I never would have used to describe Caspian before today. It was as if the facade of carefree fuckboy had been removed, and he was finally allowing me to see the man beneath.

"There we are. You're settling down now. That's my sweet girl."

His fingers trailed across the side of my face, a tender caress I hadn't expected. And the look in his eyes stole my breath.

I couldn't say which one of us moved first, only that the next thing I knew, our lips were touching. His large palm pressed between my shoulder blades, holding me against him as I gave myself over to the feel of this man and the safety of his arms.

He tried to pull away, to break the kiss even though I could tell he wanted more, but I wouldn't let him end this. Not yet. I threaded my fingers into the hair at the base of his skull and deepened the kiss, parting my lips, an invitation for more. The way he groaned into my mouth had my body on fire for him. I forgot all about the ghost, Blackwood, my past.

Right now, the only thing that existed was him.

Caspian finally succeeded in ending our kiss, but the way he kept me clutched to him, his breaths coming hard and fast, eyes filled with desire, told me everything I needed to know. We were both lost in each other.

"Why did you stop?" I whispered against his ear. He turned his head and nestled his face in the crook of my neck. I shivered every time his stubble brushed the sensitive skin.

"I'll have you laid out on your back in this hallway if I don't."

I had to admit, that didn't sound like such a bad thing.

At least then I could replace my memory of this corridor with thoughts of him instead of that . . . monster.

"I'm sure you've done more scandalous things than that."

"Far more scandalous, indeed. But none as enjoyable as this."

Getting to his feet, he held a hand out so he could help me do the same. The simple gesture, him guiding me to standing, shouldn't have been so affecting. But it was. I felt the brush of his fingers along my palm as though it were his tongue against much more sensitive skin. Caspian Hook had me in his thrall, and I was here for it.

"You need to stop looking at me like that, sweet girl."

"Why?"

"Because I'm liable to find the nearest flat surface and fuck you against it."

Without conscious thought, my eyes trailed to the wall beside us.

Caspian let out a little growl and pushed me up against it, our linked hands up over my head. "Is that what you want, darling? Me to ravish you in the hallway?" He rocked his pelvis against my belly, the thick length of his arousal pressing into me, promising hours of pleasure if I said yes.

Heat flooded my cheeks as my thighs clenched. "I . . . fuck, I don't know."

He smirked before dropping his lips to the hollow of my throat and layering kisses across my collarbone as he murmured, "Then you're not ready for me yet. You will be. But I'm not taking you until you're begging me to sink inside you to the hilt."

It was on the tip of my tongue to let him know that could be arranged when my eyes caught a shadowy movement over his shoulder. A startled cry left me, fear that the ghost had returned obliterating any and all lusty thoughts.

Caspian shifted into my protector once more, body squarely in front of mine, guarding me as he turned to face our intruder, one hand at his belt, as though reaching for a non-existent weapon.

A heartbeat later, a figure stepped out of the shadows, and Caspian's defensive posture deflated.

"Oh, it's you. I should have known you'd like to watch."

CHAPTER
SIXTEEN
CAIN

Asshole zoomed in front of me as if he knew who I sought and was leading the way. Perhaps he was. Stranger things had happened. Or maybe he just sensed that same shift in energy I did. Something crackled in the air, a restless tingle across my skin. It had started when she left the rec room, but I'd ignored the sensation until I couldn't deny it any longer.

A scream shattered the silence, and I knew without question that it was her.

Dahlia.

As we raced ahead, Asshole bounding down the corridor and me giving up all pretense of walking, the aura of malice and despair grew to unbearable levels. I couldn't catch my breath; the oppressive weight of the atmosphere was too great.

"Dahlia," I whispered, knowing she couldn't hear me, that I shouldn't care this much about a woman I'd just met.

As quickly as it had appeared, the dark sensation vanished, the air lightening and that oily coating of evil dissipating. I skidded to a stop as I rounded the corner and caught sight of her. No. *Them.* Dahlia was trembling on the floor, that bastard pirate clutching her to him like only he could save her.

Chest heaving, breaths sawing in and out of my throat as my vision blurred, I held myself back. Anger, raw and all-consuming, took over. My hands shook, little blue flames racing across my fingers in a deadly dance, while a single thought boomed through my mind.

She belongs to me.

Hook's lips found hers, and I saw nothing but blue fire as fury burned through any and all rational thought, catapulting me into a scene so real it had to be a memory.

Under a cloudless blue sky, she floated in the pristine waters of her favorite hidden lake. I saw why she loved it. The field of daffodils offered bright spots of color in the ocean of greenery surrounding the water. I, however, could focus on only one thing. Her.

Clad in nothing but a thin muslin shift that clung to every curve like a second skin, she lay in the still pool with her eyes closed as she let the water soothe her. I stood in the shadows, hidden by my magic and the trees bordering the water. She wasn't mine. But she belonged to me. She just didn't know it yet.

The bargain I'd made with her mother just this morning ensured it.

It wouldn't be long now.

Wind sent little ripples drifting across the smooth surface of the lake. She jolted as if they'd woken her from a trance. Turning onto her stomach, she swam toward the shore, more of her delectable body revealed with every stroke. Tight pink nipples pressed against the wet cloth of her shift. My mouth ran dry at the thought of what they might taste like. Of the sounds I'd be able to pull from her when I had her under me once she was mine.

I adjusted my swollen cock with an inaudible groan. The temptation to bring myself off here and now was strong, but I resisted. The next time I found release, I wanted it to be in her tight little cunt. She'd look even better filled with me. I'd paint her thighs with my spend and mark her with my scent so no one else would dare touch what was mine.

"Careful, love, you're dangerously close to scandalizing the forest."

I gritted my teeth at the sound of the man's voice, defensive magic building in my hands on instinct.

The object of my obsession let out a soft gasp, her dove-gray eyes flaring wide when she spotted the man holding her dress up like a prize.

"Henry! Stop it this instant. Give me back my gown." She covered her breasts with one arm while reaching for the garment with the other.

"I don't think I will." The handsome prick smirked and put it behind his back even as he closed the distance between them. He turned his head and offered her his cheek. "Unless you grant me that kiss I've been desperate for."

Her cheeks went a bright pink, and she looked away from him, her gaze sweeping over the copse of trees where I was hidden.

That's right, goddess. Look for your true mate. I'm right here. Waiting.

"You know we can't. It wouldn't be proper. If someone caught us, I'd be ruined."

Someone is right here, and it won't be your reputation you'll need to worry about. That boy lays a finger or any other body part on you, I'll rip it off and choke him with it. And then see about ridding you of his touch. Right after locking you up and punishing you for betraying me.

"Then I suppose there'd be nothing left for me to do but marry you." He winked at her. "Which fits right in with my plan, truth be told."

"What?" she gasped.

What! There would be no marriage between my mate and this . . . overstuffed peacock. She was mine to claim.

"All that's left to do is get your mother's blessing. I know I should wait until she agrees, but I simply can't. It's a foregone conclusion."

I watched with jealous fury rushing through my veins as he sank to one knee and touched her hand. I would cut off his fingers one by one and send them to her as wedding gifts for the first ten days of our marriage. How dare he deign to touch my bride.

"Henry . . ." she protested. But it was feeble at best. She was won over by his pompous display.

If I ground my teeth any harder, they were liable to turn to dust.

How could she possibly prefer this manchild to me?

Taking her by the arm, he tugged her down until she was kneeling before him, his fingers now tracing her cheek. "Marry me, my darling. Put me out of my misery and tell me you'll be mine?"

That was enough. Before she could answer, I siphoned power into my palms and thought perhaps I'd send it straight into Henry's heart, killing him before she got the chance to betray me. But she wrapped her arms around him, and I cursed because there was no way for my bolt of fire to miss her if I sent it their way. My goddess was a devout woman, though. She believed in messages from on high. Omens. Signs. Warnings.

Those I could absolutely do.

Blue fire still coiled in my hands, I shoved them into the ground, eyeing those flowers she loved so much as I sent it barrelling toward them. The field of cheery yellow blooms withered and died, the decaying petals littering the now dry, cracked earth.

My soon-to-be bride gasped in fear, her gaze sweeping across the land. All the color drained from her cheeks as she returned her focus to Henry.

"No. No, I cannot."

"Don't be ridiculous. Of course you can."

"No, Henry. Look around you. The gods are displeased. This is an omen. Something terrible will happen if I accept you."

Freeing herself from his hold, she snatched her forgotten dress from the ground and raced back toward her village, leaving the poor lovestruck fool staring after her.

Realizing the two of us were alone, my goddess safely out of sight, I grinned. A slow, malicious curling of my lips.

Excellent

Before he could fully stand, I sent one final blast of power his way.

Straight into his heart.

He was dead before I turned away.

"I should have known you'd like to watch." Hook's voice pulled me out of the memory that had taken me hostage.

So I was a coldhearted killer—and apparently married. Also, I think I was a bit of a stalker. A real role model for the kids. Perfect.

"Kinda hard not to watch when you're pawing each other in the middle of a fucking hallway."

Dahlia wouldn't look at me. She buried her face in Hook's shoulder, and I hated it.

"Doll . . ."

I didn't know what to say, only that I didn't want her hiding from me.

She shifted, peering over his shoulder at me.

Recognition slammed into me. Those eyes. They were *her* eyes. The woman in my memory.

As quickly as the thought took shape, I dismissed it. My mind was playing tricks on me, looking for an explanation for this unseemly obsession of mine. Trying to justify the draw I felt to her.

I was a married man. Or promised, at the very least. I could not lust after a pretty little doll.

"It's fine, Cain. We're fine."

"I felt the presence in the air. Something bad happened here. I can still see the residue of it hanging over you."

She glanced up and narrowed her eyes, searching for truth in my words. While Dahlia might not be able to make it out, I could still see the echo of the energy that tried to attach itself to her.

"You need to get her out of this hallway, Hook. That spirit could be back at any moment. It's All Souls Day, and Dahlia walked right into its web."

"How do you know this?" Hook asked, a dubious expression on his face.

I had no fucking clue. But it was true; I had no doubt. "If you won't get her out of here, I will."

Reaching for Dahlia's arm, I braced myself for the contact. I hadn't touched her yet, but there was no way feeling her skin under my fingers would end in anything but arousal on my part.

She was having none of it. The stubborn woman jerked

away from both of us. "I can get myself out of here just fine, thank you."

Just like the woman in my memory, she pulled free of Hook's hold and rushed off, not sparing either of us another glance.

"Now look what you've done. You've scared her off. I had her right where I wanted her, mate."

I wondered how much trouble I'd get into if I killed him.

My fingers tingled with power, and Asshole growled in response. Almost as if he was telling me not to do it . . . or egging me on.

Deciding it wasn't worth the paperwork—or another night in No Man's Land—I sighed and trailed after Dahlia. I had no excuse for it, but I couldn't resist the urge to make sure she got wherever she was going safely.

Looked like that was a big ol' check in the stalker column.

Something told me Dr. Masterson wouldn't count this as positive progress.

SEVENTEEN

KAI

I rrational anger clawed at me as I tore open my sketchbook and mindlessly recreated the scene I'd stumbled upon. Dahlia kneeling in front of Hook, her beautiful body wrapped in his arms, his lips on her . . .

My blood hummed in a jealous rage.

It should have been me.

She's mine.

The thought whispered through my mind, unbidden. I wasn't sure if it was purely mine, or if it was my dragon, or a bit of us both. Usually he was the possessive bastard, but I'd be lying if I tried to pretend that Dahlia didn't bring out the same urge in me.

My dad told me he knew mum was it for him the moment he saw her, lost and wandering Faerie alone and confused. It had taken everything in him to let her go, and in the end, he'd sacrificed all he had to be with her. That was how I felt. I couldn't explain it, I simply knew it to be true. So seeing Hook with his paws all over my treasure was too much to bear.

"What the bloody hell is this?" Tor snarled, snatching

the pad from my hands and glaring down at the charcoal scene I'd been in the middle of.

"None of your fucking business," I growled, matching his simmering violence with my own. If the Beast of Novasgard was looking for a fight, he'd just found one. Today was so not the fucking day to push me.

The Viking's eyes bled black with what looked like galaxies swirling in their depths as he tossed the artwork to the grass. Oh, the Berserker was ready to come play. Good. I was a dragon. Even if my power had been locked down tight, I could take him.

"Don't touch her. Don't look at her. She is mine."

On instinct, I huffed. "That's nae what it looks like to me."

Without warning, Tor slammed his fist into my face. I heard the crunch of my nose breaking and felt the warm spray of blood leaving me as my head was thrown to the side. A dark laugh left me as I wiped the blood away, my eyes catching on my sketchbook and the crimson drops dotting my latest drawing.

The drawing of Dahlia and . . . me.

Once again I'd subconsciously drawn myself into the scene. Replaced Hook with her true mate. Me.

Oops. No wonder the bastard was so enraged. He thought I was the one who'd kissed and held her.

I guess technicalities didn't really matter. I'd wanted it to be me.

Logic didn't exist any longer between us, no matter what I'd come to understand. He drew blood, threw the first punch, and now he'd have to pay. Dahlia couldn't choose him if he was dead.

My chuckle swelled, my laugh now booming through

the courtyard. "Oh, I was hoping you'd do that. Now I don't have to feel bad for doing this."

It was my turn to take a swing, but instead of my fist connecting with his cheek, he caught it mid-strike, his long fingers closing over mine and squeezing. Hard. Immediately, my bones ground together, the pressure overwhelming as they started to crack.

"What was that? I can't hear you over the sound of your bones breaking."

Agony ripped through my hand, but I continued fighting him, my free hand gripping his face. My dragon roared inside me, the power I'd thought lost to me returning and rushing through my cells. Tor bellowed as my fingers turned to talons and pierced his skin, his blood running down the model-worthy face he'd been gifted. Tor knocked my hand away, my claws scoring his visage.

"Not so pretty now, are ye?"

Tor bared his teeth in a laugh, his form changing as I watched. "If you think a little blood will save you, you've never fought against a Berserker." He tugged me forward until our faces were a mere inch apart. "We thrive on pain. You did me a favor, dragon."

"You really think she'll choose you, Beast?"

"Fate chose me."

My dragon roared in protest. It couldnae be true. Not with the way my entire being was pulled into her orbit.

"No!" Rearing back, I shoved him hard enough that his beastly form stumbled.

My skin rippled as my dragon tattoo fought its way to the surface, struggling to find some path to freedom. Unfortunately for it, the magic binding within the ink held fast, keeping the two of us separated. Though with the way I could feel his emotions and had just borrowed some of his power, it seemed the chains had weakened.

Something for me to look into later.

Right now, I had a Berserker to burn to cinders.

Tor, his body now fully changed to the monster he was feared for, came at me, running full speed.

"Fight!" someone shouted.

Another voice cried out, "The Beast is loose! He's going to kill him!"

Nae, he wasn't. I would do the killing. I'd rip his arms from his body and feed them to the creature that lived in the loch. Then I'd watch him bleed out as I claimed Dahlia right in bloody front of him.

Tor made to tackle me, but I held my ground, wrestling him as we grappled for the upper hand.

Likely summoned by the shouting of the gathering crowd, Bruno raced from the castle, his hair wet and clothes askew.

"Godsdammit it, Tor. Can I not even take a shower without you flying off the handle?"

Oz was right on his heels, looking just as unkempt as Tor's handler. "Oh fuck," he breathed. "This is bad. Someone call Dr. Masterson!"

No. I did not want the meddling doctor to keep me from ridding myself of this adversary.

"You might be an equal match physically. But there's one surefire way to finish him."

My dragon hadn't been able to speak directly to me in far too long, but I recognized his smoky growl instantly. My lips curled at his play on words.

Fire.

Yes, that would do nicely.

And if I could talk to him, I could access his strength.

Bruno and Oz were barreling down the hillside. If I waited any longer, there was a chance Bruno would intercept us. I couldn't risk losing my shot. Tor couldn't be allowed to get between my treasure and me.

Dragon fire burned hot in my chest as it built, ready to be released. Curls of smoke escaped my nostrils, heat searing my veins. My human form wasn't accustomed to the fire, but I'd survive even if it hurt.

As I released my flame, a roar accompanying the fiery breath, I saw it reflected in Tor's midnight gaze. There was no trace of fear. No acceptance of imminent death. Just a warrior's joy. Tor smirked, his teeth red with the blood still dripping down his face. Then he ducked, my fire shooting over his head, through the place he'd just been standing.

"Bru, get down!" Oz cried, knocking Bruno over as the flame sailed their way.

The stream of fire hit the rose garden and branches of the nearby ancient yew, rapidly creating an inferno as it spread through the bushes of beautiful flowers.

"No!" my dragon roared, furious that we'd missed our target. *"Again!"*

A half dozen pixies flew from the tree, little shrieks of terror leaving them as they witnessed what had happened to their home.

"Quick, somebody get a water witch. We cannae let it burn down!"

"We'll help!" a mermaid cried as a gossip of them dove into the loch below. As soon as they surfaced, they used their tails to fling water up into the burning boughs.

I didn't care about any of them. All I saw was the man who stood between me and my mate.

"End him."

"Kai! Stop!" Dahlia's voice rang out, cutting through the haze of violence clouding my mind.

My gaze snapped to her, standing at the crest of the hill, flanked by Hook and Cain, her expression horrified. She was afraid. Of me.

Two things happened at once. Bruno cast out his magic, binding Tor and stopping him from killing me, and I fell to my knees, shame at what I'd done stealing my breath.

No. Not again.

As I took in the flames and the panic of the crowd racing to extinguish them, I knew that I'd gone too far. I deserved whatever punishment they gave me.

I was a monster, every bit as much as the man in front of me. Worse, even. Because I'd known exactly what I was doing and never stopped to question it.

I couldnae be trusted.

I couldnae be hers.

Head down, fingers digging into the earth, I refused to look anywhere but at my trembling hands as I willed the claws to recede.

"Everyone, to your rooms!" Dr. Masterson shouted, her voice close enough I could have grabbed her if I'd wanted to. "You two," she bit out. "You've just earned yourselves a one-way trip to No Man's Land."

EIGHTEEN

DAHLIA

T he mood around Blackwood when they finally lifted the lockdown—I wasn't sure what else to call the mandatory stay-in-our-rooms order from yesterday—was bleak. More bleak than usual, that is. One might call it a *bleak* house. Castle? *See what I did there?*

What the fuck ever, shit was moody. Including yours truly.

I was agitated, my skin not feeling like it fit right, my body sore after a night spent tossing and turning. I couldn't even call what I did dreaming, my thoughts restless as they worried about Tor and Kai—those poor pixies. Where would they have their orgies now? Was there some kind of shelter for them?

I shouldn't have been thinking about the two completely toxically masculine alpha males and their display, but I fucking was. I liked it. Every feminist bone in my body hated that I liked it, but there it was. If they hadn't been sent to No Man's Land, there was no telling how the night would've ended.

With your mouth on Kai's dick, probably.

I wanted to scream at my brain about how that didn't even make sense when Caspian was the one I'd been kissing, but fuck me . . . ever since Kai had taken to trying to work out my smutty acronyms, I couldn't help but picture him in all sorts of colorful scenarios. I lifted my fingers to my throat, the whispered memory of him collaring me with his large, hot hand making me shiver. Not to mention the absolute anguish on his face when he realized what he'd nearly done during his fight with Tor. That one tortured look between us when he heard me call his name had hit me hard. Right in the heart.

And lady parts.

We loved a broken man, didn't we?

Yeah, it definitely wasn't just Caspian in my fictional roster.

Caspian. Kai. Tor.

And a little voice whispered, *and Cain,* not letting me forget the sexy as sin southern gentleman. His expression had been harder to read when he'd stumbled across Cas and me in the hallway. But something electric had passed between us, and I distinctly got the impression he hadn't been happy about what he found. He'd been watching us. Why did that send a thrill through me?

Girlfriend, you are a fucking mess. You need more therapy than Dr. Masterson can provide in a lifetime. You need the full-kink package. Is that a thing? It should be a thing.

My stomach growled as I headed into the dining room, the scents of coffee, fresh pastries, and fried meat hitting my nose instantly. God, I was fucking starved. I loaded a plate, avoiding the haggis because if I couldn't tell what it was by looking at it, I just wouldn't put it in my mouth.

"Not a haggis fan?" Oz asked, startling me as he came up next to me.

"I thought you could only read minds if you're touching someone?"

He laughed, thankfully not offended by my assumption. "I don't need to read your mind. Your face was speaking volumes."

I frowned down at the cake of nondescript, lumpy black stuff. "It's just so . . ."

"It's pretty good, actually. Just don't think too hard about what it's made out of."

Shaking my head, I let out a soft giggle. "Nah. Pass."

"I didn't peg you for a chickenshit."

"What part of me screams adventurous?" I gestured to my glasses and messy bun. "I look like cat lady Barbie."

He gave me a studious once-over, his lips twitching with amusement. "I'd say more like sexy librarian Barbie, but same thing, really."

"Oh fuck you, Ozzie."

"Guess what? Barbie was my secret bestie growing up, so that means you need to come sit with us for breakfast." He nudged me toward the table where Sorcha was waiting, her back ramrod straight, sleek hair falling past her shoulders, topaz eyes making me wonder if she could turn people to stone like Medusa.

"Picking up strays again, Oz?"

"Found this one contemplating murder by the breakfast buffet."

"I was not!"

He smirked at me. "Sure."

"Leave her alone, Oswald."

"I told you never to call me that."

I snorted, "Oswald? What a fabulous villain name. Like the Penguin from Batman."

He shot me a look that said if I kept going, I'd regret it.

185

"Okay, okay. Sorry. I can just take my food upstairs. That was the plan anyway."

"No, stay. We're just assholes and forget that not everybody else is." Oz snagged me by the wrist, his eyes going a bit hazy just as he let me go. He blinked quickly and shot me an apologetic smile. "I didn't peek, promise."

Something told me he was lying. Why else would his eyes have done that? But if he was going to be kind enough not to out me regarding whatever it was he'd seen, the least I could do was take the olive branch.

Sighing, I sat across the table from the beautiful vampire. Oz took the seat beside her before pushing a small container of clotted cream toward me.

"So . . ." I started.

"So?"

"What are you in for?" I blurted, mentally wincing at how socially awkward I was. I guess all the forced proximity with other people hadn't done me any favors in that regard. Good to know.

"I already told you. Murderess and brain fryer," Oz said, as he finished his bite of croissant, using the half he was holding to point to Sorcha and then himself.

"Yeah, but you just sort of glossed over it. I'm a writer, which means curious is basically my default setting. I want details."

"You want more detail than 'Sorcha killed her husband'?"

The vampire rolled her eyes. "You are such a bloody liar. I didn't do the actual killing, that was my sister-in-law. I was the one who used my compulsion to start the riot that gave her the distraction she needed for his assassination. Then my brother threw me in here and locked away the key so the vampire council couldn't find me."

When she didn't immediately smile or say something about how she was joking, I let out an awkward laugh. "Coooool."

"And since I'm literally in here because I found out something I wasn't supposed to, all I'm going to say on the matter is I peeked in on something I shouldn't have, freaked out, and accidentally made a garden of human veggies."

The way he said that made me think this place wasn't just for those whose powers were out of control. This was also a refuge. A safe house. Blackwood had its secrets, but maybe they were a saving grace for some of the people here.

Deciding to ask the question outright, I turned to him. "So you mean not everyone here is a crazed monster."

"Well, we're all a little deranged, but who isn't?" Sorcha said with a slow grin.

Oz rolled his eyes and sighed, seeming to be over her shit. "I'd say it's a mix. Some of us are here because the alternative was worse. Some of us weren't given a choice at all"—he jerked his head to a waifish girl eating a bowl of what looked like porridge—"she's the bastard daughter of some high-up shifter. He didn't want a 'mixed blood daughter' on his hands, so he sent her here where she couldn't embarrass him. And then there are the others. Like Kai and Tor."

After their very public showdown the other day, Oz didn't need to elaborate.

"Don't forget Cain," Sorcha added.

I mentally snorted. *As if we could.*

"He's all sorts of dangerous," she continued, bringing a Bloody Mary to her lips.

"Did we figure out what he is yet?" Oz asked.

My ear perked up in anticipation. I was undeniably interested in the answer. Cain may not remember I exist, but the man was a walking enigma, which basically made him my catnip. "No. My money is on dark warlock. He screams unbridled and morally bankrupt."

Oz ran his hands together. "Mmm, my favorite."

"And here I was thinking you were into those muscle-bound protective types," Sorcha teased, waggling her eyebrows.

"Bru and I are . . ." Oz trailed off, looking embarrassed. "Complicated."

"There's a reason it's a status on Faceplace," I said, slathering my croissant in the cream and some jam. I was so here for this turn in the conversation. I didn't know these two very well, but I was always here for angst-ridden tales of the heart.

"Well, yeah. And it's hard to date someone when 99 percent of your time is spent babysitting someone else." He sighed. "Besides, I'm mostly waiting for him to fall in tragic, one-sided love with Tor instead of me."

Jealousy hit me in the gut.

"Now, now," Sorcha said in a sing-songy tone. "What does Dr. Masterson always say? What's your evidence?"

Oz blew a raspberry at her. "Have you seen the guy in sweatpants? It's right there. Staring at me."

"And somehow, Bru only has eyes for you. But sure, make it as complicated as you need to." Sorcha inspected her nails before giving a long sniff and training her gaze on me. "You'd better stop by the infirmary on your way upstairs. You're going to need supplies."

Dread curled somewhere deep inside me. Was that a warning? Was she planning to hurt me?

"God, Sorcha, you're so creepy. Let a woman figure out Aunt Flo is coming for a visit on her own, Jesus!"

I groaned and buried my face in my hands.

Just what I needed. My period on top of all my other problems.

My face had to be the color of a ripe tomato as her warning crystalized. Oh. *Oh God.* She could smell my period? Jesus fucking Christ, who else could do that? Could Kai? Or Tor? They were both shifters . . . I think. They must have enhanced senses.

"There are no less than ten vampires on this property, Dahlia. You should lock yourself in your room until it's over. Some of us have less restraint than others."

Oz slapped Sorcha on the arm. "Come on, now you're freaking her out. Listen, no one is going to take your blood without permission."

Sorcha smirked, lifting crossed fingers. "We can certainly hope."

"She's just fucking with you."

I wasn't so sure, but as though she'd summoned the red demon from the depths of hell, my uterus gave a dull throb.

I was not one of those women blessed with easy periods. There were no light days or regular tampons in my future. Nope, it was all heating pads and agonizing cramps. Plus, you know the raging mood swings, wild dreams, and completely unpredictable cycles. Sometimes it was three days; others it was nine and an iron deficiency as a consolation prize.

Who won the menstruation jackpot? No, seriously, I really want to know, because it sure as shit wasn't this bitch. It sort of felt like God gave me two when he handed out the PMS genes.

"I think I'll eat upstairs," I muttered, taking my plate and excusing myself.

"Good luck! See you in five to seven days."

Sorcha sniffed the air, her eyes fluttering closed. "Six."

"You're so fucking weird. It's a wonder you have any friends."

"Friend. I have *friend*."

"Lucky me."

I would have laughed if I wasn't already dreading the next few days.

I did myself a favor and listened to Sorcha's advice, as unnerving as it was. Stopping by the infirmary proved to be easier than I expected. To my surprise, they had a whole kit available for me, including an empty hot water bottle, some painkillers, and plenty of pads and tampons. There was even a menstrual cup for people who liked those. I'd never gotten the hang of them. I was always anxious I'd end up spilling and leaving a murder scene in the bathroom.

Anxiety was so much fun.

There was a never-ending list of things to stress the fuck out over.

Another wave of cramps hit me as I got to my room, this one much worse than the last. It was going to be a bad one. I could already tell from the intensity of the ache. Maybe I could take a hot bath to get ahead of things, or at least pop a few pills. I closed my door and stripped down to my boyshorts and sports bra, but even that much effort exhausted me. No bath. Just a lie down until this passed.

I'd worry about the rest . . . later.

NINETEEN

TOR

"Nordson, you're cleared to leave," Edgar hollered as my door unlocked and swung open. It pained me that I'd spent enough time here to recognize the guards by voice alone.

They'd caged me longer in the past, but I supposed this time I hadn't proven to be the biggest threat. That honor was solely Kai's. Or it was for the moment.

With that knowledge came another realization. Kai was the only one able to stop me if Bru failed and my beast took center stage. He'd be able to protect Dahlia from me if need be. And he'd do it in a way Bru would never dare.

Kai could kill me.

Why did that fill me with relief?

Because you know she'll be protected. That there's someone else capable of keeping her safe. You saw how possessive he was over her. There's no denying the connection between the two of them.

My beast pushed, threatening to ruin all my carefully gathered control. Closing my eyes, I took a deep breath and willed it to settle. Alek shared his mate, and though it was the last thing my Berserker wanted, I could as well.

I might not have a choice.

The truth was, with every shift, more of my humanity was lost to the darkness of this bloody curse.

To the bloodlust.

I was losing.

I couldn't be everything for her, not if I was a monster.

Pulling my hair into a knot at the crown of my skull, I huffed in frustration, knowing what I had to do. Swallow my pride and ask the dragon for help.

It didn't take me long to find him. I knew exactly where he'd be. The max security cell. The one where I'd left deep claw marks in the walls as I'd raged. Sure enough, there he was, visible through the six inches of bespelled glass that separated us.

Kai sat on the bed, eyes glowing violet, the dragon tattoo pulsing under his skin. I didn't have to say a word before his eyes slid to me, the slits of his pupils elongated like his creature.

I wondered how much of the man was in control right now.

"I know you can hear me, Kai," I said as I pushed the button next to the wall to activate his intercom.

He nodded but didn't say a word.

"I need you to do something for me."

The man stood and stalked to the glass. His movements were reptilian, almost a slither. "What could I possibly do for you? And why the fuck would I want to?"

I offered him a bitter smile. "Because believe it or not, I'm about to give you exactly what you want."

"Your head on a pike?"

"Better. I want you to watch over Dahlia."

His glowing eyes narrowed. "And why the fuck should I believe you'll just hand her over to my keeping when only yesterday you tried to kill me over a picture?"

"Because I think you're the only one who *can* keep her safe . . ." Knowing I needed to give him the full truth, I added, "From me."

Kai let out a disbelieving laugh. "And you think I'm the better option of the two of us? I could have burned her to a crisp. If she'd have been any bloody closer, she would've been caught in the crossfire."

"No. You stopped. The moment you heard her, you stopped."

He held my stare, mistrust heavy in his eyes.

I gave him the rest of my truth. "If not for Bru, I wouldn't have. When the beast takes over, I . . . I can't stop. It gets worse with every shift." I exhaled heavily. "I'm losing. I don't know how much longer I'll be able to hold him back."

Then I lifted my shirt and revealed my tattoo, the rose down to its last handful of petals.

"I won't be able to protect her, not forever. She's mine, but I can't provide her the one thing I should be able to give. That's where you come in, Kai. She wants us both."

Oh, it galled me to admit it. But I'd come to terms with it during my confinement. My mate's well-being was my priority. We may not ever complete our mate bond, but I was hardwired to protect her from all harm, even if—no, *especially* if—that harm was me.

This bargain was the only way to ensure that.

"Fine. I'll watch over her."

"And you'll kill me when the time comes?"

Kai's jaw flexed before he nodded. "*If* it comes to that. Aye."

I released a breath I hadn't realized I was holding. "Thank you, Malakai."

"I'd say it was my pleasure, but I'd be lying. There's nothing pleasurable about promising to kill someone. Not even a great hulking arse like you."

Pressing my palm to the glass, I offered him a lift of my chin. Then I walked away, a very different upcoming conversation weighing heavy on my heart. She was going to run. There was no way she wouldn't. Until Dahlia arrived here, she hadn't known a whit about the supernatural world.

Or mates.

Or mate bonds.

Or how Berserkers went mad the longer they were separated from their mate.

Bully for her, I was already mad and growing more so every day. She'd hardly notice the difference.

Before long, I was back in the central area of Blackwood, taking the steps to her floor two at a time. I needed to see her, make sure she was safe, and explain more clearly why I was the way I was. I had to tell her the unbridled truth.

The copper scent of blood hit me as soon as I reached her door, sending every one of my protective instincts on high alert. Something was wrong. She was in there, bleeding.

All sane thought fled. Without bothering to knock, I sent her door flying open, using my shoulder and inherent strength to break the lock.

"Dahlia!" I shouted, casting my gaze around and half-expecting to find her unconscious form lying in a pool of blood.

I was half right.

I realized my mistake instantly, finding her not on the

floor as I'd feared, but curled up asleep on her bed, blood staining her thighs and the comforter beneath her.

She stirred, moaning in pain as I stood over her. "Tor? What are you doing in my room?"

"You're bleeding."

Sitting up, she groaned again, this time glancing down her body. "Oh no. Fuck."

I was no stranger to females' cycles. I'd been raised understanding and respecting this particular monthly trial they had to endure. Hell, more than once, I'd been sent to gather supplies for my mother or sister.

The adrenaline pumping through me was slow to retreat, although the beast within seemed content to stand down. For once we were of the same mind. We wanted to care for the beauty fate had bestowed upon us.

It might be our last and only chance.

"Stay there," I ordered, my voice gruff and a bit harsher than I'd intended.

"Sure, come on in. Make yourself at home."

Not replying to her sarcastic tone, I stalked into the bathroom to collect everything she'd need. A warm, damp towel, her robe, and last but not least, I started a bath for her.

I returned, setting her robe at the foot of her bed and moving purposefully toward her.

"Uh, what do you think you're doing there, big guy?" she asked, eyes going wide as I pried her knees apart.

"Caring for you."

She blinked up at me as I used the towel to wipe away the blood. "Uh . . . I can do that."

"Please, Kærasta. Allow me to help you?"

"Why?"

"I need to."

"Is this some weird fetish? Do Vikings have a period kink?" she teased.

I met her gaze with all seriousness. "Blood is an aphrodisiac for Berserkers, yes, but this is not sexual. This is me serving you."

"Serving me?" she parroted, sounding dubious.

Tell her. It's why you're here, and she deserves to know.

"My mate," I clarified, eyes still locked on hers.

She swallowed, throat bobbing as she processed my confession. She didn't appear surprised by the admission, just caught off guard. I supposed the situation was a bit unusual, at least to someone like her who'd only just discovered this world. Especially since this was only our second time truly interacting with one another.

It was hard to explain the pull a Berserker felt toward his mate. But to me, it didn't feel sudden or rushed at all. It was as if my world's axis shifted the moment I'd laid eyes on her. Between one heartbeat and the next, my entire reason for existing changed. I no longer lived for myself, but for her. She was the sun my world revolved around. The gravity that held me steady. The air in my lungs.

In a word, she was everything.

"I'm your *mate*." She tried the word on for size. "So I'm married?"

A tender laugh escaped as I continued cleaning her thighs. "It's so much more than that.

As I already told you. It's rare. Life changing. Forever. Now that I've found you, I'll be yours until the day my soul goes to Valhalla."

"Could you maybe stop wiping me and give me a second? This is a whole fucking lot for being awake for about two minutes."

Backing away, I fought the urge to pull her into my

arms and kiss her until she believed me. "Of course, Kærasta."

She slipped from the bed, wincing when she looked at the comforter. "Gross."

"I'll deal with this. You go clean up. I'll be here when you're done."

She shot me a look that spoke volumes. She wasn't sure how she felt about me taking over her life this way, but she was too out of sorts to push the issue. That worked in my favor.

As my beauty cleaned herself up, I pulled the blankets from her bed and replaced them with the fresh set stored in the wardrobe. By the time I was done, it was like nothing had ever happened. That handled, I peered at the broken door and grimaced.

I wasn't usually one to resort to magic; I preferred the simplicity of using my fists to get my point across, but I couldn't deny its usefulness. My mother was a reality shaper, or more specifically, an animagi infused with the ability to shape the world in any way she chose. It was a rare and powerful gift.

Drawing on some of the power she passed down to me, I fixed the weave of reality and restored the door to its prior status. Then, before I released the magic, I used it to bring into being a few other items that might benefit my beauty.

She opened the bathroom door, her cheeks pink and little wisps of hair curling at her temples that had escaped her bun. Dressed in a long, plush robe, she offered me a sheepish smile.

"I'm okay now. You don't have to stay."

I'm not going anywhere.

Rather than saying that and getting her back up, I

aimed for something closer to a request. Or at least as close to one as my beast would allow.

"I'd like to."

"You changed the sheets?"

"Of course."

"And . . ." She looked at the offerings on her desk. "Chocolate, potato chips, wine?"

"Yes. And the hot water bottle is filled and ready for you. The temperature will stay the same."

She narrowed her eyes. "How?"

I couldn't stop my smirk. "Magic, beauty."

"I thought you were just only into beast stuff."

"Beast stuff?"

"You know what I mean."

Raising a brow, I shook my head. "I don't. Please, enlighten me."

She flexed like she was in a bodybuilding competition and made a sound I could only assume was a growl. "Beast stuff."

"You are fucking adorable. Has anyone told you that?"

"Don't distract me with your sexy accent and flirty eyes. You've been so broody and intense up until now. What's changed?"

"I understand now. I'm giving in to fate instead of fighting her. And I feel a certain peace when you're with me. I can't explain it."

She canted her head, giving me a once-over. "I like this version of you. A lot."

"Enjoy it while it lasts. I'm more beast than man these days." If my bitterness coated the words, she didn't comment on it.

"Did I say I don't like the beast?"

The admission shocked me. Perhaps it shouldn't have;

she was my mate, after all, but it did. I was so used to everyone hating the beast, myself included. It was a constant struggle every second of every day not to give into those basest urges. And here she was, unassuming and perfect and ready to snuggle up with him.

A low rumbling built in my chest.

"Are you . . . purring?"

"No," I grumbled, embarrassed. "Maybe."

Handing her the water bottle, I stretched out on her bed, arms open for her to come to me. Was it presumptuous of me to expect her to join me? Yes. But I knew from the tension surrounding her eyes that she was in pain. I could help ease that.

"You remember I'm on my period, right? There was a literal bloodbath in the sheets you changed."

"Yes, of course I remember."

"So you realize I am not having sex with you."

"Who said anything about sex?"

She blushed. "You're in my bed."

"And?"

"Don't guys in beds want sex? The ones in my books usually do."

"We'll get there one day, when you're ready to give yourself to me. Until then, I'm content to care for you as a mate should."

"You realize that this is weird, right? That people don't just go around barging into strangers' rooms and declaring them their mate and cleaning blood off them like it's fruit punch."

"You say weird, I say natural."

Heaving an exasperated sigh, she shook her head and shrugged. "I guess it's just lucky you didn't try to lick it off me."

We could save that for next time. Orgasms were known pain relievers, but something told me she wasn't ready for that little bit of information. I wasn't afraid of blood. Not in the least.

We called it bloodlust for a reason.

"Fine. Just let me get some panties on. I can't lie there with you knowing all that's keeping my virtue safe is a robe."

My cock throbbed in response to her statement. "Your virtue is safe with me."

She snorted. "If you really believe that, I have some magic beans for you."

"Why do you have magic beans? Giants are fearsome creatures, not to be toyed with."

"No, ugh, it's an expression."

I watched her snag a pair of knickers from her drawer before she held up one finger to signal me to wait as she dashed into the bathroom again. When she returned, she joined me on the bed, tucking herself into my side so I was spooning her, my palm slipping over her lower belly. That blissful calm washed over me at the contact, and she sighed in response as well. Our bond was already stronger than I ever expected, and it was soothing us both.

"I'm sorry, beauty."

"Sorry for what?" She turned to face me, big gray eyes staring into mine.

"For the display with Kai. For pushing you away. For everything that's to come. I'm unpredictable where my beast is concerned. You deserve more from your mate."

Her answering laugh brought a smile to my lips; it was as if her joy was infectious. I'd smiled more with her in the last hour than I had in weeks.

"Considering I didn't even know I had a mate, I'd say I

lucked out. Who doesn't want their very own over-the-top protective alpha? And one with a tragic curse to boot. It's like winning the romance novel lottery. Now all I need for you to do is get all growly and say 'mine' right before you thread your fingers into my hair, bend me backward, and kiss me like I'm your reason for breathing."

"Consider it done." Heart pounding, I gathered her hair in my fist and tugged until she craned her neck and her lips were right bloody there.

A low growl rumbled in my throat when the movement pressed her soft belly against my raging erection, and it was all I could do not to rock into her. "You're mine, Kærasta. Fucking mine."

Her breath hitched as she parted those full lips in invitation, and I took them without a second thought. Gods, she tasted exactly as I imagined. Sweet and delicious. Like my favorite treat. I wanted more. So much more, but she wasn't ready yet.

Breaking the kiss, I pressed our foreheads together, and we simply breathed each other's air as we let the moment sink in. Once our bond was complete, our breaths would sync, her exhales becoming my inhales.

"What does it mean?" she whispered.

"What?"

"Kærasta. You've said it to me so many times now."

"It's the title the men in my family have used for their mates since Odin first blessed them with his gifts. The meaning has changed throughout the centuries, but for us, it's reserved specifically for the one who carries the other half of our soul. The one who brings our life purpose and meaning."

"That's . . . a lot more important than babe."

I laughed, pressing a kiss to her forehead. "Yes. Much more important."

"Tor?"

"Yes, beauty."

"Can you stay with me until I fall asleep? I feel better when you're touching me."

"It would be my honor to watch over you, Kærasta."

I put a little more emphasis on the word now that she understood what it meant. Her smile lit up her whole face as I wrapped my arms around her and pulled her closer.

"Does that make you my Kærasto?" she teased.

"Absolutely not."

"All right, all right. Fine. Beast it is."

Somehow, when she said it, it didn't sound like a curse. I actually quite liked it from her lips.

"Go to sleep, my beauty. I'll be here, I swear it," I whispered against her hair.

As she drifted off in my arms, I prayed to the gods I was telling the truth and that if there was any justice left in this world, they wouldn't take me from her for good. Just because I'd gotten Kai to give me his vow, didn't mean I wanted him to have to keep it.

But just in case, I intended to savor the feel of my mate in my arms. Fate only knew how many more opportunities I might have.

CHAPTER
TWENTY

HOOK

"Two bleeding nights, wasted sitting in a moldy graveyard waiting on a fucking petulant ghost who . . . ghosted me. We had an appointment. It's bad form," I grumbled as I entered Blackwood's courtyard. "I could have been seducing a pretty little writer instead of freezing my bollocks off in that dank, dark tomb."

He was supposed to be my in. I couldn't get what I needed without him. Fucking arsehole. All that pixie dust, wasted. I was going to have to arrange another meeting with Adonis. The fucker owed me.

Spotting a light still blazing in one of the resident's windows, I paused and performed a quick count. My lips curled up in surprise when I realized the resident in question was my delectable Dahlia.

I'm sure you're wondering how I know the window belongs to her. Would you believe me if I told you it was simply research? A pirate must always have his escape route planned, you know. And I intended to get myself in a compromising position with her sooner rather than later.

"Why are you up so late?" I mused. Then again, I suppose she could have risen early. It was just before dawn, best I could tell. Either way, the fact remained that she was awake.

Maybe the night wasn't such a loss after all. Perhaps I could pay her a little visit. Maybe help her find inspiration for one of her spicy love scenes. Oh, every single part of me stood up and applauded that idea.

I pushed through the front door and made a beeline for the staircase, a strange giddy anticipation running through me at the thought of seeing her again. She would smile, and her cheeks would go pink as I leaned against the doorframe, waiting for her to invite me inside.

I'd woo her thoroughly. Tuck a strand of that long blonde hair behind her ear. Croon sweet nothings into her ear as I slowly walked her backward toward her bed. And then, by some weird twist of fate, I'd land on top of her, those bountiful breasts of hers bouncing delightfully.

Oh yes. This was a brilliant idea. My cock thought so too.

It had been eons since I'd bedded a woman. Coming to Aurora Springs had been an adventure, and I'd worked my way through every willing female there, but Blackwood changed everything. It'd been nothing but a very long dry spell since then.

Not that I haven't had opportunities. The mermaids were a handsy bunch, more than willing to grant my every whim. I just hadn't wanted to. I had to remain focused on the reason I was here.

Or so I'd thought until my sweet girl arrived. For her, I would allow myself to be distracted. She wasn't simply a dalliance, and that scared me a little. I'd never wanted more than one night to sate my lust. Perhaps I could use a session with Dr. Masterson to examine that. She was always yammering on about how I needed to dig deeper and examine my dark urges.

But first, Dahlia. I stood at the end of the long hallway, zeroing in on her door. Yes. Dark urges first. Then therapy.

Smirking, I undid one extra button on my shirt, making sure I looked the part of rakish pirate before I ran my fingers through my hair to ensure it was tousled just so. Then I began my slow saunter toward her room.

A jungle cat on the prowl.

Me-ow.

Just when I was really getting into the mood, her door swung open and a very different blond head appeared in the doorway.

I jumped back, crouching behind a fern to remain out of sight. That blasted Viking had gotten to her. He'd spent the night, by the look of his rumpled clothes. If I hadn't spent the last six hours waiting for an inconsiderate poltergeist, I'd have this codfish on the ground, begging me for mercy.

He turned, eyes wild, shoulders trembling as his body shifted and he became the beast he tried so hard to contain. I flattened myself against the wall, barely breathing as he snarled and rushed past me.

As soon as he was gone, I stood, raked my hand through my hair once more, and took a steadying breath. Had he been in his beast form when he was with my darling? Had he hurt her? I'd flay him alive if he so much as harmed a hair on her head.

He'd rue the day he'd got on the wrong side of Captain Hook.

Feeling quite dashing—nay, heroic—I crept as soundlessly as possible to her room, keeping an ear out lest the beast came back to finish what he'd started.

"Darling, are you all right?" I said, pushing the door fully open and peering into her room, terrified of what I might find.

Her desk lamp was on, explaining what I'd seen from her window, but the woman in question was curled up peacefully on her bed.

Maybe too peacefully.

Was she even breathing?

A gentleman would check.

Creeping toward the bed, I whispered her name but got no response, so I stood over her and pressed my palm to her sternum in search of a heartbeat. Her skin was warm and velvet soft, the telltale rise and fall of her chest easing my worry. She moaned and shifted onto her back, the robe she wore sliding open wider and exposing the curves of her full breasts.

The temptation to flick that little bit of cloth further so I could learn the color of her nipples was strong. One of my fingers stretched out, likely intending to do just that, but a sleepy sigh had me freezing in place.

"C-Cas?" she murmured, my eyes shooting to her face at the sound of my abbreviated name.

No one had ever called me Cas. I bloody liked it coming from her.

"Am I dreaming you?" The sleepy question went straight to my dick.

"Yes, love. Even your subconscious wants me in your room. Now back to your dreams, my sweet girl."

Her eyes fluttered as she obeyed. "Mmkay."

She looked so innocent that I couldn't resist the urge to lean down and press a chaste kiss to her temple. "Would that I still belonged to the Sea Court so I could whisk you away and make you my princess. Dream of me, darling. They don't have to be sweet. I know mine won't."

It took a strength of will I didn't know I possessed to leave her, but I did it. See? Heroic. Noble, even. So what if I was going to have to wank off in the shower as soon as I got to my quarters? I could have done it next to her bed and glossed her lips with my spend so I'd be the first thing she'd taste when she woke.

Hmm . . . maybe I should reconsider. The thought held undeniable appeal, and my cock was raring to go. I turned back toward her room—I was a villain, after all—and reached for the doorknob, but a bloodcurdling scream echoed from downstairs, stopping me in my tracks.

"Oh, bloody hell," I muttered, turning to race back to the stairs and see what all the commotion was about.

I wasn't the only one. Bleary-eyed creatures poked their heads out of their rooms, asking each other what was going on. I ignored them, intent on learning the truth for myself.

A crowd had gathered in the foyer, a sobbing mermaid in the center, hands bloodied, eyes glassy, hair a bedraggled mess.

"Nautica . . . sh-she's dead. I found her by the lake when I went for my morning swim. Th-the Ripper got her. Oh gods, she was still warm."

Dr. Masterson's head of curls appeared, the crowd parting for her as she moved to the center of the room, her expression grave.

"Is it true? Has the Ripper found us?" a pale witch asked, her voice shaking.

"Aye. He's here."

SESSION TRANSCRIPT: NOVEMBER 7TH

Dr. Masterson: This is Dr. Elizabeth Masterson. It is November seventh, and the time is 1:00 p.m. This is a recorded session with resident Caspian Hook. Caspian, it's been a while since you've attended a solo session, even though you're scheduled weekly. Why now?

Caspian: I dunno, Doc. You tell me. Your goons are the ones who hauled me in. Didn't really give me much choice in the matter.

Dr. Masterson: Do you think it has something to do with you selling a banned substance to your fellow residents?

Caspian: Who me? I'm not selling anything. Search me all you'd like. I'll even strip for you. You won't find a thing. Well . . . you might find *something*, but nothing illegal.

Dr. Masterson: *clears throat*

Caspian: I can assure you, Doctor, no money has exchanged hands. What on earth would I do with money here?

Dr. Masterson: Be that as it may . . .

<<rustling clothes>>

Caspian: Oh, come now, don't tell me a beautiful woman such as yourself has never broken a silly rule or two.

<<pen clicking>>

Dr. Masterson: Tell me about your need to break the rules, Caspian. Why does it thrill you?

Caspian: *sighs* Doesn't it thrill everyone? The possibility of being caught? The excitement of knowing you could get into trouble? Oh, I can feel the rush now. It burns through me, and the gratification of getting away with it is even bigger.

Dr. Masterson: Did you get into trouble a lot as a child?

Caspian: I don't know. I can't recall much of my time as a child. Immortality, you know.

Dr. Masterson: Fae are not immortal, Caspian. They are long-lived.

Caspian: It amounts to the same thing, really.

<<pen clicking repetitively>>

Dr. Masterson: Nervous, Caspian?

Caspian: *chuckles* No. Why would you ask that? I'm perfectly splendid.

Dr. Masterson: You're fidgeting with that pen an awful lot. Seems like you're anxious. Worried about something. Maybe you aren't getting enough sleep at night. There've been reports of you wandering the halls after hours. You're not a vampire, nor are you a shifter. Perhaps a sleeping draught should be added to your nightly regimen?

<<chair scrapes against floor>>

Dr. Masterson: What do you think you're doing?

Caspian: Just getting a little closer, doc.

Dr. Masterson: This is highly irregular, Caspian. Please take two steps backward.

Caspian: But that's not what you truly desire, is it, Doctor? Not if the way your pulse is fluttering in your neck and the flush on your cheeks is any indication. You want me to come closer so I can tell you exactly what I need to be happy here. Isn't that right?

Dr. Masterson: *gasps* I . . . I don't . . .

Caspian: Shh, it's all right, darling. This is a safe place, remember? Feel free to make any confessions you'd like. I won't tell.

<<chair falling over>>

Dr. Masterson: *uneven breathing* That's quite enough. This session is over, Caspian.

Caspian: Aw, shucks. Just when I was starting to enjoy myself. You're such a tease, Doctor.

<<footsteps door opening and closing>>

Dr. Masterson: Despite binding potion, subject still retains full access to his glamour and fae influence. My recommendation is to increase the dosage. Session terminated at 1:05 p.m.

<<static>>

End of transcript.

CHAPTER
TWENTY-ONE

KAI

"Motherfucking Scotland and your motherfucking stairs! Has . . . no one . . . heard of . . . elevators?" Dahlia stumbled through the doorway that led to the battlement where I was currently hiding out.

Her face was flushed as she gasped for breath, eyes not yet finding me where I was seated on the parapet. She had a tote bag covered in a bright unicorn print slung over one shoulder and a hoodie that read, *I'm silently judging your grammar.*

Part of me mourned the lack of a puzzle to work out. It was a small victory every time I did. I could use a small victory today. Fucking hell, I could use a minuscule one.

Tensing, I waited for her to notice me because I knew the moment she caught sight of me, I'd see fear in her eyes. How could I not? I'd nearly destroyed Tor as she watched.

I should be used to it by now. Goddess knows I had more than enough experience with looks of loathing and terror aimed my way. And I'd earned each and every one.

No one despised my lack of control more than myself.

I was my father's son. I should be better. Stronger.

Instead . . . I was the ultimate failure.

I may be beautiful on the outside, but I was horrifying on the inside. A creature who ruined everything he touched. At least Tor wore his curse for all to see. Mine slithered under my skin and reveled in destruction, with none but myself the wiser.

The instrument of their demise lurking in plain sight.

"Jesus, it's high up here. Windy too." Dahlia's hair whipped into her face, forcing her to spit the errant locks out of her mouth. "Maybe this was a bad idea."

Yes, gem. Turn around and leave me be. Don't force me to watch the light leave your eyes when you see me.

She cast a baleful look back the way she came. Poor thing looked so put out at the thought of going down the stairs that I couldn't contain my chuckle.

"Kai?" she called, her voice strong and steady, not fearful at all. "Is that you?"

I couldn't exactly deny it, but I didn't want to encourage her either, so I remained silent.

"Is this where you've been hiding?" She glanced around. "I guess it makes sense. A dragon high atop a tower."

Oh, lass, this is not my tower. I would never leave my hoard so unprotected.

"Are you really not going to talk to me?"

"What would you have me say?"

"Hello might be nice. Maybe a how the hell are ya? It's great to see you again. I see you're having an asthma attack. Are you dying and in need of mouth-to-mouth or other forms of first aid?"

I stood, leaving the paperback I was reading on the stone floor at my feet. "Well, are you?"

"No. I'm fine. My asthma cleared up when I was a kid. I'm just not used to climbing five thousand stairs."

Shrugging, I said, "It was only thirty-two."

"Same difference. Especially when it's a turret and you're spinning in a circle with nothing but a pathetic bit of rope to cling to. Could you imagine if I had luggage?"

"Tell me how you really feel."

"Scotland can bite me."

I'd like to bite her, right on her plump arse.

"You should write a strongly worded letter to the Prime Minister. Let him know how you would solve these problems."

"Elevators, Kai. They're called elevators."

"I—"

"And while I'm at it, AIR CONDITIONING! What is it with the entire UK and not having AC? I'm sweating my tits off. Do you know how gross boob sweat is? I can tell you, it's not sexy. Nothing kills a lady boner like boob sweat."

Surely I'd misunderstood her. Sometimes it felt like we didnae speak the same language.

"Ladies get boners?"

"Oh yes. Especially when someone is . . . competent."

"Competent? Explain."

She waved her hands around, really getting into it now. "You know, like talented and capable people. Men with tools and hard hats who can put stuff together, or better yet, build something from the ground up. Women who are super smart and good at their jobs. Dudes that get shit done. Correctly. The first time. Or fuck, ones that can ask for help if they need it and aren't threatened by a successful woman. That's the hottest of all."

I raised a brow. "Is this something you're in need of? Men with hard hats?"

"Oh baby, you don't even know."

Baby? I liked hearing her call me that. "Can I . . . put something together for you, lass?"

"Don't tease."

"I'm not. I donae have my tools here, but I'm a *competent*"—she smirked at my intentional use of the word—"wood carver and glass blower, though that doesn't come in handy nearly as often."

"Are you really?"

"I'm great with my hands. And anything relating to fire." I shrugged as if it was no big deal, though inside I was fighting back the urge to impress her. To gift her with one of the pieces I'd left at my parent's home in Faerie.

If I hadn't already decided to live in denial, I might have paid more attention to that urge. To what it meant not only for me, but my dragon.

"Pictures or it didn't happen."

"What?" We definitely had a cultural, if not language, barrier between us. She'd lived her life in the human world, I out here in the Highlands with all manner of supernatural creatures. Everything was different.

She shook her head. "Never mind. Why are you hiding up here?"

"I'm not hiding. I'm on the lookout. Watching over the grounds."

"You say watching, I say hiding. No one has seen you for days."

"I was only released this morning."

Her brow furrowed, and an apology shone in her eyes. She hadn't expected that.

"But Tor was out the next day."

"He wasn't the one who almost burned down the yew tree."

In three strides, she was directly in front of me, her eyes blazing as she stared into mine. "You stopped."

"That's what Tor said too."

"It's the truth. You stopped, and no one was hurt in the end."

It was on the tip of my tongue to tell her I wouldn't have if not for her interference. But I couldn't give her that truth just yet. It was too big. Too meaningful. I wasn't ready to deal with the consequences of it right now.

"Not until the Ripper showed up, anyway," she whispered. "Is that why you're up here?"

"Aye. We need eyes watching for any suspicious creatures. It was part of the conditions of my release from No Man's Land. Consider it my probation."

"I guess I do feel safer knowing you're up here ready to flame roast any potential baddies." She released a sigh and cast her gaze across Blackwood's grounds. "Want some company?"

Before her eyes returned to mine, they snagged on the paperback I'd left face up on the ground.

"Malakai Nash, are you reading my book? And not mine like I own it, but mine like I wrote it! You sneaky, sneaky dragon."

I fought the wave of embarrassment careening through me at being caught, but I wanted to know her better. To understand how her beautiful mind worked. Reading her words was like a glimpse into her imagination, and what a place it was.

"So what if I am, lass? Plenty of people seem to like it. They made a movie, didn't they?"

She slipped past me and scooped up the book, trailing her fingers over the title. "I always loved this cover. I hate that they changed it to the movie-tie-in version."

Since she didn't seem embarrassed by my reading choice, I figured it couldn't hurt to ask her about it. "I find it odd that you didn't realize you were a medium when you wrote about one. And with so much . . . detail."

"Well, they say write what you know. I guess my subconscious was trying to tell me something. I'm a lot more like Rebel than I thought."

"Why the pen name?"

"Why not? Almost all authors have one. And I doubt anyone would take Dahlia Moore, daughter of the infamous cult leader, very seriously. Unless it was a cash grab biopic or something."

I hated the darkness in her eyes when she mentioned her past. In an effort to turn the conversation away from that topic, I latched onto her characters instead. "So, you're more Rebel than you thought. Does that mean you want to have your very own group of ghosts?"

She wrinkled her nose. "I can barely tolerate being in the same room as one ghost. I think I'll give the ghost dick a pass. I want a man I can hold on to."

Fuck.

I swallowed through the lump in my throat.

"Ye have one right here, gem."

Her face fell. "I know. But I also have this weird mate thing with Tor and kissed Caspian. I saw the hurt look in your eyes when I mentioned Tor and the connection we have. I don't want to do something rash and end up hurting any of you. Not until we're all on the same page about what these connections are or aren't."

She wasn't wrong. I didn't share as a rule, but if it meant the difference between having part of her heart or nothing at all, would I be willing?

Fuck, what did it even matter when I knew I could

never truly pursue her? Eventually I'd be called back to the fae realm, and even if that was decades from now, there was still my dragon to contend with. One day I'd have to leave her, and it may very well kill me if the two of us got even further entangled.

Or her.

Dragons were possessive by nature. If I allowed myself to get close to her, he may do something rash, like kill her so no one else could have her. It wouldn't be the first time a dragon went insane. We weren't exactly the most noble or rational creatures. Our kind was mostly extinct for a reason.

"I'm sorry, lass. I wasnae thinking beyond the here and now. You're spoken for. Tor claimed you loud and clear. I cannae get between a Berserker and his mate."

Unless I have to kill him to save her. I mentally shook my head, still shocked that he'd sought me out and made me vow to do it. Somewhere between trying to rip my head off and getting sent to No Man's Land, his attitude about me changed. We were no longer adversaries, but more like temporary allies. I wasn't sure how long the uneasy truce would last between us, but I'd seen the raw honesty in his eyes when he'd begged me to end him if he fell slave to his beast. His soul was as tortured as mine, but his love for his mate was pure. Even if the bond was new and untested.

"Kai," she protested, reaching for me.

The moment her fingers made contact with my exposed forearm, my heart lurched. She tied me up in knots. Her scent. Her touch. Her presence. This wasn't normal attraction by any stretch of the imagination, making it all the more difficult to fight. She couldn't possibly be mine. Not if she was already Tor's.

Or could she?

The Shadow Queen had four males. Tor's own brother

was part of a group relationship as well. Hell, she wrote about a woman with multiple lovers. Was it really that out of the question?

The temptation to chase that thought was almost irresistible. But I couldn't.

I'd already proven that I was incapable of sharing. I'd nearly murdered Tor when he'd made a claim on her. What would happen if someone touched her in front of me? Another razed village?

I couldn't risk it.

It was time for me to accept the truth. No matter how strong her call, Dahlia Moore would never be mine.

TWENTY-TWO

DAHLIA

My eyes darted to the door for the sixth or seventh time in as many minutes. *Where is he?* Our group session was starting any minute, but I hadn't seen Tor since the night he'd broken into my room and taken care of me. I still can't believe I just rolled over and let him clean my thighs and run me a bath, but honestly, I'd just been so fucking surprised I didn't know what else to do. No one had ever cared for me like that. The first time I started my period, I thought I was at death's door as my body revolted against me. Fear I'd offended my goddess or that something was deeply wrong with me had taken hold, and I'd sobbed until my throat was raw as I curled up in the shower, watching the blood swirl down the drain.

I was starved for affection. A total whore for any and all acts of selfless kindness. I don't think I could have sent Tor away if I'd wanted to. And I hadn't. The fact that he was a sexy Viking man was only the cherry on top.

The tenderness was so out of character with the simmering violence he battled every second of every day.

I'd have said it was unnatural, but if anything, he seemed right at home in the caretaker role. Almost as if it's who he'd been prior to his curse.

Maybe Dr. Masterson pulled him after what happened during the last session.

I bit down on my lower lip; it was certainly plausible, but I'd be lying if I said I hadn't been hoping to see him.

After the second day post-forced period cuddles without so much as a sighting, I'd started questioning the whole thing. Was it just some weird hormonal fever dream? Did I make it all up? It wasn't outside the realm of my imagination. And if I was being objective, Tor hadn't exactly behaved the way a "normal" man would. What with the washing and fussing. Who even did that?

A sexy-as-sin Viking from a mystical realm, that's who.

He'd swooped in and love-bombed me with his Kærastas and mate talk. But then he ghosted. Was this typical in his culture? To tell a woman she was his mate and do the swoony things with the kissing and the touching and then vanish into thin air?

"Is this seat taken?" Kai asked as he stood in front of the empty chair next to me.

"Now it is," I said, grinning as he offered a gentle smile. There was something in his eyes, though, a guardedness I didn't like.

It was the same wary expression he'd had when I found him on the battlements yesterday. He was slipping away from me instead of getting closer.

He was never yours to begin with, dummy. You can't lose what you never had.

I was dangerously close to delusional if I thought my life and my character Rebel's were at all the same. She may have a group of men who worship her, but that wasn't real. That didn't happen to regular people like me.

"Gang's all here," Cas said as he sat across from me, eyes heated, roguish grin twisting his lips. "Where's the doc?"

I blushed and had to look away as a hazy memory of him kissing my forehead filled my mind. I had one guy building walls, one avoiding me, and another undressing me with his eyes. I took a quick peek at Cain. And another who I was pretty sure didn't know I existed at all.

Definitely not Rebel.

"Tor's missing," I argued, forcing myself to come back to the present.

"Tor won't be joining us," Dr. Masterson said as she strode into the room.

A pang of loss went through me, which was ridiculous. I barely knew the man. But even still, I wanted him here. "I thought this was part of the program."

"It's voluntary. All of this is. You choose what you get from being here," Dr. Masterson offered, taking her seat at the head of the group.

"Except No Man's Land," Cain chipped in. Asshole growled, tiny but fierce. As if sensing my eyes on him, the little floof craned his head my way, his tiny tongue lolling out the side of his mouth. I would have sworn he was begging for a *boop*.

The doctor leveled an unamused glare at Cain. "That's a security measure. You know that as well as everyone."

"And it's not voluntary. Are you telling me I can leave whenever I want? That any of us can walk out the door without being hauled back?"

"Once you complete your treatment as required by your

sentence from the High Council, you may. Not all of you are here under a council order, but enough of you are." Her gaze swept the room, landing on Kai as she finished her sentence.

Technically, I could leave whenever I want. "I elected to be here."

"Oh, you may think so, but that's only because you don't have all the information."

"What the hell is that supposed to mean?" I asked, my back snapping ramrod straight.

The doctor met my furious glare without flinching. I suppose, given the other personalities in this room, I was hardly a major threat. But I'd stab a bitch with my pen if I had to.

"There's a video, love." Cas's expression was somber, which I hadn't expected.

"A video?"

"Yes."

"We will address it in your next solo session if you wish, Dahlia. But for now, let's focus on the goal of this group meeting, shall we?" Dr. Masterson pulled out her phone and went through the routine of introducing herself as the device recorded the session.

"This is Dr. Elizabeth Masterson. It is November eighth, and the time is 11:00 a.m. This is the second session of our peer accountability group V."

"V?" Cas echoed, his flirty gaze leveled on me. "As in vagina? My favorite."

Why? Why did that make me blush?

"V as in there are twenty-one other groups on record," Dr. Masterson corrected.

"So why not call us group twenty-two?" Cain drawled, his long fingers idly playing with his puppy's fur as he challenged her alongside Caspian.

Dr. Masterson's expression was pinched, but to her credit, she took a deep breath and calmly replied, "Because I didn't. Now, are there any other off-topic questions you'd like to ask, or can we get on with today's business?"

"Is that an actual offer? Because I've got a list a mile long," Cas started. The doctor glared at him in response, but he only grinned unrepentantly. "Guess not. Carry on, then."

"Thank you for the permission to run my own group." She sighed and opened her notebook, pen poised and at the ready. "Today we are going to discuss vulnerability. Namely making yourselves uncomfortable on purpose."

As usual, Caspian was the first to reply. Nose scrunched, he let out a soft sound of disgust. "Why would I ever do that? And on purpose, of all things. No. I don't think I will."

"All right, your loss. The rest of you, I want you to think back on a time you felt discomfort because of a situation you were in."

Kai scoffed. "How about this one right here?"

"Same," Cain agreed. "Also, I have no memory. My list is gonna be mighty short."

"Let's start with you, Dahlia."

Great.

"How about every time I have to be social ever?"

"Let's dig into that. What about social situations specifically makes you uncomfortable?"

"The people," I answered without hesitation.

Dr. Masterson waved a hand around the room. "You're in a social setting now and are perfectly fine."

I gave her a smile that was little more than a baring of teeth. "That's what you think. I've had a lot of practice faking it."

"You'd never have to fake it with me, love."

"I'll believe it when I see it," Cain grumbled.

Ignoring what the thought of him seeing me not faking it with Cas did to my downstairs lady garden, I shook my head. "I struggle with so much anxiety before, during, and after. What if I say something wrong or do something to annoy them, and I get punished for it? What if they all judge me? Add the press to the mix, and I have to worry about being canceled. And it's not enough that I might just say something wrong. I also have to deal with my appearance being picked apart. I can hardly frown in public these days without it being dissected."

"You can imagine us all naked if that helps," Cas offered.

"That's public speaking, you fucking idiot," Cain muttered.

"She has my full permission to imagine me naked whenever her heart desires."

"Knock it off, pirate." Kai spread his legs wide enough his thigh pressed against mine. I couldn't tell if he was aware of the contact, but I sure as hell was.

"Let's explore that deeper, Dahlia. Do you feel as though you're being judged right now?"

"Uh, yeah. You're literally judging my responses and writing shit down."

Her smile was gentle. "Yes, but only so we can help you work through this. It seems all of us in this room need to work on parasocial relationships."

Kai snorted.

"Understanding how quickly these situations can escalate from low-level stress to a full breakdown of control is vital to assimilating into the human world. To that end, I want you to pair off and use the rest of our time to practice being vulnerable, open, and connected to your partner, even though you're uncomfortable."

Cain raised his hand and cleared his throat. "May I please reiterate that I have nothing to share? No memories. No baggage."

Cas was already on his feet, striding toward me as though ready to claim me as his partner.

"Not so fast, Caspian. You will be paired with Malakai. Dahlia, you're with Cain."

The broody southerner crossed his arms over his chest and trained his gaze on the floor in front of him.

Cool cool cool.

Can't wait.

What's one more awkward conversation to agonize over?

I stood, striding to the farthest corner of the room, the area with a lovely window seat and cushions I could hold for security. Cain could come to me. Grumpy fucker.

He looked over at me, the slight incline of his eyebrow his only reaction.

I see your eyebrow, and I raise you a second. I sent the thought his way with a haughty lift of my brows. Almost like I was saying, well, what are you waiting for?

The standoff would've been funny if he wasn't so damn hot.

I could practically hear him crooning in my ear. *"I don't go to anyone, Dahlia. They come to me. Now get over here before I make you."*

Jesus, that voice was potent even when it was just in my mind. I had to clamp my thighs together to alleviate some of the building ache.

Fed up with our nonsense, Asshole came bounding over and jumped straight into my lap. Paws on my shoulders, he started licking my face and drawing a giggle from me.

That's right. I'll get you my pretty, and your little dog too.

The witchy cackle that accompanied the thought was thankfully just in my mind.

Cain gave a weary sigh and unfolded his frame from the chair before he stalked over and joined me. Victory was mine.

"Regardless of this little assignment, I should warn you, this will be a one-sided affair. I don't have anything to share."

Ah, yes. One-sided. Just like my attraction to him.

"Is there a reason you despise me? Have I done something to piss you off?"

"I don't know. Have you?"

"Not that I can tell."

"Give me back my dog."

"He came to me. I didn't snatch him."

Cain held his hands out for Asshole, but the pup stood in my lap, made a circle, and plopped back down instead.

"Traitor."

Asshole panted happily. Maybe he had special puppy senses that told him I needed him more than his owner at the moment.

"Fine. I'll start so we can get this over with. My memories are spotty too. You're not alone there. My childhood was so traumatic I blocked most of it out, and when we uncovered one of my repressed memories, I was locked in an anxiety spiral for days."

"Why?"

I exhaled heavily and stared out the window without really seeing anything. His fiery gaze was unnerving, and it was hard to look at him while admitting to things I hadn't fully accepted myself.

"I grew up in a death cult. Not death like the Helter

Skelter Manson people, but as in they worshiped the goddess Death. They tried to sacrifice me."

"Jesus."

"Yeah, so, you know, you're not the only one here with hidden truth bombs in your brain."

He had nothing to say to that, so I just kept going.

"It gets better. My dad was the one holding the sacrificial dagger. Literally. He even handpicked the boy that was going to rape me first. I think maybe he and I were engaged or something. It's really hazy, but the betrayal I felt that it was the two of them holding me down . . ." I had to trail off and clear my throat, shoving away the tears that were threatening at the reminder.

Cain's jaw clenched hard enough I saw the muscles flexing. "How old were you?"

"Twelve."

His hands sparked with blue fire as he sat with my confession. Asshole nudged my arm until I began petting him and something in me calmed.

"I don't trust people, and that's why I can't stand to be in public. If my dad could do that to me, what's to say a stranger won't do worse?"

"Is that even possible? For a stranger to treat you worse than he did?"

"I guess not, but I don't really want to find out." I blew out another heavy breath. "The thing I remember most, besides the fear, is that all I wanted to do was make him proud because then maybe he'd want to spend time with me. He kept me at arm's length. Never really wanted me around, or at least that's the sense I had from the memory. There was this other woman who raised me. So I guess I have some abandonment issues too. Like not only did he not want to raise me, he wanted to get rid of me in the most permanent way possible. And again, if my own dad didn't want me around, why would anybody else? Why bother getting attached?"

"Everyone is going to leave you at some point. It's the nature of life and the inevitably of death."

There was something about his voice when he said that. A weight that I hadn't heard there before.

"Speaking from experience?" I asked, finally looking up at him again.

He shrugged, the side of his mouth curving up in a mocking grin. "I dunno. I can't remember."

I huffed out a laugh. "I wish I still didn't remember. It fucking sucks carrying all of this around. No wonder young me boxed it all up and threw away the key."

"Boxes don't have keys."

"You sound like my editor. Let me mix my metaphors if I want to."

We shared a soft smile, and for a second, I felt closer to him. I guess Dr. Masterson's exercise wasn't so stupid after all.

"So why are you here? Being anxious doesn't seem like enough of a reason to be in the supernatural version of Arkham Asylum."

"Hey! Look at you. That's a pop culture reference. Some memories must be coming back."

He pressed his lips together and shook his head. "None that are of any use to me."

"Like what brought you here."

"Exactly."

That seemed to be all he was going to say on the matter, so I gave him a little shrug and answered his earlier question. "You know why I'm here. I freaked out at my premiere.

Saw a ghost, screamed bloody murder, thought I killed everybody . . . Oh shit."

"What, what is it?" he asked, body tensing as if he needed to jump into action.

"I only just now realized. At the movie premiere, I hallucinated that everyone died, just like they did at the ritual. I . . ." I shook my head, frustrated that I was losing my train of thought. I was onto something, I was sure of it, but the harder I tried to grasp it, the quicker it slipped away. "I wonder why I did that. If my subconscious was trying to remember something."

"Your mind is protecting you. That's no surprise. But that's the thing about boxes. Eventually someone is going to open them."

"Do you think your mind is protecting you?"

Just like that, he shut down. I watched the carefully constructed mask of disinterest slip into place. "Session's over."

I glanced at the clock. "No, it's not. We still have ten minutes."

He scooped Asshole out of my lap and stood. "It's over because I say it is."

"But—"

"Don't push me, little flower. I'm not your friend. I don't want to fuck you. And I don't owe you a damn thing."

He walked away before I could respond, but honestly, what could I say? He'd just proven all my fears right. He was judging me. He thought I was stupid and took all the vulnerable pieces I'd shown him and thrown them in the trash.

The sound of his voice calling me little flower still echoed in my traitorous brain. The endearment sent a wave of longing through me.

Stop it, Dahlia. You are not Rebel. This is not a romance novel where the broody one finally comes around and confesses he's been in love since the moment he saw you. And the holdout isn't actually interested. He isn't holding out on anything. He doesn't want you.

This is real life.

And in real life, happy endings are never guaranteed.

~

CAIN

I WAS A FUCKING ASSHOLE. I was worse than Asshole, even. As if he picked up on my thoughts, the puppy in my arms emitted a fierce little growl.

"Oh, get over it," I muttered, my mind still churning. "She's a grown-up. She'll be fine."

She didn't deserve my cutting remarks, but I hadn't known what to do. Dahlia wasn't for me. I already had someone. Hell, I'd been dreaming of her.

How could I lead one woman on when another might be out there somewhere waiting for me? One I was likely married to.

I couldn't deny the way my skin buzzed with protective energy as she'd shared her darkest memory with me, though. All I wanted was to make them all pay for hurting her. Burn them to ash and send them straight to hell where they'd answer for their sins.

"Who do I have to pay to get in on the action? Just me, him, and five minutes in a cell."

"You really need to get a handle on those flames, pal."

My steps faltered, eyes dropping to my hands before shifting to the demon leaning against the wall, a cigarette behind one ear and a lighter in his hand. He flicked it open, then shut, open, then shut, almost compulsively.

"Be thankful all I can do is hold this fire right now. You sneak up on me, there's no guarantee I won't send it straight at you next time."

The James Dean wannabe smirked at me. "I'm shaking in my boots."

I wasn't sure what it was about the demon that got under my skin. I didn't like him. He hadn't done a thing to me, yet he set off every alarm bell in my mind. Almost like he was my enemy. Or working for him.

But that didn't make any sense. I didn't have any enemies.

"She really riles you up, doesn't she, boss?"

Boss? Why would he call me that?

"Everyone riles me up."

"Not like her. Your eyes do this weird flashy thing. Better be careful. Someone might see her as a way to get to you."

I stiffened, not appreciating the assumption or the threat. "People would have to be really fucking stupid to do anything to get to me. You don't want my undivided attention, Drax. I promise."

He lifted both hands. "I didn't say *I* was going to do anything. Just offering you a friendly bit of advice."

"You've never been friendly a day in your miserable life," I said, the words rolling off my tongue before I had a chance to consider them. The statement brought me up short. How would I have any inkling as to who he was prior to this? "Do we know each other?"

Drax's smile was sharp enough to cut. "I'm not going to

lie to you and say no."

"Tell me who I am."

"Nah, this is way more fun. Watching you put the pieces together. Knowing I could give it all to you."

"If you value your life, you'll tell me what I want to know."

"I might be afraid if you were even half the man you truly are."

Power surged through my veins, building in the palms of my hands. "Do. Not. Toy. With. Me."

"But that's a demon's favorite game, *boss*. Remember? Oh . . . right." He pretended to pout, his dark chuckle filling the air between us. Then he winked. "See you around."

I wanted nothing more than to rip his tongue out of his head and watch him choke to death on his blood. But an orderly came around the corner as I took my first step toward the demon.

Drax laughed and began humming. It took a second, but I recognized the tune: "You're the Devil in Disguise."

My eyes narrowed, unease coiling in my gut.

Is he giving me a message? Is that why he called me boss? Everyone knows demons report to Lucifer.

No. I couldn't possibly be.

Was I?

TWENTY-THREE
DAHLIA

You'd think after my big beastly Berserker (I do love alliteration) abandoned me, I'd just let him go and stop fantasizing about him. But no.

After the things he'd said, I struggled to believe he'd just up and walk away.

What if he's Farmer Georging you again?

Is he a tragic hero with terrible fears that he'll hurt you?

The answer was right there in front of me. I had no fucking clue.

I simply didn't know him well enough to make a call either way. He could very well be a decent dude pushing me away in some sorry attempt to spare me. Or he could be a raging asshole who got off on playing with my feelings.

No, Asshole would never do that to me. He was a sweet puppy. I needed to come up with a new word for the level of douche-fuckery such behavior called for.

Sweaty taint?

Salty scrotum?

Oh, shriveled scrotum.

Yes, there it was.

Tor might just be a shriveled scrotum. *Ugh*. When I tell you I had a full body shudder at the mental image that caused. Just two dangling balls of flesh with Tor's broody face on them. Yeah, no thanks. There's no way I'd ever look at a ball sac the same way again.

Because you look at them regularly now, you fucking weirdo?

Realizing I was starting to spiral, I forced myself to take a series of deep breaths. I needed to get out of my room, go for a walk or something. Get a change of scenery and just get out of my head for a while. Dr. Masterson would be so proud of me.

"Walk and think. Stop picturing scrotums."

"Do you often picture them?" Bru's smoky voice caught me off guard as I strode down the hallway, aimless and restless. I hadn't even realized I'd been speaking out loud.

He just smiled and looked at me intently, clearly waiting for an answer. Feeling suddenly defensive, I snapped, "Do you?"

He surprised me by smirking. "When the mood strikes."

Heat blazed in my cheeks at his admission, but before I could do anything with it, his presence registered. Oh fuck, if he was here, Tor had to be close by. My belly swooped at the thought.

"Is he . . . here?"

"No."

Disappointment punched me in the gut. "Oh. Okay." Disheartened, I almost turned away and let it go, but that's not who I was. It certainly wasn't who I wanted to be. "No, you know what? It's not okay. Where is he? He came into my room, dick swinging, took care of me, told me I'm his freaking kareesta, or whatever, and then left without a word. So no, okay isn't an option. Where. Is. He?"

Bruno's eyes filled with sympathy. "He's with the doctor."

"Which doctor? Dr. Masterson?"

He pressed his lips together and shook his head. I couldn't tell if he was saying no or if he was trying to telegraph that he shouldn't have spoken at all.

"Is he sick?" I asked, gripping the man's forearm so hard I was sure my nails would leave little crescent imprints.

"He is with the doctor. She's helping him."

The steely look in his eyes told me everything I needed to know. He wasn't going to give me anything else.

"Is he always like this? Hot and cold? Ready to shove me up against the wall and claim me, then act as frozen as the polar ice caps. Well . . . maybe that's a bad example. They're melting."

"I couldn't say. I've never seen him shove anybody against a wall. Unless he was in the middle of trying to pummel them. But I don't think that's what you meant."

It took a second before I could clear my mind of the images of Tor having his way with me up against a wall. Clearing my throat, I murmured, "Er, no. Not exactly."

"He's doing what he must. That's all I can share."

I narrowed my eyes. "Well, when you see him, you tell him he's a shriveled scrotum."

"I can emphatically assure you I will do no such thing."

"Scaredy-cat."

"Have you seen him when he's angry? Why purposely provoke him?"

"Yeah," I said, but it was more like a sigh. He was fuck hot when he was angry.

"Yeah . . . no. He's ripped limbs from bodies."

"Who among us?"

Bru did a double-take at my breezy response. Okay, to

be fair, I hadn't ripped any limbs in the literal sense. But I'd definitely done it in the fictional sense. I was basically a serial killer. But a nice one. With cookies and cozy blankets and no real murder. Emotional annihilation only. This was the reason I'd been gifted a mug that said *Tears of my readers* on it.

"When can I see him? I need to talk to him about . . . everything."

Bru shook his head and offered me a wan smile. "I have no idea when he'll be finished with this round of treatment. All I know is they're harder each time, and he will need a day or so to recuperate."

"I hate this."

Sympathetic eyes met mine. "As do I. But he's making a valiant effort to be whole again."

For you.

His unspoken words hit me like a kick to the cunt.

"Will you at least tell him that I . . ."

That you what? Are pining for him like a heroine in a Julia Quinn novel?

"That I miss him?" I finished lamely.

He nodded. "Yes. That I will do."

With a heavy sigh, I gave him a little nod. "Thanks, Bru."

"Of course."

There wasn't really anything to say after that, so I continued with my aimless wandering. I hated this. I may have been a hermit, but I never had to deal with men and managing my emotions relating to them. Now I had four who were nearly always on my mind. Honestly, my brain was already busy enough. I really didn't have room for four sexy dudes.

Walking past the media room, I stopped short at the sound of Caspian's incensed rant.

"Never in my life have I worn a fucking pair of tights, and don't get me started on his dreadful mustache!"

"Oh, this is bound to be good," I muttered, peeking around the open doorway to find my pirate and dragon inside. Kai was holding a remote, the movie *Hook* frozen on the big screen.

Cas snatched the remote. "You know, I forgot to tell you, your mum called earlier. She said we should watch *Puff the Magic Dragon* so you can relive your childhood."

"Oh, you're fucking hilarious, you know that? You should pack up all your crap and take your show on the road. In fact, I'll help you."

"You know what? I have a better idea. Why don't we let our sweet darling choose?" Cas slid his gaze to where I was watching in the doorway.

"Busted," I muttered.

"I knew you were there the whole time, love."

Shuffling into the room, I shrugged. "I wasn't eavesdropping on purpose."

"Pretty little liar," he crooned.

"Okay, fine, you caught me. What's my punishment? The rack? Shall I walk the plank, Cap'n?"

"That sounds more like a *fun*ishment."

My nipples perked right up at that idea. Horny bitches.

"So you said I get to choose, huh?"

"Aye, gem. Your choice, but you have to come over here and sit with us." Kai was manspread on one end of the sofa, his big frame a very tempting pillow.

Caspian patted the cushion to his left, i.e., the one furthest away from Kai, who was seated on his right. "Got your seat right here, love."

I technically could try to squeeze myself between them, but something warned me against it. One smoking hot male was enough of a distraction. Mama didn't need two of them overriding her senses. As an extra precaution, I decided to lie on my stomach across the chaise lounge, which put my feet as the only part of me near either of the guys. You couldn't do much with feet.

Boy, I really thought I did something there. Turned out, I was way off.

This might not have been the best position to put myself in—two of the hottest men I've ever met, a cozy couch, and pheromones galore, but after talking to Bru and just being more confused about Tor, I wasn't sure I'd be able to turn in for the night and get any sleep. A movie with two guys I liked to be around—and who weren't avoiding me—was a much more palatable option. Besides, I wasn't really married to Tor. We'd interacted less than a handful of times. But that kiss was one for the books . . .

I could argue that Cas's was too.

Fuck, I was confused.

"Relax, Dahlia. You're wound so tight I can sense it from over here, lass."

"Yes, darling. We won't bite."

Releasing my breath, I kept scrolling through our movie options when I found quite arguably the best possible selection. There was no containing my self-satisfied smirk as I announced, "Okay. I'm ready. I've made my choice. Now you must endure like the big, strong males you are."

"Oh goddess. What is it?" Kai asked, his eyes locked on me instead of the screen.

"Lady Chatterley's Lover," I said with a shit-eating grin as I hit play.

Caspian's aggrieved sigh reverberated through me.

"Bollocks. What's that expression, Kai? Lie back and think of England?"

"Trust me, boys. You'll like this version."

I know I did. That sexy groundskeeper lived rent-free in my mind.

I propped my head in my hands and settled in as the credits began to roll. Cas stood almost instantly, and I nearly protested, but he switched off the lights and shut the door before returning with a thick blanket. He draped it over me and rested his palm on my exposed ankle, one finger tickling the delicate bone on the inside.

Almost instantly, my attention was riveted on that small bit of flesh. My eyes might have been locked on the screen, but I was absolutely absorbed by the little circles Cas drew against my skin. I definitely shouldn't have worn this baseball tee nightie tonight, but I really didn't think I'd see them because I was just trying to settle my mind before bed.

Should I stop him? There wasn't a single part of me that wanted to.

But should I? Was I breaking some unknown mating oath?

You didn't take an oath, stupid.

Right, that settled it. I wasn't doing anything wrong, and he couldn't be assed to so much as send me a carrier pigeon, so fuck it. I was going to relax and enjoy myself. Or, more specifically, enjoy whatever Cas was doing to my leg.

His palm shifted up my calf, touch still gentle and sending tingles straight between my legs.

What is he up to?

It didn't take long for me to find out. Caspian's touch remained completely respectful. At least it did until the first time Lady Chatterley and her hottie started taking clothes off. Then he slid his hand up my leg and curled it around my thigh under the blanket. I swear on all that is holy that I did not part my legs intentionally. I. Did. Not.

Out of the corner of my eye, I caught sight of Kai shifting and adjusting himself, but Cas's face appeared, blocking my view. He flashed me a wicked grin before holding one finger to his lips as he scooted forward on the sofa.

"Our little secret, darling," Cas mouthed.

A thrill ran through me. Any moment, Kai could catch us. What would he do? Feed me his dragon dick?

Oh God.

There was absolutely no discounting the surge of wetness that accompanied that thought.

And in case you were wondering, Sorcha was right. I was one day post-shark week. Thank fuck.

This torture continued as I tried, and failed to focus on the screen instead of the way Cas stroked my inner thigh. But then he moved, and I almost moaned when his long finger traced the edge of my panties. Lady Chatterley was getting railed again, and I wriggled my hips, parting my thighs a little more so I could invite Cas to give me what I needed.

My pirate was more than happy to oblige, but boy, he made an event out of it. He teased me with slow glides of his fingers along my panty line, then over my cotton-covered pussy.

"Mmm, perfectly plump," he whispered.

As far as Kai knew, he could have been talking about the actress on the TV. Only I knew the truth. It sent another wave of arousal through me, pooling between my legs.

My heart thundered as Cas continued to feather his fingertips over my labia, avoiding the place I really wanted him to touch. All the while, his fingertips would venture ever closer to my throbbing clit. My breaths turned into soft pants, and I was acutely aware of Kai's stony presence on the far side of the couch. I stole glances at him out of the corner of my eye, but he never once looked our way, his attention captured by the erotic display on the screen.

"Quiet, sweet girl."

I had to bite down hard on the inside of my cheek when he finally swept his fingers along my seam. I was so wet I was certain there'd be a puddle beneath me when I stood. Then he gave me what I wanted. The way I was desperate to cry out his name when he brushed my clit was nearly painful. But I stayed quiet and as still as I could while Captain fucking Hook circled that bundle of nerves over and over. He timed his movements well, keeping me on edge and not allowing me to come until the couple in the movie did.

As much as I hated his game, I loved it.

It was unexpected, a little depraved, and absolutely sexy.

Knowing Kai could catch us at any moment only made it more so.

And all the man was doing was playing with my clit. He wasn't even fucking me with his fingers, though I wished he would. I desperately wanted something to clamp down on while riding out the high of my orgasm. As the waves of pleasure began to crest, Cas adjusted his position once more, and it was exactly what I needed. He continued his attention on my clit, but his thumb was there, tracing my entrance, sending shivers through my body. I came with a faint whimper as the pair on the screen cried out in ecstasy.

Cas faked a stretch and twisted my way, brushing his lips over the skin not quite covered by the blanket. It was practically chaste, but it sent a second wave careening through me, the heat of his lips against my skin as intoxicating as the brush of his fingers over my sensitive folds.

"Well, that was much more enjoyable than I anticipated," he said as he stood and stretched.

Glancing over my shoulder, I caught sight of the straining bulge in his pants. He smirked, then ran his fingers under his nose, inhaling long and deep as his eyes fluttered.

"I think I'll turn in. Perhaps have a shower."

He didn't bother waiting for either of us to respond. He just walked out like he did everything else, dick first.

When I managed to calm my racing heart, I risked another glance in Kai's direction.

This time, however, his eyes weren't focused on the TV. They were on me, and they were filled with desperate hunger.

Oh fuck.

TWENTY-FOUR

KAI

That shifty pirate thought he was getting away with something right under my nose. He wasn't going to get a damn thing past me, not when I could scent Dahlia's arousal as clearly as if she were naked and spread before me.

It was the test of my life to stay put and let them carry on, acting all the while as if I didn't know what was happening beneath that blanket.

Oh goddess, but I did.

And it may have been more torturous in my imagination.

Nae. It was painful sitting here listening to her little gasps and restrained whimpers, pretending I was unaffected. But I wouldnae ruin this for her. Watching my treasure be brought to her climax was a thing of beauty. Especially since she was trying so hard to hide it.

There was no hiding it from me.

I was aware of each catch of her breath. Every swallowed murmur. The narrowing of her eyes and the way her teeth bit down into her bottom lip. I even picked up on the wash of color over her cheeks and down her chest, thanks to my dragon's uncanny sight.

If I'd been a weaker man, I would have palmed my dick. Hell, I would have pulled it out of my joggers and stroked it in time with her soft cries. Knelt in front of her and fed my aching length into that lush mouth so she could put an end to my misery.

She shuddered, and Caspian pulled back before he stood and stretched, his body turned away from me. "Well, that was much more enjoyable than I anticipated. I think I'll turn in. Perhaps have a shower."

The movie continued, but neither Dahlia nor I were focused on it. Not after Caspian left us alone together. This time I did palm my dick as she repositioned herself so she was curled up on the sofa.

I never once looked away, even though I really should have. All I could think about was how wet her cunt must be. How Caspian knew exactly what he was doing by leaving us here.

As soon as the credits rolled, Dahlia took a shaky breath and peeked at me. Her eyes flew wide as they caught and held onto mine.

"Uh . . . um . . ." She jerked her thumb toward the door. "I should probably get to bed. Early worm and all that. Deadlines. Editors." She made a face and rolled her eyes, like they were the reason she was attempting to flee from me.

No fucking way was she running from me now.

I was up and across the U-shaped sofa before she'd even set one foot on the floor. I caught her by the hair, my fingers tangling in the silky strands as I whipped her around to face me, her gasp washing over me as my lips crashed into hers.

I adjusted us until she was under me, at my mercy, all

fucking mine. She melted against me, her mouth opening as I held her head where I wanted it. I took her kiss and made it mine. Her little whimpers of need sent fire through my veins. Or maybe that was my dragon rising to the surface.

Either way, I burned for her.

Her hips rocked upward, rubbing against my stomach as she searched for friction.

"Desperate little thing, aren't ye, lass? One climax isn't enough to sate you?"

Hands gripped the hem of my shirt, tugging upward in a silent request for more skin.

"You're so warm," she whispered against my lips.

"I'm a dragon, gem. Of course I'm warm."

Her nails dug into me as I moved down her body.

"Wait, where are you going?"

I didn't answer until my shoulders were positioned between her thighs, my eyes slow in their perusal of her form. "I'm going to clean you up. You better speak now if that's not what you want."

"C-clean me?"

I smirked, not breaking eye contact. "Aye. With my tongue. You made quite a mess of yourself during the film."

"I didn't think you—"

"You honestly thought I wouldn't know? I could smell your need the moment he touched you."

"Are you mad?"

Pressing my nose between her thighs, I inhaled the intoxicating scent of her pussy, and she squirmed in response. "No. But I am painfully aware you need more than what he gave you." Running my nose along her damn cotton knickers, I rolled my eyes upward again until I could see hers. "Do ye want me to give you more, Dahlia? Can I taste the treasure between your thighs?"

She gulped, her tongue darting out to wet her lips. "Y-yes?"

"Answer me honestly. I won't take you against your will."

"I want it."

Thank the fucking goddess. My hips rocked into the sofa cushion without my permission.

Tucking my fingers into the waistband of her knickers, I peeled them down her legs, tucking the scrap of fabric into my back pocket for safekeeping. Those would come in handy later.

"Pull up your nightgown," I demanded, not wanting anything to get between me and my prize.

She did as I bade, her chest rising and falling in rapid breaths as she watched me with hungry eyes.

"Kai," she whispered, her fingers going to my hair and tangling in the strands. "I . . . no one has ever—"

"Then I'd better ensure it's unforgettable. Let me make you come on my tongue, my priceless gem. Let me show you how you should be adored."

I kissed her inner thigh, nipping lightly as I grew closer to the place I wanted to be more than anything, and when I finally did arrive, she was already fluttering in anticipation. The way her back arched as my lips closed over her swollen clit was a thing of beauty.

She cried out, her fingers diving into my hair and pulling me closer to her writhing hips. Goddess, yes. I would happily suffocate if it was her cunt robbing me of breath.

I ate her like a man possessed, and truthfully, I was. An innate urge to keep her clawing at me, calling my name, begging for more, drove me on. My fingers sank inside her slick opening, first one, then a second, and she clamped down on them as though asking me to stay forever.

"Yes," she chanted softly above me. "More."

A rumble of pleasure built in my chest, the vibration rolling through me into her.

"Oh God," she moaned, her body quaking against mine.

Curling my fingers, I pressed against that secret spot inside her and couldn't stop my grin as she nearly pulled my hair out in response. But I wanted to fuck her with my tongue, taste her from the source. Drink her down until all I had to sustain me was her nectar.

Sliding my fingers free, I switched places, moving them up to circle her clit while I licked my way up to her channel. Noticing the drops of arousal running down her skin, I didn't want any of it to go to waste, so I collected each and every one before allowing myself to bury my tongue inside her.

"God, Kai! What are you doing to me?"

I rolled her clit over and over as my tongue filled her until she couldn't stand it anymore. She came with a ragged cry, walls gripping me and promising more pleasure than I could imagine if only I sank my aching cock home.

I didn't let up until the fingers buried in my hair started to tug up instead of pressing down.

"Too much," she whimpered.

I pulled away, turning my face to the side so I could press a kiss to her trembling inner thigh before looking up at her.

Her breaths were uneven, her arm draped over her face.

I didn't like that I couldn't see her expression.

Something felt . . . off. Like she wasn't one hundred percent the sated woman I'd intended her to be.

"Gem? Everything okay?"

Her answering laugh was shaky. "Are you kidding? It's fan-fucking-tastic. Never in my life have I ever had an orgasm I didn't have to work for. Until tonight. And now I've had two. That was . . . you are . . . wow. It was so much better than the ones I give to myself."

I couldn't help myself. I smirked. "Happy to help."

Bringing my fingers to my mouth, I sucked her slick off them, but knew I'd be stroking my dick to the scent of her as soon as she was safely in bed. As much as I wanted to give her another mind-blowing climax, I could see she was already overwhelmed. We'd gone as far as we'd go tonight. There was always tomorrow. And all the days thereafter.

I didn't think I could ever let her go now that I'd gotten a taste of what being with her was like. My plan to stay away was shot to hell the moment she walked into this room. I was hers.

I may be a condemned man, but I would cling to Dahlia with my dying breath and smile when the goddess came to collect because every day with her would be one that I would treasure.

And if anyone recognized treasure when they found it, it was a dragon.

TWENTY-FIVE

TOR

Eighteen months earlier
FARRELL PACK RANCH, COLORADO, USA

"Give me my daughter back," Alek said, trying to pluck the tiny bundle of blankets and baby from my arms.

I twisted away from my twin. "You'll have her forever. Give her favorite uncle five more minutes."

"You're her only uncle. She has to call you her favorite."

"Technically that's not true. My brother will love her to bits once he gets to meet her. West is great with babies. They love him." Noah Blackthorne strode into the room, Sunday on his arm, the two of them all smiles. She looked radiant. You'd never have known she'd given birth such a short time ago, and in such a traumatic fashion.

My eyes flicked across the room to the former priest, who was pretending to be reading. I knew the blood he'd given was part of the reason for her expedited recovery.

Vampires might not be my favorite of the other supernatural species, but they certainly were handy to have around if you needed healing.

"What are you looking at, Mr. Nordson? Can't a man read in peace?" Caleb's stern brow furrowed even deeper.

"Irish, Irish, Irish," Sunday teased.

"Are ye sassing me, wife?" he snapped his book closed and trained his gaze on her.

"Maybe. What are you going to do if I am?"

Noah squeezed her tighter to him. "Don't provoke him. You could barely sit down the last time he made you repent for your sins."

I glanced from Noah to Caleb, then back again. I wasn't sure how they did it, but this sharing dynamic really seemed to work for all of them.

"Okay, Sunbeam, are you ready for Daddy to get you changed for bed? I've got your favorite wolf jammies all ready," Kingston Farrell, the alpha of the Farrell pack and Sunday's fourth mate, said as he came inside from his evening run. The man was covered in a sheen of sweat and streaks of dirt and had clearly been in his wolf form until he arrived home.

I'd thought it was strange when I arrived that there were folded piles of his clothes on the front stoop and the back porch, but now I understood. Shifters might be comfortable walking around naked, but now that they had a baby, modesty was something they protected.

Sunday gave Noah a kiss on the cheek before unwinding her arm from his and moving to Kingston's side. Reaching up, she pulled a stray leaf from his hair. "Not so fast, mister. You need a shower before you go anywhere near our baby."

"You gonna wash my back, Sunshine? I can't promise I'll get you clean."

Noah scoffed. "You're too late. I already took care of her."

Without missing a beat or sparing any of us a glance, Caleb flipped a page and added, "So did I. Three times."

"Where in Odin's name was I?" Alek complained.

"With your brother," Noah said with a smirk.

Alek punched my arm. "I knew I never should have invited you to stay with us. You ruin everything."

I turned away and cradled Eden closer to my chest. "Careful, I've got a baby here, brother."

"Oh, come off it, you wouldn't drop her. Father trained you better than that."

"He'd better not. I'll tear his fecking arms off if he does." Caleb was on his feet, all righteous protective anger burning in his eyes.

"Okay, okay, everyone just settle down. No one's dropping the baby." Sunday offered me a sweet smile. "It's fine, Tor. Alek, it's your night to be big spoon. You can more than make up for being distracted."

He rubbed his hands together, eyes twinkling. "You better believe it, Kærasta. It's a good thing Caleb's on baby duty tonight because I don't intend to let you get a wink of sleep."

Pressing my palm to Eden's ears, I spun away from the happy family. "All right, my little Valkyrie, that's enough of that. You don't need to hear your parents say such naughty things. I'll just take you outside and tell you a bedtime story, shall I?"

Before I could get out the back door, Caleb was in my face, expression deadly.

"What? Am I not to be trusted with her outside these walls?"

Caleb held up a bottle, waiting for me to take it. "Here. She's always hungry before bed. Don't forget to burp her."

Eden weighed barely more than a feather, so it was easy to cradle her in the crook of one arm and accept the vampire's offering.

Kingston's amused voice carried behind me. "Well, would you look at that. A manny with a man bun. We should hire him on full-time."

"No. One Viking is plenty for our home," Noah protested.

Alek snickered. "Glad to know I always get the job done."

Halting, I turned back to face him. "Only because I taught you everything you know."

Alek rolled his eyes. "You're minutes older than me, you arse. You didn't teach me shit."

"Maybe we could trade you in for Tor, Alek. He's really much more useful than you are. He's not even afraid of ghosts," Kingston teased.

Sunday came up to me, her eyes twinkling with pure happiness. She traced the line of Eden's little button nose before giving me her gaze again. "It really is remarkable how much the two of you look alike. If it weren't for your scar, I wouldn't be able to tell you apart."

Alek came up behind her and nuzzled her neck. "Most can't, Kærasta. But I can guarantee you, you'd know it was me the moment I touched you. You feel it . . . here." He pressed his palm over her heart and feathered a kiss on her shoulder.

"I do."

"See? We don't need him at all," my twin said, tossing me a wink to take the sting out of the words. "One Viking is all anyone needs."

"Don't listen to them, Valkyrie. I'd be happy to stay and watch over you. Uncle Tor is ready and willing any time you need me."

Smiling, I took my niece outside, where I shared the stories of the stars with her, pointing out constellations and educating her on the fierce battles of her ancestors. She'd finished her bottle and had finally drifted off to sleep by the time Sunday joined me on the back porch.

"It's beautiful here, isn't it?" she asked.

"It is. Nowhere near as breathtaking as Novasgard, but there isn't a place that holds a candle to home."

"Do you miss it?"

"Yes."

"Will you go back now that things are settled here?"

I thought it over for a moment before shaking my head. "No. I don't think my destiny lies in Novasgard. I belong here."

She sighed and cupped my cheek. "I'm lucky to have you. We all are."

"Glad you recognize that."

Her laughter startled the baby, and she began to fuss in my arms.

"Here, let me take her. I'll put her to bed. Kingston will have a fit if he doesn't get to sing her the lullaby he wrote."

I handed my niece to her mother and watched them go inside with a contented smile. It had been nice spending time with my twin and his family, but I was getting restless. I hadn't been lying when I'd said that destiny was calling to me. I could smell it in the air.

The urge to move overtook me, and I strode toward the trees lining the back of the property. I'd need to figure out my next steps soon. I couldn't stay here watching my brother live his life while failing to do the same with my own. He had found his purpose, and I was grateful one of us had been gifted a mate. They were so rare, so few and far between, it was undeniable I'd never receive the same. My purpose was still unknown, but I'd find it.

"Nordson," a smooth voice called out from the darkness.

On high alert, I turned toward the sound and froze as a golden-haired man with intense green eyes stepped out of the trees.

"Who the fuck are you?" I asked, wishing I had a weapon at my hip.

"I am justice. My name is Finbar, and I have been sent by my queen to make you answer for your crimes against our people."

"I didn't do anything to your people."

"Deny it all you want. The Shadow Court fae you killed had families. You decimated them, destroying their bodies so there was nothing left to bury. Now you must face the consequences."

Fucking hell. He thought I was Alek.

Clarity spread through me faster than one of Odin's lightning bolts. This was it. This was the reason I'd felt fate's call so strongly tonight. The gods intended for me to be right here, in this exact moment.

Alek had paid his dues and earned his happily ever after. I would take his place. I would pay for his perceived sins.

Spreading my arms wide and opening my hands in a gesture of complete surrender, I tipped my head back and laughed at the universe. "Well, what are you waiting for? Kill me if you must. Mete out your justice. Just make it swift."

Finbar chuckled. "Justice you shall have, but it will not

be swift. You will suffer for your deeds and be reduced to nothing but the monster you truly are."

A ball of green magic hit me in the chest, burning through me and bringing me to my knees. The sting intensified and spread, leaving me gasping for breath as Finbar stared down with righteous fury in his eyes.

"From this night on, you will be stripped of your humanity, a slave to the violence you could not control, a danger to everyone around you, including those you hold dear. There will be no hiding what you are behind a handsome facade. Everyone will see the truth. You will suffer, Nordson. You will be an outcast. From now on, you will never know a second's peace. You will be lost forevermore. A hunted beast, a fallen prince, a shame to your father's legacy."

Finbar turned and faded into the shadows, his night's work done.

I was not as lucky. He'd reduced me to a huddled mass in the field. The pain burning inside me was absolute. My fingers dug into the earth, searching for purchase as my body trembled. Something was terribly wrong.

Sweat poured from my forehead, dripping into my eyes as the shaking in my limbs intensified. It felt like something had woken inside me and was trying to claw its way out. I could barely breathe. My skin no longer felt as though it fit. I was dying. I had to be.

"Tor?" Alek called, his voice far away but growing closer. "I was just joking about wanting you to leave. Come back into the house. We can crack open that last bottle of Father's mead."

I could not let him see me like this. He could never know what I'd done.

Staring down at my arms and hands, I panicked as they

shifted from human to beastly. Talons ripped through the soil as scales erupted across my forearms. My head throbbed so fiercely I wondered if it was splitting open, and pure rage buzzed in my brain.

I had to leave before I did something I couldn't take back.

With what little control I still possessed, I clumsily made my way to my feet and stumbled into the forest, out of Alek's line of sight and away from everything I knew and loved.

~

Present day

"AGAIN," Bruno demanded, his voice not leaving room for any argument.

I'd lost track of the days I'd been locked in here. I knew Dahlia would be furious with me, would see my absence as abandonment. And deservedly so.

But finding her changed everything.

Never once had I regretted taking my brother's place and accepting the curse that had been intended for him. Never once, until I met her.

Learning I had a mate opened my eyes to a future I never imagined for myself.

If I'd known, if I'd thought for a second there'd been a chance, I might have thought twice before I'd welcomed the Shadow Court's vengeance. It was hard to say for sure, because even now I can't imagine leaving my brother to that fate. And if I hadn't, who's to say she and I would have ever crossed paths?

Mates were a gift from the gods, true. But with such gifts came trials. My parents had theirs, Alek and Sunday their own. Now it was my turn. No longer could I blindly accept the inevitability of this curse. I needed to break it.

It was the only way I could be with her.

"You're a pathetic excuse for a man, Tor. It's no wonder she wants them instead of you," Bru pushed, collecting an orb of magic in the palm of his hand.

I growled, my skin rippling as it sought the change, but I clenched my jaw until I could taste blood pooling in my mouth.

"No, she is mine," I snarled.

"Prove it. She won't want you if you're a disgusting killer."

Breathing hard, I fought against the creature within. The one whispering in my ear. Crooning about violence and bloodshed and all the ways we could kill and dismember those who sought to take what was ours.

"Tor!" Bru shouted, recognizing that I was on the brink. "Fight it, you fucking coward. You do not deserve her if you cannot show even the slightest resistance."

My palms clenched into trembling fists as I did exactly what he said. I fought.

"She's probably under him right now, moaning his name. You're not even on her mind."

My head throbbed, the pain so intense little sparks danced in my eyes.

"They both are. Kai . . . and Caspian. Touching her. Fucking her. Giving her everything a pathetic monster like you cannot."

"No!" I roared, hating every word that came out of his

mouth. I couldn't do this. The hateful words he was spewing were so filled with possible truths my heart over-ruled my head. We'd learned quickly Dahlia was my trigger, and Bru was relentless in exploiting it.

"She. Loves. Them."

I fell to my knees, stomach sick, limbs trembling, but still mostly human.

"Enough, please, enough," I begged.

Bru moved to my side, and I stiffened as if bracing for a blow. I was so twisted up by my emotions and so worn down from fending off my beast that I could not bear a strike of any kind. Emotional or otherwise.

But all he did was hold out a bottle of water. "Here, take it."

"How much longer must we do this?" I asked, skin sticky with sweat, body aching.

"As long as it takes."

"But look at me, I'm a mess."

"I am looking at you. You're a mess, but you're also still human. It's working, Tor. Trust me. Now get back up."

I stood on shaking legs, mouth still tasting of blood as I gave him a slow, determined nod.

Eyes holding mine, he snapped, "Again."

TWENTY-SIX

DAHLIA

"I'm going to nominate you for canonization."

I laughed at Kiki's dead-serious announcement. "What? Why? I'm not even Catholic."

Kiki waved a hand as if that was a minor inconvenience. "I hereby dub thee the patron saint of dry vaginas. You could get even the dustiest vag wet again. Good lord, girlfriend. Where the hell did that chapter come from? It was so hot, it made *me* blush. And then I burnt my damned stir fry and didn't even care enough to do more than toss the whole-ass pan into the sink and turn on the tap so I could finish the rest of what you sent over without my apartment going up in flames."

"So it's safe to say we should keep that one in?" I teased, tossing myself on the bed.

"No. We should definitely cut it. It's terrible. Straight to the trash."

That tiny piece of me that would always worry I was a trash writer and someone was going to figure it out any day now had a mini panic until I let her sarcastic tone sink in.

"But how will they make that one work for the inevitable movie deal?"

"Creative draping?"

Kiki giggle-snorted. "You can't *creatively drape* four big ol' donkey dicks."

It was my turn to snort. "I don't know. Maybe we need to pitch it to those spicy anime studios first?"

"God, yes. They need more dicks in their productions. It's all tits and cake. Like, we deserve the good sausage too."

"Tits and cake? Like butts?"

Kiki shook her head. "Never mind. Let me worry about the deals. You just focus on sending me more chapters. Although, we might want to consider a partnership with a condom company or something. Your readers are going to wake up pregnant with no idea how it happened."

"There are going to be so many babies named Ren and Kit next year."

"Excuse me . . . where's my sexy drummer? Harrison is an amazing name."

"You can use it for your firstborn."

She gagged. "Blech. No, thank you. I am the quirky aunt who teaches them things they shouldn't know about. Not the mom."

"We all have our parts to play."

"Exactly. Someone's gotta be the bridesmaid. Speaking of . . . how's that husband of yours doing? You consummate the marriage yet?"

My cheeks flamed so hot there was no way to hide from her. "He's fine. I guess. Also not my husband."

"What? No! Divorced already?"

I made a face that she easily interpreted.

"What did he do? Do I need to teach him a lesson? Is

this a fly over there and kick him in the balls situation, or should I send a smelly fish via post?"

"No, it's really complicated. He's complicated."

She rolled her eyes. "Of course he is. The hot ones always are. That's why we say hot mess. But also, you're in fucking rehab. Everyone there is a disaster. Come to think of it, isn't there a rule against dating people? Seems like you're begging for trouble."

"Who's side are you on?"

"Yours obviously. I was just thinking out loud."

"We're . . . well, he says I'm his mate, but I don't know how that can be true when I also . . ."

"Want to be railed into next week by those other two hotties I met?"

I released a heavy breath. "That's one way to put it."

"Babes, it's okay to be confused. You have a lot going on, and until you iron out the details with your God of Thunder look-alike, you don't owe him anything. You don't owe *any* of them anything. So play the field if that's what you want to do. Give each of their massive shlongs a joyride or whatever. But whatever you do, make sure you're putting yourself first. Have fun. You're there to take care of you."

I shrugged. "You know what? You're right. It's not like I'm really married. Tor might have kissed me until I was dizzy, but Caspian fingered me on the couch while Kai watched, and then Kai ate me out until I came so hard I thought I died."

The camera tilted, and Kiki's stunned expression slid out of view as her laptop hit the ground. "What?!" she screamed as her face came back into focus. "Dahlia Moore, you absolute cunt. Way to bury the lede! I. Want. Details."

"I just gave them to you."

"You gave me the abridged version. Now get yourself

comfy because I need to know every single thing from the moment that Thor guy kissed you until the hot Scot finished you off."

I couldn't look her in the eye as I recounted the three absolutely incredible but totally different experiences. And then, because I was still twisted up in knots about it, I told her about my therapy homework with Cain.

She was swooning by the time I was done, her hands pressed to her chest and a dopey grin on her lips. "Okay, I get why you can't say goodbye to Hemsworth. He really took care of you like that? God, If I'd have been there, I would have shoved you out of the way and wifed him up so fast."

"Yeah, but then he disappeared."

"Because he's working on himself. We love a man who takes self-development seriously."

"Is that what he's doing? How do we know for sure? It's not exactly like he's been around."

"Sweetie, what else is he going to be doing? He's locked up there, same as you. It's not exactly like he hopped on a plane and skipped town."

"True," I mumbled, biting the inside of my cheek.

"And that Hook guy is fuck hot. I never understood the exhibition thing, but I fucking get it now. Whew! Sexy sneaky pirate. Are you gonna ask him when he intends to plunder your booty?"

"My booty is off limits."

"You say that now, but you only have so many holes and at least three men who want to fill them. I think that Cain guy does too."

"He hates me."

"Does he? Is that what you're telling yourself? Enemies-to-lovers, babes. Enemies. To. Lovers."

"But this isn't a book, Keeks. This is my life."

"How's that relevant? Tropes come from somewhere."

"Yeah, but . . ."

"No, no, no. I think you were onto something. Maybe what you need to do is treat this exactly like one of your books. Remember when you started thinking about Rebel and needed to do all that research on rock bands? Or that time you had to go get a bikini wax just so you knew what it felt like? This is like that. You need to do your research. Go out with these guys. Spend some quality time with them— without any sex organs involved—get to *really* know them."

I frowned, but I honestly didn't hate the idea. "Go out with them."

"Yeah. Let them show you why you should be with them. There's more to a relationship than physical attraction. You have to connect in all ways for it to last. Or . . . maybe you just let the pirate plunder you if that's all you want. But I know you. You're not made for casual flings and random hookups. That's never been you. Not in your books, and if you'd been able to be out in the world, not in real life. Your connections with people are only made when the relationship is meaningful. Give them the chance to prove they are worth being meaningful."

"All of them?"

Kiki shrugged. "Maybe one will come out the winner. Maybe only a couple of them will hook their claws into you. Maybe none of them will. The only way to know is to try. And if, in the end, you want all of them, fuck what everybody else says. You do what works for you. Polyamory is way more common than people think. But that's for you to figure out when you get there."

She was onto something, not me. "Now I just have to

figure out what kind of dates are possible here. It's not like we can leave."

"Stargazing from the tower? Strolling through the gardens? Paddleboats on the lake? A picnic in the—"

"Okay, fine. I get it."

"Good. Now, get out there and make mama proud. Just make sure you stretch first. They're big enough you're gonna need it."

We hung up, and I dropped my phone on the bed, wondering if I should have told her I'd never been on a date before. I didn't know how to do this. Any of it.

Most days, I felt like a barely functioning adult. Until I arrived here, my days consisted of living in my PJs, eating dry cereal out of the box, writing a chapter or two, and having to do a sniff test to remember if I put on deodorant. I was not good with the people-ing. People were complicated. And scary. And they always betrayed you in the end. Which was why I avoided them at all costs.

At least, I did until Blackwood took that option away from me. Now people were thrown in my face at nearly every opportunity.

As far as trials by fire went, I suppose it could be worse. I was definitely out of my element, but I'd be lying if I said I hadn't come to look forward to my interactions with Kai and Caspian. I hadn't had enough with Tor or Cain to put them firmly on the list, but I was definitely drawn to them, which was more than I usually felt around anybody else.

Before Blackwood, my world had been so small, and then I got sent here and it sort of blew up. Now my life was new and terrifying and . . . exciting.

For the first time in as long as I could remember, I was excited to see what the day would bring. Unless it was another ghost. You could cancel my subscription to the vengeful ghosts, please. Thankfully none had seen fit to bother me since the episode in the hallway, and I was really hoping it stayed that way.

So yeah . . . I was safer alone, but did I want to settle for safe? Or did I want to risk everything and embrace the excitement?

The answer was obvious. It was time for me to let someone other than Kiki in.

The only question left was, which one of them would it be?

TWENTY-SEVEN

HOOK

It's been four days since my fingers were in Dahlia's slick cunt. The memory played in my mind on a loop. I'd caught myself countless times on the cusp of going to her, only to let out a string of curses and march myself back to my room.

I was Captain bloody Hook, for fuck's sake. I didn't chase *anyone*. They came to me, and I barely needed to so much as crook a finger to encourage them. If I wanted to get my dick wet, all I had to do was wink in a mermaid's direction. Case in point, the four sirens standing near the edge of the loch, dressed in the colors of a stormy sea, shells woven into their long tresses.

"Oh, Caspian, would you like to say a few words? Nautica always said you were going to marry her one day."

What? I certainly was not.

"She loved you even though you two couldn't be together. I always thought you and I would share her."

"I'm sorry, what the fuck did you just say? I couldn't possibly have heard you correctly. You thought *you* were going to share her with *me*? Assuming I was even interested in monogamy, what the hell makes you think you're on my level, fish boy?"

The merman blanched, eyes casting around for assistance. "Well, you know, clearly you're destined for greater things or . . . or . . . something," he finished lamely, so clearly out of his league that it was hard not to laugh.

"She was a lovely creature, I'm sure. But I barely interacted with her. I most certainly wasn't planning to . . . marry her. That's ludicrous."

"Oh please, Caspian. Just a few words. It would mean so much to her. To all of us."

"Oh yes, please do! You have such a lovely way with words."

"Oh, bleeding hell." I shook my head and took a step forward, readying myself to knock them off their fins. "There once was a lady with fins. Who loved to make all the men sin. She sucked on my cock, and drowned in the loch. Never to be heard from again."

Damn, I was good.

I'd infused just enough of my glamour into the performance that despite my irreverent words, the gossip all applauded loudly.

"Bravo! Bravo, Captain."

"She would have loved that," one of the females said, her eyes shimmering with tears.

"We'll have it engraved on her tombstone," the merman said, wiping his own eyes as he worked to control the emotion in his voice.

"Yes, yes, that's lovely. Am I free to leave now?"

They sniffled their agreement, and I made haste, eager to get on with my evening's festivities. Most notably, getting the delectable Dahlia under me. I'd gone to my room that night with my fingers smelling of her and come so hard in the shower I was worried one of the orderlies might have burst in on me because they were afraid I'd been attacked by the Ripper.

That devil was really starting to piss me off. Security had noticeably tightened after the mermaid was slain on the grounds. It was hard enough coming and going without anyone being the wiser. The last thing I needed was a damned guard poking his nose where it didn't belong.

Especially tonight.

Tonight I was going to try and corner a deadman. Adonis, that is.

I adjusted my leather bracelets as I made my way back to the living quarters so I could collect the pixie dust I'd need to pay off the guard, but I stopped when Dahlia called my name.

"Well, hello there, darling. Fancy seeing you here. Out for a sunset stroll?" I worked to keep my swagger at the usual level of smolder. For whatever reason, she seemed to disarm me, and I felt like a fool floundering to find my words when I was around her.

She tilted her head, her hair down tonight and spilling over her shoulder. I hated that I noticed. When had I ever fucking noticed a woman's hair and the way the sun's last few rays made it glimmer like starlight? It took everything in me not to lean in and smell it.

"I guess you could say that. I was actually looking for you."

"Oh, you were, were you?" *That's more like it; she comes to me, not the other way around.* But then I reached out and took hold of her white-gold tresses, and my fucking heart flipped in my stupid chest at the feel of their silken texture.

If I didn't get over this affliction right the fuck now, I was going to punch myself in the face.

"You're taking me on a date tonight."

"Am I?"

"Yes. I figure since you've had your fingers inside me, it's the least you could do."

Annnd I was hard as a godsdamned rock. Fuck, she was going to catch sight of my cockstand any moment.

"Well, you see, as much as I would love nothing more than to take you out and show you the night of your life, I have an appointment this evening."

"Here?"

"Not technically."

Her brows lifted, and she took a quick peek around before leaning in and whispering, "You're making a break for it?"

The scent of honeysuckle assaulted my nose, answering my earlier musing. I would give all the treasure in Davy Jones's locker if she didn't look down and notice the wet spot on my trousers from how she made my cock weep.

"I like to think of it as a mutually beneficial arrangement."

"You're bribing a guard and leaving the grounds? Now I have to go!"

"I'm not sure if that's the best . . ."

But she was already spinning away and beelining back to her quarters. "Let me just grab a jacket. I'll be right back. Don't you dare ditch me, or so help me, you will never get in my panties again."

Oh, she knew exactly where to aim her punches, didn't she? Little minx. Fuck, I liked her. And I didn't see the harm in her joining me since I was reasonably sure I could keep her safe. So long as the Ripper didn't happen upon us. Then I was only *mostly* sure, but I'd do my damndest to keep her out of his sights.

"Far be it from me to do anything that might jeopardize my access to your knickers. I have to go back to my room first. Meet me by the pixie tree in five minutes, love."

She nodded, her hair fluttering behind her like a kite I wanted to chase. Her likeness would make a beautiful figurehead for my ship, with those curves and her angelic face.

I had to bite down on my knuckle to keep from groaning aloud. I wondered how Dahlia felt about ships. Did she get seasick? Or would she embrace the . . . motion of the ocean, as it were?

Focus, you bilge rat. Go collect the pixie dust from your hideyhole, and then get back here. You don't want her to think you've abandoned her. Especially if she's serious about making good on her threat.

I told her five minutes; I was back there in two, waiting while heaving for breath because, yes, I'd run like a complete tool.

By the time she returned with her aforementioned jumper in hand, there was no containing my smile. I pushed off the tree and met her halfway, offering her my elbow.

"Well, sweet girl, are you sure you're ready for a night of drinking and debauchery?"

"Oh yes."

"Are you sure? You seem like such a good girl. I'd hate to corrupt you."

I wouldn't, I'd fucking *love* it.

Dahlia's laughter filled the air. "Oh please, I write about women who get railed in every hole. I'm not that sweet. Get moving, pirate. We have a date."

≈

"The Hag's Tooth? Really? That's what they decided to go with?" Dahlia asked, disgust crinkling her nose.

"A band of ghosts called The Haunts? Those who live in glass houses . . ."

She gave a little gasp, wide eyes shooting to mine. "Oh, that's how it is? You really want to do this, Captain *Hook*?"

I waved both of my intact hands at her. "That was only the first guy."

"What do you mean, the first guy? There's more than one guy? How many guys are there?"

"No clue. Dozens, at least. Or at least there were. I'm the current and only iteration for the time being."

"Dozens? How does that even work?"

"It's called belief, darling. Faeries are fueled by it. Captain Hook exists because people believe he exists. As long as there is belief, there will always be a Hook."

"I *do* believe in faeries," Dahlia teased.

I pinched her ripe behind. "And we love you for it."

"So how did you become him? Hook, I mean."

Shrugging, I reached for the door. "I can't remember. But all I know is when one dies, another replaces him. I am him, and will be until my time comes."

"Better avoid Florida, then."

"What?"

"Florida . . . gators . . . crocodiles? Never mind."

Pressing my palm on the swell of her hip, I ushered her inside the bustling pub.

"Wow, this place is way busier than I expected for such a sleepy town in the middle of nowhere."

"That tends to happen when it's also the *only* place in town."

"Fair point. Lead the way, good sir."

I feigned an affronted scowl. "I'll have you know that I have never been good a day in my life."

She hummed, her eyes flashing with mischief. "Oh, I dunno about that. You were pretty good the other day."

If she only knew how sexy her voice was when she dropped it the way she did. That husky whisper colored with a bit of need went straight to my cock. I couldn't help but wonder how set on this date she was. Maybe I could convince her to fool around in the washroom. Or if there was live music, maybe I could take her on the dance floor. Or beneath one of the tables. After the way she dripped all over my fingers during our impromptu movie night, I just knew she'd get off on the thrill of being caught.

I had to adjust myself as we walked to the bar. Pressing her up against the wood, I leaned close and rocked my hips into her as I breathed in her scent. "I can be exceptional tonight, sweet girl."

"Why, Captain Hook. Is that a plank in your pocket, or are you just happy to see me?"

Taking her earlobe between my teeth, I bit down just enough to make her groan, then I backed away. "I'm always happy to see you, love." Unable to resist myself, I winked and added, "But if you're in search of a bit of wood, I can definitely supply some."

Catching the eye of one of the bartenders, I waved her over. She gave me a little nod, finishing up the drink she was pouring and hustling over, completely ignoring the line of customers that had gotten here before us.

Eyes locked on me, the bartender asked, "What can I get ya, love?"

Offering her my most dazzling smile, I gave her my order. "Two pints of whatever's on draft, my lovely."

"Oi, how come he's got head-of-the-line privileges?" a bearded man complained from the back of the queue.

I didn't say a damn thing, simply winked at the barmaid and took the glasses she offered before handing her a couple of notes.

Accepting the nearly overfilled glass, Dahlia cocked a brow. "You're just a shameless flirt, aren't you?"

"Yeah, why?"

She laughed and shook her head. "You would completely miss the point. I bet you can't go a day, hell, a single hour without trying to get into a woman's pants."

"Care to wager on it?" I asked, certain I'd prove her wrong and end up balls deep inside her perfect heat as a reward. Fuck, I might have to excuse myself to the loo and have a moment to myself to take care of the way I was reacting to being with her. I hadn't been this pent-up in ages.

"I'll take that bet." She held her hand out, but just before I could grasp it, she pulled it back. "But first, let's be clear on the rules. No flirting. No sexual innuendos. I expect a proper conversation, eyes on my face, and you keep your hands and other body parts to yourself unless I invite you."

"And when I win? What are you going to reward me with, darling?"

"Guess you'll just have to wait and find out. But when *I* win, I'm claiming one secret of my choosing."

"That's all?"

"Something tells me it's going to be more than you want to part with. Which makes it priceless."

Never one to shy away from a wager, I held out my hand. "Shake on it?"

"I can't wait to take you down."

Her palm fit into mine so perfectly, and it took everything in me not to lean in and tell her she could take me down and ride me until the sun came up. But that would have lost me the bet already. I was far more clever than that.

"Shall we find ourselves a little booth in the back?"

"Sounds like the perfect place to talk and get to know each other better."

Part of me wanted to gag at how positively boring that sounded. Another part was undeniably curious about the woman in front of me. She was a riddle I couldn't quite solve. Equal parts innocent and vixen. Haunted but free. Independent yet in need of a protector. I wanted to learn more.

In truth, I wanted to learn everything.

Maybe then I'd finally be free of this fascination with her.

A little voice inside my head told me I was a fool to think I'd be able to live without her now that I'd tasted her lips and felt our connection, but that was the same voice that always ruined every plan I made. Who needed a conscience when you had all this swagger? No one.

Sliding into the booth, I waited for her to join me, equal parts hoping she'd nestle into my side and take the complete opposite end. She opted for the latter, which made keeping myself in check much easier, until she stripped out of that jumper she'd brought and leaned forward. Gods, her tits were right there, ready for ogling.

No. No, Caspian. You are stronger than this. You never lose. Don't give in to her flagrant attempt to foil you.

"Cas?" Her voice broke through my internal struggle.

"Sorry, sorry. Yes, I'm listening."

"What were you so focused on over there? Did you lose the bet already?"

"You'd know if I lost, Dahlia," I said, purposely using her name instead of my usual endearments.

I drained my pint with my eyes never leaving hers. A challenge I wanted to see if she'd meet. She smirked and did the same, wincing as the last of the carbonated beverage went down her throat.

"Another?" I asked, flagging down a barmaid.

"Don't think I can't see straight through you. Getting me drunk won't make me forget the rules."

"You play your way, I'll play mine," I said, eyes drifting over to the woman sidling up to our booth.

"Another round? Did ye want to order something while you're at it?"

"I think we're good on food," I said, eyes shifting to Dahlia to confirm. She nodded, so I turned back to our server. "Just two pints, please."

"All right then, just a reminder that the kitchen is closing early tonight due to the curfew. So if ye change yer minds, do it soon."

"Curfew?"

"Aye, on account of the Ripper being so close. Where have ye been hiding? Under a rock?"

"Sort of."

"Well, there's only a madman on the loose, dismembering folks and stealing bits of them as trophies. This last one . . . he took one of her ribs, the poor lamb. Take care when you're walking home tonight. Don't go alone. You're just his type."

Dahlia paled as the woman walked away to get our drinks. "Maybe we shouldn't be out here."

I glared at the barmaid's retreating back. She just completely ruined the mood.

"You have nothing to worry about. I'll keep you safe."

"Do you think he's out there? Lurking in the shadows, waiting for his next victim?"

Aye. I did, but I wasn't about to tell her that. Seeing the fear in her eyes, I realized she was going to continue to fixate on the macabre turn of the conversation unless I distracted her. There was nothing for it. I had to lose the bet.

It was the only way to get the night back on track and chase away whatever nightmares currently featured in her mind. So I stood, held out my hand, and waited for her to give herself over to me. I was a master of redirection. It was part of my occupation, after all.

"What are you doing?"

"Dancing with the prettiest girl in the pub."

She blinked a few times, a slow smile curling her lips. "If you touch me, you lose."

Taking her hand, I pressed my lips to the back of it, eyes never leaving hers. "I know. But if I don't touch you, I've lost already."

TWENTY-EIGHT
DAHLIA

This swoony motherfucker. It wasn't enough for him to be handsome and charming; he had to say things like, "If I don't touch you, I've lost already." Who talked like that? No one. Okay, maybe a fictional person, but no one in real life.

"There's no musi—" I began, but a fiddle player started up in the corner, and Cas grinned, tugging me close.

"What was that, darling? I can't hear you over the music."

"Very funny."

He twirled me across the floor, one hand on my waist, holding me closer to his body while the other was linked with my own.

I'd never admit it out loud, especially after giving him shit about being a shameless flirt, but I loved this side of him. Playful and a bit silly. We weren't out here trying to impress anyone, nor was he being over the top by slow dancing when the beat didn't call for it. Instead he was spinning me around, twirling me away from him and then pulling me back into his body until we were both howling with laughter.

And I knew he was doing all of it for my benefit.

Hook took his wagers seriously; it was part of the reason I'd agreed to his bet. I'd seen him playing cards in the rec room more than once. He hated to lose, and yet tonight, he'd done so willingly. Just to make me feel better.

Not that he'd said that in so many words, but what other reason could there be?

"You didn't tell me you could dance," I said breathlessly when the song ended.

The man was grinning down at me, mirth shining in his eyes. "I can dance. There. Now you know. Do you need another pint?"

"What I need is the bathroom before I do more drinking." I pressed my palms to his chest and gently pushed him away. "You get our pints. I'll meet you at the table."

He was still watching me with that sexy smirk when I walked away, so I put a little extra sway in my hips for him. Right before I disappeared down the little hall leading to the bathrooms, I glanced over my shoulder to see if he was still watching.

There was no containing my smile when I saw that he was. And that he looked about two seconds from following me. Sweaty bathroom sex with Captain Hook? In theory, it sounded fun, but I really didn't want a bar washroom to be where I lost my v-card. I'd add it to the list of things to try later.

After taking care of my needs, I fluffed my hair and made sure the girls were still perky and in position, then I sauntered back toward the table.

Before I made it three steps, a hand wrapped around my wrist and yanked me back.

For a second, I thought it might be Hook, so I was laughing when I spun around. A quick look was all I needed to realize my mistake. The sallow-skinned man with crimson eyes was no pirate. I was still pretty new at interacting with supernatural creatures, but the fangs glistening in his mouth gave him away.

Vampire.

"Where do you think you're going, little one?"

Once upon a time, that dark, rumbly Eastern European accent would have done me in, but not today. I had more than enough handsome on my plate.

"Fuck off, Dracula. I'm not interested." I yanked my arm free of his hold and continued toward the table.

Not taking no for an answer, the asshole grabbed me by the nape and turned me around to face him. His eyes locked on my throat before he leaned close and inhaled while dragging his fangs along the tender skin of my neck. "Fuck, you're pure. You'll be delicious. Look into my eyes, precious."

A strange tickle flitted across my brain. It was such a strange sensation that I froze, my eyes blinking like the act could brush off the shadowy touch. As soon as my eyes snapped back open, the sensation was gone.

And so was the vampire.

My breath caught in my throat at the sight of Cas holding the pasty fuck at knifepoint, the man's exposed sternum sizzling where the blade touched him. We'd be having a conversation about that once we were back at Blackwood.

Before I could take a step toward Cas, I was engulfed in a powerful set of burly arms, and the scent of clean, cold air mixed with the wild charge of an oncoming storm. It was fresh but feral all at the same time. It was undeniably Tor.

"Go. Get her away from here," Cas demanded, sparing us the briefest glance before nicking the vampire's skin. "I've got this handled."

A low growl erupted from Tor, and I twisted in his arms in time to catch him baring his teeth. It was obvious by the wild look in his obsidian gaze that he hadn't registered Hook's words.

"Kærasta," he rumbled, holding me so tight to him I had to fight to draw a breath.

"Tor," I squeaked. "Can't. Breathe."

He shook against me, clearly fighting hard against an impending transformation. If his beast took over now, this pub would turn into a slaughterhouse. I had to try and redirect his attention.

"Tor, baby. Look at me."

A low growl vibrated from deep in his chest, but he gave me his eyes, his expression tortured as he desperately fought to control himself.

"I'm safe. You and Cas saved me from him. You did everything right, baby. Everything."

He sucked in a deep breath, his eyes fluttering closed as he dropped his forehead to mine. His hold on me loosened just enough I was able to wiggle my arms free so I could cup his cheeks.

"I'm right here. I'm safe. He didn't hurt me. You got here in time."

That seemed to be what he needed to hear because with each ragged inhale, he relaxed further. When his eyelids finally opened again, the whites were back, and there was the tiniest sliver of midnight blue ringing his dark irises.

"Dahlia," he whispered. "You're all right."

"Yes. Not a scratch on me, big guy."

He pressed his lips to the crown of my head and

inhaled, his arms tensing around me. "You smell like pirate. Hook was all over you."

I can't say I'd ever been sniffed by a guy before. It was surprisingly erotic, and I was more than a little flustered when I managed to reply. "I *am* on a date with the guy."

"But you're mine."

"Okay, caveman. God, you alpha males really do like to stake your claims, don't you? Why don't you just pee a circle around me while you're at it?"

"You mock me, but don't think I wouldn't if I believed for a second it would protect you."

Well then. At least he was stringing together complex sentences again. Progress. I didn't mind the grunts, though.

"You disappeared on me. *Again*. What was I supposed to think?"

"I am your mate. So long as I live, I will always return to you."

The vow was swoony as all hell, but his matter-of-fact delivery left a lot to be desired. I didn't appreciate him talking to me like I was the one who'd fucked up. He ghosted me. He didn't get to be upset.

"Ugh, you're so frustrating. How was I supposed to know that? We haven't talked about it beyond you calling me kareesta and saying I'm yours."

"Kærasta."

"Yeah, that."

"I've shared with you the importance of that name. What else is there to talk about? We are fated."

I scoffed. "You say that like we're Viking married. News flash, we're not. I wasn't there. No one pronounced us husband and wife."

"Easily remedied. We're in Scotland. I could have us handfasted before morning."

301

"Handfasted? Big guy, it's the twenty-first century. No one handfasts anymore."

At least, I didn't think they did. I made a mental note to check.

"Ah, Viking, thank you for taking care of my girl while I disposed of the rubbish." Cas appeared at my side and held out his hand. "Come on, darling. Ready to continue our date?"

Tor's menacing growl made the hairs on the back of my neck stand on end.

"Mine," he snarled.

Caspian quirked a brow. "Is that right? I don't see your mark on her body or your ring on her finger. Correct me if I'm wrong, but by every law that matters, that means she's unspoken for."

"Jesus, you two are stifling. I can barely breathe through the pheromones." I wriggled out of Tor's hold and returned to our table, where a full pint awaited. Belatedly, I acknowledged that if Tor hadn't wanted me to go, I'd still be locked in his arms. I was no match for his strength, which meant he didn't see Cas as a true threat.

But maybe he should. Just because the pirate would probably lose in a fistfight didn't mean he wasn't as capable of stealing my heart. I was trash for more than just brawn. A witty mind and sharp tongue lit up all kinds of pleasure centers in my brain. Cas had those in spades.

"Sit down, you two. This date just became a threesome."

"Oh goody," Caspian murmured, while Tor . . . brooded.

My Viking was having the most epic sulk. It was sort of cute. Or it would have been if I wasn't the reason for it.

"Lighten up, Hemsworth. She's got space for both of us in her heart. Don't you, sweet girl?" Cas flagged down a server and ordered a pint for Tor, then downed half of his. "Now, what shall we do to pass the time? A game? Perhaps a bit of healthy competition to see which of us can properly seduce her?"

Tor grunted. "I'm her mate. There's nothing you could do to best me."

I finished my pint and let out a tiny ladylike burp before giggling. "Me Tor. Me angry. Grrrrr."

"She's pissed. I do love a lightweight. So entertaining."

"Was that your plan all along? Abscond with her and get her to lower her inhibitions so you can take advantage of her?"

"Hey now! Captain Hook does not need to take advantage of anyone, thank you very much."

"He's right. I absconded with myself. He's just a sexy bonus."

Tor grumbled under his breath, "*I'm* a sexy bonus. He's a dirty pirate."

Patting him on the thigh, I sighed. "You know, that was almost a whisper. I'm a big fan of whispers."

Cas leaned forward, his voice dropping until it rolled over my skin like the faintest caress. "Is that so, love?"

I nodded. "In one of my favorite romantasies, the hero and his scrappy sidekick have a whisper off to see which is the more epic Cicero. No . . . Lipshitz? No, that's not right either. You know, the guy with the nose who fed the other one lines to help him get in the chick's pants. Sirius. Ugh, you know who I mean."

Hook tried to fight his laugh but failed. "Cyrano."

"That's the one!" I shouted. Then I giggled again. "I don't know if you realize this, but I have a bit of a word kink."

"What's a word kink?" Tor asked, his brow furrowing adorably.

"Why so serious?" I asked, deepening my voice in my very best Joker impersonation.

"What is she doing?" Tor glanced at Cas for help, but the pirate only stared at me lovingly.

"She's pure chaos when she's been drinking. Brilliant."

I didn't remember being such a lightweight, but I also couldn't remember the last time I'd gone out drinking with anyone. All I knew was this was the most fun I'd had in months. Maybe longer.

"Okay, enough posturing. There's only one way this can end. Two of you enter, one emerges with the prize."

Cas continued grinning. "What's the prize?"

"Me. Obviously."

"I'm listening."

"Whisper to the death. Whoever ruins my panties first wins."

"I don't need to whisper to do that," Tor said smugly, reaching for me.

I scrambled away from him. "Nuh-uh. No touching. Use your words, just like your mommy taught you. Well, maybe not *just* like she taught you. That might be weird."

"Allow me to demonstrate, Viking." Cas leaned in and locked eyes with me before lowering his voice to a seductive rasp. "If I could, I'd write a song about the way your lips taste. Would you let me feel them if I promised to make you come? Again?"

Lightning flashed in Tor's eyes, and I knew Cas was seconds away from losing his tongue if I didn't act fast. Giving him a little golf clap and a small nod, I teased, "Solid first attempt. What have you got for me, sexy?"

Tor gave a resigned sigh, but his gaze was hot when he

leaned in, taking his time to brush my hair off my neck and lean in close. Jesus, was it hot in here? I was sweating.

"Would that I could lay you out across this table and worship between your perfect thighs until you trembled under me. Would you like that, beauty? My tongue inside you while the pirate watched on in dismay?"

I think I swallowed my tongue.

"Uh . . . um . . . o-okay."

Tor chuckled. "I think we can both agree I'm the undisputed winner."

"Not so fast. You touched her, which was clearly against the rules. Bad form. I win by default."

"Let's, um . . . let's call it a draw, boys. You both can have me. I mean, take me. I mean . . . fuck. Walk me home."

"I think I preferred it the first way," Cas said with a soft laugh.

"Settle the tab, pirate. We're taking my mate home and tucking her in bed."

We got up, and I immediately wobbled, far more unsteady on my feet than I'd expected. I guess four pints was a lot for me. Before I could attempt a graceful exit again, Tor had me in his arms, cradling me as he carried me out of the bar.

∿

TOR

DAHLIA'S EYES fluttered shut almost instantly, her arms slung around my neck, her face pressed against my chest. She made content, sleepy noises as she inhaled my scent. I don't think she realized she was doing it or that she was currently talking in her dream state.

"Yummy Viking."

Fuck, the feel of her body on mine was intoxicating. I wanted to keep her with me always. Perhaps I'd bring her back to my room so she could roll around in my sheets with me instead of returning her safely to hers.

"It seems our little writer has a scent kink too. Noted." Hook sauntered down the road by my side, but his steps faltered as a ghostly figure appeared under the lamppost. "Hold on. Adonis, you and I need to have words!"

Dahlia stirred in my arms as Caspian wandered away. The spirit was making her restless.

Not wanting her rest disturbed, I called out, "See to your business. I'm taking her back."

He gave me a distracted nod, his attention pinned on the smirking ghost.

"I made you no promises, you scallywag. It's not my fault that poltergeist stood you up. I'm not his keeper." The spirit cackled, strange mirrored eyes flashing in the yellow light.

We were too far away to catch Caspian's clipped reply.

The walk back to Blackwood was long and required me to carefully pick my way through dense forest and rocky terrain. But I hardly noticed it. I had my mate in my arms. I would have walked to the ends of the earth if I had to, so long as I could keep her safe and with me.

Thankfully I knew the way back, having had to track Caspian and Dahlia, who'd used some sort of magical means to cover the distance. They never realized I'd been following them, but the second I saw her place her arm in his, I'd been helpless to do anything else. Where my mate went, I followed.

Jaw clenched, my eyes traveled across her moonlit face, a little snarl escaping at the shadowy bruises marring her lovely neck. That fiend had touched what was mine. If I'd been there like I should, it never would have happened. The bloodsucker would never have had a chance to get close to her. I'd almost been too late.

Never again.

No one touched what was mine and lived.

The pathetic guard who'd let Hook and Dahlia leave was still unconscious at his post after I'd put him in a sleeper hold so I could follow. Come to think of it, should he have woken by now? Worried I might have killed him, I gave him a not-so-gentle nudge with my boot. A loud snore escaped as he fell over onto his side.

Not dead, just out cold. Perfect.

Striding confidently across the grounds, I kept my eyes trained on the surroundings, not wanting anyone to stop us or question what the beast was doing with her. Not that I needed to worry. The hour was late, and those lurking in the shadows didn't care about any business but their own.

Dahlia's sleepy fingers toyed with my hair as I climbed the staircase, and all I wanted was to feel her clutching the strands and tugging as she found her release against my mouth. If I could prove to her she didn't need anyone other than me, I would. Seeing her with that pirate, smiling and laughing as though he was the only man in her world, raised a very real fear that I was failing as her mate. And honestly, I absolutely was.

My brother had found his fated mate and had done everything he could to keep her. Which included sharing her with three other men. The only time he'd left was because he'd been shackled and removed from this plane. But me? I continued to distance myself from Dahlia, afraid the monster within would harm her. How could I say she was mine if I wasn't present for her? If I wasn't warrior enough to win this battle, did I even deserve her?

Her door came into view, and against all my urges, I opened it and placed her on the bed, hoping she'd stay asleep just as much as I wanted her to wake.

She looked so beautiful lying there. Peaceful. Trusting. Mine.

"I'll do right by you, Kærasta. I swear it. I will spend the rest of my days atoning for the ways I have failed you. I vow that I will be your devoted mate from here on out. I will be the man you deserve, or I'll die trying."

Leaning down, I brushed my lips across her forehead and allowed myself to breathe in the sweet scent of her hair before pulling back.

"Are you going to claim me now, Tor?"

I shook my head, my jaw clenched tight as I pressed a tender kiss to her lips. Godsdammit, I wanted more. I wanted to take that kiss and turn it from something chaste and romantic to something carnal and primal. But I forced myself to regain control. "Not tonight, my beauty. One day, yes. But when I do, you will be in a position to remember every last moment."

"Will you at least stay until I fall asleep? I'm peaceful when you're near."

The earnestness of her request shattered my resolve. There was only one answer I could give her. "As you wish."

SESSION TRANSCRIPT: NOVEMBER 15TH

Dr. Masterson: This is Dr. Elizabeth Masterson. It is November fifteenth, and the time is 10:00 a.m. This is a recorded session with resident Malakai Nash. Kai, it's been a while since our last session.

<<rustling paper>>

Kai: Got your notebook ready for me, I see. And here I thought I wasn't your biggest problem child. Guess I proved that wrong.

Dr. Masterson: What makes you think that you are?

Kai: Well, I nearly burned down your damn tree and murdered those wee pixies. Not to mention the Novasgardian. Murderous rampages tend not to go over very well in places like this.

Dr. Masterson: Is that what it was? A murderous rampage? What an interesting choice of words, Kai. Especially given the current climate.

Kai: Are you implying I'm the Ripper, Doctor? I'm flattered you'd think I was able to use as much restraint as he does. I think I've proven myself to be much more of the burn-it-all-to-the-ground variety of monster.

Dr. Masterson: *clears throat* Yes, well. You know what they say about assuming.

<<dead air>>

Kai: *dark chuckle*

<<clothes rustling>>

Kai: Do you really think I'd tell ye if I was?

Doctor Masterson: You seem to be more playful than you have been in our past sessions. Why do you think that is?

Kai: Aren't you the doctor? You tell me.

Dr. Masterson: I think you're reconnecting with your dragon.

Kai: It'd be best for all involved if you're wrong.

Dr. Masterson: I see you didn't deny it.

Kai: It's complicated. He's been . . . talking to me. Knocking at the door between us. Asking for things.

<<book snaps shut>>

Dr. Masterson: There you are.

Kai: What?

Dr. Masterson: Your dragon tattoo. He opened his eyes. He's listening.

<<zipper>>

Dr. Masterson: Why are you hiding him away, Kai?

Kai: I'm not. I'm just cold.

Dr. Masterson: *tsking* We both know that's a lie. Dragon shifters run hot. You could walk stark naked through a snowstorm and not feel it.

Kai: Maybe I just don't appreciate your eyes on me, Doctor. It's one thing to play around in my head. It's another to stare at my body.

<<fingers drumming on a table>>

Dr. Masterson: Why have you become uncomfortable displaying your form? We used to have to beg you to wear a shirt until recently.

Kai: Things have changed.

Dr. Masterson: How so?

Kai: My eyes are open to the future I want.

Dr. Masterson: And what future do you see that you didn't before?

<<Knocking on door>>

Joffrey: I'm sorry to interrupt, Doctor Masterson. We have a situation.

Dr. Masterson: I'm in the middle of a session.

Joffrey: It's an emergency.

<<chair scraping>>

Kai: Duty calls, doc. Guess we'll have to save that for our next session.

Dr. Masterson: *sighs* Yes, I guess we will. Until next time, Malakai. Session terminated at 10:07 a.m.

<<static>>

End of transcript.

Tucking in the front of my *Buy me books and tell me I'm pretty* tee, I grabbed my chunky cardigan and then moved toward the door. Breakfast was calling my name. Actually, it was screaming that I really needed a bagel with cream cheese and a gigantic cup of coffee.

To say I'd been disappointed when Tor wasn't in my bed this morning would be an understatement. Everything smelled of him, though. Like . . . everything. My clothes, my hair, the blankets. It had been hard to get up and wash him away.

Fighting hard to ignore the ache in my chest, one I attributed to his ghosting me a-freaking-gain, I opened the door with a little more force than necessary.

Something small and black caught my eye a millisecond before I stepped on it.

"It's either a bomb or a present," I murmured.

"It's a present. From one of your handsome lads." My skin crawled as the voice of the spirit who frequented my bathroom floated to my ears from behind me.

"Stop spying on me, Myrtle."

"My name isn't Myrtle."

"Don't care."

She huffed, but that buzzing sensation I hadn't realized I'd been feeling disappeared as she faded away. I was starting to get more accustomed to day-to-day interactions with spirits. I hadn't felt anything like the attack on All Souls Day. As much as I hoped I never would again, I knew my reprieve wouldn't last. I was a magnet for fucked-up shit. Sooner or later, it was going to catch up with me.

Bending down, I plucked the box off the floor and opened the lid, letting out a shocked gasp at what I found inside.

"You said it was a gift!" I shrieked at my bathroom friend, even though I knew she was gone. Nose crinkled in disgust, I muttered, "Are these fucking teeth?"

"Fangs."

I snapped my head up as Tor swaggered down the hallway, a travel cup of coffee in his hand.

"Fangs? Why are there fangs in a box at my doorstep, Tor?"

"Because I didn't think you'd appreciate a decapitated head."

I gagged. "E-excuse me?"

"He put his fangs on you. I ripped them out," Tor said, as if it was the most natural thing in the world. There wasn't an ounce of remorse to be found.

"You are a fucking psychopath."

"I prefer Berserker, but they are not mutually exclusive."

I shook my head, grumbling under my breath, "First boyfriend you've ever had, and you get the serial killer."

Tor moved close, tipping my chin up until my eyes found his. "It is my honor as your mate to present you with the blood of your enemies. I will not apologize for protecting you or avenging your honor. You are *mine*. You may not know yet what that means, and that's my fault, but you will. For as long as I live, none shall harm so much as a single hair on your head."

My knees went weak as his words wrapped around me like a big Norse blanket. Also, I made a mental note to cancel all future haircuts. My stylist didn't deserve to die because I needed a trim.

"Did we . . . uh . . . you know?" I'd been drunk, but not so drunk I couldn't remember what we'd done. I hoped. But I still needed to check.

"I held you until just before dawn, and then after I dealt with the vampire, I met Bru for a workout."

Relief flooded me. Not that I didn't want to be with him physically, but I really didn't want my first time to be lost in a haze of alcohol.

"Speaking of Bru, where was he last night? I thought you weren't allowed to go anywhere without your babysitter?"

"I passed a series of tests this week. Bruno and Dr. Masterson decided to extend my leash. So long as I check in at regular intervals, I no longer require my *babysitter*." The last word was sneered, as if it offended him to say it.

"That's great. So no more—" I held up my hands and growled.

His grin was infectious and made me smile too. "It's an effort to contain, especially when my mate is the object of affection for every creature in the bloody room, but yes."

"So I bring out your possessive side, huh? You know, in some communities, that's considered the ultimate hot guy quality."

His gaze dropped to the fangs in my palm, then returned to meet mine. No words, just a raised brow.

"Oookay, noted. You're the ultimate hot guy. Excellent."

"Glad we have that cleared up."

Look at him making jokes. "You're in a good mood this morning."

"Why wouldn't I be? I held you in my arms all night."

Fucking swoon.

My stomach chose that moment to interrupt a good thing by growling loudly and with abandon. You'd think the grisly gift left on my metaphorical doorstep would have put me off my breakfast, but apparently I was into that sort of thing. I wasn't sure what that said about me, but I was going to take a page out of Tor's handbook and pretend it was totally normal.

He wrapped his arm around my shoulder and tucked me into his side, somehow successfully making me feel petite next to his enormous frame. I loved the way it felt to be his, there was no denying that, especially not when we walked down the stairs together and Sorcha and Oz stopped their conversation to watch us.

Feeling like every eye in the room was on us, I cast my gaze around, immediately clocking Kai, Caspian, and Cain. Why did my attention find them like they were homing beacons? Kai had a plate of food in his hands, a charcoal pencil tucked behind one ear, and a level of intensity in his stare I'd grown to crave as he walked toward a table and took a seat. Cas was in a state of pure dishevelment, his clothes wrinkled and absolutely the ones he'd worn last night. The dark circles under his eyes had nothing to do with his guyliner and everything to do with fatigue, and he lacked his usual swagger. Then there was Cain. Brooding? Check. Devastatingly handsome? Check. Staring at me with a loathing only made possible by an enemies-to-lovers romance writer? Checkity check.

A little shiver rolled down my spine. I wasn't sure what I'd done to earn that look. Or what caused the little muscle feathering in the side of his jaw. My eyes dipped down, noting how he compulsively snapped his fingers to create a blue flame and then released it. Almost like it was a lighter he was fidgeting with.

Before my mind decided to do anything, I found myself angled in his direction, foot lifted as though I was going to go to him.

But that didn't make any sense.

Asshole chose that moment to rescue me. The little dog came barrelling at me with a series of excited yips. I scooped him up, cuddling the living snowball close as he climbed my shoulder and gave me his version of a doggy hug. He let out an almighty growl as Tor stepped near, and I couldn't help but giggle. Tor's beast would eat this dog for breakfast.

Hell, he might not even need to chew first.

Entirely unfazed, Tor reached out and tugged the hair elastic off my wrist, earning himself a couple of warning barks and near misses with Asshole's tiny teeth. Lazily pulling his hair up into his man bun, Tor bared his own teeth and let out a growl of his own.

I was shocked that Asshole didn't cower. If anything, he seemed to approve of the machismo display, his little tail wagging.

When I turned my attention back to Cain, I was startled to find him standing in front of me, eyes blazing.

"You keep trying to steal my dog."

"It's not my fault he likes me. Maybe you should take it as a hint that I'm not your enemy."

"Everyone is my enemy until proven otherwise, baby doll."

And there went my fanny, fluttering all over the place.

Tor let out a dry cough, reminding both of us he was right there. Cain ignored him, those eerie blue eyes locked on me.

"What do you want, Cain?" I asked, handing him the dog.

"I tried to come to you last night."

Oh Jesus. Why? Also, why did that send a thrill through me?

"Because?"

"Doc told me I had to. Apparently I didn't complete the exercise in group. So you and I need to work things out."

"Work things out? You say that like we had a fight. Did we have a fight I'm forgetting? Because I'm pretty sure you stalked off without a word. Fighting requires words, doesn't it?"

Annnd I was rambling. This guy. What was it about him that immediately twisted me into knots?

"If I want to get out of this fucking place, I need to play nice. That means you and I have to spend some quality time with each other so I can show Doc I'm making progress."

"If I recall correctly, I *did* play nice. You were the one who didn't want to try."

"Which is why I am the one coming to you."

"Is this supposed to be some weird apology for the way you ditched me after I poured my heart out to you? 'Cause it's not a very good one. If anything, it feels more like a demand."

Tor draped his arm across my shoulders, and Asshole growled again. "She only has room for one domineering alpha male in her life."

Cain finally looked Tor's way. "And I suppose you think that title belongs to you?"

"I don't think anything. I know."

Cain offered him a smile that was far from friendly. "Lucky for you, I have no intention of taking that role. But if I did, rest assured, it would be mine."

Oof, that hurt. I wasn't sure why. It's not like I needed any more male attention, and yet the thought that he didn't want me cut deep.

"I'm afraid I don't have time for you right now, Cain. Tor and I have a date."

The way my Viking's chest puffed up almost made me giggle. He was proud to be with me. Unlike the sweaty scrotum in front of me.

"Look at you. Playing at being the sweet, untouched virgin when you've got them rotating out of your bed night after night."

"What?" I asked.

"I saw you leave with Hook and return with Tor last night. And correct me if I'm wrong, but wasn't it Kai who escorted you back to your room a few nights past? My, my, baby doll, you're collecting quite a stable of willing studs."

"You sure seem to be paying an awful lot of attention for someone who says they don't care."

"I care only in as much as it affects me. Dr. Masterson wants us to work together, which means despite my feelings on the matter, the two of us will have to spend time together. Your constant flitting about from man to man makes you unavailable to me, which also means you are currently impeding my ability to leave this place."

"Keep telling yourself that, Cain. I hope you have the day you fucking deserve," I shot back. I would not let him boss me around.

I could feel his stare on me all the way to the table Oz and Sorcha had claimed. Once again, the two of them stopped talking the moment we approached, and the uncomfortable silence paired with Cain's ridiculous disdain made me snap.

"What! God, what is it?"

Oz gulped, his face drained of all color, eyes haunted. "Don't you know? The Ripper struck again last night."

THIRTY

CAIN

"God's teeth, can you control your hamster?" Sorcha snarled as she hopped over Asshole on her way . . . well, I didn't give a damn where she was going.

Asshole let out a little bark, clearly unhappy with the comparison. Or maybe he was just reacting to the tone of her voice. I was still unclear on how much the puppy understood.

I glared at the vampire as she stalked off, crouching and lowering my voice as my constant companion stood up on his hind legs and rested his little paws on my knee.

"Don't let her get to you. She only treats you that way because you're giving off little dog energy. You need to be fierce, remember? Don't take any shit. Bite first, apologize later." He wagged his tail so hard he fell off my knee, then stared at me, pink tongue peeking out of his mouth. "Big dog energy, pup. That's what you need. Every morning, we'll make sure you start your day with BDE."

Asshole yipped as if in agreement with my plan.

It was hard to fight the smile threatening to break out

on my face. The dog was still a pain in my ass, but lately he'd grown on me.

"As long as I'm here, no one's gonna fuck with you, buddy."

He trotted in front of me, head held high, tail—what little there was of it—standing tall. When Joffrey came around the corner, Asshole growled and snapped at him. The squatty man grumbled but jumped away to avoid my dog.

"Good boy. Who's the biggest badass in the room? It's you. Yes, you are. Yes, you are."

Caspian's low chuckle had my hackles rising. "Baby talk? Really, Cain? I didn't know you had it in you."

I rose to my full height slowly, jaw clenched as I met and held his gaze. I dared him with my eyes to mock me further.

"Posture all you want, but that image of you talking to the fluffball like he is your precious wittle babykins will live rent-free in my head so long as I'm alive."

I took a menacing step forward. "You breathe a word of this to anyone . . ."

Caspian laughed again. "Oh, I'm telling everyone I know."

"Not if you don't have vocal cords."

Before the pirate could reply, a man I couldn't recall seeing in Blackwood's halls strode toward us. His hazel eyes met mine, and I couldn't shake the sense of familiarity that shot through me.

I'd seen him somewhere before. I'd bet Asshole's lunch on it.

"Oh, new blood. We do love fresh meat, don't we, Cain? I wonder what he's in for." Caspian elbowed me, and I almost broke his arm on principle.

I think the only reason I didn't was because I was too busy cataloging every detail I could, the empty expanse that was my memory desperate for the one thing that would bring it all back. He was fairly nondescript. Clean-shaven, mouth curled in a pleasant smile. Not too tall, muscular, but not overly so. His hair was a light brown with a few golden highlights and a slight curl. The only thing that remotely stood out about him was the small scar above his temple.

By all accounts, he'd blend into a crowd, but something about him said I needed to pay attention. Figure out why he lit up my brain with recognition.

As he passed us by, his gaze flashed to meet mine, and I saw the same acknowledgment from him. Yes. He knew me. Who the fuck was this guy?

He disappeared around the corner, taking any answers with him.

"C'mon, Cain. We'll be late for our session."

"Since when do you care about punctuality?"

"Since I can't wait to share my good news with everyone."

"What good news?"

"That the big bad mysterious Cain is a dog dad."

"Fuck off."

He smirked. "Don't mind if I do. Dahlia is going to love it when I whisper this into her ear. It's too bad she hates you. This might've been the one thing that softened her toward you."

Annoyance knotted the muscles in my shoulders and neck. I wanted to hurl this man across the room. He was like a gnat, constantly buzzing around my face. Every time he opened his fucking mouth, my eye twitched.

He reached the therapy room before I did, striding in

and claiming one of the empty seats in the circle of folding chairs. So far, Kai was the only other person in the room. The dragon barely spared us a glance, his expression closed off and distant.

"Oh goody. You're in a foul mood too? Aren't we a merry band of sailors?" Hook settled with one chair between him and Kai, which put the pirate directly opposite me.

He spread his legs in his customary power pose and smirked at me. I rolled my eyes and almost ordered Asshole to go bite him in the junk.

As if my annoyance brought him joy, Caspian smirked and leaned back comfortably in his seat, arms thrown out and resting on the back of the empty chairs on either side of him. "It must gall you."

"The sight of your face? Why yes, actually it does."

Hook's upper lip curled. "No, I mean the fact that we've all had a taste of her. And you never will."

I knew exactly who he was talking about but forced my expression to remain impassive. "Who? There are plenty of women here at Blackwood."

"You know exactly who. Kai is the only lucky bastard who has feasted on her, but I can attest to the fact that her cunt is sweet and slick for all of us."

"Don't talk about her like that, pirate." The words left my lips before I could call them back. I shouldn't care, but I did. The knowledge burrowed deep and festered right alongside my temper. Knowing Dahlia had willingly let them touch her did something to me.

"Rein it in, Cas. She's not a chess piece you can use to win this stupid game you're playing," Kai warned. "She means more to us than that."

A shadow moved through Caspian's eyes. There and then gone. I'd say it was guilt, but that would require the pirate to have a conscience. By definition, they were morally bankrupt. Taking whatever they wanted whenever they wanted without apology. Why should he worry at all about the carelessness of his words? That would require him to *care* full stop. The only person he cared about was himself.

But he stopped talking all the same, instead turning his attention to adjusting the many rings on his fingers with as much care as a jeweler. Interesting. So the pirate had feelings, after all.

The door opened, and we all swung our heads toward the entrance, as though we instinctively knew it would be her. And it was. Dahlia walked in, face fresh and clean, eyes bright, hair pulled up into a bun atop her head. She was still in jeans and that loose shirt that read, *Buy me books and tell me I'm pretty*, but she'd lost the cardigan somewhere between breakfast and now. I didn't mind; now I had a glimpse of her shoulder as the shirt slouched off to one side.

She cast me a baleful glare before taking the seat between Kai and Hook. It wasn't like I'd wanted her to sit with me anyway. Asshole immediately jumped off my lap and scurried over to hers, abandoning me with no guilt whatsoever, just like he always seemed to whenever she was around.

Sadly, my dog was no more immune to the woman than I was. What was this hold she had over us? I hated that I was so captivated by her. By all accounts in my spotty memories, I already had a woman. One I loved obsessively. I shouldn't be drawn to Dahlia.

Tor strode into the room then, interrupting my spiraling thoughts. I'd have liked him for that reason alone. But then he took one look at Dahlia parked between the other two men and growled, reminding me that he wasn't a man at all. None of us were. We were all villainous creatures hiding beneath the skin of mortal men.

Lately I got the sense I wasn't even mortal. There was something about this power running through my veins that felt ancient. Timeless. And my run-in with that shifty demon, Drax, only seemed to confirm it. Not that I was certain I was the Morningstar. Surely someone would have come looking for me by now if that was the case.

But still . . . I couldn't shake the idea either.

Tor stood in front of Hook, exuding waves of threatening energy. "Move."

Hook simply draped his arm around Dahlia and smirked. "No."

"I said, move."

"And I said . . . no. You had her all night—at the tail end of *my* date, mind you. Fair is fair, Viking. It's my turn."

The now familiar buzz of my magic tingled in my fingers while Dahlia squirmed uncomfortably in her seat. I'd already known she'd taken off with the bastard last night and that she'd returned with the Viking, but I didn't appreciate having my nose rubbed in it. Kai didn't seem particularly thrilled either, though he managed to keep his expression neutral. If not for the appearance of Dr. Masterson and the stranger from the hallway, I think the other two men would have come to blows.

"Tor, good to see you back with us. Have a seat, please," Dr. Masterson said, her tone brooking no room for argument from the burly demigod.

He held her stare for a beat, looking like he might challenge her too, but then grumbled under his breath and cracked his neck before claiming the seat on the other side of Kai.

The man from the hallway was dressed in a lab coat

now, a notepad in his hand and an unassuming smile on his face.

"Doctor Hiddleston," Dahlia whispered, eyes locked on him.

"It's Temperance, actually, Ms. Moore. It's lovely to see you looking so well. Your time at Blackwood seems to have agreed with you."

She blushed, eyes darting down as she regrouped. I shouldn't know her well enough to so easily interpret her microexpressions, but I did. A part of me felt as if I knew her better than myself.

Then again, I didn't know myself at all, so that wasn't exactly a high bar.

"You knew?" she asked, her gaze flitting from one doctor to the next. "About . . . me?"

He smiled. "Of course. Like recognizes like, my dear. I knew the only place that could help you was Blackwood. I'm pleased to see I was right."

Dr. Masterson rested her hand on his arm like they were old friends. "Nate is visiting us for a couple of weeks at my request. I wanted to introduce you all to him today so you'd know why he was here and feel comfortable sharing with him as you do in our other sessions. Please treat him as an extension of me."

"Thank you, Lizzie." He turned his focus back to us and said, "I try to get to Blackwood at least once every year. So much to learn from your esteemed doctor's work."

Caspian and Kai exchanged a look that I echoed. These two were so far up each other's asses it was a surprise one of them wasn't wearing the other like a puppet.

Cas mouthed, "They're fucking," at Kai, and the dragon snickered.

Just as the doctors took the last remaining open seats,

the door swung open again, and Joffrey stuck his head in. "I'm sorry to interrupt, Dr. Masterson, but there's a constable here asking to speak with Mr. Nordson."

Everyone's attention snapped to the Viking.

"Why?" Dr. Masterson asked.

"Apparently he was spotted leaving the forest in the early morning hours." Joffrey cleared his throat, unable to look at Tor. "Alone. Covered in blood. And quite close to where the Ripper's latest victim was discovered."

Dahlia paled, her eyes growing wide as she made to stand, gently placing Asshole on the floor. "No. You don't understand."

"Hush, Kærasta. I'll deal with this."

What the devil was going on here? They seemed to speak to each other in nothing but tortured looks before he walked toward the door.

"Joffrey, send for Bru. Meet us downstairs momentarily." Dr. Masterson got to her feet and cast us a weary glance. "I suppose we will need to reschedule this session. Never a dull moment around here. You can see why I called for reinforcements."

Tor and the doctors left the room as abruptly as they'd appeared, leaving the rest of us to look on in confusion.

"He didn't do it," Dahlia whispered fiercely. "I mean, he did attack a vampire, but only because he attacked me first. Tor had nothing to do with the Ripper killing."

"How do you know?" Kai asked.

"All he did was take his fangs. That's it. He . . . gave them to me."

"Like a courtship present?" Caspian asked. "That's ghastly. But I suppose coming from a beast, there's a certain . . . poetry in it."

A hint of Kai's dragon flashed in his eyes, turning them

a blazing violet. "Gem, this latest kill *was* a vampire. And the souvenir the Ripper took this time was fangs."

"No," she protested, shaking her head in adamant denial. "No. It wasn't him. He was with me all night."

"Except for when he was out murderin'," Kai said.

"This has to be a mistake."

Surprisingly, Caspian was the first to try and calm her. "If it is, they'll prove it soon enough. The Ripper has been active for weeks. We all know Tor's been locked away up here. Bruno and *Lizzie* will sort it."

Dahlia's face contorted into a mask of worry, and damn it all, I wanted someone to soothe her. Me, if I was honest with myself, but I couldn't be the man to do that. It wasn't in the cards for me.

Besides, she had three others. Two of which were also in the room.

She didn't need me.

"I can't just sit here and wait. I'm going for a walk," she finally said.

"I'll go with you," Kai offered. "There's no sense in you being alone right now."

As soon as she was out of the room, he glanced back at Hook and me. "We've all seen him beast out. He can't be trusted around her."

"Do you really think he'd have the finesse to take a souvenir?" I asked.

I hadn't seen what happened when Tor was in his other form, but I could hazard a guess. And he didn't strike me as the type to carefully remove pieces of his victim. Rip them limb from limb, sure. But surgically extract?

Then again, he'd given her a set of fucking teeth so . . .

"I'm not willing to take the risk. She needs protection, and we are hers, whether we've all accepted that or not."

He rushed out of the room, and then it was just Caspian and I, Asshole sitting at my side staring expectantly. Not eager to prolong my time with Hook, I got to my feet and started for the door.

"Cain, just one more second of your time."

"What the fuck do you want now, pirate?"

Hook's smile was all teeth when I spun to face him. "Oh, just for you to remove that massive stick up your arse. Maybe then you'll be less abrasive than a barnacle on a whale's cock."

Before I could ask what he meant, he stood mere inches from me, his flattened palm in front of his mouth as he blew sparkling dust into my face. His parting words were delivered amidst a round of furious barks.

"Enjoy your evening, Cain. Can't wait to hear all about it."

THIRTY-ONE

DAHLIA

Dahlia,

While this message isn't written directly by Tor's hand, please accept it from mine. He wanted me to ensure you knew his exact whereabouts so you weren't under the assumption he'd left you again.

He and I, along with Dr. Masterson, are accompanying the constable to the Inverness police station so Tor can provide his full cooperation and statement proving his innocence. He is not being arrested or charged with anything, and the doctor assures us this is the right decision for everyone's safety.

This may take a considerable amount of time, as we have to travel by mortal means to avoid traumatizing the human constable. Please rest assured you will be Tor's first stop when he returns.

337

Best,
Bru

I set Bruno's note down with a heavy sigh. I'd already read it about seven times since it had been delivered an hour ago. Some of the worry that had sat heavy in my chest since this afternoon had eased thanks to Bru's reassurances. Some . . . but not all.

Tor wasn't out of the woods, but it seemed like things were going in that direction. I had to trust that Bru and Dr. Masterson would keep him safe.

Or maybe he'd turn into a raging lunatic and murderate everyone and it wouldn't matter.

Fuck. I was a hot mess. No, I was a spicy goddamned disaster. A whole-ass disasterpiece. But I couldn't do anything to fix this, which is exactly why Tor had Bru write me this note. The sun had been down for half an hour already, and still my Viking hadn't returned. There was no way I'd be able to sleep, even with the information they'd given me. Not when he was out there with a promise to come to me.

So now I had to find a way to fill the hours from now to then without driving myself to drink. That left me with only one option. I'd do what I did best in times of stress. I'd snack and read.

Curled up on my bed with a soft, fluffy blanket, I let myself fall into a fantasy world where a heartbroken warrior and the brainwashed assassin he loves have to fight to the death. Apparently, I was really in the mood to get my feelings hurt.

Misery loves company, wasn't that the saying?

Popping a couple of cheese crackers into my mouth, I

opened my reading app and scrolled back to chapter one. I'd read this series countless times; it had turned into a bit of a comfort read for me. There was something special about books that continued to twist you up into knots even when you knew they'd end with an HEA. Sort of like a security blanket, I guess. My life may be out of my control, but I knew for a fact these two would find their way back to one another.

That's what I needed right now. The promise of a happy ending.

Right as I was reading about how the hero was ready to fall on his own blade, a knock sounded on my door.

"There better be a special place in hell for people who interrupt readers."

As soon as the grumbled words left my lips, I was off the bed and racing for the door, thinking maybe it was Tor and I'd take it all back.

"I thought you'd never get h . . ." The words died on my tongue as I was met with the one man I never expected to darken my doorway. "Cain?"

"Knock, knock, baby doll," he murmured. "I come bearing gifts."

Was he *leaning* against my doorframe? Holy Hades.

One arm was propped against the frame, two crystal glasses dangling precariously between his long fingers. The other arm hung down at his side, a bottle of expensive-looking brandy held by its neck. What really struck me was his rumpled state. His hair looked like he'd been freshly fucked. The collar of his shirt was open to his sternum, and one side of the hem was hanging out while the other was still neatly tucked in. But what really got me was the forearm porn. He'd rolled up those sleeves to the elbow and, sweet baby Jesus, the veins.

It made me think of other body parts with thick, pulsing veins.

Mouth suddenly dry, I had to drag my eyes back up to his. "Gifts?"

Without waiting for an invitation, he pushed past me into my room. "You and I are going to spend some quality time together."

"We are?"

He set the glasses down on my side table and filled each one halfway with the amber liquid. "I've figured out our problem."

"You did?"

His eyes lifted to mine, a mischievous smile quirking his lips. "Are you capable of declarative sentences, or are we only speaking in questions tonight?"

"Uh . . . I'm better on paper."

"I'm not. I'm far better in person." He took his glass and brought it to those smirking lips before downing a sip and sighing.

"Are you . . . drunk? You hate me."

"I don't hate you. I hate what you do to me."

I didn't have a response to that. I must have entered the Twilight Zone somewhere between Bru's letter and my book. Or maybe I fell asleep, and this was all a dream.

I pinched myself, wincing with a mumbled, "Ow!"

Okay . . . not a dream, then.

"Explain, please. Our last interaction versus what's going on right now does not add up. You wanted to wring my neck during our last one-on-one, and you've been a miserable grump ever since. That, plus whatever the fuck this is, does not equate."

"Equate, huh?"

"What do you want me to say? The math isn't mathing."

"Well, to be honest, I'd love to get my hands around your neck, baby doll. That's the problem."

Oh.

Oh.

"But you hate me."

"We've already covered this. I hate how you make me feel, and I'm tired of pushing it all down."

There was nothing in his eyes but sincerity. I didn't know what to do with that. Usually he was so damn hard to read.

"So this is what, exactly? A truce?"

He shrugged, taking another sip while simultaneously handing me the second glass. "Call it whatever you want."

"Well . . . have a seat, I guess. We can play twenty questions."

He plopped down on the end of my bed in the most graceless way I've ever seen. Very out of character for this man who seemed to glide through life like a god. Usually it seemed like the very air moved out of his path. Not tonight. Tonight he was all mortal.

I returned to my spot at the head of the bed and gingerly brought the alcohol to my lips, fighting a cough as the stuff burned my nose hairs on my first sniff.

"Ugh, where did this come from?"

Twisting so he was facing me, one of his legs folding on the mattress, the other bracing him on the floor, he gave me another lazy shrug. "Dunno. It was in my room with a little card. It's called Brimstone Whiskey. Ever heard of it?"

"Definitely not."

He knocked back a large gulp of the stuff and grinned. "I think it's my favorite. It tastes like my favorite, anyway. I don't know anything about myself." Leaning forward, he whispered, "I'm a mystery."

If his words had been even the tiniest bit slurred, I'd have said he was wasted. But other than a looseness of limb and a lightness about his face, he seemed completely coherent.

"That you definitely are," I agreed.

Using the hand cradling his glass, he pointed a long finger at me. "You're a mystery too, one I intend to unwrap."

The choice of words had a sexy shiver working its way down my body until it settled between my legs.

Oof, the guy was as potent as the whiskey. And twice as dangerous.

Swallowing, I shook my head. "I'm not a mystery. I'm just private. In this day and age, that makes people curious, but I promise you I'm quite boring."

"No."

"No?"

"No," he repeated, his eyes drifting over my face and then down. "I'm sure you are many things, baby doll, but boring is not one of them."

The man scooted closer until his knee was touching my foot, then he reached out with his free hand and traced my ankle so lightly I should have barely felt it. Except I did. All the way between my legs, like he was doing something dirty.

"Soft. So fucking soft," he murmured.

"Cain?"

"Do you have any idea?"

I was waiting for him to finish that sentence, but the rest never came. Instead he leaned toward me, close enough that I wondered if he might try to kiss me, but instead he set his glass on the table, returning to his previous position with one of my cookies in his hand.

"Hey, those are mine."

He took a big bite, his smile almost childlike in its joy. This was not the man who snarled and growled at me in the dining hall only this morning. He was far too relaxed. Unguarded. No, uninhibited.

"Cain . . . are you high?"

"Hmm?"

"Are you high? You know, stoned. Did you take something?"

"Nope."

I narrowed my eyes before reaching out and grabbing him by the chin. "Look me in the eyes, Cain."

He did, the blue so bright it all but glowed as his tongue darted out to lick a crumb off his bottom lip.

I was stupidly jealous of that crumb.

"If you wanted to play, you could have just said so," he whispered, hand now trailing up my bare calf. I really should have worn yoga pants instead of bike shorts. "I may not be a pirate, but I'm sure I could find your hidden treasure."

Yeah, he was high as a fucking kite. His pupils were blown; the blue sliver of his irises, while bright, were little more than thin rings. He also seemed to have trouble focusing, and all he wanted to do was touch me.

"Cain, you're not thinking clearly."

"Yes, I am."

"No, you're not. You don't even like me. Someone slipped you something, probably in this magic whiskey that just appeared in your room."

He shifted so he was on his knees in front of me, close enough to cage me in if he wanted, and it took everything in

343

me not to part my legs. But as his face drew closer, I stopped wondering if he might kiss me and focused on the few sparkles that caught the light when he turned into it.

"Why are you wearing glitter?"

"Oh, that? It's the sparkly dust Hook blew in my face earlier. I thought I washed it all off."

"Ooh fuck, he didn't. He wouldn't."

But it wasn't a question, because I knew for a fact that's exactly something Hook would do. I'd watched him hand over a vial of sparkling pixie dust to the guard just the other night in exchange for letting us slip out.

The pang of disappointment I felt that this was all some drug-induced haze was impossible to ignore. Cain didn't actually want me. That was the pixie dust talking. I could be anyone, and he'd react the same. He wasn't in any frame of mind to consent right now. But I was, so I needed to make sure neither of us did something we'd regret. Scooting away from his touch, I moved to get off the bed and put some distance between us, but he stopped me with a hand on my wrist.

"Don't leave."

"Cain, sweetie, I'm going to get you some water, okay?"

His brow furrowed. "I don't want water."

"You'll thank me in the morning, I promise."

"No. I want to drink from between your thighs."

Oh, my stars, this man.

"Not an option."

"We don't have to tell them."

"This isn't about them. It's about you not being in your right mind."

"Agree to disagree, baby doll. For the first time since I got here, I'm exactly where I want to be." Then he smirked. "Well, not exactly."

He yanked me toward him until I awkwardly fell against him, then somehow, he maneuvered us so I was flat on my back with him on top of me.

"Part your thighs like the goddess you are, Dahlia. If you won't let me have you, at least let me feel you."

Don't do it.

Don't do it.

I did it.

Of course I did it.

There was one reason and one reason alone that I didn't want to do this, and it was pixie dust. If this had been him with all his faculties, I'd already be naked.

"Cain . . ."

"Dahlia," he countered, his voice wrapping around me like velvet.

"You're making this so hard."

He rocked into me, a wicked smile on his lips. "You're making *this* so hard."

The way his rigid length rubbed along my center had me aching for release, for more, for him.

"Kiss me, baby doll. Let me know what it's like. I can't be the only one who doesn't."

I was trash for him. I'd give anything for this to be really him talking.

He hovered over me, his mouth only a breath from mine, when I caught the glimmer of dust on his lip. I turned my face to the side as he began feathering kisses over my jaw. He let out a low, rumbled groan that I felt all the way down my body.

"Gods, you taste good," he whispered.

"Cain, we need to stop. This isn't right. You're not your-self. This is the pixie dust."

Rolling his hips again, he moaned as his teeth dragged

along my neck. "Tell me what pixie dust does. How do you know this isn't me?"

"It . . ." Oh shit, was he going to make me come like this? He rolled into me again. Yeah, he just might. I didn't know the specifics, but from what I'd seen, it acted a whole lot like ecstasy. "It lowers your inhibitions. Makes your skin hypersensitive. Frees you to make yourself feel good."

"And do you think it makes you do things you don't want to do?"

"I-I don't know. But—" I broke off with a strangled gasp as he rocked into me again, this time with a bit more force.

"I know exactly what I want, Dahlia."

"And what's that?" I forced out as pleasure built in my core.

"To make you come. Can I give that to you, baby doll?"

I shouldn't have. I really fucking shouldn't have. But I gave in to this intense experience and simply nodded.

"Thank fuck."

His hand went to his belt, but I stopped him.

"Clothes stay on."

It was the only way I could keep myself from feeling like I was taking advantage. Sort of my own version of 'just the tip.'

"Make me come, Cain. But I want you to feel good too."

"We'd both feel better if you let me get us naked."

Realizing the only way he'd agree was if I made it some kind of challenge, I forced myself to sound unimpressed. "I mean . . . if you don't think you can get the job done . . ."

He let out a low chuckle. "I see what you're doing. Okay, baby doll, have it your way. Challenge accepted."

His lips returned to my neck, exploring my skin in

teasing little nips as his palm skated over my hip and up until he cupped my breast through my shirt.

"Gods, you are so soft and full. Fucking perfection."

He continued his sensual exploration, all the while rocking his hips into me with growing intensity. Shit, I was close. I finally gave him something in return by rocking my pelvis into him, giving us both an added layer of friction.

"Fuck, baby doll. Fuck. Come. Please. I need it," he gritted out, his breaths a harsh rasp.

That was all it took. I shuddered against him, my body lighting up from the inside as an orgasm ripped through me. He stiffened, grunting his own pleasure as his cock throbbed and pulsed from behind his fly, and I swore I felt the heat of his release through the fabric.

I was going to hell for this. But I didn't care.

"That was . . ."

I didn't quite have the words. Technically it was the most basic sex act, but somehow Cain had turned it into something forbidden and sexy. He'd made us come with nothing more than the grind of his erection against my clit through at least two layers of clothing. I could only imagine how mind-blowing he'd be when he had access to all his best tricks.

Instead of responding, he rolled off me and onto his back on the empty side of my bed. I thought perhaps it was over, that he'd come to his senses and would leave. Instead, he pulled me with him until I was half sprawled on top of his body, my cheek resting over his heart.

"Sleep, baby doll," he ordered, fingers trailing through my hair.

"It's too early to go to bed."

"Shhh, don't make me spank you."

Before I could unpack my reaction to *that* fun little

nugget, I decided a nap might do me some good. It wasn't lost on me that I'd have some explaining to do when I woke up, but being here, breathing in his scent and hearing his heartbeat beneath my ear, I told myself I'd cross that bridge when I got there.

I thought Cain had already drifted off, so I jolted when his sleepy voice reached me.

"You feel so good in my arms, baby doll. Don't think I'll ever let you go."

Well, what the hell was I going to do about that?

THIRTY-TWO

DAHLIA

C ain was still passed out on my bed when my bladder demanded I extract myself from the cage of his arms. I was dreading the part where he'd wake up and look at me with that mask of disinterest back in place.

Not wanting to speed that confrontation along, I opted to sit at my desk instead of back on the bed beside him, using the quiet time to open an email from Kiki.

From: Kiki.Jones@ravenscroftpress.com
To: Ruby@rubyspector.com
Subject: Premiere night video

Dee,

You said you needed to see this, but I'm warning you, it's bad. Like, creepy bad. And I don't say that lightly because I know you're one of those people who only wants to do something more when people tell you not to. But I really mean it.

Don't open it unless you want to be freaked the fuck out, ok?

Keeks

My cursor hovered over the attachment as I debated whether to heed her warning. I could just leave it alone, stay in the dark, and not have any kind of true imagery burned into my mind. Currently there were bits and pieces floating around up there, but the line between what was real and what my mind conjured up was blurry. This was my chance to know for sure what happened that night. And honestly, could it be any worse than what I'd already imagined?

Technically I'd already seen it all. If it was real, if any of what I'd experienced at the premiere had happened, I needed to know.

Cain groaned softly as he rolled onto his side, facing the wall. Part of me missed being able to see his peaceful expression. The brooding frown gone, he looked like a different person, perhaps a glimmer of who he'd been before whatever traumatic events he'd experienced had shaped him. But, the reminder that he was still very much in my bed had me putting on my headphones so I didn't disturb his rest with the sounds from this video. If it was anything like I remembered, it wasn't quiet.

Fingers trembling, breath escaping on a heavy sigh, I forced myself to click the link and get it over with.

The picture was shaky, and the quality, while clear, was far from HD. This wasn't filmed by one of the mainstream reporters who attended the event. If I had to guess, it was probably taken by a guest on their cell phone. Or maybe a pap, but they had better equipment these days, so my money was still on a regular attendee.

My suspicion was confirmed when an excited voice squeaked, "Oh my God, there she is! It's Ruby!"

Not even a second later, I appeared in the frame, walking along the carpet with Keeks at my side, a nervous smile on my face as my gaze swept the crowd. I had to admit, Kiki had been right, I looked fantastic in that red silk gown. It'd been the right call to let her dress me.

As the video went on, nothing out of the ordinary happened. The woman filming continued to ramble excitedly as actors from the film joined me on the red carpet. Pictures were taken, people hugged, and then the entire cast and crew joined me for *the* photo. The one where all hell broke loose.

I saw it the instant I recognized my father in the crowd. My face paled, and my expression went from tense smiles to blank. Then Kelsey Young, the actress playing Rebel, put her hand on my shoulder.

I flinched watching it happen because I knew what came next, but seeing it from the viewpoint of a spectator was so much worse. Kelsey gasped, eyes wide as she fell to the carpet, dead on the spot. It happened so fast that the crowd didn't react at first. The silence gave me time to take in the details I'd missed in the moment. I'd been braced for what happened to Kelsey and was prepared to see it, but what I hadn't expected was how my own eyes appeared on that screen. They'd gone an eerie milky white as my hair began to float around my face and panicked breaths sawed in and out of me.

"Holy shit. What's happening? Is this a publicity stunt?" the videographer asked.

One by one, the people near me died, and the shouts of

shock and dismay popcorned throughout the crowd. But then *I* screamed, the sound an echo of the one I'd let out in my recovered memory of the cult. My wail bowled over all the others like an avalanche, eclipsing everything else as it went on for far longer than I remembered.

The camera shook, then fell to the ground, giving me a chaotic view of the people dead on the pavement before the picture went black.

"Fuck!" I shouted, ripping the headphones clean off my head and throwing them on the desk, not caring if I woke Cain this time.

My stomach churned as a terrible sense of dread created a pit inside me. Skin breaking out in a clammy sweat, I took a deep breath, then a second, but there was no stopping the bile rising in my throat. I ran for the bathroom, falling to my knees at the toilet just in time.

I was a crying, snotty mess when my stomach finally stopped trying to claw its way out of my body. It felt like a combination of the worst food poisoning I'd ever had and a horrible hangover. My head hurt. My body hurt. My heart hurt.

All those people. I'd *killed* all those people.

Why was no one talking about it? How had they covered all of this up?

But then another voice whispered through my mind. *But you didn't kill them, remember? Kiki was there. She's still alive. Kelsey is still alive.*

The video had to be a fake. Photoshopped or CGI or whatever. People were doing crazy things with those AI deep fakes these days.

There was no way this would have escaped the notice of the entire world if it hadn't been faked. Unless it was played off as a publicity stunt, just like the person with the camera had said.

I vomited again.

Standing on shaky legs, I stumbled to the sink and splashed cold water on my face before rinsing my mouth and shutting off the tap. Unfortunately, my towels weren't where I'd put them, so I had to go to the linen cupboard and snag one. I went back to the sink so I could brush my teeth, frowning at the water running full blast.

"I turned you off," I muttered, reaching for the knob and twisting until the flow was cut off. "You better not be fucking with me, bathroom ghost. Today is so not the day."

But if my non-moaning Myrtle was around, she was keeping quiet. I stared down at the sink, waiting for . . . something. When nothing happened, I reached for my toothbrush and shivered at the intense cold suddenly surrounding me. The knob on the faucet squeaked as it slowly turned on its own, and water began flowing once more.

"Nope. Not today, Satan."

I tried to get my hand to reach for the faucet, but I was too busy clutching the porcelain and keeping myself upright. I'd gone from one shock to another in rapid succession, and my body was struggling from the surge of fear and adrenaline. It seemed like my fight-or-flight response was busted. Or maybe I had the third, never spoken about variety: freeze.

My breath puffed out in a little cloud, and as my eyes lifted to the mirror, I noticed the way it fogged. Like I was outside in negative-degree weather, not in the magically temperature-controlled suite I'd been assigned. I'd felt this before, the innate sense of menacing unrest, when I followed that presence out of the rec room and down the maze of hallways. It was back.

Voice caught in my throat, I stared on as an invisible finger dragged across the fogged mirror, slowly creating a distinctive letter D. I wanted to scream, to run, or throw something at the mirror, but I couldn't. My knuckles ached from the intensity of my grip on the basin, and every breath I took felt like a boulder was sitting on my chest.

Just as the invisible finger got to work on the next letter, sharp, insistent barks broke me out of my trance. It was like I'd been drowning and someone had just pulled me out of the water.

I gasped for breath, my knees gave out, and I went down. Hard.

God, that was going to leave a bruise.

The temperature in the room returned to its normal comfortable warmth, and I made myself get up because I could not stay here for Cain to find. Giving my mouth a quick rinse with mouthwash, I spit—refusing to look in the mirror—and hustled to my door to stop the dog from waking the entire floor.

As soon as I cracked it open, the ball of fur raced inside. His little body quivered with tension as he paused, sniffed, and then bounded into the bathroom. I didn't even have a chance to follow him before he growled, barked once for good measure, and then shot back across the room and onto the bed. I thought he'd flop next to Cain, but no. Never one to do anything in half-measure, Asshole jumped onto Cain, who'd rolled onto his back, turned in a couple of circles, and then curled up on his chest, his tiny nose pressed against his master's neck.

I'd say it was cute if I didn't know Cain would sneer at the word. Then again, I did love to poke the bear.

Back against the wall, I slid down until my ass hit the floor, and I just sat there, knees tucked against my chest, arms wrapped around them, eyes not leaving the man who slept on my bed with his adorable puppy. Asshole had scared the spirit away once; maybe he'd keep her from returning.

It was very likely my logic was faulty, but one thing was certain: I wasn't going anywhere near that bathroom alone. I was just going to sit here and watch Cain sleep like a weirdo stalker, and then when he woke, I'd beg him to stay so I could take a shower and wash away everything that had happened.

I didn't know if it was because of the video or my run-in with the ghost, but I no longer felt safe on my own. And for a woman who'd spent nearly her entire teenage and adult life that way, it was a serious blow to my pride.

Call it paranoid, but I couldn't shake the sense that something bad was out there, and that it was out to get me.

THIRTY-THREE

CAIN

Sharp rapping on my office door pulled my attention from the logbook on my desk. I laid down the quill and shot my gaze to the interloper who'd already poked his head inside.

"My lord, we have a problem with your bride."

The low-grade headache that hadn't fully diminished since my return home flared up at the words. "What now?"

"I think you better come see for yourself. She's . . . upsetting the residents."

Rolling my eyes, I shoved back my chair and cracked my neck as I readied myself to do battle with my wife. Again.

She'd seemed so docile and sweet, but that had all been an illusion.

The woman was a harpy.

She fought me at every turn, yet I'd still grow hard the second I caught her scent.

Why didn't she understand that she belonged to me? It would be so much better for us both if she'd just give in.

My footsteps echoed down the hall, a sharp staccato I

hoped she heard. I hoped she was counting my steps and readying herself for the fight that was brewing.

Maybe I should have knocked before flinging the room to her bedchamber open, but it was my godsdamned domain. I could go wherever the fuck I pleased. I answered to no one.

The room was utterly ransacked, dozens of priceless artifacts shattered from being flung across the room. All the garments I'd selected for her were shredded and tossed into a heap on the floor. And in the middle of it all, there she stood, back to me, shoulders rising and falling with her heaving breaths.

My temper surged. "I grow tired of your childish tantrums."

She picked up a crystal chalice and hurled it at me. "And I grow tired of *you*."

"You'd have to spend time with me to tire of me."

"Why would I do that? You gave me no choice but to marry you, and now you keep me captive in this dark, terrible place."

"You've made yourself a prisoner. I offered you an entire kingdom, wife. You are the one who chooses instead to cower in here."

"We may be married, but I will never be your wife."

"You have been mine since the day you were born. One day you will admit it, and you will love me as I love you."

She scoffed and poured herself a nearly overflowing glass of wine. "Your idea of love leaves plenty to be desired, *husband*." Knocking back the drink, she gritted her teeth and hurled a second chalice at me, this time hitting my shoulder. "I will never love you."

For the first time since I barged in, she allowed herself

to look at me. When her eyes locked on mine, somewhere in my subconscious, I realized this was a dream.

"Dahlia," I whispered as everything faded away and was replaced by the sensation of a tiny wet tongue licking my cheek in earnest.

My eyes fluttered open, and I was greeted with Asshole's grinning face hanging over mine. I shoved his head away with a groan. "Ugh, your breath smells like your ass. What did I say about licking me?"

"I think you like it," a soft voice said, causing me to sit up and hold the dog under his front legs so I could inspect him.

"What did you say?" I asked, my attention locked on Asshole's beady eyes.

"I said you like it," the feminine voice came again. This time, I was better able to triangulate the location. It hadn't come from my dog, as I'd feared, but from the floor.

Dahlia.

Everything snapped back into place. My arrival at her room last night. The whiskey. The pixie dust. Her soft body under mine as I dry humped her to . . . fuck, I couldn't get an erection.

A bolt of lust shot through me, quickly followed by a wave of guilt, neither emotion one I had any interest in dealing with right now.

"What time is it?"

"Early."

"Why are you on the floor? And why do you look like you've seen a ghost?"

"Because I have."

She was lacking her usual fight, and that, more than anything, woke my foggy brain the rest of the way up.

"Is it still here?" I cast my gaze around the room,

searching for the same residue I'd seen the last time an encounter left her like this.

"The bathroom. It was in there. It's been gone a while. Asshole scared it off."

I patted my dog on the rump. "Good boy. There's that BDE we've been working on."

The puppy preened, sitting taller at the praise. Our little pep talks each morning were doing him a world of good.

"Excuse me?" Dahlia spluttered. "Did you just tell your dog he has big dick energy?"

"No. He has big dog energy. What is wrong with you?"

She blushed, her shoulders curling forward as she dropped her chin back to her knees. "Oh. My bad."

I didn't like the sight of her on the floor in that defeated pose. It scratched at something within me. Something I didn't have a name for.

"Do you need me to check the bathroom? Make sure the ghost is gone?"

She shook her head. "I know it's gone. I would feel it if it was still here. That's not something you forget."

"Then why are you cowering?" My voice came out sharper than I'd intended, but I really didn't like her like this. It was . . . upsetting. And that pissed me off.

"I'm not cowering."

"Yes you are, damn you. Now get the fuck up."

She gaped at me. "This is my room, you soggy scrotum. I'll sit on the floor if I want to!"

"It's so early the sun isn't even up yet, Dahlia. Get up and get your ass back in bed. There's no reason for you to be hiding in your own room."

"Why are you mad at me? Is this because of what happened . . ." Her eyes shifted down to my pants. The pants I'd definitely come in last night.

I huffed, frustrated. "I don't know. I think I should leave. Coming last night had been a mistake."

I didn't specify whether I meant in my pants or to her room. One I regretted, the other I absolutely did not. But she didn't need to know which was which.

She stood, her entire attitude hesitant as she glanced from the bed to the bathroom door.

"What is it?"

"I just . . . I need a shower after everything."

"Then take a fucking shower."

Her lower lip trembled just a fraction before she schooled her expression. "I don't want to be alone in there."

"I'm certainly not showering with you."

There was no way I could be trusted around her naked, dripping wet body. I hadn't even been able to contain myself around her fully clothed one.

Anger swelled in my gut, my power pulsing in my veins. The first thing I was going to do when I left her was hunt down that fucking pirate. On second thought, I'd find a change of clothes first, but then his ass was mine.

"You'll be fine."

She took a shuddering breath and nodded, crossing the room until she stood, shaking like a leaf in front of the partially open door.

"Oh, for fuck's sake. Fine. I'll sit in there while you shower. Will that make you feel better?"

"Yes."

"Perfect. Let's go."

The way she held herself had me half expecting something to jump out at us, but the bathroom was empty.

Dahlia started the shower, then turned to me as the water heated. "I'm sorry about last night. I tried to put on the brakes."

She was beating herself up thinking she'd taken advantage, but she hadn't. I remembered every single second of our stolen night together. I was the one that had pushed. That had hungered and craved.

"Let's never speak of it again."

For one unguarded second, she allowed me to see her shattered expression, but then she cleared her throat and spun away. "Of course. Whatever you want."

I leaned against the sink, averting my gaze as she slipped out of her clothes, and only when she gave the all clear did I look up. I shouldn't have. Her silhouette was the perfect torture in the white shower curtain that went around the entirety of the claw-footed tub.

I should be ashamed of my behavior last night. Of the fact that I'd come to her room intent on plying her with alcohol and getting her to agree to finish that stupid assignment with me. I hadn't counted on losing myself as soon as I felt her skin beneath my hand.

To be fair, that was the pixie dust's fault, but nothing would have happened if I hadn't wanted it. The drug only enhanced one's desires; it didn't create them out of thin air. It was like an erotic truth serum. I didn't want to face the truth. I couldn't touch her again. Not only for her sake, but for the sake of the woman I'd married. The one from my dreams and my memories.

I may not remember her name or her face or even know how much of what came to me in my dreams was real. But I was still hers. Which meant Dahlia Moore was not an option, no matter what my body said.

HOOK

. . .

"WHAT THE FUCK is wrong with you?" Cain's voice boomed from behind me as I sat at my desk and studied the map of Blackwood I'd nicked from Dr. Masterson's office.

My fingers were stained with ink from jotting down notes in my book and crossing off the places I'd already searched. Nothing but dead ends and false leads. If that poltergeist had sent me on another wild goose chase, I'd . . . do absolutely bleeding nothing because he was dead and I couldn't hurt him. Fuck.

I didn't even look back at the man who'd so rudely interrupted me. I simply continued puzzling together the ghost's jumbled nonsense to try and find an answer.

"You've chosen the wrong morning to pick a fight, Cain."

"You're the one who picked the fight, pirate. In what world is drugging someone acceptable behavior?"

This time, I swiveled in my chair so I could face him. "Pirate," I stated matter-of-factly. "We're a morally gray lot by nature. The only code of honor that matters is my own."

"You have no honor."

Now that annoyed me.

"Would you like to say that again?"

"I don't need to. You heard me."

Getting to my feet, I squared my shoulders. He might be taller than me, but we were a close physical match. I could take the pampered southern rooster. "I expected you to thank me, if I'm being honest. Most people pay good money for a mere taste of what I gave you last night. But I guess you didn't find anyone to pull that stick out of your arse after all. Pity. You look like you could be fun if you just blew off some steam."

"If you think you're going to convince me you were just trying to help, you're wrong."

I rolled my eyes. "You can cease the poor victim act any time. I know why you're locked up here, Cain. You are far from innocent."

"We've established that. Gods, you love to hear yourself talk, don't you?"

"Who doesn't?" I said with a smug grin. My popularity spoke for itself.

"Try drugging me again, and you won't be able to speak."

Taking a step closer, I let out a low laugh. "And why is that?"

"You'll be dead and buried where no one will find you."

"Then I suppose it's a good thing Dahlia can see ghosts, because even killing me won't keep me away from her."

Cain ground his teeth so hard I could hear it from my seat.

Ah, touched a nerve, did I?

Leaning forward, I allowed my shit-eating grin to stretch. "That's why you're really here, isn't it? Because it fucking kills you that I've touched her and you haven't? Is the big bad villain jealous that I know what she sounds like when she comes apart?"

Blue fire lit in his eyes as he stared me down, and I'm not ashamed to admit a little flicker of apprehension came to life in my chest. But then he smirked.

"No. I'm not fucking jealous. Especially not after last night."

I quirked a brow, studying him, but his expression gave nothing away. "Bullshit. If you'd had her, you'd be in a far better mood."

"What makes you think I ever wanted her to begin with?"

"I might be self-important, but I'm not blind. I see the way you pant after her like your little dog. Say, where is Asshole this morning?"

"With Dahlia. Where I left him."

"Don't want her, my arse."

"Have you heard her whimper yet? It's such a perfect little cry. Now that she's had a sample of what I can do to her, she'll be addicted. You just turned the focus on me, and she'll never be the same. I gave her one night, and that's all she gets, but she's going to forget all about her pathetic little pirate."

I laughed in his face this time. He thought he was going to make me jealous? Ridiculous.

"Please, you were merely an appetizer. An amuse-bouche if you will. But me? I'm the main fucking event."

Cain's lip curled up in a snarl.

"Do you know what happens when a full-blooded fae takes a human lover? What we can reduce them to? If you think Dahlia will ever forget me, you're a bigger fool than I thought. I could have our pretty little rabbit on her knees crawling for me with little more than a crook, or should I say hook, of my finger."

"Fuck you," he spat.

"Is that all you have to say? A real wordsmith, you are." I ran a hand through my hair and rolled my shoulders. "You know, I'm feeling rather hungry. I have a real craving for cherry pie. If we're done here . . ."

I moved to brush past him, but he caught me by the bicep and gripped me hard. "Don't fucking touch her."

"Did you forget so soon? I already have."

That seemed to be the final straw. In less time than it

took me to draw in a breath, Cain's eyes glowed with blue fire, and his touch *burned*. A surprised gasp left my lips as the sound of searing flesh hit my ears. The agony of his touch was exquisite. For while he was physically burning me, that's not where it ended. Oh no. I felt it all the way to the depths of my blackened soul.

"Wh-what is th-this?" I forced out as he continued to burn me from the inside.

"She's mine," he snarled, his eyes a raging blue inferno.

"S-stop."

The agony was like nothing I'd ever felt as his power burned its way through my veins and into my very being. If he didn't let up, I feared I might actually perish. Me and my immortal soul. There'd be nothing left behind to haunt sweet Dahlia.

Cain only grinned. It was in that moment I realized how completely I'd underestimated him. I'd thought Tor was unhinged, but Cain was the true monster. He might be the most depraved of us all. And I'd helped him slip his leash.

"Cain, stop!" a harsh male voice barked as tattooed hands gripped his shoulders and jerked him away from me.

Kai held the man back, confusion on the dragon shifter's face and fury on Cain's.

"This isn't over, pirate. Leave her be. I'm warning you."

I wish I could say that I had a snappy comeback at the ready, but the second he let go of my arm, I sagged to the ground.

Cain let out a chilling, villainous laugh. Kai dragged him away, but the sound of his wicked amusement at what he'd done to me echoed down the corridor.

Perhaps I pirated too close to the sun? I'd always thought my greatest nemesis was Peter Pan, but now . . . was Cain Alexander the one I should truly worry about?

THIRTY-FOUR

KAI

"Look at the two of them. Pretty as a fucking picture," I grumbled, watching from high atop my tower as Tor and Dahlia strolled through the grounds.

It had been four days since he was questioned in the Ripper investigation, and from the time he returned, Dahlia wasn't far from his side. Or rather, *he* wasn't far from *her*.

As much as I'd been trying to talk myself into the idea of sharing her, it was clear the four of us had our work cut out for us. Such an arrangement required all of us to be on the same page, and with the way Cain had gone after Hook and the jealousy currently prickling in my veins, we weren't even in the same library.

Part of my issue was the strength my dragon had amassed since Dahlia's arrival. He may not have manifested, but he was there, influencing my emotions and reactions and, in some cases, burning the fucking place down. My rational brain understood groupings like this fledgling one we had. It was common in Faerie for many men to service a single woman. It was an honor if she was your mate. But most fae weren't also burdened with a dragon. Possessive, wild creatures ruled by instinct rather than logic.

It was going to be a battle, every second of every day, until he and I made peace. Not that we ever would. I simply didn't trust him. I couldn't. He was the reason we'd slaughtered all those innocent people. Glancing behind me at my shameful hoard, I took a shuddering breath, resigned to what I had to do next. My dragon needed his chains reinforced, and the only way to do that required pain and blood. My pain and blood, to be exact.

I checked the lore book one final time, double-checking the runes I'd selected, and then made a few last adjustments to my outline. Satisfied it was ready, I copied it onto my skin, covering my entire forearm in the intricate design that would create a cage for my beast. He knew exactly what I was doing. The way he thrashed within the containment of my skin on my back caused a painful sort of pressure which made me grunt and shift in order to bear the discomfort. It hadn't been this bad since he was first bound within me.

He was a powerful creature, my bloodline all but ensuring that he'd rival one of the ancients. After all, I was destined to guard the Shadow Queen's crown if ever I was called upon. Just like my father before me.

I reached for my tattoo gun, thankful for the magic that modernized every aspect of Blackwood when necessary. This tower had clearly been used as someone's lodgings a time or two in the past, and I took full advantage of the comforts it provided. The gentle buzz of the gun as I switched it on was a welcome sound in the quiet space, an old friend coming to greet me. As always, I sank into that half-meditative space where all that existed was the patch of skin I worked on and my art.

I lost track of time as I etched the elaborate swoops and flourishes, taking great care to ensure they were perfect. With magic such as this, one wrong dot and the results could be disastrous. Especially with the way the golden, magic-infused ink would disappear into my flesh once the spell was set. There'd be no do-overs. I had one shot.

Which made my dragon's insistent scratching at the barrier between us even more of a problem. He wanted me to fail. He hated that he'd been locked away, all but left to rot in his magical prison.

"What are you doing? You traitor! I could claim her for us. I could make her love us."

"You can't be trusted. You nearly killed those pixies."

"And? Pixies are nothing to us. Ants to be crushed beneath our majesty."

"And this is why you can't be given the reins," I muttered, continuing on with my work, wincing as he lashed his tail down my arm in an attempt to stop me.

"Don't you understand? You're weaker without me. We are two sides of the same coin. You can't protect her without me. What happens when the beast is all that's left of that Viking? You won't stand a chance."

A swell of fear hit me as I brought the ink-filled needles to my skin for the final bit of the design that would set my spell and lock him away. But I would just have to deal with that when the situation arose.

Because no matter how much progress Tor'd made, there was only a single petal left, which meant it was a matter of when and not if. One day, likely soon, something would set him off, and then we'd all have to live with the consequences.

I started up the gun again, drawing the lines slowly and carefully, meticulous in my artistry as I worked.

"What the hell, Kai? Is that my sweatshirt?"

The hand holding my tattoo gun jerked, and it was years of experience that had me lifting up instead of accidentally inking a rogue line into my skin. It was all ruined. In one small flinch, all my hard work was fucked because I knew that even if I hadn't ruined the design, I'd broken the power of the spell. Each line had to be continuous until it met a stopping point. That was part of the binding. Dahlia had just given the dragon exactly what he wanted.

My dragon's laugh was a smoky caress in my mind, his pleasure unmistakable as he slithered into a new position on my body. Without needing a mirror, I knew he'd ensured he was visible and that he had at least one of his eyes trained on the object of our shared obsession.

A roar of desperate fury escaped before I could contain it. Dahlia startled, her eyes as round as two marbles as I shouted, "Do you have any idea what you've done?"

"No!" she shouted back. "Fuck, Kai."

I was instantly contrite. The last thing I wanted was for her to fear me. And maybe I was also a little ashamed that she'd learned I was the one who'd been stealing her things.

"I'm sorry, gem. I didnae know it was you. Ye startled me."

"You didn't have to yell at me."

I caught the gloss of tears in her eyes and felt like a right arse. "You're right. I shouldn't have. Will you forgive me?"

Her eyes narrowed. "Will you tell me why you have a pile of my stuff in here?"

I loosed a heavy breath. "I'm a dragon. We hoard things."

"Treasure, I thought."

I just held her curious stare, allowing her to come to her own conclusions.

"My sweatshirt and silk scrunchie are treasure to you?"

"They're yours. They carry your scent."

She let out a little noise I'd come to know as showing interest. "And you . . . like my scent?"

"Aye."

"You could have just asked. I would've done something less felonious, like spray my perfume on your pillow or something."

"It's petty theft at best, and also, it's not your perfume I'm after."

Color crept into her cheeks. "I see. If you collect these because of how I smell, why do you have these other things?" She strolled toward my hoard and I nearly came out of my skin when she touched the old typewriter I'd taken from a former resident who'd left it behind.

"They're lost treasures. Things that were valued once but lost in the shuffle."

Her fingers ghosted over a few other items, like a necklace crafted of rare gems and a magic-infused dagger.

My muscles were coiled, ready for me to spring into action and protect the items I'd so carefully collected. But there was no denying the other part of me. The one that had my cock thickening in my pants and my pulse racing. The one that wanted her to pick up the jewels and drape them across her naked body.

"See?" my dragon crooned. *"She is ours."*

"So you see them as special even after they've lost their shine?"

"Aye, lass. Every one of these items is precious to me."

"You have more of mine than anyone?"

"Of course I do."

Because *you* are precious to me. I kept the words locked inside, but she might have plucked the truth from my mind.

Her breath hitched as she took her lower lip between her teeth and stared into my eyes. "Do you have to steal it, Kai? Or can it be freely given?"

My throat was dry. Why was my throat so fucking dry? I swallowed hard before croaking, "It can be freely given."

Her expression shifted then, melting from shy to coy in the blink of an eye. Not looking away from me, she hooked her fingers into the material on either side of her hips. It took a second for my brain to catch up with what I was seeing.

I had to try twice before I was able to form words as she eased the pink silk down her calves. "I already have a pair of your knickers."

"So you don't want these ones?" she teased, holding out the scrap of fabric on the tip of one finger as her dress slipped back into place.

Before she finished her question, I bolted across the room and snatched them, cradling the fabric like it was spun gold. "These can stay here. The others are . . . elsewhere."

"Naughty dragon."

"Yes, my treasure. You have no idea."

Instead of echoing my dragon's statement, I simply draped the knickers atop the pile of pilfered items. "Don't tease, lass. I cannae take it."

"Who's teasing? I'm after a trade."

"A trade?"

"I want my sweatshirt back. It's my favorite. In exchange, you can keep those." She tipped her head toward the pile.

"No deal."

"But—"

"Mine," I growled, some of my dragon slipping into the word. "Dragons don't share their treasure."

"Yes, they do." Once again, I ignored the persistent voice in my mind. It was far too soon to think about that line of thought.

"I can give you something else in return."

I narrowed my eyes. "Like what?"

"You said you loved my scent. Clearly you're a panty thief." Biting down on her lower lip again, she scanned the room. Eyes alighting on the nest of blankets and pillows in the corner, she grinned. "What if I leave it on something else. Something special and just for you?"

"What do you have in mind?"

She was up to something. Something that excited her. Her pulse was fluttering along the side of her neck, and her eyes glittered with mischief. I think I'd say yes for that reason alone.

"Talk me through it, Kai. I love the sound of your voice."

"I would, if I knew what you were up to . . ."

What the bloody hell was this vixen doing? My question was answered when she wandered to the nest in the corner and selected a small rectangular pillow before she straddled it.

"Have you ever dated a girl who had a special pillow, Kai? Or maybe it was a stuffed animal?"

It wasn't until she rolled her hips into the pillow and allowed her eyes to flutter closed that it all clicked. Oh goddess, she was riding it, pleasure chasing across her face like it was my cock she was ground down onto.

"Mmm, Kai. Would you believe mine was a dragon?"

Oh. Oooh.

"Tell me what you would do to me. Tell me why I should give this to you when I finish."

"Better yet, I could show you."

"But then you won't have a special souvenir to add to your collection."

"You drive a hard bargain, gem." I couldnae remember a time I'd been this hard in my life. Or one where I'd been so torn. Watch her hump my pillow and soak it in her arousal? Or have her take me for a ride instead?

"Take your cock out, dragon. I want to see if it lives up to the fictional dragons I've written."

She rocked her hips and tossed her head back, moaning as I stood there like an untried youth. What the hell were we doing? But then I did exactly as she asked and pulled my aching length free.

Giving myself a cursory stroke, I shuddered as my palm ran over the multitude of ridges along the shaft.

"Well, does it live up to your imaginings?"

Her pupils were blown wide, her face flushed with hunger as she eyed me. Her gaze lingered on my shaft, and I knew she was taking in the draconian symbols encircling the base. "So much better. I didn't know you were tattooed there too."

"I had to practice on someone."

She swallowed and licked her lips, her hips working over the cushion between her thighs faster. "Are those ridges?"

This time I smirked as I tightened my grip around my shaft. "For your pleasure."

She rolled her eyes but laughed as well. "We'll see about that."

"Trust me, lass. You'll forget your fucking name the

second I'm buried inside you. I will make you feel so good you'll see stars."

"Mmm, now who's teasing?"

"Show me how you'd ride me. Give me something to think about when I use those knickers you gave me to bring myself off tonight."

Cupping her breasts with her hands, she rolled her nipples beneath the fabric of her dress, drawing a harsh gasp from deep in her throat.

Fuck, she was beautiful. As much as I wanted to be the one giving her pleasure, watching her steal it for herself was everything I'd dreamed of. She looked so free. I'd never forget this gift she was giving me.

Lost to the sensations, she moaned and rocked into the pillow as I watched, only giving myself the occasional stroke because I was saving my cum for tonight.

"Watching you touch yourself, god, it's better than porn," she groaned, her hips rocking even faster.

"Same, lass. Fucking same."

"Oh, I'm close," she rasped.

"Come for me, gem. Leave your juices on the pillow for me to remember this moment by."

As if that was all she needed, her eyes rolled back, and the most erotic moan was torn from her. It was all I could do to stave off my own climax. If I thought she'd let me, I'd mark her in my spend and watch it drip down her body, coating her the way she was coating my pillow. Marking her as mine for all to see.

The primal thought had me squeezing myself at the base to keep from coming then and there.

She stood, her knees still shaking as she righted her dress and took a steadying breath. Then, the sassy woman stalked toward me, handed me the pillow, and snatched her jumper from my pile before sauntering away.

"Pleasure doing business with you, Kai."

I was still standing with my mouth hanging open and my cock in my hand when she turned back and winked before disappearing down the staircase.

As soon as she was gone, I brought the pillow to my nose and inhaled deeply, my dick twitching and dripping at the scent of her arousal. Arousal caused by me. Because she was mine just as she was theirs, and Dahlia had just proven it.

Now we all just had to figure out how not to kill each other.

THIRTY-FIVE

DAHLIA

W ow. I was a fucking bad bitch. Who knew I had it in me? I hadn't gone up to Kai's secret tower with the intention of doing anything more than exploring. After spending the morning with Tor, I hadn't been excited about going back to my room and staring at a blank white screen. I was pretty sure my cursor was a tiny blinking devil at this point, mocking me for the lack of words on the page.

They say write what you know . . .

They also say write drunk, edit sober, but you don't do that.

Maybe it's because my subconscious was searching for ideas for my next chapter. Or maybe it's because Kai's growly voice and pretty purple eyes got my blood flowing, but as soon as the idea took root in my mind, I knew I had to do it. *Me*, not the character in my book.

His expression alone was worth it.

God, the yearning. It was delicious. I could spend days trying to find the words to explain the precise look of desperate longing and never quite get it right. I'd never wished I was an artist more so I could immortalize the way his brows furrowed and his jaw clenched. At least I had my memories.

Sigh.

I was nearly down the tower stairs when I felt it, that pressure in my head, a buzzing along my skin. A ghost was nearby. My heart jackhammered as panic threatened to take over, but I was able to beat it back. This energy didn't feel the same as the terror that'd haunted me twice now. Angry, desolate, confused. That's what I got from this entity.

The swirling emotions were only getting stronger, and I was in a literal tower complete with its very own spiral staircase, so there was no way to get around it. Not unless I wanted to flee back up to Kai, but that would only prolong the inevitable. The ghost was here whether I liked it or not.

Bolstering my strength, I continued down the stone steps, bracing for the moment this specter came into view.

In the almost month I'd been at Blackwood, I'd had my fair share of ghostly encounters, but I wouldn't go so far as to say I'd gotten used to them. I'd only just started to pick up on the differences in their energy. There were the harmless ones, like the girl who lived in my bathroom. Her energy was like a butterfly's wings across my skin. Non-threatening, playful even. The ones who quietly floated about, either because they didn't know they were dead or because they had some other agenda that didn't involve the living, had similar vibes. Then there were angry ones whose confusion and fury sat on me like a weight, but I knew they couldn't actually hurt me. I wish I'd known that when I met the wolf who'd wanted to hunt me that first night. But the worst were the malevolent ones. Spirits of true evil, like the one I was pretty sure was haunting me. I didn't know for certain, but it felt like that kind could really do damage.

This was all intuition, though, little more than a very uneducated guess. I was hardly an expert. It's not like there was a class I could take, but maybe there was a book or two in the library. I should look into that. If these one-on-ones were going to become a regular thing, I should probably be better prepared to handle them. If there was a class, I definitely would have lodged a complaint that of all the ghost archetypes, we were sorely lacking in the *sexy* variety.

"This one doesn't want to hurt you. It's confused. It's not going to do anything." Sometimes I had to give myself pep talks, like affirmations every morning in the mirror, to keep going. This was one of those times.

Just as I made it to the first landing, I found her. I staggered back, my elbow smacking painfully against the stone.

"Jesus," I whispered, my pep talk not doing a damn thing to prepare me for the horror in front of me.

The woman had been murdered. Recently, if I had to guess. She was dressed like I usually was, in a pair of leggings and a long-sleeved sweater. Her hair was a loose braid down her back. I could have easily imagined her as one of the residents. She seemed as though she'd be right at home in our ranks.

If not for the bloody black holes that were supposed to be her eyes. And, you know, the whole floating in place, see-through thing she had going on. That was sort of a dead—pun intended—giveaway.

"What do you want?" I asked, my voice trembling.

She reached for me, floundering in midair as she tried to find me. "H-he took my eyes. M-my Sight."

This had to be the work of the Ripper. What were the odds there was a second supernatural serial killer running around Blackwood stealing his victim's body parts? Someone had mentioned that his souvenirs were related to his victim's gifts, but I blame my shock over finding her for my inability to put two and two together.

Something else clicked in place for me, though, and a rush of excitement swept through me. "What does he look like? Tell me. Help us stop him."

Bringing her hands to her empty eyes, she covered her face and wailed. "I can't. I can't. I . . ."

She began to flicker in and out of view, the humming in my veins fading. Fuck, I was losing her.

"What's your name? Where is your body? How can we find you?"

Shaking her head, she faded away, but before I could blink, she was back, right in my face and shouting. I fell back onto the stone steps, my reflexes wanting me as far away from her as possible.

"He's not going to stop until he gets what he wants. I've Seen it. I've Seen him. He's building his strength. Hunting." She was flickering rapidly, her body barely retaining her form as she whispered, "For you."

Oh. Fuck. No.

I was officially done entertaining the idea that I could handle this on my own.

I needed help.

I needed Dr. Masterson. She'd know what to do.

With that thought in my mind and little aftershocks of terror pumping through my veins, I took off like a bat out of hell.

SESSION TRANSCRIPT: NOVEMBER 19TH

Dr. Masterson: This is Dr. Elizabeth Masterson. It is November nineteenth, and the time is 9:00 a.m. This is a recorded session with resident Tor Nordson. Tor, please have a seat. I will strap you into the chair.

<<buckling sounds>>

Tor: How much longer do I have to endure this? It's clearly not working.

Dr. Masterson: We've been over this. Our sessions must continue until you've proven you've learned control.

Tor: *bitter laughter* I only have one fucking petal left. I think we're way beyond that now. The next time I turn, it's over. The man I once was lost forever to the beast within.

Dr. Masterson: Which is exactly why this session is more important than ever. We must persevere, and you have to control your beast rather than let it control you. One day, you will shift again. It's inevitable, but if you're in charge, it is my theory that you'll be able to find yourself again.

Tor: *disbelieving scoff* Have you never seen a Berserker who lost his mate? Mindless. Out of control. Dangerous. Wholly without a conscience. When this beast takes hold, that's what I'll be. She will be out of my reach even if she's right in front of me.

Dr. Masterson: She? She who?

<<restraints rattle>>

Tor: It doesn't matter. Once I go, I've made arrangements to ensure I don't hurt anyone else again.

Dr. Masterson: Arrangements? What kind of arrangements? Tor, that all sounds very bleak and final. I'm concerned.

Tor: No, you're not. I am nothing more than a frog for you to dissect. You want to study me. Fix me so you can be a footnote in some silly book. But you'll fail. We're all doomed to fail.

Dr. Masterson: Well, with a mindset like that, it's no wonder you haven't made any progress.

Tor: Can we please get this over with?

<<restraints rattle>>

Dr. Masterson: I thought you were worried you'd change?

Tor: I won't.

Dr. Masterson: What makes you so sure all of a sudden?

Tor: You reminded me what I'm fighting for.

Dr. Masterson: And what is that?

Tor: My mate.

Dr. Masterson: *sighs heavily* All right. Here, bite down on this. We don't want you cracking any of those pearly whites, now do we?

<<switch being flicked>>

Tor: *grunts*

<<hum of electricity>>

Dr. Masterson: This will only hurt for a moment. I'm starting at the lowest setting.

<<zapping noise>>

Tor: *muffled cry of pain*

Dr. Masterson: That's it. Not even a flicker of black in your eyes. Beautiful. Let's try the next setting, shall we?

Tor: *panting*

<<zapping noise for a longer span of time>>

Tor: *pained groan*

Dr. Masterson: Good. Very good, Tor. You're doing so well. Keep it up. Just one more setting to go.

<<zapping intensifies and goes for even longer>>

Tor: *muffled scream*

Tor: *animalistic growl*

Dr. Masterson: You're so close, don't give in now. Fight, Tor.

Tor: *snarls fade to heavy breathing*

Dr. Masterson: Well done, Tor. You did it. I can't believe it. You were shifting right in front of me, but you contained the beast. Here, let me take that out of your mouth.

Tor: I almost *breathes heavily* lost *breathes heavily* control.

Dr. Masterson: But you didn't. That's the important thing. Now you know that it's possible for you to stop it. The next time you find yourself in a triggering situation, remember what you did here.

<<door slams open>>

Bruno: No, you can't go in there.

Dahlia: Just try and stop me, beefcake. I need to see her.

Dr. Masterson: Dahlia, I'm with a resident. Please schedule an appointment.

Dahlia: Tor? W-why are you restrained like that? What's happening here? He's sweaty and shaking.

Dr. Masterson: It's all aboveboard, I assure you. Just part of his treatment plan.

<<rustling of clothes>>

Dahlia: He doesn't deserve to be tied down like some kind of animal.

Tor: *sharp inhale*

Tor: *low animalistic growl*

Dr. Masterson: Tor, remember what we just went over.

Tor: *growling intensifies*

<<restraints snap and clatter to the ground>>

Tor: I can smell him on you. You're mine.

Dahlia: *gasps* Tor! Tor put me down!

Dr. Masterson: Tor, get back here!

Tor: Session's over.

<<static>>

End of transcript.

THIRTY-SIX

TOR

"Tor, what are you doing? I needed to talk to her. It was important!"

Dahlia's voice barely registered as I gripped her thighs tighter and continued storming toward the first secure room I could find. She was mine. She needed to understand it. How could I make her see?

Instinct overrode rationality as I took turn after turn through the labyrinth of hallways that would take me deeper into No Man's Land. I was in search of privacy, and the closest—not to mention best—place for that was in the hallway of high-security cells. No one would think to look for us here.

"Tor, stop ignoring me. Put me down!"

She wriggled atop my shoulder, so I hitched her higher and smacked her soundly on the arse to stop her squirming.

"Did you just *spank* me?"

"I'll do it again. Stop moving."

Dahlia let out a frustrated growl, her temper spiking to mirror my own. If she thought me intimidated, she clearly hadn't been paying attention. My beast loved the fight. Craved it. All she was doing was getting me—

A sharp flash of pain at the back of my waist had me growling.

My mate bit me. She may have even marked me. Fuck, maybe I could get Kai to ink her teeth marks into my skin so I'd always have a reminder.

I was so fucking hard, my sweats tented obscenely, and there was no way I could hide my reaction to her. Not with my hands full.

I didn't care. Not one damn bit. Let them all see what a Berserker's mate could do.

The empty cells came into view; no guards were necessary because the doors were locked by both mortal and magical means. Only a fool would come down here willingly.

A fool, or a Berserker.

One and the same, really.

I carried my mate into the first free cell and kicked the door closed behind me. It wasn't locked, but it didn't need to be. The only thing in danger was her virgin cunt.

"What the hell are you doing?"

"What I should have done from the first."

Standing her on her feet, I fought the tremors in my limbs that signified my beast was close to taking hold. I was already weakened from the doctor's tests, but the sliver of control I still had snapped the second she'd come into the room reeking of another man.

"Tor? Your eyes . . ."

I knew what she saw: the swirling galaxies, the promise of bloodlust and violence.

"You smell like him," I bit out, my voice more growl than anything.

Her eyes widened with understanding. "That's what this is about?"

"You're mine."

"Tor . . ."

"Mine!" I roared, my beast rattling my bones in his attempt to break free. "Not his. Not theirs. MINE!"

I'd thought the confined space would help, knowing that it was only her and me, but it only made the fact that she had another man's scent on her more obvious. Fury unlike anything I could remember took over me, and I rent her dress in two, my trembling fingers turned to black claws. Her shocked gasp should have stopped me, but it only spurred me on.

Somewhere in the back of my mind, I knew this would be the last time I'd be anywhere close to myself. I'd lose my humanity and, in the process, lose her. But the drive to claim her was so strong, I could think of nothing else. Nothing would keep me from my mate. No consequence, not even the possibility of the change, was strong enough to stop me.

Her soft hand slid over my cheek, eyes trained on mine. "Yes. I'm yours, Tor. Yours."

The racing of my heart eased, my anger ebbing a little at those words. "Mine."

She feathered her lips over my jaw, murmuring her agreement.

My eyes closed as the relief of her touch brought the tiniest flicker of sanity. But then I caught another whiff of *him,* and it came roaring back.

"You smell like him," I repeated, desperate for her to understand. The need to replace his scent with my own overcame me, and I rubbed my cheek against the crown of her head and then lower along each side of her neck. My hands stripped her of the remains of her dress while I used the rest of my body to press up and rub against every inch of bare skin I could.

"Wh-what are you doing?" she stammered, her voice breathy, the tone mirroring the arousal I scented in the room.

"Fixing it."

Dropping to my knees, I continued to run my cheek along her smooth skin. When I reached her belly, I added little licks, trailing my tongue up and along the rounded swell of her hip before nipping her hard enough that she yelped.

I rolled my gaze up her form, meeting her eyes. "Don't tell me to stop, beauty. I can't bear it, not claiming you."

Nipples tight and skin flushed, she couldn't disguise the lust painted across her body. But she didn't try. Her hands went to my thick hair, and she tugged so I came to my feet.

"What does claiming mean?" she asked as she wrapped her arms around my waist and held me close.

I ran my hands over her, stroking the long blonde hair I wanted splayed across my chest every night, trailing down her back until I reached the swell of her full, round arse. I cupped the globes hard enough that my fingers left indents. It wasn't just my scent I wanted all over her; it was also my marks. I wanted everyone in this bloody place to know who she belonged to by the time we left this cell.

Her fingers on my bare skin made me thankful the doctor needed me shirtless for her treatment.

"I marked you," she murmured, tracing the indentation her teeth left on my side.

On reflex, my hips jerked, pressing my erection into her. "I liked it."

"Clearly."

"To answer your question, beauty, claiming means you accept me as yours for all time. You consent to be mine. My mate. My Kærasta."

She pulled back so she could look up at me. "Is this like a vow thing? I just say a couple words and it's done, or is there more to it than that?"

"No. It's so much more. We come together fully: bodies, hearts, souls. We will be entwined so tightly our bond can never be severed."

"And what about the others?"

I stilled my perusal of her body, a white-hot flash of jealous rage racing through me. "I don't . . ." What could I say in response to her wanting them? Clearly my twin and his mate had made such an arrangement work, so it was possible, but with the way I was feeling . . . I didn't know if I was capable of the same.

"You have known about them from the beginning, Tor. I have . . . connections with them too."

I made a sound that was some combination of a roar and a growl.

"Don't ask me to give them up," she whispered. "Not before I know what those connections mean. It would be like one of them asking me not to want you."

"You'd choose me if they demanded it of you?"

"I couldn't give you up. It would be an impossible choice, like choosing between air or the blood in my veins. I can't live without either."

Nodding, I closed my eyes and took a deep breath, the scent of her and I now the only thing in the room. "And you will be mine regardless of what happens with them? No matter the outcome, you and I will be joined as one forever?"

"Isn't that what being your kareesta means?"

"Kærasta."

She smirked up at me. "I know. I just really wanted to hear you say it again."

Dipping my head, I found the shell of her ear and whispered, "My Kærasta."

She melted into me. "Yes, yours. I'm yours, Tor."

I cupped the nape of her neck and kissed her then, the beast inside me fully at ease with the reassurance she'd offered. No matter who else she accepted into her heart, I would have a permanent place in her soul. I could live with that.

Then she uttered two of the most perfect words in existence.

"Claim me."

THIRTY-SEVEN

Tor's eyes flared with unadulterated hunger the moment the demand left my lips, his hand at the nape of my neck tightening as he pulled me in closer.

His beast was still close to the surface. One wrong word, and I had little doubt he'd lose the battle within. The thrill of knowing he was balanced on a knife's edge between deadly creature and man wasn't lost on me. But the truth was, I wanted him—all of him—in any form.

"I can't believe I found you, Dahlia."

"You can't believe it? You could basically be a fictional character I created. I can't believe you're real." I traced the taut lines of his chest, following the ink of his tattoo with my finger before trailing down, down, down to his waistband.

Oh, hello.

Jesus, was that a fucking tube of cookie dough in his pocket?

Suddenly nervous, I kept my palm pressed against the burning skin of his stomach, afraid to find out the answer to that question. I'd played with my fair share of toys, and I was pretty sure I had obliterated my hymen over a decade ago, but this wasn't me alone in my room. This was real. This *meant* something.

"Why don't you push down my joggers and find out exactly how real I am?" He offered me a wolfish grin, and butterflies fluttered in my belly in response.

Once I did that, this would be happening. There was no going back.

No, Dahlia. Don't forget, consent can be revoked at any time.

But that thing in his pants was huge. Even though I'd felt it against me before, wriggled my butt up along the length of it, the thought of seeing him, touching him, taking him into me was daunting. What if he didn't fit?

Usually the thought of a growly alpha hero promising me he'd make it fit had me giggling like a schoolgirl. It was less cute when he was rocking a two-by-four.

Tor's lips, which had been blazing a trail across my shoulder and up my throat, paused, and he pulled back to assess me. "You're shaking, beauty. What's going on inside your head?"

"I know you think I'm some kind of sex goddess, but I . . . well, I haven't ever done this before. I mean, with another person. And I know virginity is a construct or whatever, but you're clearly a card-carrying member of the tripod club, which means this is going to hurt, and I'm a little scared. But I want to do it. God, I really want you to rail me into the fucking mattress, but I'm also aware that means to get to said railing, we need a lot of foreplay. Like a lot. Niagara Falls levels of a lot, otherwise I think you might be in danger of tearing something—"

To his credit, Tor didn't laugh. He just rested the blunt

tip of his forefinger over my lips and gazed into my eyes. "Trust me to take care of you, Kærasta. You will feel nothing but pleasure, I promise."

Swallowing, I gave myself a moment to center my thoughts. Trust him. I had to trust him. Just because it was my first rodeo didn't mean it was his. I'm sure he figured out how to wield his Nordic broadsword years ago.

"A little pain is probably okay," I whispered.

"Nothing you don't ask for."

He took my hands in his and directed them to his waistband again, but this time we shoved his joggers down together, freeing said broadsword and proving that none of my toys had prepared me for what Tor was packing.

"Am I supposed to get down on my knees and pray to my new lord and savior, a.k.a. your fucking massive dick? Seriously, how do you walk around with that thing in your pants all day? Does it have its own zip code? Do you have to tie it off to one side to keep it in place? Is it fucking sentient?"

"Dahlia," he groaned with a laugh. "We don't have to do this. Though it may kill me not to. If you're not ready, I understand."

"Excuse me? What happened to beast Tor? The guy who was all, *I'm going to claim you*, and *you're mine*, just a minute ago?"

"Oh, he's still here, just eclipsed by my need to see that my mate feels safe. Believe it or not, my need to protect and care for you overrides my need to fuck you."

The way his lips framed that word had my thighs clenching. There was something so damn good about a guy with a sexy accent saying naughty things.

"Can you do both?"

His lips curled into a sinful grin. "Yes, beauty. Lie back on the bed, and let me get you ready."

Not to be outdone, I tossed him a saucy wink as I moved to the room's twin bed. "I've used that line too, you know. Though usually in reference to back door activities." I froze mid-climbing onto the bed, my eyes growing wide. "That's off the table for the foreseeable future, by the way. At least until I know you aren't going to split me in half."

His lips twitched with amusement, his eyes roaming over my body and locking onto my ass, which was up in the air like I was offering it to him. Without a word, he moved to stand behind me, his big hands curving around my waist and locking me in place as he leaned over and started trailing kisses down my spine. Every press of his lips was like a brand on my skin, hot and tingling, lighting me up from the inside.

"Mmm, I know I said lie back, but this is too perfect to resist," he murmured, large palms skirting the fronts of my thighs before gripping my legs and pulling them apart. "Drop your chest down, my beautiful mate. Give me access to what I want most."

I knew this position. I'd written it more than once. My mate wanted me to *present*.

A full-body shiver worked its way through me. Without even knowing it, Tor was helping me live out one of my top ten fantasies.

"Tor, what are you doing?"

"Shh. Trust, beauty. Let me make this everything you ever imagined. Let me love you."

I had to bite down on my bottom lip to keep from crying out when those big palms of his spread my ass cheeks wide. I couldn't decide if I was embarrassed or super fucking turned on when he just shoved his face right on in there and got to work.

Super fucking turned on. Yup, that was the answer.

I moaned loud enough it bounced off the cement walls, but I didn't care one bit. Tor's lips and tongue feasted on me, sucking my pussy like it was giving him life. His tongue delved inside as he pressed on my lower back with one hand to keep my ass in the air while his other hand drifted around my front to find my clit.

Some strange garbled noise escaped me as I tried to beg him for . . . something. To stop? To never stop? I wasn't sure.

Tor must have been the Dahlia pussy whisperer, because he clearly understood the message. His pressure on my clit was perfect, as was the thrust of his tongue in and out of my dripping core.

You said you wanted Niagara Falls.

An answering flood of wetness spilled from me as he flicked my clit just right.

"So fucking sweet," he rumbled against my cunt. "Give it to me."

I was on the edge, my whole body trembling, and then he growled as his tongue fucked my pussy. That was it. I fell hard, screaming his name like it was a benediction.

"That's it, beauty. Take what you need. Give it all to me. It's mine."

Walls still fluttering as my orgasm faded, I wasn't prepared for him to sink one large finger inside me. The groan I released was indecent in the best possible way.

"I'm going to need you to come at least one more time before I give you my cock, beauty."

Even drunk from my climax, I couldn't keep the sass out of my reply. "Oh, shucks. How ever will I endure it?"

He smacked my ass, earning a little yelp from me.

"Mmm, you liked that. Your pretty cunt squeezed my finger so tight just from a slap on the arse. I can't wait to feel that on my cock."

After a few glides of the single digit, he added a second one, my body already protesting the thickness.

"Relax," he breathed against my spine, his movements controlled and steady as he kept working me. It wasn't long before he had me mewling and pressing back into him, silently begging for more. Without upping his pace, he added a third, and I was panting against the stretch. It was delicious, but way more than I'd ever dealt with.

"Tor, it's . . . fuck, it's a lot."

"Too much?"

He stopped moving his hand, waiting for my answer. I glanced at him over my shoulder, fingers gripping the sheets so hard my knuckles were white. "No. Just . . . go slow."

"Whatever you need," he promised.

My eyes nearly rolled back in my head when he used his other hand to work my clit and get me relaxed and pliant against him once more. He didn't alter his pace until my hips started to rock, begging him for more.

That's when he added a fourth finger, and I saw stars at the edge of my periphery.

"Jesus, Mary, fuck."

"Are you okay?"

"Yes. God. Yes. Keep moving."

He worked his fingers in and out, the wet sounds of my desire for him filling the room.

"You're being such a good girl for me, mate. Taking everything I give you so beautifully."

I would've been embarrassed at the mewl of pleasure his words caused, but I was too lost in him to think of anything else as I came on his hand, crying out and turning my head to bite my arm just to give me something to ground me.

"Now you're ready, Kærasta."

I was only partially aware of him slipping out of me and gently rolling me onto my back.

His grin was pure male satisfaction as he stared down at me. I knew I had to be a sweaty mess, my face the color of a ripe tomato, but you'd never know it based on the hunger in his gaze. Hunger for me.

"Do you know what I love the most about your body, Dahlia?" he asked, positioning himself between my thighs, his rigid length already nudging at my entrance.

"Right now, I'm thinking it has something to do with my pussy."

He shook his head. "It's in my top five favorite parts of you, but no, it's how easy you are to hold on to. I can grab onto your full hips, your thick thighs, your perfect fucking tits, and not worry about breaking you. I'm a large man with large appetites, and you're more than woman enough to satisfy my every craving. My perfect match."

His hips pressed forward, the swollen crown of his cock breaching my entrance. "I . . . oh God, it's big."

"Yes, but you can take me, Kærasta. You were made for me."

With deliberate slowness, he sank into me, his dark eyes trained on mine, watching for any hint I needed him to stop. It burned as his thickness filled me, but in the most delicious way. I was so worked up, so intensely aroused, that when he was sheathed fully inside me and his pelvis brushed my clit, I nearly came again.

"Gods, Dahlia," he rasped, his body trembling above me. I couldn't tell if it was from how hard he was fighting against his need to rut into me or if he was fighting against something else.

His eyes glittered with a depth of emotion I wasn't ready for, but it was the way his face had begun to change that sent a tendril of arousal-laced fear through me. He was on the edge of shifting.

Closing his eyes, he breathed slow and deep, and the pewter scales I hadn't noticed until now that ran across his forearms retreated.

I needed him to move, needed friction to ease the unbelievable fullness inside me. So I rolled my hips to adjust my position. Big mistake.

Tor groaned as if in pain. "Don't. Please don't move. You're so fucking tight, I can't—"

His eyes found mine, and I could see lightning flicker in the obsidian depths. He was barely holding onto his control.

"I need more," I whispered.

"And I need you to trust me. I will not rut into you like a beast. Not until I can keep myself restrained."

Smirking, I wrapped my arms around his broad shoulders and lifted my head so I could kiss him. Of course, that moved our position, and we both moaned. Well, mine was more of a whimper. "I like the beast, Tor," I murmured against his lips.

Tor's body quaked, the veins in his arms bulging. "Temptress."

"You started it with that big dick of yours."

He laughed, but it was more of a tortured rasp than anything. "Fuck, don't make me laugh."

"Then distract me so I can't be funny. I'm a nervous talker. We've established that."

I dragged my fingernails down his back, making him

shudder as he kissed me again. "Hold on to the headboard," was his only warning before he pulled out part way and then drove himself home.

For once I was glad I listened. The power of his hips thrusting into me shoved my body backward, and if I hadn't been holding the bars, I would have slammed into the headboard without warning. As it was, my head was still knocking into my fists, but better that than metal. I didn't want a concussion as a parting gift.

"Fuck, Dahlia, you take my cock so well. Fucking perfect. I never want to leave. Gonna bury myself so deep in you you'll never forget me."

Usually I'd make a joke about how his dick had already imprinted itself on my womb, but my heart was currently melting into a puddle of goo. I was also *thisclose* to orgasming again, and I couldn't think much beyond focusing on the man inside me.

"It's so good, Tor. You're mine. God, you're mine."

"Yes," he growled, the words seeming to unlock something inside him as he pumped harder and faster, chasing the same pleasure I was on the cusp of finding.

My brain was the equivalent of cotton candy soaked in water. It was pink and sparkly and knew only pleasure as Tor lit me up inside out. He was fucking me, sure, but there was no doubt the big strong Viking was making love to me while he did it. Each powerful thrust, each roll of his pelvis against my clit, each pleasure-filled groan, was proof enough of that.

"Say you'll be mine, Dahlia," he demanded. "Say it."

"Yes, I'll be yours. I *am* yours."

"Kærasta," he cried, his hips losing their smooth rhythm as they pistoned erratically. "Come for me."

I'd never thought I could come on command. Obviously, I hadn't accounted for Tor. Never say never. I fucking shattered, my pussy fluttering and squeezing his steel length, milking him for everything he was going to give me.

With a ragged groan, he gave one more hard thrust, his tip pressing against my cervix in a way I found strangely pleasurable as well as painful. I felt the jerks of his cock as he pulsed inside me and flooded me with his release. But even more so, I felt the connection between us like an impenetrable chain binding our souls. We may not be witches, but we'd cast a spell made of sex magic tonight. One we'd never be able to break.

THIRTY-EIGHT

My attention was trained on Asshole rather than the psychiatrist currently blathering on about the importance of self-reflection. Honestly, she could have been talking about the proper way to castrate a bull for all the attention I was paying her. I was much more interested in the little devil gnawing on the toe of my shoe.

"Leave it," I snarled, but he just looked at me and growled. Fucking big dog energy coming back to bite me in the ass.

I fought an aggrieved sigh. It was probably my fault he was acting out. I'd forgotten to pick up his treats and a fresh bone from the kitchen this morning.

"Cain, are you listening?" Dr. Masterson asked, tapping her pen impatiently on her notepad.

"No."

"How are you ever going to prove that you are capable of returning to society if you refuse to do the work necessary to get there?"

Before I could answer, a high-pitched tinkling sound filled the air, and my attention was drawn to the unassuming glass orb sitting on her desk. It could've been a paperweight for all its bland decorative purpose. But now, rather than crystal clear, an eerie blue smoke blossomed inside.

"What the fuck is that?"

The doctor seemed as surprised as I was. "Oh, would you look at that? I'd started to think it was broken."

"What is it?" I repeated, a gnawing sense of dread filling me.

She blinked and returned her gaze to me. "It's a bond detector. As you are likely aware, mate bonds, especially in their early stages, are tenuous things. For creatures who already struggle with control, it's essential that they be monitored. The orb notifies me of any new bonds as they are solidified so that I may act swiftly and ensure the safety of the new mates as well as the rest of the residents. This is the first time I can recall Blackwood ever having a mated pair." Her gaze turned inward. "I'll have to see about getting them new accommodations, of course. And some sessions to help them nurture their bond. They'll likely need to be alone for at least a few days before their emotions settle enough for them to be around others. Well, his anyway, she's probably not a threat."

My stomach churned, my heart lurching as a certain gray-eyed beauty's face came to mind. "Who—" I had to clear my throat and try again before I could get the words out. "Who are the mated pair?"

"Tor and Dahlia, I'm assuming. After what I witnessed this morning, I'd be surprised if it was anyone else."

I felt sick, my skin going cold and clammy at the thought of her with him. Not just *with* him, but bound to him. Asshole yipped before raising onto his hind legs and pawing at my knee. I glanced down at him and found blue fire tipping my fingers without my permission.

"Cain, are you all right?" the doctor asked.

I closed my eyes and breathed deeply, willing the power to recede into my hands.

"Very good. That took a lot of control. Well done."

If she only knew how out of control I still felt. I was reeling. Cast adrift. Un-fucking-done.

I needed to get out of here. "Sorry, doc, time's up. See you next week," I said, standing and heading straight for the door.

"Cain, wait—"

But I ignored her and kept going.

Dahlia had ruined me, and she hadn't even done anything other than exist in my orbit. My every waking thought was clouded by her. My fucking dreams had turned into replays of random scenes in my past, but where the woman had been my . . . wife, she now wore Dahlia's face. I was dangerously preoccupied with a woman I barely knew. All while being bound to one I couldn't remember.

Guilt tore at me. I was a married man, at least so far as I could remember. I shouldn't feel this way about anyone other than my bride. Not if those feelings in my flashback had been real. She deserved better than this. Better from me.

So why was I so destroyed over Dahlia finding a mate? A better man would have welcomed the knowledge that I couldn't have her. That she'd never be mine. The temptation forever and irrevocably removed because she was soulbound to another.

Apparently I was not a better man. If there ever was an angel on my shoulder, I'd long ago set that little bastard on fire. Because even though I told myself I wanted to let

Dahlia go, it was a lie. One I'd perpetuated until the night I'd finally had her in my arms.

Now I *had* to.

And the knowledge had me ready to burn this place to the fucking ground.

～

KAI

I'D BEEN on edge since Dahlia left my tower, my skin feeling like it was two sizes too small, apprehension thick in the air. Originally I'd chalked it up to sexual frustration, because she was a fucking tease with that pillow, but now I wasn't so sure. I shouldn't still be feeling this way because of a case of blue balls.

Technically, they weren't even blue. I'd used her knickers to fuck my fist the second she'd fled.

So this was something else. Something that pricked along the back of my neck telling me to pay attention, to be on guard for a threat.

Cain's tall form came barreling down the corridor, icy flames sparking from his fingers as he did. The dog at his heels growled every few steps, his mood mirroring his master's.

Before I could get out of the way, the twat shouldered past me, knocking into me hard enough that I hit the wall.

"Watch it," I grumbled. "What's wrong with you today?"

Instead of answering, he asked a question of his own. "Have you seen Dahlia?"

"Not since this morning."

"So she really could be mated to that fucking Viking. Godsdammit."

My stomach turned into a pit. "What are you on about?"

Cain's lips curled up in a mockery of a smile. "Guess you should have made your move when you had the chance. Now it's too late. Tor mated her."

My dragon roared, his voice a lash as it whipped through my mind. *"I told you to claim her, but you were too weak. You let our mate slip away."*

I didn't. I'd been courting her. Giving her the time she needed before locking her into something so incredibly permanent. He'd taken the chance from me. For all that I'd come to accept that I might have to share Dahlia, I never considered that time was against me or that I wouldn't be the one to take my place at her side as her one true mate. Why would I? She was mine. Both my dragon and I recognized the pull, even if I'd been too scared to admit that's what it was. A woman could have multiple lovers, but multiple mates? How could that ever work? Had Tor even explained what he'd done? What it meant? Had he forced the bond on her?

"Kill him. Get her back. She's ours."

"How do you know this?" I all but snarled.

"Doc Masterson got an alert during our session. She's moving them to their own little love nest."

"We need to get to her. It might not be too late to break the bond."

That had to be true. It *had* to. Maybe if I bit her before the bond with Tor fully settled, it would override the usurper's claim. The goddess wouldn't give my mate to me only for me to lose her like this. Would she?

"Okay, there, buddy. You're dragoning out on me. Get yourself under control, at least until I'm out of the line of fire." Cain backed away slowly, his dog growling as he went.

I glanced down at Cain's blue-flame-covered hands. "You're telling me to get myself under control, fire fingers?"

He shot me a baleful glare but managed to suppress his flames.

"Now, where is she?" I demanded.

Cain raised a brow. "I asked you that, remember?"

"Find her." My dragon roared, clawing at the barrier between us. He was desperate, furious, and tearing apart my defenses.

"We need to find her. Who might know where she is?"

Even as I asked the question, an answer came to me. Apparently, Cain was of the same mind because, as one, we said, "Hook."

Hook

WHERE WAS my delectable little writer hiding herself? I'd planned to take her off on an adventure this evening, but she was eluding me. The minx. I'd have to put her over my knee. Well, that sounded like a fantastic way to spend my time. I'd simply have to locate her first.

Moving to the map, held open courtesy of two knives I'd borrowed from the chef, I muttered the incantation Adonis had so kindly given me and sacrificed one drop of blood to activate the spell. Then I waited for the object of my affection to appear on the parchment. She'd be nothing but a little red dot, but that was all I needed. If she was on the grounds, I'd find her.

When it appeared, I blinked twice to be sure I was seeing correctly.

"Whatever did you do to get yourself locked up in No Man's Land, naughty girl? Allow me to rescue you. Feel free to thank me on your knees."

Anticipation already sending my blood rushing south, I adjusted myself and snagged the skeleton key I'd pinched from Masterson's office during my very first session, then took off in search of Dahlia.

Not wanting any delays, I took one of several hidden passages I'd discovered in my early days. Blackwood had very few secrets I'd yet to uncover, save the only one that mattered. But that was a problem for another day.

Getting inside No Man's Land was simple. The high-security doors only served to keep the most dangerous of us in, not keep the rest out.

One day people would stop underestimating me. Thankfully, today was not that day.

I strolled down the first of many halls, making note of the open cells and thinking this couldn't possibly be right. Then I spotted the one nearest me with its door noticeably closed.

"Found you, little rabbit. What a reunion this will be."

I pulled out the key and crouched down to verify it was, indeed, my darling. The sight that greeted me was like something out of my fantasies. Dahlia, nude and draped on the bed, pink-tipped nipples just begging for attention. But that's where the similarities ended. Instead of me pumping between her spread thighs and making her cry out, Tor was currently sliding out of her, shifting their bodies so he could reposition her to his liking.

Bloody hell, he's a crafty arsehole.

I would just have to take care of this problem right fucking now. If he thought he could keep her all to himself when a pirate wanted her as his own, he was dead wrong. I'd simply steal her back. No one could resist the charm of Captain Hook. But first, I needed a distraction. A big one.

Tor was far from the worst creature residing in Black-wood's halls. I'd just find someone bigger and scarier than him to do the dirty work for me.

Rolling the key back and forth over my knuckles, I headed straight to the back of the hall, knowing the worst of the bunch would be kept the furthest away from the main exit.

Without prejudice, I started unlocking doors. The inhabitants took wary steps my way, most blinking in the light. I could only assume they'd been locked up for a great while.

I knew I'd come to the right place as soon as I clocked the first two creatures. One was a hulking brute of a demon. All red eyes and scarred skin. One of his horns had been sawed off, and where bat wings used to hang on either side of his spine were jagged bones. Beside him, almost comically small compared to his towering form, was a creature no less deadly. The man's beard nearly reached the floor, a crusty red-hued cap clutched between his gnarled fingers.

"Gentlemen, I have a proposition for you . . ."

THIRTY-NINE

TOR

"Why do they call it a twin bed when it's clearly built for one person?" Dahlia's amused voice filled me with a calm certainty for the first time since I'd met her.

I wasn't twisted with the fear my mate would leave or unsure if I could be the man she deserved. I knew now, beyond the shadow of a doubt, she wasn't going anywhere. Not without me by her side.

"I stopped fitting in a twin bed when I was four." I pulled her farther across my large frame, loving how soft her skin was on mine.

"I'll bet. You're a big boy," she purred, her fingers tracing the lines of my tattoo.

I'd never had a chance to tell her what it represented, but I supposed it no longer mattered. My beast was quiet in a way I'd never felt before. He was sleepy and sated within me. Content now that our mate was well and truly bound to us. While my curse could never be broken, it was, in a manner of speaking, blocked. I had control of my Berserker, a grip on the rage that dirty fae had unleashed. The cliff

425

that was the final petal was as clear as day, but I wouldn't jump off it. Dahlia would anchor me. My love for her wouldn't allow anything else.

She gazed up at me from beneath her lashes. "You look happy."

"I am. I found my mate, have her in my arms, and will never let her go."

Her smile was quite possibly the most beautiful thing I'd ever seen.

"You sure you don't have any regrets? I mean, you haven't seen me when I'm on deadline. I turn into an absolute bridge troll. I forget to shower and speak in complete sentences. I'm basically feral. It's not pretty."

I leaned up and nipped the side of her neck in a dominant display that had my cock thickening between us. "It's a good thing I'm also part feral then. My beast will have someone to play with."

"Oh, that sounds fun."

"It will be."

A scream ripped through the air from beyond the door, causing everything in me to tense.

"What was that?" Dahlia asked, sitting up as I slipped from the bed.

"Don't move from that spot, Kærasta. Something isn't right."

She clutched the sheet to her chest, giving me a wary nod. I was thankful she didn't question me.

Another terrified screech, this one rapidly cutting off with an unmistakable gurgle, came from outside, closer, much closer.

"I smell . . . virgin blood. What manner of delectable treat do we have here behind this door?" The demonic voice brought my Berserker to the surface. My beast was no longer lounging in the background. He was alert and ready, my body already trembling from the surge of his bloodlust in my veins.

He would not touch what was mine.

"Tor?" she whispered, fear laced in her tone.

"I will protect you to my last breath. Stay where you are." My words hardly sounded like I'd uttered them, they were so filled with rage and gravel.

"Here, kitty, kitty," the demon said, scraping claws along the metal door that separated us. "Let us play with you, won't you?"

The door swung open, revealing a group of the most sinister creatures Blackwood contained. The ones for whom freedom was never an option. The demon leading the pack grinned, his sharp teeth in a too large mouth dripping with blood.

"She has a playmate already. Not to worry, pretty, we'll dispatch him before we take care of you."

It was her whimper that sounded the death knell in the end. Not the monsters in the doorway hurling their threats. The sound of my mate's fear sent me flying off the edge, humanity be damned. In that moment, she didn't need the man. She needed the beast.

He was the only one who could save her.

Heart pounding, I gave over control, knowing this was the last time I'd have with her as my true self. Knowing she wouldn't understand, but that she would at least survive this. Knowing I would protect her, even if it meant I lost myself to do so.

The transformation was swift, but far more painful than any I'd undergone before. It felt as though the Berserker ripped me in two, clawing himself out from beneath my skin, remaking me in his image. I roared as my bones and flesh rearranged themselves to accommodate his larger form, his horns curling up and back from my temples, his scales racing down my arms and torso.

I didn't even feel the demon's claws as they slashed across my chest. The only clue my skin had been broken was the spray of blood on the stone floor. With an almighty battle cry, I gripped his disgusting head between both hands and twisted until it was rent from his shoulders and his pathetic body fell to the floor.

"T-Tor?"

Tossing the head at our would-be attackers, I turned to face my beauty, my skin coated in the blood of our enemy. Her eyes flew wide at whatever madness she saw blazing in mine, but it was obvious she understood.

None of these creatures would survive me.

She was my mate.

And I . . .

I was her monster.

FORTY

DEATH

I loved it when everything fell into place as it should. This plot was my greatest achievement, thirty years in the making. My sisters had called me foolish, but the proof would appear any minute now. They wouldn't be able to deny the facts when my Apocalypse took hold.

They always said that death was inevitable. That I had it easy, never had to work for anything, and everything just fell into my lap. Well, I'd show them. Not only was I as cunning as War and as devious as Pestilence, but I was more twistedly brilliant than them all.

I'd figured it out, you see. Why we always failed. I'd cracked the code, and now it was only a matter of time. My board was set. My pieces in place. Now it was time to watch them fall, one by one.

The hairs on the back of my neck stood on end, the atmosphere in my lair changing as though lightning was about to strike. Giddy anticipation built in my gut as a smirk twisted my lips. Those lovestruck fools had stumbled right into my trap. But then, I knew they would. It was expertly laid for them so I'd get what I wanted. The first rite was complete.

A low grunt came from behind me and my smile widened as I spun around in my chair. There, locked away in a special cell of my making, stood one of our greatest allies and adversaries, his power only matched by his counterpart—my sister.

"Well, well, well. If it isn't War, horseman of the Apocalypse. Fancy seeing you here." I glanced at the remaining empty cells floating in the chamber I'd made my own. "One down, three to go."

He slammed his fists against the magical barrier keeping him secured, his eyes burning with fury, but I knew I was safe. He couldn't break free. Not unless I chose to let him out.

"Better make yourself comfortable, Chaos. You're going to be here for a while." I winked as he snarled. "Don't worry, old friend. You won't have time to get bored. I've got so many plans for you."

Don't worry, the world isn't ending...yet.
The Mate Games : Death will continue in Hunted Beast.

In the meantime, curious about what happened after Hook dosed Cain with pixie dust? Download your Haunting Beauty bonus scene at www.thematEgames.com/ BeautyBonus or get the audio version at www. thematEgames.com/BeautyAudioBonus

THE MATE GAMES UNIVERSE
BY K. LORAINE & MEG ANNE

MORE BY MEG & KIM

Also by Meg Anne

THE KEEPERS

A GUARDIAN/WARD HIGH FANTASY ROMANCE

THE DREAMER (A KEEPER'S PREQUEL)

THE KEEPERS LEGACY

THE KEEPERS RETRIBUTION

THE KEEPERS VOW

THE KEEPERS BOXSET

THE FORSAKEN

A REJECTED MATES/ENEMIES-TO-LOVERS ROMANTASY

PRISONER OF STEEL & SHADOW

QUEEN OF WHISPERS & MIST

COURT OF DEATH & DREAMS

∼

GYPSY'S CURSE

A PSYCHIC/DETECTIVE STAR-CROSSED LOVERS UF ROMANCE

VISIONS OF DEATH

VISIONS OF VENGEANCE

VISIONS OF TRIUMPH

THE GYPSY'S CURSE: THE COMPLETE COLLECTION

∼

STANDALONES

MY SOUL TO TAKE: A FORBIDDEN LOVE MEETS FATED MATES PNR

ALSO BY K. LORAINE

~

STANDALONES

C<small>URSED</small> (MFM S<small>LEEPING</small> B<small>EAUTY</small> R<small>ETELLING</small>)

~

REVERSE HAREM STANDALONES

T<small>HEIR</small> V<small>AMPIRE</small> P<small>RINCESS</small> (A R<small>EVERSE</small> H<small>AREM</small> R<small>OMANCE</small>)

A<small>LL THE</small> Q<small>UEEN'S</small> M<small>EN</small> (A F<small>AE</small> R<small>EVERSE</small> H<small>AREM</small> R<small>OMANCE</small>)

ABOUT MEG ANNE

USA Today and international bestselling paranormal and fantasy romance author Meg Anne has always had stories running on a loop in her head. They started off as daydreams about how the evil queen (aka Mom) had her slaving away doing chores, and more recently shifted into creating backgrounds about the people stuck beside her during rush hour. The stories have always been there; they were just waiting for her to tell them.

Like any true SoCal native, Meg enjoys staying inside curled up with a good book and her fur babies . . . or maybe that's just her. You can convince Meg to buy just about anything if it's covered in glitter or rhinestones, or make her laugh by sharing your favorite bad joke. She also accepts bribes in the form of baked goods and Mexican food.

Meg is best known for her leading men #MenbyMeg, her inevitable cliffhangers, and making her readers laugh out loud, all of which started with the bestselling Chosen series.

About K. Loraine

USA Today Bestselling author Kim Loraine writes steamy contemporary and sexy paranormal romance. **You'll find her paranormal romances written under the name K. Loraine and her contemporaries as Kim Loraine.** Don't worry, you'll get the same level of swoon-worthy heroes, sassy heroines, and an eventual HEA.

When not writing, she's busy herding cats (raising kids), trying to keep her house sort of clean, and dreaming up ways for fictional couples to meet.